BARBARA ERSKINE

Midnight *is a* Lonely Place

HARPER

This novel is entirely a work of fiction. The names, characters and incidents portrayed in it are the work of the author's imagination. Any resemblance to actual persons, living or dead, events or localities is entirely coincidental.

Harper
An imprint of HarperCollins*Publishers*
1 London Bridge Street
London SE1 9GF

www.harpercollins.co.uk

This paperback edition 2016

First published in Great Britain by
HarperCollins*Publishers* 1994

Copyright © Barbara Erskine 2016

Barbara Erskine asserts the moral right to
be identified as the author of this work

A catalogue record for this book is
available from the British Library

ISBN: 978-0-00-728077-3

Printed and bound by CPI Group (UK) Ltd, Croydon, CR0 4YY

MIX
Paper from
responsible sources
FSC
www.fsc.org FSC C007454

For A.J.
who thought of the title

'Where'er we tread 'tis haunted, holy ground'.

Byron

'C'était pendant l'horreur d'une profonde nuit . . .'

Racine

PROLOGUE

Her hair was the colour of newly frosted beech leaves; glossy; rich; tumbling from its combs as he pulled her against him, his lips seeking hers. His skin was tanned by the sun and the wind, hers, naked against him, white as the purest marble.

The heavy, twisted silver of the torc he wore about his arm cut into her flesh. She did not notice. She noticed nothing but the feel of his body on hers, the strength of his muscular thighs, the power of his tongue as he thrust it into her mouth as though he would devour her utterly.

'Claudia . . .'

He breathed her name as a caress, a plea, a cry of anguish, and then at last a shout of triumph as he lay still, shaking, in her arms.

She smiled. Gazing up at the sky through the canopy of rustling oak leaves she was utterly content. The world had contracted into the one small clearing in the deserted woodland. Child and husband were forgotten. For this man in her arms, she was prepared to risk losing both; to risk losing her home, her position, life itself.

He stirred, and, raising himself onto his elbows, he stared down at her, his face strangely blank, his silvery eyes unseeing.

'Claudia . . .' he whispered again. He rested his face between her breasts. It was the little death; the death a man sought; the death which followed coition. He smiled, reaching his fist into her hair, holding her prisoner, tracing the line of her cheek-bones, her eyelids, with his lips. What would this woman's husband, a son of Rome, an officer of the legion, say if he ever found out? What would he do if he learned his wife had a lover, and that the lover was a Druid Prince?

I

'I hate being famous!' Kate Kennedy confessed as she sat on the floor of her sister Anne's flat. They were sharing a takeaway with a large Burmese cat called Carl Gustav Jung.

When her biography of Jane Austen was published Kate had found herself a celebrity overnight. She was invited onto talk shows, she was interviewed by three national daily newspapers and two Sundays, she toured the libraries and bookshops of Britain and she met Jon Bevan, described by the *Guardian* as one of England's most brilliant young literary novelists and poets. The reason for all this interest? What the *Times Literary Supplement* called her 'sizzling exposé' of Jane's hidden sensuality; her repressed sexuality; the passion in those well-loved, measured paragraphs.

Three weeks after meeting Jon she moved into his Kensington flat and her life changed forever.

Her elder sister and former flatmate, Anne, had remained philosophical about being deserted. ('My dear, it was bound to happen to one of us sooner or later.') Herself a writer – a Jungian psychologist whose library, especially the Freudian bits, Kate had ransacked when writing *Jane* – she had watched with amusement as Kate coped with fame. And found it wanting.

'If you hate it so much, bow out. Become a recluse. Decline to appear, my dear. Cultivate a certain boorishness. And wear a veil.' Anne licked soy sauce off her fingers. 'Your sales would double overnight.'

'Cynic.' Kate smiled at her fondly. 'Jon says I'm mad. He loves it, of course.'

'I can see Jon giving up writing in the end to become a media person,' Anne said thoughtfully. She wiped her hands on a paper napkin stamped with Chinese characters and, wrapping her arms around her legs, rested her chin thoughtfully on her knees. 'He's bad for you, you know, Kate. He's a psychic vampire.' She grinned. 'He's feeding off your creative energy.'

'Rubbish.'

'It's true. You've slipped into the role of housewife and ego masseuse without even realising it. You're besotted with him! It's months since you got back from Italy, but you haven't even started writing the new book yet.'

Startled by the vehemence of the statement Kate was astonished to find that she felt guilty. 'I'm still researching.'

'What? Love?' Anne smiled. 'And does Jon still think you're mad to write about Byron at all?'

Kate nodded fondly. 'Yes, he still thinks I'm mad. He thinks Byron is too well known. He thinks I should have plumped for someone obscure – and not so attractive,' she added as an afterthought. 'But I'm glad to say my editor doesn't agree with him. She can't wait for the book.' She shook her head wearily, giving Carl Gustav the last, carefully-saved prawn. She had been secretly pleased and not a little flattered to find that Jon was jealous.

'Is that why you chose Byron? Because he's attractive?' Anne probed further.

'That and because I love his poetry, I adore Italy and he's given me a chance to spend wonderful months travelling round Europe to all the places he lived.' Kate gathered up the empty cartons from their meal. 'And he was a genuinely fascinating man. Charismatic.' She was watching Carl Gustav who, having crunched his prawn with great delicacy, was now meticulously washing his face and paws. 'Actually, I am ready to start writing now. My notes are complete – at least for the first section.'

Anne shook her head. 'I suppose I can think of worse ways of earning a living!' She stood up and went to rummage in the fridge for a jar of coffee beans. 'Tell me, are you and Jon still happy?' she asked over her shoulder. 'Really happy.'

Kate nodded.

'Getting-married happy?'

'No.' Thoughtfully. Then, more adamantly, 'No, I don't think either of us are the marrying type. At least not at the moment.'

'But you can see yourself living with him for a long time.'

There was a moment's silence as Kate regarded her sister with preoccupied concentration. 'Why do you want to know?'

'I've been offered a job in Edinburgh. If I take it I'll have to give up the flat.'

'I see.' Kate was silent for a moment. So, it was burning bridges time. 'What about Carl Gustav?'

'Oh, he'll come with me. I've discussed it with him at great length.' Anne bent down and caressed the cat lovingly. He had always been more hers than Kate's. 'He's quite pro-Edinburgh, actually, aren't you, C.J?'

'And he approves of the job?'

'It's a good one. At the University. A big step up that dreadful ladder we are all supposed to mount unceasingly.'

Kate turned away, astonished by the pang of misery that had swept through her at the thought of losing Anne. 'Have you told Mum and Dad about this?'she said after a minute.

Anne nodded. 'They approve and I can see them just as often from Edinburgh. It's not as though it's the end of the world, Kate. It's only four hundred miles.'

Kate smiled. 'Well, if C.J. approves, and Mum and Dad approve, it must be OK. Get rid of the flat with my blessing and I'll try and hang on to Jon for a bit!'

But she didn't.

It was sod's law, she supposed, that the day after Anne moved into her new flat in Royal Circus she and Jon had their first serious row. About money. Hers.

'How much are they going to pay you?' He stared at her in astonishment.

She pushed the letter over to him. He read it slowly. 'It's an American contract! You must have known about this for months.' He was hurt and accusing.

'I didn't want to tell you until it was definite. You know how long these things take –' She had saved the news as a surprise. She had thought he would be pleased.

'Christ! It's iniquitous!' Suddenly he was on his feet. 'I get paid a paltry few hundred dollars' advance for my last book of poetry and you –' he spluttered with indignation, – 'you, get that!' He threw the letter down.

She stared at him, shocked. 'Jon –'

'Well, Kate. Be realistic. You write bloody well, but it's hardly literature!'

'Whereas your books are?'

5

'I don't think anyone would dispute that.'

'No. I'm sure they wouldn't.' She took a deep breath.

'Oh, hey, come on.' Suddenly he realised how much he had hurt her. Silently he cursed his flash-point temper. He put his arm round her shoulders. 'Look, you know me. All mouth. I didn't mean it. You are bloody good. You do enough research! Take no notice. I was just miffed. No, let's face it, jealous.' He gave her a hug. 'I might even go so far as to swallow my pride and borrow some of that money off you.'

It was the first time she had heard even a hint of his financial problems.

He managed it by making her feel guilty. She saw that later. It was a subtle manipulation; a masterpiece of manoeuvring. She pushed the money at him; threw it at him; gave it to him and lent it to him, with every cheque tacitly apologising that she made money while he did not. When the end came she had less than a thousand left in the bank and no prospect, though he had promised faithfully to repay her, of any more until her next royalty cheque in the summer.

Even so, it was not the increasing pressure over money which came between them in the end. It was something sudden and quite unexpected.

It was a cold, miserable day in early December when Jon found her in the Manuscript Gallery of the British Museum standing looking down at the flat glass case where an open book stared up at her, Byron's crabbed, slanting hand, much crossed out, flowing across the page of the dedication to 'Don Juan'. The atmosphere of the gallery, the air conditioning, the strange false light with its muted hum were giving her a headache. She had been concentrating too long and the unexpected tap on her shoulder had given her such a fright she let out a small cry before she turned and saw who it was and remembered Jon had said he would meet her for a quick coffee.

The restaurant was, as usual, packed and as they sat down at a table near the wall she had no idea that this would lead to the outbreak of war. A couple of Japanese tourists, hung with cameras, inserted themselves, with bows and apologetic smiles, into the two spare chairs next to them. Coffee slopped into Jon's saucer. A tall man, his own legs had folded with difficulty beneath the table as he pushed himself into the corner opposite Kate. His tray balanced in one hand, a letter in the other, his long, lanky frame and floppy hair lent him an air of languid elegance, something to which one look at the keen darting of his eyes as he stared around the room immediately gave the lie.

Still thinking about Byron, she had not immediately sensed his excitement. 'You're coming with me, Kate!' He picked up the letter which he had put on the table between them and waved it at her. There was a gleam of triumph in his eyes.

'Coming with you? To the States?' Giving him her full attention at last, Kate looked at him in surprise. 'I can't.'

The expression of baffled anger which for a moment showed in his face confirmed her sudden suspicion that he was not going to understand.

'Why?' He was hurt and astonished by her response. He had thought she would be as excited as he was. He scowled. Why was it that she never reacted the way he expected? 'This is the most important time of my life, Kate. My new novel being published in the States. A lecture tour. Publicity. Perhaps real money at last. Isn't that what you want for me?'

'You know it is.' Her tone lost its defensiveness. She regarded him fondly. 'I'm terribly pleased for you. It's wonderful. The trouble is I am writing a book too, if you remember. And I can't just swan off on a tour at the moment. My research is complete. My notes are ready. I am about to start writing. You know I can't go with you. It's out of the question.'

'For God's sake, Kate, you can start the book any time.' Jon flung the letter down. He had counted on her; he could not visualise himself without her. 'I'm not asking you to give it up. I'm not asking you for a vast amount of time. We would be in the States less than a couple of weeks.'

Kate glanced at the Japanese woman sitting opposite her. Her eyes tactfully lowered, the woman was unwrapping a vast multi-layered sandwich, from which tranches of ham and cheese and various highly-coloured salad leaves hung in festoons. The air filled suddenly with a mouthwatering aroma of cooked meats.

'You know as well as I do that a couple of weeks is a hell of a long time when you are writing,' she retorted crossly. Her headache had worsened, she felt tired and depressed and she could be as stubborn as he on occasions. 'Don't be an idiot, Jon. Anyway,

7

you would get on much better without me.' Somehow he had managed to make her feel guilty.

'But I need you. Derek has got some terrific things lined up for me.' Jon stubbed at the letter with his forefinger. 'Telly in New York. And some wonderful parties. An interview with the *New York Magazine* and *Publishers Weekly*. You would meet everyone. He is expecting you to be there, Kate. We're an item on the literary circuit –'

A wave of impatience swept over her. 'I don't care if your publisher is expecting me, Jon. I don't care if the President of the United States is expecting me. You may be an item, but I am not. Nor am I a natty little accessory to complement your glittering image. If I tour New York it will be to publicise *Lord of Darkness*, not to be photographed smiling at your elbow. I'm sorry, but I'm going to stay here and work.'

Jon shook his head. His voice was suddenly bleak. 'You can't stay in the flat, Kate.'

'What do you mean? Of course I can.' Even then she took no notice of the warning bell clanging away at the back of her head.

He folded his arms, the familiar stubborn expression beginning to settle on his face softened by a hint of anxiety. 'Derek has asked me to lend the flat to Cyrus Grandini while I'm away.'

Kate was speechless for a moment. 'And who, may I ask, is Cyrus Grandini?' she spluttered at last.

'Oh, Kate.' He was impatient. 'The poet. For God's sake, you must have heard of him!'

'No. And I don't wish to share a flat with him.'

His reply was apologetic. 'There's no question of sharing the flat. I'm sorry, Kate, but I have agreed he can have it for two weeks.'

'But what about me? I thought it was my home too.' She fought to keep the sudden panic out of her voice.

'It is your home.' He sounded angry rather than reassuring. 'You know it is. Derek expected you to come to New York; so did I. I thought you would jump at the chance!'

'Well, I haven't.'

'Then you will have to find somewhere else to go for a couple of weeks. I'm sorry.'

So, that was it. She knew where she stood. A lodger. A lover. But not a partner.

8

She stood up, scraping her chair back on the floor with such vehemence that the Japanese man next to her nearly dropped his pastry. He too leaped to his feet, climbing from behind the table so that she could squeeze inelegantly past him. A wave of frustration and anger and unhappiness swept over her. 'If I go, I go for good,' she stated flatly as her neighbour subsided once more into his chair and reached rather desperately for his pastry.

'OK. If that's the way you want it.' He had turned away from her and sat, chin in hand, staring up at the horsemen from the Parthenon on the frieze on the wall above him, suddenly and shamefully near to tears. Correctly interpreting his rocklike stance the Japanese lady who had been preparing in her turn to rise and allow him to leave the table relaxed and took a large mouthful of sandwich.

It was after eleven when he returned to the flat that evening.

The front door led straight into the small sitting room where she was sitting reading, cosy in the warm light of the single table lamp. Outside she could hear the sleet hitting the window. The shoulders of Jon's heavy jacket glistened and sparkled with unmelted ice. 'Well, have you changed your mind?' he asked.

For a moment she was confused, still lost in the world of Lord Byron and his friends. Unwillingly she dragged herself back to the present. 'No. I haven't changed my mind.'

'It's not working, is it?' He stood in front of the electric fire and began slowly to unwind his long scarf.

'What isn't working?' She kept her eyes on the book before her. Her stomach had clenched uncomfortably at his tone and the print blurred into an indistinguishable black haze.

'Us.'

She looked up at last. 'Because I won't go to the States with you?'

'That and other things. Kate, let's face it. You're too obsessed with your damn poet to have time for me. Look at you. Even now you can't take your eyes off some bloody text or other.' He swooped on her and grabbed it out of her hand. 'See!' He held it up triumphantly. '*Victorian Poets*!' He hurled it down onto a chair. 'He –' by implication Kate gathered that 'he' meant Byron, '– comes between us all the time. You have no time for us; for our relationship, Kate.'

'Jon –'

She was stung by the injustice of the remark but he swept on. 'No, hear me out. You're completely obsessive. You have no time for me at all.'

She leaped to her feet. It had taken her much of the afternoon to calm down after their exchange at the British Museum earlier. She had thought they could work things out amicably once he came home, once he had had time to think about the justice of everything she had said. 'You . . . you say that, when all you ever talk about is your own work. Your friends, your parties, your TV interviews! You admitted that you only wanted me to go with you to the States as an appendage! The Jon Bevan literary circus. The wonderful, clever, stunning novelist and poet Jon Bevan and his cute girlfriend who writes such glitzy biographies – though heaven forbid that they should be taken as seriously as Jon's *oeuvre*.' Her hands had begun to shake as she realised the implications of what she was saying. She was condemning their relationship unequivocally to death. There would be no going back on this, no making up, no withdrawing of hurled insults. 'You're right, Jon, This relationship is not going to work. It's over. Finished!' Pushing past him, she flung out of the room.

Their bedroom was very small. The double bed, pushed against the wall, left space for a desk – her desk. On it her laptop sat amongst piles of books and papers. Jon's desk was in the sitting room she had just left. Jon's sitting room. Jon's flat. She stared round in despair. Then she reached for her coat. Throwing it on, she turned and ran to the front door.

'Kate. Don't be childish. We can work this out.' Jon followed her. Suddenly he was terrified by what he had done. 'For Christ's sake, where are you going?'

'Out.' She was fumbling with the deadlock.

'You can't go out. It's nearly midnight and it's snowing.' His anger had gone. He saw himself suddenly as she must see him – selfish, arrogant, thoughtless, cruel. 'Kate, please –' He stretched out a hand towards her.

She did not answer. Slamming the door behind her she had run down the steps and out into the street.

10

II

She missed him.

The flat was tidy, already empty though she was still there, and the days were ticking by. She had to find somewhere, somewhere she could afford, to live, to lick her wounded self esteem, to write.

She tried to justify what had happened; to explain it to herself. He was right. It had not been working. There had been too much conflict, too much competition between them. And all the sacrifices had been hers: her time, her concentration, her money and her commitment.

Well, now it was over. All her time, her concentration, her commitment could be focussed on one thing. One man. Byron. She stood, spreading honey on a slice of bread, watching the wholemeal crumbs disintegrate. Frowning, she tried to stick the crumbs back together. She couldn't stay in London, that was obvious. Her money – the money she had leant him – had been her sole source of income. She had spent a morning scouring her bank statement and building society book, calculator in hand, trying to see how far she could make the last few hundred pounds stretch. Thank God she had had the sense to stick some of it into a tax fund which, even for Jon, she had not touched. Without that she would be in trouble indeed. It was all her fault. She was a sucker, a classic, besotted mug. She had no one to blame but herself. And Jon. She had tried calling him names. It helped, but always she came back to the empty space in her life and the fact that she missed him.

But life had to go on, which was why, two days later, she found herself at Broadcasting House, where her old friend, Bill Norcross, ran one of the production departments.

'So, is what I hear on the grapevine true? You and Jon are a couple no more. The beautiful Kate Kennedy has turned at bay and bitten the hand that fed her.'

Bill leaned back in his chair and waved Kate into its twin, angled on the far side of his desk.

Swallowing a retort Kate sat down, aware of his eyes sliding automatically from the top of her black leather boots to the line of her hem. Secure in the knowledge that her thighs were thickly and unglamorously shrouded in black woollen tights she crossed her legs, deliberately provocative. 'He never fed me Bill. I paid my share,' she said calmly.

Bill grinned amiably. She was tall, like Jon, and with a similarity of build which had led many people to take them for brother and sister. Where on Jon the look was loose-limbed and laid back, on her it was elegant and graceful, an impression compounded by her long brown hair, tied loosely at the nape of her neck with a scarlet silk scarf, and by the slender fingers which at the moment dangled the pair of spectacles which she had put on to scrutinise Bill's face and then removed as though a ten second scan was enough for a lifetime.

'I need your help, Bill. I need somewhere to live for a bit.' She paused and gave him a slow, reluctant smile. 'I wondered if I could stay in your cottage.'

Bill frowned. 'My God! You must be desperate. Do you know where my cottage is?'

She laughed. 'It's up in North Essex, isn't it?'

'It's in the most beautiful corner of Essex, which is, to my mind, the most beautiful corner of England. But alas, at this time of year, it is also the most inaccessible and cold. I have only a minimum of so-called mod cons, the bedroom's full of rubble, the roof leaks and it's very damp and cold. You'd be miserable. Has Jon thrown you out?'

'In a manner of speaking.' She narrowed her lips. 'I thought we shared a flat, but apparently not.'

'So, you have split up?'

She nodded. 'The histrionics are over. We're both being frightfully civilised.' It hurt to talk about it.

She had known Bill for fifteen years, since they had been freshers together at university. He was one of her best friends, but she was not going to tell him about the money. What she had done with her savings to render her unable to pay a decent rent was none of his business. Besides, Jon had promised he would pay her back when he received his next advance. Or the next . . .

12

Cheerful, generous, feckless, selfish bloody Jon! and she was the mug who fell for him!

Bill leaned back and folded his arms across his chest. A stout, balding man in his mid thirties, he had a humorous, likable face which to his chagrin, failed to convey anything other than a perpetual, cheerful bonhomie.

'Am I right in thinking Jon has relieved you of most of the dosh you made with *Jane*?'

She raised an eyebrow. 'Is that what he told you?'

'Not in so many words, no. I guessed. I've known you both a long while, after all, before you even met each other. Are you completely skint or can you afford some rent?'

'Some,' she said guardedly. 'But not London prices.'

'No. Near me. In Essex. Up at Redall Bay. My neighbours have a cottage they want to rent to someone for six months. It's a couple of miles from mine; a lot more civilised. Quiet.' He gave a sudden laugh. 'Quiet as the grave.'

'Would they rent it to me?'

'I'm sure they would. They were talking about it last time I was up there. They need the money. If I recommend you and if you can rustle up a cheque for three months' rent in advance I'm pretty certain I can fix it for you.' He leaned forward abruptly and pulled open a desk drawer. The sheaf of photos he threw onto the blotter in front of her were crumpled and much thumbed. 'It's bleak, Kate. You'd better think hard about it. You would be terribly lonely.'

She picked them up with a glance at his face. 'I know it's bleak. I know the coast. I've been up there once or twice.'

The pictures featured a series of holiday scenes: people, boats, dogs, children, sand, shingle and always the sea – a grey-green, muddy sea. In one she saw a small cottage in the distance. 'Is that your place?'

He nodded. 'I don't go there much in the winter. I can't stand the cold and the desolation.'

'It looks lovely. But too crowded.' She glanced up at him mischievously. 'I want solitude. I am writing a book, don't forget.'

'What else?' With an expansive gesture of his arms Bill stood up. 'If I can find a tenant for Roger and Diana who can pay good solid money for the privilege of staying in that God-forsaken cottage of theirs freezing their balls off – saving your presence –

I shall earn loads of Brownie points with them and they'll be in my debt forever. Give me a couple of days to phone them and send them your cheque and I can assure you that provided it doesn't bounce, they will welcome you with open arms.'

She stood up. 'Don't tell Jon where I'm going, Bill, assuming he's even remotely interested,' she said as she left. 'At least for now I want it to be a complete break. On my terms.'

'Bitch.' It was said with great affection.

'Well, why not. He's dropped me in it.' She was surprised at her own lack of anger.

'Silly sod.' Bill grinned amiably. 'I'll tell you what. I'll drive down with you at the weekend. It won't do any harm for my place to have a quick airing, then you can drop me at the station on Sunday night and I shall abandon you to the east wind and return here to my creature comforts.'

It did not take long to clear her stuff out of Jon's flat. There didn't seem to be much of it – apart from her books, of course.

They had discussed it all amicably in the end, just as she had determined that they should. They had been adult and business-like and utterly calm in the division of their affairs – a divorce without the complications of a marriage – and with a cool kiss on her cheek Jon had departed for New York several days earlier than he had originally intended. He did not ask her where she was going; they had not mentioned the money.

A half-dozen boxes and suitcases packed into the back of her car, a carton of plants, carefully wrapped against the cold wind, and an armful of unwanted clothes. That was the sum total of her life in London which she ferried to the attic of Bill's house in Hampstead – all to be put in store except the plants which were to be pampered and coddled by him far from the East Anglian wind. That left her laptop and printer, her books, her boxes of filing cards and notes and a couple of suitcases packed with jeans and thick sweaters and rubber boots. It was not until she had piled them into her small Peugeot and gone for one last look around the flat that the small treacherous lump in her throat threatened to choke her. She swallowed it sternly. This was the beginning of the rest of her life. Slamming the front door behind her she pushed her keys through the letter box, hearing them thump onto the carpet the other side of the door with a dull finality which suited her mood exactly. She had not enquired how Cyrus Grandini would gain entry to the flat and Jon had not told her. Turning the collar of her jacket up around her ears she ran down the steps towards her car. She would pick Bill up at the Beeb on her way across London and then together they would head north-east.

III

The tide crept higher, drawn inescapably onward by the full moon lost behind ten thousand feet of towering cumulus. Softened by the sleet in the ice-cold wind the sand grew muddy and pliant beneath the questing fingers of water. The shingle bank was deserted, lonely in the darkness. As the water lapped the stones in silence, gently probing, a lump of sand broke away from the mound behind it and subsided into the blackness of the water. Behind it, a further fissure formed. Matted grass strained and tore, a network of fine roots pulling, clinging, interlocked. The grass hissed before the wind, grains of sand flicked into the air by a gust, veering round into the east. Now the wind and the tide were of one mind and, inexorably, the water crept forward.

The small pocket of clay, left on the floodplain of the River Storwell after the glaciers had melted, had two thousand years ago, been at the bottom of a freshwater marsh. Long ago drained, the marsh had gone and the rich pasture which replaced it had turned, over the centuries, to arable then to scrub and to woodland, and then, as the sea advanced inexorably on the eastern coasts of England, to shingle beach. Now, after nearly two millennia of change and of erosion the soil, sand and gravel which still separated the clay from the air and the light was only centimetres thick.

IV

Diana Lindsey's plump figure was swathed in a thick pair of trousers, an anorak and a vast lambswool shawl as she stood in the doorway of Redall Cottage watching her eldest son lighting the fire. She was a small fair-haired woman, pretty, with light green eyes and reddened, work-worn hands.

'Hurry up. Lunch will be ready soon, Greg. I've already wasted enough of this morning with all your fuss.' She cast a professional glance around the small living room. Watery sunlight poured through the window, illuminating the bright rag rugs on the floor and the small sofa and chair which had been pulled up around the fire. She was pleased with the room. They had only had twenty-four hours to tidy the place, to move Greg's belongings out of it and to replace them with a few pieces of respectable furniture: a table and two chairs for the kitchen; a small Victorian nursing chair for the bedroom where the double bed had been the only fixture; sheets, towels, a box of basic groceries – Bill's idea and well beyond the landlord's brief, but she had agreed with him that the place would be cold and lonely enough without finding there was no food or coffee in the cupboards and no shops for miles, and those there were, not open until Monday morning. The final touch had been to light the woodburner which was settling now to a steady roar, and fill a vase with winter jasmine for the kitchen table.

Greg latched the burner's doors and stood up. His burly presence filled the small room and he had to bend his head beneath the ceiling beams. 'Right. Satisfied now, Ma? Lady Muck will be comfortable as a bug in a turd here.'

'Don't be vulgar, Greg.' Her reproach was automatic. Bored. She went through into the kitchen and had a final look round there, too. The pots and pans and plates were almost unused – Greg had never bothered to cook anything except coffee as far as

17

she could tell. The knives and forks and spoons she had brought over from the farmhouse. 'Right. Let's get back. Bill phoned to say they would probably be here by tea time. He wanted her to settle in before it got dark.'

'How wise.' Greg pulled open the front door. Behind them the flames in the woodburner dipped and flared and steadied behind the blackening glass of the doors. 'Shall I call Allie?'

Leaving his mother to head for the Land Rover parked at the end of the rutted track which led through the half mile or so of bleak woods separating the cottage from Redall Farmhouse, he turned and walked around the side of the cottage. The small, timber-framed building, painted a soft pink, nestled in a half-moon of trees. Behind it, short rabbit-cropped turf formed an informal lawn which straggled towards the sand and shingle spit separating the estuary of the River Storwell from the beach and the cold waves of the North Sea. It was a windy, exposed site, even today when the sun was shining fitfully from behind the broken cloud.

'Allie!' Greg cupped his hands around his mouth and bellowed for his sister. As his mother opened the door of the Land Rover and climbed in, he disappeared around to the far side of the cottage into the teeth of the wind.

Alison Lindsey, fifteen years old, her blonde hair tightly caught by a rubber band into a pony tail tucked into the neck of her yellow windcheater, was crouching in the lee of one of the shingle and sand dunes which stood between the cottage and the sea. She glanced up as her brother appeared and raised her hand, the wind whipping tendrils of hair into her eyes.

'What have you found?' He jumped down the small sandy cliff to stand beside her. Out of the wind it was suddenly very quiet, almost warm in the trapped sunlight.

'Look. The sea washed the sand away here. It must have happened at high tide.' She had been scrabbling at the sand; her fingers were caked with it. He could see where she had caught her nail. A small streak of blood mingled with the golden red grains stuck to her skin. She had dug away the side of the dune and pulled something free. 'See. It's some kind of pottery.'

He took it from her, curious. It was slipware, red, the glaze shiny with a raised pattern, hardly scratched by the sand.

'Pretty. It must be something someone chucked out of the

cottage. Come on Allie. Ma's in a ferment. She wants to feed us all before she goes off to Ipswich or wherever it is she is going this afternoon, and I want to get out of here before Lady Muck turns up.'

Alison took the piece of pottery from her brother and wedged it into her anorak pocket. She glanced up at him. 'Why do you call her that? She's famous, you know. She's written a book.'

'Exactly.' He smiled grimly. 'And no doubt will feel herself superior in every way to us country bumpkins.' He gave a short laugh as he scrambled up the bank and turned to give his sister a hand, hauling her bodily out of the sandy hollow. 'Well, she'll soon find out that living in the country at this time of year is not the same as swanning out for the odd picnic in the summer. Then perhaps she'll go away.'

'And let you have the cottage back?' Alison surveyed him shrewdly, her green eyes serious.

'And let me have my cottage back.' He looked at her thoughtfully. 'Don't say anything to Ma, Allie, but I think between us you and I can find a way to chase Lady Muck away from Redall Cottage, don't you?' He smiled. 'Perhaps we can give the weather a helping hand. Scare her off somehow.'

'You bet.' She laughed. Then she frowned. 'But don't we need the money?'

'Money!' Greg snorted. 'Doesn't anyone think of anything else around here? For the love of Mike, there are other things in the world. We're not going to starve. Dad's pay-off and his pension are more than enough to last us for years. We can afford petrol and electricity and food. They can afford to buy booze. My dole money buys my paint and canvas. What does every one want all this money for?'

Alison shrugged dutifully. She knew better than to argue with her elder brother. Besides he was probably right. She sternly pushed down a sneaking suspicion that his views were simplistic and wildly immature – he was, after all, twelve years older than she – and, pushing her wispy hair out of her eyes for the thousandth time as they reached the Land Rover, she pulled open the door and hauled herself into the front seat beside her mother.

In the farmhouse the third Lindsey offspring, Patrick, had been laying the table for lunch, walking silently around the kitchen in his socks as his father dozed in the cane chair before the Aga, two cats asleep in his lap. The silence of the room was broken only by the ticking of the grandfather clock in the corner and by the gentle bubbling from the heavy pan on the stove. The air was rich and heavy with the fragrance of the cooking chicken in its thick herb-flavoured gravy. Two years older than Alison, Patrick was the studious member of the family. Upstairs in his bedroom – the north-facing end room above the kitchen, according to Alison the best room in the house because of its size – computer, printer, calculating machines and hundreds of books vied with one another for space, overflowing from tables and chairs on to the floor and even from time to time out into the corridor outside his sister's room. At the moment Patrick was lost in thought, his mind still fully occupied with his school project. He noticed neither the noise of the engine as his brother drove up outside and parked the Land Rover around the side of the house, nor the speed with which Number Two cat, Marmalade Jones, jumped off his master's lap and onto the worktop where he proceeded to lick the pat of butter which Patrick had incautiously withdrawn from the fridge.

The opening door woke Roger, startled Patrick and gave the cat an unwonted and sudden attack of conscience.

'My goodness it's cold out there.' Diana went straight to the heavy iron pan simmering quietly on the Aga and peered inside it before she took off her coat.

'Bill rang.' Roger stretched and reached for the newspaper which had slid from his inert fingers as he slept. Indignant at the move, Number One cat, Serendipity Smith, slipped from his knees and diving through the open studwork which separated the kitchen from the living room, went to sit on the rug in front of the fire, staring enigmatically into the embers. 'They should be here by about three. Apparently she's an absolute cracker!' He grinned at his eldest son and gave a suggestive wink. 'You might try charming her, Greg, just this once. I can't believe as your mother's son you are completely devoid of the art.'

'Oh you.' Diana gave her husband a playful tap on the head.

Greg ignored them both. Sealed in an intense inner world of frustrated imagination he frequently missed his parents' affectionate banter. Walking through to the fire he stooped and threw on a log. 'Half the old dune behind the cottage has gone,' he called through to them. 'You know the one which shelters it from the north-easterlies. A few more tides like that one last week and we'll need to worry about the cottage being washed away.'

'Rubbish.' Diana, having hung up her coat was now tying a huge apron over her trousers. The apron sported a giant red London bus which appeared to be driving across the rotund acres of her stomach. She shook her head. 'No way. That cottage has been there hundreds of years.'

'And once upon a time it was miles from the sea, my darling.' Roger stood up. Painfully thin, his face was haggard with tiredness, a symptom of the illness which had forced him to take early retirement. 'Come on. Why don't I open a bottle of wine. That stew of yours smells so good I could eat it.' He smiled and his wife, on her way back to the Aga with her wooden spoon, paused to give him a quick hug.

'Show Dad the piece of china you found in the dune, Allie,' Greg called from the next room. His sister, still wearing her anorak, had seated herself at the table, her elbows planted amongst the knives and forks which Patrick had aligned with geometric neatness. She fished in her pocket and produced it.

Roger took it from her and turned it over with interest. 'Its unusual. Old I should say. Look at the colour of that glaze, Greg.' He held it out towards his eldest son. Reluctantly, Greg left the fire. Taking the fragment he turned it over in his hands. 'You could take it into the museum some time, kiddo,' he said to Alison. 'See what they say.'

'I might.' Alison stood up and they were all surprised to see her eyes alight with excitement. Her usual carefully-studied air of ennui had for a moment slipped. 'Do you know what I think? I think it's Roman. There's stuff just like it in the castle museum.'

'Oh, Allie love, it couldn't be. Not out here.' Diana had produced four glasses from the cupboard. She handed her husband the corkscrew. 'The Romans never came this far out of Colchester.'

'They did, actually. They've found a lot of Roman stuff at Kindling's farm,' Roger put in. He tore the foil from the top of the wine bottle. 'Do you remember? They found the remains of a villa there. Some rich Roman chap from Colchester retired here. They found an inscription.'

21

Alison nodded. 'Marcus Severus Secundus,' she said, intoning the words softly.

'That's right.' Roger nodded. 'There was an article about him in the local paper. And they found even older stuff too. Iron Age, I think it was, or Bronze Age or something. Are you still thinking of doing something archaeological for your project, Allie?' He smiled at his daughter.

'Might.' Her sudden burst of enthusiasm had apparently run its course. She sat down again and spread her elbows, scattering knives and forks. Patrick frowned, but he said nothing. He had learned a long time ago that a comment from him would produce a tirade of abuse from his sister which would upset everyone and end up with the whole meal being spoiled. It had happened before too often.

'I'm going to excavate the dune.' Alison's sudden announcement stopped Roger's hand in mid air as he poured the wine.

'That sounds a bit ambitious, old girl,' he said cautiously. 'There would be a lot of hard digging and you might not find anything.'

'I found something before.'

'In the same place?' Greg looked across at her, disbelieving. 'Why didn't you say?'

'None of your business.' Alison reached for a glass of wine which left Patrick without one.

'Hey, that's mine –'

'Pour yourself one.' When neither parent said anything she raised the glass defiantly to her lips and took a sip.

'What did you find, Allie?' Roger's voice took on the conciliatory tone he often used with his daughter – soft, persuasive, almost pleading.

'I'll show you.' She rose to her feet, and, her glass still in her hand, trailed towards the staircase which led from the living room behind the door in the corner by the inglenook.

'There's loads of books on archaeology in her room,' Patrick put in in an undertone when she was out of earshot.

'You haven't been in there again.' Diana was exasperated. 'You know she doesn't like it –'

'She nicked my Aran sweater. I needed it.' Patrick's mouth settled in a hard line, exactly like his sister's as Alison reappeared with a shoe box in her hand.

'Look. I found all these on the beach there, or in the cliff or in

22

the saltings, and these two I dug up from the dune.' She tipped the contents of the box onto the table amongst the knives and forks. For once there was no comment about the shower of dirty sand which descended over the cutlery on Diana's scrubbed table top: several shards, a few pieces of carved bone and one or two unrecognisable fragments of twisted, corroded metal. 'I think it's a grave. A Roman grave,' she said solemnly.

There was a moment's silence.

Slowly Greg shook his head. 'No chance. If it's anything at all, it's one of those red hill things – to do with ancient salt workings. Not that that isn't extremely interesting,' he went on hastily after a glance at the rebellious set of his sister's face. 'Perhaps we should get someone over here who knows about these things.'

'No!' Alison rounded on him furiously. 'I don't want anyone knowing about it. No one at all. It's mine. My grave. I found it. You're not to tell anyone it's there, do you understand. Not anyone at all. I am going to dig there. Anything I find is mine. If you tell anyone it will ruin everything. Everything!'

Sweeping her treasures back into the box, she clamped the lid on it and flung out of the room.

'Let her be.' Diana turned comfortably to the stove. 'She'll grow bored with it when she realises how much hard work is involved. And I'm sure there is nothing there. Nothing at all that would interest anyone sane, anyway.' She smiled tolerantly. 'Clear up that mess would you, Patrick darling and then let's eat, otherwise our guests will be here before we've finished.'

V

His nails had cut deep welts into the palms of his hand; the veins stood out, corded, pulsating on his forehead and neck, but his silence was the silence of a stalking cat. Not a leaf crisped beneath his soft-soled sandals, not a twig cracked. Soundlessly, he parted the leaves and peered into the clearing. His wife's long tunic and cloak lay amongst the bluebells, a splash of blue upon the blue. The man's weapons, and his clothing, lay beside them. He could see the sword unsheathed, the blade gleaming palely in the leaf-dappled sunlight. He could hear her moans of pleasure, see the reddened marks of her nails on his shoulders. She had never writhed like that beneath him, never uttered a sound, never raked his skin in her ecstasy. Beneath him the woman he adored and worshipped would lie still; compliant, dutiful, her eyes open, staring up at the ceiling, on her lips the smallest hint of a sneer.

He swallowed his bile, schooling himself to silence, watching, waiting for the climax of their passion. His sword was at his waist, but he did not reach for it. Death at the moment of fulfilment would send them to the gods together. It would be too easy, too quick. Even as he watched them he felt the last remnants of his love curdle and settle into thick hatred. The punishment he would inflict upon his wife would last for the rest of her days; for her lover he would plan a death which would satisfy even his fury. But until the right moment came, he would wait. He would welcome her back to his hearth and to his bed with a smile. His hatred would remain, like his anger, hidden.

Watery sunlight filled Roger's study, reflecting in from the bleak garden, throwing pale shifting lights across the low ceiling with its heavy oak beams. Greg flung himself down in his father's chair and stared round morosely. He would never be able to paint here. Somehow he had to get Lady Muck out of the cottage – his cottage – so he could go back. She must not be allowed to stay.

The small room was stacked with canvasses and sketch pads.

24

His easel filled the space between the desk and the window; the table was laden with boxes of paints and pencils and the general debris he had fetched down from the cottage; a new smell of linseed oil and white spirit overlaid the room's natural aroma of old books, Diana's rich crumbling pot pourri and lavender furniture polish. Thoughtfully he stood up. He leafed through a stack of canvasses and lifted one onto the easel, then he sat down again, staring at it.

The portrait bothered him. It was one of a series he had done over the past two or three years. All of the same woman, they were sad, mysterious; evocations of mood rather than of feature; of beauty by implication rather than definition. This was the largest canvas – three feet by four – that he had tackled for a long time and it had given him the most trouble.

He sat gnawing at the knuckle of his left thumb for several minutes before he glanced round for brush and palette. It was the colours that were wrong. She was too hazy; too indistinct. Her colouring needed to be more definite, her vivacity more pronounced. He stood close to the canvas, leaning forward intently, and stabbed at it with the brush. He had made her too beautiful, the bitch, too seductive. He ought to paint her as she was – a whore; a traitor; a cat on heat.

His tongue protruding a little from the corner of his mouth, he worked furiously at the painting, blocking in the face, shading the planes of the cheeks, sketching lips and eyes, touching in the line of the hair, his anger growing with every brushstroke.

It was a long time before he threw down the brush, wiping his hands carelessly on the front of his old, ragged sweater. He stood back and stared at his handiwork through narrowed eyes, aware that as the sun moved lower in the sky, slanting first across the estuary and then across the bleak winter woods, the light was changing once again and with it her face. He glared down at the palette he had slid onto his father's desk, aware that the anger was leaving him as swiftly as it had come and wondering, not for the first time, where it came from.

VI

Turning the car off the road Kate found they were bumping along an unmade track through a wood. Before them the sky, laced with shredded, blowing cloud had that peculiar intensity of light which denotes the close proximity of the sea.

'I hope we don't have to go far down here,' she commented, slowing to walking pace as the small vehicle grounded for the second time on the deep ruts. Winding down the window she took a deep appreciative breath of the ice-cold air. It carried the sharp, resinous tang of pine and earth and rotting leaves.

'I'm afraid it gets worse.' Bill grimaced. 'And you'll have to leave your car at the farmhouse. Roger or Greg will run all your stuff up to the cottage in their Land Rover.'

The track forked. In front of them a rough wooden gibbet held two or three fire brooms – threadbare, broken. She brought the car to a standstill. 'Which way?'

'Right. My place is up there to the left – about half a mile. The farmhouse is down here.' He gestured through the windscreen and cautiously she let in the clutch once more. The track began to descend sharply. They bounced again into the ruts as the wood grew more dense. Pine was interspersed with old stumpy oaks, hazel breaks strung with ivy and dried traveller's joy and thickets of black impenetrable thorn.

The farmhouse itself stood at the edge of the woods, facing east across the saltings. Behind it a thin strip of field and orchard allowed the fitful sunshine to brighten the landscape before another wood separated the farmhouse gardens from the sea. There was no sign of any cottage.

She halted the car beside a black-boarded barn and sat for a moment staring out. The farmhouse was pink washed, a long, low building, covered in leafless creepers which in the summer were probably clematis and roses. Even in the depths of winter the place looked extraordinarily pretty.

'What a lovely setting.'

'Not too wild for you?' Bill glanced beyond the farmhouse to the mudflats. As far as the eye could see there was nothing but mud and water and grey-green stretches of salting. A stray low shaft of sunlight shone from behind them throwing a sunpath over the mud towards the water. The rich colour lasted a moment and then it had gone.

Bill opened the car door allowing biting, pure air into the warm fug. 'Come on. It will start getting dark soon. I think we should get you settled in.'

Kate surveyed her hosts as she shook hands with them. Roger and Diana Lindsey were both in their fifties, she guessed. Comfortable, quiet, welcoming. She found herself responding immediately to their warmth.

'I thought you would like some tea here before you go up to the cottage,' Diana said at once, ushering her towards the sofa. 'Make yourself comfy – move those cats – and then I'll give my son a call. He is going to take your stuff up there for you. It's a long walk carrying luggage.'

'And she's got a heap of it,' Bill put in. He was standing with his back to the fire, his palms held out behind him towards the smouldering logs. 'Computers and stuff.'

'Oh, my goodness.' Diana frowned. 'In which case you'll certainly need help.'

'Where is the cottage?' Kate, while enjoying the soporific comfort of the tea and the warmth of the fire, was eager to see it. Over the last couple of days her excitement, though partly dampened by the thought of how much she was missing Jon – a thought she had deliberately tried to erase – had been intense.

'It's about half a mile from here. Through the wood. You're right on the edge of the sea out there, my dear. I hope you've brought lots of warm clothes.' Solicitously Diana refilled Kate's cup, inserting herself between Kate and the staircase door where she had spotted a movement. The kids were spying. No doubt any moment now they would appear. She sighed. Kids indeed. She meant Alison and Greg. Patrick would no doubt be upstairs by now with his computers and would not reappear until called

27

for supper. It was her elder son – a grown man, old enough to know better – and her daughter, who were, if she were any judge of character, going to cause trouble.

She glanced over her shoulder at Roger. 'Give Greg a call. I want him to help Miss Kennedy –'

'Kate, please.'

'Kate.' She flashed Kate a quick smile. 'He could start loading her stuff into the Land Rover.'

'I don't want to be a nuisance.'

'You won't be.' Was it Kate's imagination, or was there a certain grim determination in the way Diana said those words?

Greg, when called, turned out to be a man in his late twenties or early thirties, Kate guessed, which made him around her age or slightly younger. His handsome features were slightly blurred – too many beers and too little care of himself – and his thick pullover was smeared with oil paint. He shook hands with her amiably enough but she sensed a hint of reserve, even resentment in his manner. It was enough to make her question her first impression that here was a very attractive man.

'I'm sorry. It's a nuisance for you to have to drive me to the cottage,' she said. She met his eyes challengingly.

'But necessary if our tenant is to be safely installed,' he replied. His voice was deep; musical but cold.

Bill must have felt it too. She saw him frown as he levered himself to his feet from the low sofa. 'Come on, Greg. I'll give you a hand. Leave the others to finish their tea, eh?'

As the front door opened and the two men disappeared into the swiftly-falling dusk, a wisp of fragrant apple smoke blew back down the chimney.

'You can park your car in the barn, Kate,' Roger said comfortably. He leaned back in his chair, stretching his legs out towards the fire. 'It'll be out of the worst of the weather there. Pick it up whenever you want, and if you have any heavy groceries and things at any time give us a shout and we'll run them over for you. It's a damn nuisance the track is so bad. I keep meaning to ask our neighbour if he'll bring a digger or something up here and level it off a bit, but you know how it is. We've never got round to it.'

'I've come for the solitude.' Kate smiled at him. 'I really don't want to be rushing up and down. I'll lay in some stores at the nearest shop and then I'd like to cut myself off from the world for a bit.' The thought excited her. The great emptiness of the country after London, the sharp, clean air as she had climbed out of the car, had heightened her anticipation.

'You'll be doing that all right. Especially if the weather is bad,' Roger gave a snort which might have been a laugh. 'There is a telephone over there, however. You might find you're glad of it after a bit, but if you want peace you'd better keep the number quiet.' He looked up as the door opened.

'All loaded.' Bill grinned at them. 'I think what I'll do, if you don't mind, Kate, is begin to make my way back to my place. It's quite a walk from here. I'll leave you to Greg and I'll wander over tomorrow morning if that's all right. Then I can show you the way back on foot in daylight, and perhaps we can have a drink together before you drop me off in Colchester to catch the train for London.'

The Land Rover's headlights lit up the trees with an eerie green light as they lurched slowly away from the farmhouse into the darkness. Kate found herself sliding around on the slippery, hard seat and she grabbed frantically at the dash to give herself something to hold on to, with a worried thought for the computer stored somewhere in the back.

'Sorry. Am I going too fast?' Greg slowed slightly. He glanced at her. He had already taken note of her understated good looks. Her hair was mousy but long and thick, her bones good, her clothes expensive, but he got the feeling she wasn't much interested in them. The undeniable air of chic which clung to her was, he was fairly sure, achieved by accident rather than design and the thought annoyed him. It seemed unfair that she should have so much. 'I take it you're not the nervous type. I can't think of many women who would want to live out here completely alone in the middle of winter.'

Kate studied his profile in the glow of the dashboard lights. 'No. I'm not the nervous type,' she said. 'I enjoy my own company. And I've come here to work. I don't think I'll have time to feel lonely.'

'Good. And you're not afraid of ghosts, I hope.'

It had been Allie's idea, to attempt to scare her away with talk of ghosts. It was worth a try. At least until he thought of something better.

29

'Ghosts?'

'Only joking.' His eyes were fixed on the track ahead. 'This land belonged once to a Roman officer of the legion, Marcus Severus Secundus. There's a statue of him in Colchester Castle. A handsome bastard. I like to think he strolls around the garden sometimes, but I can't say I've ever seen him.' He grinned. Not too much too fast. The woman wasn't a fool. Or the nervous type, obviously. 'I'm sure he's harmless.' He narrowed his eyes, concentrating on the track.

Beside him Kate smiled. Her excitement if anything increased.

The cottage when it appeared at last seemed to her delight to be a miniature version of the farmhouse. It had pink walls and creeper and was, she could see in the headlights as they pulled up facing it, a charmingly rambling small building with a peg-tiled roof and smoking chimney. Beyond it she could see the dull gleam of the sea between towering banks of shingle. Leaving the headlights on, Greg jumped down. He made no effort to help her, instead going straight round to the rear of the vehicle, leaving her to struggle with the unfamiliar door handle. When she at last managed to force the door open and jump down, he straightened, his hair streaming into his eyes in the wind. Before she realised what he was doing, he threw a bunch of keys at her. She missed and they fell at her feet in the dark.

'Butterfingers.' The mocking words reached her through the wind. 'Go and open the front door, I'll carry this stuff in for you and then I can get back.'

The door had swollen slightly with the damp and she found she had to push it hard to make it open. By the time she had done it Greg was standing impatiently behind her, his arms full of boxes. She scrabbled for a light switch and found it at last. The light revealed a small white-painted hall with a staircase immediately in front of her and three doors, two to the left and one to the right.

'On the right,' Greg directed. 'I'll dump all this for you and you can sort it out yourself.'

She opened the door. The living room, low-ceilinged and heavily beamed like its counterpart in the farmhouse, boasted a sofa and two easy chairs. In the deep fireplace a wood burning stove glowed quietly, warming the room. The other three walls each had a small-paned window, beyond which the black windy night was held at bay by the reflection of the lamp as she switched it on. She crossed and drew the curtains on each in turn. By the time she had finished Greg had brought in another pile of stuff.

'Well, that's it,' he said at last. He had made no attempt to tidy it or distribute things for her. All were lumped together in a heap in the middle of the rug. 'If you need anything you can tell us tomorrow.'

'I will. Thank you.' She gave him a smile.

He did not respond. With a curt goodnight he turned and ducked out of the front door, pulling it closed behind him. Resisting a childish urge to run to the window and watch him leave she saw the glow of the headlights brighten the curtains for a moment as they swept across them, then they disappeared. She was alone.

Walking out into the hall she pulled the door bolt across and then turned back. The sudden wave of loneliness in the total silence was only to be expected. She sighed, looking round. Somehow she had expected that Bill would be with her this first evening. Or that the new landlord would invite her over for supper.

It had all been such a rush up until now. The packing, the storing of her stuff, borrowing books from the London Library, arranging her new life, separating herself from Jon; she had had little time to think and she had welcomed her exhaustion each evening. It meant she did not dwell on things. Here there would be plenty of time to dwell unless she was very careful. She straightened her shoulders. There would also be plenty of time to work, but first she would explore her new domain.

The cottage was very small. Downstairs there was only the one living room with a small kitchen and even smaller bathroom next to it. Upstairs there were two bedrooms, almost identical in size. Only one had a bed. In that room someone had made an attempt at cosiness. There was a chest of drawers and a small Victorian chair upholstered in rubbed gold velvet, with a couple of soft cushions tossed onto it. There was a new rug on the sloping floor and a wardrobe, which touched the low beamed ceiling. Inside was a row of wire hangers. Kate went downstairs again. Her initial excitement and sense of adventure was slipping away. The silence oppressed her. Taking a deep breath she went into the kitchen and reached for the kettle. While it boiled she lugged her two suitcases upstairs and left them. She would hang up the dresses and two skirts which she had brought with her later. All her other clothes – jeans, trousers, sweaters – she could stuff into the small chest of drawers tomorrow. She did not feel like unpacking this evening.

After sorting out some of her books and papers, stacking them all neatly on the table in the living room, and putting the food and the bottle of Scotch she had brought with her into the kitchen cupboards she felt too tired to do any more. She made herself some tea, selected a couple of tapes and sat down, exhausted, on the sofa near the fire, her feet curled up under her. Her hands cupped around the mug, she sat listening to the strains of Vaughan Williams on her cassette player, strangely aware of the giant heave and swell of the sea outside beyond the shingle bank, even though she could not hear it.

She should have felt pleased with herself. She was in the country at last. She was ready to begin work. She had the peace and quiet she desired – Greg's attitude had not left her in any doubt that her privacy would be respected – and yet there was a nagging sadness, a feeling of anticlimax which had not a little to do with Jon, curse him. Only three weeks before, she had been living with him, researching the book, settled, a Londoner at least for the foreseeable future, and now here she was in a small cottage on the wild north-eastern coast of Essex with strangers for neighbours, no money, no man, no fixed abode and only Lord Byron for company.

Glancing at the floor where her boxes of books lay in a pool of lamplight she stood up again restlessly. She went over and, groping for her glasses in the pocket of her jeans, she began wearily to tear the sticky tape from the top of one of them. She must stay positive. Forget Jon. Forget London. Forget everything except the book.

The door banging upstairs made her jump. She glanced up at the ceiling and she could feel her heart thumping suddenly somewhere in the back of her throat. For a moment she did nothing, then slowly she straightened.

There was no one in the house so it must have been the wind, but at the foot of the stairs she paused, looking up into the darkness, the thought of Greg's legionnaire suddenly in the forefront of her mind.

Taking a firm grip on herself she walked up onto the landing. Both doors stood open as she had left them. Switching on the light she peered into the bedroom where earlier she had put her cases side by side near the cupboard. She looked round the room, satisfied herself that nothing was amiss and turned off the light. She repeated the action across the landing, staring round the empty bedroom, her eyes gazing uncomfortably at the two windows which were curtainless. The glass reflected the cold light of the central naked bulb and she was very conscious once again of the blackness of the night outside.

Frowning, she went downstairs. There had been nothing that she could see to account for the noise. She peered into the bathroom and the kitchen and then turned back to the living room.

The room was distinctly chilly. Walking over to the woodburner she peered at it doubtfully and, seeing the reassuring glow from within had disappeared, she stooped and reached for the latch. The metal was hot. She swore under her breath and looked round for something to pad her hands. Finding nothing she tugged at her sleeve and, wrapping the wool of her jersey around her fingers, she jiggled the latch undone and swung the doors open. The stove contained nothing but a bed of embers.

She glanced round but she had already realised that her tour of the cottage had yielded no coal; no log basket. She had grown spoiled living in London; the subject of heating had never crossed her mind. Central heating arrived for her these days at the flick of a switch. The hot water and heating in this cottage, it dawned on her suddenly, probably all depended on this small stove. Why hadn't Greg mentioned it? Surely the first thing he should have told her was how to heat the place. She shook her head in irritation. The omission was probably deliberate. She would have had to be very dense not to have sensed his hostility and resentment. Teach the townie a lesson. Well, if the townie wasn't going to freeze to death she would have to find some fuel from somewhere. A swift search produced one box of matches in the kitchen drawer, – thank heaven for that. As a non smoker it had never crossed her mind to bring matches. But there were no fire lighters, and there was no torch. There was nothing for it. Cursing herself for her own stupidity she realised she was going to have to explore outside in the dark.

Firmly putting all thoughts of the unexplained noise out of her head, she pulled on her jacket and gloves and with some reluctance she walked into the hall, unbolted the front door and pulled it open, fastening the latch back as she peered out into the darkness.

The wind caught her hair and pulled it back from her face, searing her cheeks. It was fresh and sharp with the scent of the sea and the pine woods which crowded across the grass towards her. She stood still for a moment, very conscious that she was silhouetted in the doorway. Reminding herself that there was no one watching she stared out at the path of light which ran from her feet in a great splash along the track before it dissipated between the trees. On either side of it the darkness was intense. She could see nothing beyond the muddy track with its wind-blown grasses and tangle of dead weeds.

Reluctantly, she stepped away from the door and began to walk along the front of the cottage, one hand extended cautiously in front of her touching the rough plastered walls. As her eyes grew used to the dark she could see the stars appearing one by one above her, and patches of cloud, pale against the blackness, and she became aware slowly of the sea shushing gently against the shingle in the distance and the wind sighing in the trees. She was straining her eyes as she reached the corner and peered round. Half way along the wall there was a small lean-to shed which must surely be some kind of fuel store. Moving a little faster as her confidence increased, she felt her feet grow wet in the grass.

Her fingers encountered the boards of the lean-to at last – overlapping, rough, splintery through her gloves. She groped her way around it until she came to the open doorway where she stopped, hesitating. The entrance gaped before her, the darkness intensely black and impenetrable after the luminous dark of the night, but she could smell the logs. Thick, resinous and warm, the scent swam up to her. Stooping, she groped through the doorway. Her hands met nothing but space. She reached out further and suddenly her fingers closed around something ice cold. A handle. Whatever it was slipped from her grasp and fell to the ground with a clatter. She stooped and picked it up. A spade. It was a spade. Leaning it against the wall, she took a cautious step forward, bending lower, and found herself right inside the shed. There at last her groping fingers encountered the tiers of stacked logs, their ends sharp, angled, their sides rough and rounded. Cautiously she pulled at one. The whole pile stirred and she leaped back. 'From the top, you idiot.' She found she had actually spoken out loud and the sound of her voice was somehow comforting. Straightening a little, she raised her hands, groping for the top of the pile and one by one she reached down four logs. That was all she could carry. Clutching them against her chest she stumbled out of the shed backwards and retraced her steps towards the corner of the wall. Once there the stream of cheerful light from the hall guided her back to the front door. She almost ran inside and throwing the logs down on the floor she turned and slammed the door shut, shooting the bolt home.

It was only as she looked down at the logs, covered in sawdust and cobwebs that she realised how frightened she had been. 'You idiot,' she said again. Shaking her head ruefully she began to pull off her anorak. What had she been afraid of? The silence? The wood? The dark?

She had been afraid of the dark as a child in her own little bedroom next to Anne's in their Herefordshire farmhouse. Night after night she would lie awake, not daring to move, hardly daring to breathe, her eyes darting here and there around the room, looking – looking for what? There was never anything there. Never anything frightening, just that awful, overwhelming loneliness, the fear that everyone else had left the house and abandoned her. Or died. Had her mother guessed in the end, or had she confessed? She couldn't remember now, but she did remember that her mother had given her a night light. It was a china owl, a white porcelain bird with great orange claws and huge enigmatic eyes. 'You'll scare the child to death with that thing,' her father, a country doctor with no time for cosseting his own family, had scoffed when her mother produced it from the attic, but Kate had loved it. When the small night-light candle was lit inside it the whole bird glowed with creamy whiteness and its eyes came alive. It was a kind bird; a wise bird; and it watched over her and kept her company and kept the spooks at bay. When she was older the owl had remained unlit, an ornament now, but her fear, tightly rationalised and controlled, had remained. Sometimes, even when she was a student at university, she had lain in her room in the hall of residence, the sheet pulled up to her chin, her fingers clutched in the pillow she was hugging to her chest as she stared at the dark square of the window. The fear had gone now.

Only one hint of it remained. She always opened the curtains at night. With them closed the darkness gave her claustrophobia. Jon had laughed at her, but he had conceded the open curtain. He liked it open because he loved to see the dawn creeping across the London roofs as the first blackbirds began to whistle from the television aerials across the city.

Well, that Kate was grown up now, and on her own and not afraid. Pulling herself together, she gathered up the logs and, walking through into the sitting room, she stacked them neatly in the fireplace beside the stove. Opening it again she peered in. The embers were very low. She looked at the logs thoughtfully. If she put one of those in it would just smother the small remaining sparks and put the whole thing out. She had no fire lighters. What she needed was newspaper and some dry, small twigs to rebuild the fire. She stared round.

In the kitchen the vegetable rack in the corner was lined with newspaper. She grabbed it, showering a residue of mud from long gone potatoes over the kitchen boards. There was enough to crumple into four good-sized wads. Stuffing them in around the log she lit it and closing the doors, slid open the damper. The sudden bright blaze was enormously satisfying but she held her breath. Would the paper burn and then leave the log to go out?

She glanced over her shoulder at the room and shivered. It had lost its appeal somehow. Her lap top computer and printer lying on the table rebuked her; the boxes of filing cards, the notebooks, the cardboard boxes full of books. She glanced at her watch. It was eight o'clock. She was hungry, she was tired and she was cold. A boiled egg, a cup of cocoa and a hot bath, if the wood-burner could be persuaded to work, and she would go to bed. Everything else could wait until morning. And daylight.

VII

It was bitterly cold and barely light. Well wrapped up in a Shetland sweater and thick jacket with two pairs of socks inside her boots and a pair of her younger brother's gloves, Alison Lindsey stood staring at the cottage from the shelter of the trees. It was in darkness. Downstairs the curtains were drawn, but upstairs both the front windows which looked down across the garden appeared to be uncurtained. She frowned, then plucking up her courage she sprinted across the grass. Heading straight for the log shed she ducked inside and groped around in the darkness. After a second she gave an exclamation of annoyance. Her tools had been moved. She kicked crossly at the firewood and leaped back with a mixture of fright and malicious satisfaction as one of the piles began to slip. Dodging the cascading logs she watched until they had stopped moving, waiting for the noise to die away. The dust settled, but there was no sound from the cottage. 'Lady Muck's asleep,' she whispered to herself and she gave a superior smile. She turned to the doorway again and then she saw her spade. It had been propped up in the corner.

Picking it up she peered out into the silent dawn. It was well before sunrise. The morning was damp and ice cold and there were still long dark shadows across the sea, stretching out into the black mist.

Running lightly she headed across the shingle and leaped down into the hollow on the seaward side of the dune. Her dune.

The tide in the night, she saw with satisfaction, had not been very high. The sea wrack on the shore, still wet with spume, was several feet short of her excavation and had come nowhere near the place where she was digging. Her tongue protruding slightly from between her teeth she set to, cutting the soft sand into sections and scooping it away from the side of the dune. From somewhere in the darkness along the shore she heard the scream of a gull.

Her hands were frozen after only a few moments in spite of the thick gloves and already her headache had come back. With an irritable sigh, she paused to rest, leaning on her spade as she blew on her wool-covered knuckles. The sand was crumbling where she had attacked it and as she watched, another section fell away by itself. With it it brought something large and curved and shiny. Throwing down the spade she bent over it and gently worked the object free of the sand. It was another section of pottery. Much larger this time. Large enough to hold the curve of the bowl or vase of which it had once formed a part. Through her gloves, as she dusted away the damp sand fragments, she could feel the engraved decoration. She stared at it for a long time, then carefully she put it to one side and attacked the sand with renewed vigour. Minutes later something else began to appear. It was thin and bent and a corroded green colour, like a rusty bit of old metal. Forgetting the pain in her temples she pulled at it in excitement. Thick as a man's thumb it was several inches long, with a rough knob at one end. Turning it over in her hands she stared at it for a long time, then, scrambling out of the hollow of her sheltered digging place she ran over the shingle towards the sea. The shingle was wet and smelled of salt and weed, the night's harvest of shells and dead crabs lying amongst the stones. Nearby she could see the gulls picking amongst them. Crouching down, her feet almost in the water, she swished the object back and forth in the edge of the tide and then she stared at it again. It was no cleaner. The greenness was a part of it. She took off her glove and ran a cautious finger over it, feeling a certain symmetrical roughness on the cold metal as though at some point in the distant past it had been carved, though now the incrustations of time and sea and sand had covered it forever.

Excited, she turned back towards the dune and stopped in her tracks. A freak gust of wind had risen. It had whipped the sand up and spun it into a vortex which danced for a moment across the beach and then dropped back to nothing. Behind her the first rim of the sun had appeared above the horizon. For a moment she hesitated, frowning. She was frightened, with the strange feeling that there was someone nearby, watching her. Shrugging, she huddled into her jacket, wedging her find into the pocket as she stared round. If there was someone there it would be a friend. Joe Farnborough from the farm, or Bill Norcross if he had decided to go for an early walk, or even Lady Muck herself or someone out walking their dog along the tide line.

Her spade was still lying where it had fallen in the sand and she took an uncertain step towards it. The skin was prickling on the back of her neck. It was a strange feeling, one she couldn't remember experiencing before, but instinctively she knew what it was. She was being watched! The words of a poem flitted suddenly through her head. Her mother had read it to her once when she was very small. The blood of the small, impressionable Alison had curdled as she listened wide-eyed, and the words had stuck. It was the only poem she had ever learned.

> When sunset lights are burning low,
> While tents are pitched and camp-fires glow,
> Steals o'er us, ere the stars appear,
> The furtive sense of Jungle Fear . . .

Primitive fear. Fear of danger which you cannot see.

She licked her lips nervously. 'Silly cow,' she said out loud. It was herself she meant. 'Stupid nerd. Move. Now. What's the matter with you?'

The sun had risen further. A red stain began to spread into the sea and imperceptibly it grew lighter. She clenched her fists and took a step towards the spade. Her mouth had gone dry and she was shaking. With cold. Of course it was with cold. Gritting her teeth she jumped back into the hollow and grabbed the spade, holding it in front of her with two hands. The wind had begun to blow again and it lifted the skirt of her jacket, billowing it around her, whipping her hair into her eyes. The dust was spinning again, rising near her feet. She rubbed her eyes with the back of her wrist. The sand was lifting, condensing. Almost it was the shape of a human figure.

Slowly she backed away from the dune and, scrambling out of the hollow, she began to move towards the cottage. Seconds later she broke into a run. Hurtling across the lawn she dived down the side of the building, threw the spade into the shed and pelted down the track towards the trees.

In the dune the piece of red-glazed pottery lay forgotten, covered already by a new scattering of sand.

VIII

Kate lay for a moment disorientated, staring up at the heavily-beamed ceiling, wondering where she was. Her dream had been so vivid, so threatening. Huddling down into a tight ball under the bedclothes she tried to piece it together, to remember what had been so frightening, but already she was having difficulty recalling the details and at last with some relief she gave up the attempt and, sitting up, she gazed around the unfamiliar room. It was ice cold. A diffuse grey light like no light she had seen before filtered in from between the undrawn curtains. It was eerie; luminous. Dragging the quilt around her she climbed out of bed and going to the east-facing window, she peered out. The sea was slate black, shadowed with mist and above it a low sun hung like a dark crimson ball shedding no reflection and little light. It was a cold, unenticing scene without perspective. She shivered and turned back into the room. Gathering up her clothes she ran down the stairs on ice cold feet and looked into the living room. There the curtains were still closed. After drawing them back she opened the doors of the woodburner and stared at it, depressed. The fire was out and the metal cold.

'Sod it!' She looked down at the single log. It was barely scorched from last night's paper blaze. To light it she would need firelighters, twigs, more paper . . .

Of course there would be no hot water either. Shivering, she abandoned the idea of washing and pulled on a pair of jeans. Thick socks and a heavy sweater and she was ready to forage once more in the log shed.

The outside world was bitterly cold. The garden – no more than a piece of rough turf and a couple of small bare flower beds – appeared to surround the cottage in a small compact circle; beyond it in the cold early-morning light the grass grew wilder and more lumpy and matted before almost at once giving way to the dunes and shingle banks which backed the sea.

As she stepped out of the front door a movement at the side of the cottage caught her eye and she stopped, astonished to find that her heart was beating faster than normal again. The fear in her dream was still with her and the silence and emptiness of the woods unnerved her. Forcing herself to walk outside she peered around and realised, relieved, that what she had seen was a rabbit. Three rabbits. They all straightened for a moment as she appeared, their ears upright, their eyes bulging with terror and then they bounded back into the trees. She smiled, amused and not a little embarrassed by her own fear. She was going to have to take herself in hand.

In the doorway of the shed she stopped. The spade was lying across the threshold. Stooping she picked it up. There were clods of wet muddy sand attached to the shoulders of the blade. Someone had used that spade recently – certainly since she had come out to the shed last night. She surveyed the woods but as far as she could see they were silent and still. Even the rabbits had gone.

Shrugging her shoulders, she gathered up another armful of logs and, this time spotting the pile of neatly stacked kindling in the corner of the shed, filled her pockets with twigs and small slivers of wood to help light the fire.

Hot coffee and a blazing furnace in the woodburner did much to restore her optimism as did the discovery that there was an electric immersion heater in a cupboard in the bathroom as a backup to the more esoteric uncertainties of hot water from logs. She ate a bowl of cereal and then set about unpacking in earnest.

Several times as she glanced through the windows she noticed that the day was clearing. The mist was thinning and the sun had gained a little in strength. By the time her bags and boxes were empty and she was storing them in the spare bedroom, the sea was a brilliant blue to match the sky.

Turning from the curtainless window her eye was caught by a stack of canvasses behind the door which she hadn't noticed earlier. They stood, face to the wall, in a patch of deep shadow. Curious, she turned one towards her. The painting was of the sea – a strangely surrealist, nightmare sea. With a grimace she pulled out another canvas. It repeated the theme as did the next and the next. Then came two more, scenes of the cottage itself, one in the autumn where a bland chocolate-box house was surrounded by a curtain of flame, the other a representation of the house as it

41

would look beneath the nightmare sea. She stared at the latter for a long time and then with a shudder she stacked it back against the wall. They were all painted by the same hand, and a hand which commanded a great deal of talent and power, but she did not like them. They were cruel; twisted in their conception.

Closing the door with a shiver she ran down the stairs and back into the sun-filled living room where her books and papers were laid out on the table ready to start work. Putting the paintings firmly out of her mind she stood looking down at the table.

The book was there, in her head, ready to start and it was going to be even better than *Jane*. Kate smiled as she pulled her notepad towards her and switched on her word processor.

The knock on the front door two hours later took her by surprise. She had completely forgotten Bill.

'Hi!' He grinned at her as she led the way into the living room. 'How are you? Ready for lunch?'

She stared at him, miles away, reluctant to lose the mood, aching to go on writing.

Bill was watching her. 'Penny for them,' he said softly. 'You didn't hear a word I said, did you? I've boobed. I've intruded on the writer with her muse.'

'Oh, Bill, I'm sorry. Of course I heard you.' Kate dragged herself back to the present and gave herself a little shake. 'Blow the muse; she can go back in her box for a few hours. And yes, that's a super idea. I'd love lunch.'

The walk through the wood was thoroughly enjoyable and eagerly she looked around, noting the crisp air, the soft muddy track, the whispering fragrant pines, the winter-dead oak, and birch and hazel bright with young catkins, as she plodded beside him, her hands in her pockets, throwing off her preoccupation with the background of the poet's father, mad Jack Byron, in order to recount her adventures of the night before.

'That's typical of Greg, I'm afraid, not to tell you about the fire or leave you any logs,' Bill said, shaking his head. 'There's a petty streak to him. He's angry about having to give up the cottage for you.' He kicked out at a rotten branch which lay half across the track.

'I didn't realise he lived there.'

'Oh yes. Greg is a brilliant painter. He dropped out of university about six years ago, halfway through getting a Fine Art degree, came home here and more or less squatted. That was before Roger had to give up work – I don't know if you realise, but he's got cancer.' He paused for a moment. 'Anyway, the Lindseys indulged Greg disgracefully, there is no other word for it, and I think Roger gave him some sort of allowance, but when he had to stop work himself there were a few heavy hints that Greg might get off his backside and get a job to help the family coffers. He was impervious to them all, I gather. He has lofty views on the sacredness of talent and the fact that the rest of the world owes him a living so he can indulge that talent. Poor Diana, I don't know how she's coped until now. The idea of renting the cottage did not go down well with old Leonardo, as you can imagine. I gather he was dragged out kicking and screaming. So, don't take his animosity personally. But don't expect him to come calling with bunches of flowers either.'

Kate frowned. 'You might have told me all this before, Bill.'

'Why? Would you have changed your mind about coming?'

She shook her head. 'No, but it explains a lot.' She paused. 'I found some paintings in the bedroom. He must have forgotten them.'

'I doubt it. If he left them there, he left them there for a reason. Which means he wanted you to see them.' Bill glanced at her. 'His paintings are pretty grim, to my mind.'

She nodded. 'I didn't like them. There was one which showed the cottage under the sea. It was –' she hesitated, trying to find the right word '– morbid – threatening.'

'Take no notice. We'll ask Diana to take them away.'

'It seems wimpish to make a fuss.'

'Not at all. You're as much of an artist as he is, remember. A better one, because you are disciplined. And you are entitled to feel as sensitive and touchy as he is.' He grinned. 'Are you feeling sensitive and touchy?'

'Not in the least. Hungry covers it rather better.'

'Good. In that case, let's find your car and go eat.'

The farmhouse was empty. After a cursory glance through the windows to convince themselves that there really was no one at home they turned their attention to the barn. Kate's Peugeot was there, neatly parked next to an old Volvo estate.

'Diana's,' Bill said. 'They can't have gone far if they are all

43

packed into that fiendish Land Rover, not if they value their teeth.'

By the time they had reached the end of the track and gained the metalled road, Kate was beginning to think he was right – and that perhaps when her next royalty cheque came she should sacrifice a few teeth in the interest of her car's springs and buy an ancient four-wheel drive of her own for the duration of her stay.

They ordered curry at The Black Swan, a delightful long, low, pink-painted pub a mile or two from the lane, and sat down pleasantly near to a huge inglenook fireplace with a gentle smouldering log which filled the room with the scent of spicy apple. Save for the smiling pink-cheeked girl behind the bar they were the only people there. 'So. Are you going to like it at Redall?' Bill sat down on the high backed settle, and sticking his legs out towards the fire he gave a great sigh of contentment. He raised his pint glass and drank deeply and appreciatively.

Kate nodded. 'It's the perfect place to work.'

'The loneliness doesn't worry you?'

She shook her head. 'I must say it was a bit quiet last night. Just the sea. But I'll get used to it. It will be wonderful for writing.' Picking up her own glass – she had opted for a Scotch and water – she looked at Bill for a moment. In a thick brown cable-knit sweater and open-necked shirt he reminded her faintly of a rumpled sheepdog. 'Did you speak to Jon at all before he left, Bill?'

He glanced at her over the rim of his glass. 'Only once. He rang to ask me if I knew where you were going.'

'Did you tell him?' She looked away, not wanting him to see how much she wanted him to say yes.

'No.' There was a thoughtful pause as he sipped his lager. 'We had a few words on various themes related to male chauvinism – his – and misplaced chivalry – mine – and professional jealousy – all of us – and at that point I told him to bugger off to America and let you get on with your life. Did I do wrong?'

'No.' She didn't sound very certain.

She was thinking of their last meeting. Jon had been about to leave for the airport. The taxi was at the door, his cases stacked nearby and she, not wanting to say goodbye, not wanting to see him again before he went in case her resolution wavered, had

44

arrived back at the flat thinking he had already gone. For a moment she had been tempted to turn and run – but he had seen her and they were after all both grownups. For a moment they had looked at each other, then she had smiled and reached up to kiss him on the cheek. 'Take care. Have a wonderful time. I hope it's all a great success.' For a moment she had thought he would turn away without a word. Then he had smiled at her awkwardly. 'You take care too, Kate, my love. Don't get too wrapped up in old George. And remember to look after yourself.' They were both hurting; miserable; stiff-necked. And that was it. Picking up his cases he had walked out to the cab and climbed in without a word or a backward glance. There was no way that she could know that there were tears in his eyes.

'I had an Irish grandmother, Kate,' Bill said after a moment's sympathetic silence. 'She was always full of useful aphorisms. One of her favourites was: "if it is meant to be it will be." I think it just about fits the case.'

Kate laughed. 'You're right. We need a break from each other at the moment.' She glanced up as a waitress appeared with their knives and forks, wrapped in sugar-pink napkins, a huge bowl of mango chutney and large pepper and salt sellers contrived to look like a pair of old boots. 'But if he phones again, perhaps you might tell him where I am this time.' She caught Bill's eye and they both smiled comfortably.

'Is there a woman in your life, Bill?' She hadn't meant it to come out quite so baldly as she sought for a change of subject, but he didn't seem put out.

'Only Aunty Beeb at the moment – the goddess I work for. There was one once, but she buggered off too.' He paused reflectively, taking another deep drink from his glass. 'You are not offering, I take it. Flattered and tempted though I would be by such a possibility, I think it would be bad for both of us.'

'I'm not offering. But I need a friend. Someone who will walk through the woods now and then and drag me to a pub for a curry.'

'Done. But not alas for a while after today. I've got a tight schedule until Christmas.'

She was astonished at how devastated she felt at his words. She had known he was going back to London and yet somehow she had counted on him being there again next weekend.

'Want another Scotch?' He had been watching her face closely and saw something of the loneliness which had shown in her eyes for a moment.

She nodded and held out her glass. 'Then we can drink to Lord Byron. By the time I see you again, he will be, with a lot of luck, several chapters long.'

After dropping Bill at Colchester station she took the opportunity to drive on into the town, curious about the place which would be her nearest large centre for the next few months. Pevsner, in the edition of the book she had briefly consulted in the London Library, had waxed lyrical about it, but nineteen-sixties red-brick shopping centres now seemed to vie with nineteen-eighties glass and concrete where much of what he had described must have been. Saddened, she turned her attention at last to the castle museum.

The huge squat building was shadowed already from the late afternoon sun as she made her way across the bridge and inside the great door to buy her ticket. The place was strangely empty. In the distance she could hear the disembodied, dramatic voice of a video loop – the sound effects and urgency of the narrative strangely out of place amongst the glass cases beneath the high-beamed roof of the castle. She walked slowly around the ground floor exhibits gazing at Bronze Age and Iron Age artefacts, gradually growing closer to the sound.

For several minutes she stood watching the video – which told of the Romans in Colchester – then turning away, she began slowly to climb the stairs. At the top were Roman exhibits, life-size models, colourful, larger than life panoramic pictures on the walls, and then another video enactment, this time of Boudicca's attack and the sack of the town.

Poor Boudicca. Kate wandered round slowly studying the exhibits, piecing together her life: the wife of Prasutagus; her children; the political background of first-century Britain; her husband's death; the rape of her daughters and her humiliation as she was flogged by a Roman – the final insult after years of unrest and dissatisfaction in a country under foreign occupation, which caused the revolt which had nearly ended the Roman occupation of Britain. What a story her life made. Suddenly Kate found herself watching the video with heightened excitement. What a biography it would make; what a book, when George

Byron was finished . . . The burning of Colchester, the rampage of Boudicca's forces across Essex and Hertfordshire as they made their way towards London, and the final hours when she realised that all had failed and she took her own life. And Colchester was the centre of it all – a city where the flames had burned so hot that nearly two thousand years later a layer of blackened death was still clearly visible in the foundations of the town.

She watched the video through twice, alone in the darkened booth – seeing the huge sketched shapes of the warriors, hearing their shouts and screams, then she stood up and left, intensely aware suddenly of the vaults far beneath the castle which were all that remained apparently of the Temple of Claudius – the temple Boudicca had burned to the ground with most of the population of the town inside it.

She recognised this feeling: the tight, bone-tingling, breathless excitement as ideas jostled in her head, and under her breath she swore. She had had this feeling before, after she finished *Jane*; not until she had finished *Jane*. To get it now, while she was still at the beginning of *Lord of Darkness* meant she was going to suffer months if not years of suppressed, hidden frustration and worry in case someone else had the idea first; in case her publisher didn't like the idea; in case the idea took root in her sleep and developed and began to encroach on the work in progress.

Shaking her head in a small gesture of irritation she moved on past the exhibits. How could a woman – any woman – however hurt and humiliated, order the slaughter of other women, of children, of babies? What kind of person was she, this remote queen who offered human sacrifice to her gods before going to war?

She stopped abruptly. She was standing in front of a statue of a Roman citizen and her eye had been caught by the name. Frowning, she read the inscription: 'MARCUS SEVERUS SECUNDUS, one of the very few recorded survivors of the Boudiccan massacre. Instrumental in the rebuilding of Colchester after its sack in A.D. 60, he died full of years and honour and was buried next to his wife Augusta in the year A.D. 72. Their graves were excavated in 1986. See exhibit in case 14.'

So this was Redall's former owner. She stared hard at the stone face of Marcus with his patrician nose, slightly chipped, his warrior stance, the carefully sculpted folds of his toga and she wondered what kind of a man he had been. He had been one of those who had survived the massacre and returned to pick up the threads of his life. She felt another sudden frisson of excitement. Had he seen Boudicca? Could he have described the warrior queen of the Iceni with her flowing red hair and her massy torcs, her body armour and her war chariot?

She jumped suddenly as a disembodied voice, echoing around the castle, announced that the museum would soon be closing and she gave Marcus a last regretful glance. But not too regretful. She had the feeling she would be coming back to see him again.

IX

The youngest son of the late King, he had stood head and shoulders above his brothers and he knew he had been the favourite. His love of learning, his memory, his wit had marked him out as a child for study and initiation. His priesthood gave him power. His royal blood marked him for destiny. That was why he had been given lands and authority, and why he was trusted as advisor at Camelodunum to the Roman settlers, even though his brothers led revolt in the west. He wore Roman clothes; he spoke their language; he assimilated their learning and their ways. And he had fallen in love with one of their women. But he hated them and he bided his time.

He frowned when he saw the detested overlords raising their temple in the heart of Camelodunum: a temple to Claudius; a temple to a man who had declared himself a god. But he kept his views silent. One day the time would come, one day the Romans would be expelled from the land of his ancestors. When that day came, he would kill Claudia's husband and he would take her back to his hall. But until then, ever the diplomat, he would smile.

His duties as druid were light. He was royal, rich, in love. The gods would understand. He would serve them in due time when the bluebells had faded and the blood ran more slowly in his veins.

The old priests disapproved. They frowned and shook their heads first at him, then at the signs from the gods; the gods who despised the Romans who would venerate a man and make him one of them.

He did not know that the gods, too, were growing angry.

It was almost dark as Kate drove down the track and into the barn and parked her car next to Diana's Volvo once more. The farmhouse, she had noticed at once and with a strange sense of loss, was in complete darkness. She had not realised until that moment how much she had been counting on being asked in to sit by their cosy fire and have a cup of tea before she set out on the walk through the wood to her cottage.

On the drive back she had found a farm shop open where she had managed to buy some bread and milk, crumbly local cheese and Essex honey and, to her great delight, some firelighters and matches.

Hefting her plastic carrier over her shoulder she was already on the track when she stopped. The torch was still in the car. Turning back she pulled open the barn door once more and, unlocking the Peugeot she rummaged in the glove compartment. The torch was there, and – experimentally she flashed it up into the high rafters – it worked. Comforted, she locked up again and set off at a determined pace into the woods.

The track ran straight for a few hundred yards and then curved eastwards, narrowing until there was only room for the rutted marks of the Land Rover's wheels. Her feet slipped and she found she needed the torch to see where to put them in the mud. The evening was very still. There was no wind and the trees were silent. In the distance she heard the warbling call of a curlew from the marshes. The sound echoed in the falling darkness and was answered by the shriek of an owl. She clutched her bag more tightly, her eyes riveted to the track.

May the gods of all eternity curse you, Marcus Severus Secundus, and bring your putrid body and your rotten soul to judgement for what you have done here this day . . .

The woods were still silent, the trees unmoving. The words, as clear and well enunciated as those of a BBC presenter, had been inside her own head. Kate stopped dead, a sheen of sweat on her skin, her heart hammering in her ears. She stared round, her eyes straining into the darkness between the tall tree trunks, very conscious of the smell of rotting wood and damp, dark earth which surrounded her.

Stupid. The darkness and the silence after the celluloid drama of the museum and the excitement of the new idea had set her imagination working overtime, that was all. She resumed walking, a little more quickly this time, her torch clutched so tightly in her hand that her fingers grew numb.

When the cottage at last came into view she was breathless. Fumbling in her pocket for her key she let herself in and turned on the light, then she put her shopping bag down on the kitchen table, ran upstairs and grabbed one of her empty boxes from the spare bedroom. Dragging it after her she went straight outside again and made for the log shed. Before she did anything else and before she lost her nerve completely she would stock up with firewood.

Flashing the torch beam around the small shed she piled logs into her box, and then a huge heap of kindling. The shed was very neat, the ranks of logs undisturbed beneath their net of spiders' webs save for a few that had fallen at the end of the pile, the spade still leaning where she had left it in the corner. With one last look round she turned off the torch and returned it to her pocket. She needed both hands for the box. Hefting it up with a groan she made her way out into the cold garden, conscious of the brooding woods so close to the front of the cottage. It was impossible to run with the box. As swiftly as she could she walked back indoors and then she dropped it on the hall floor. Turning she slammed the door shut and shot the bolt home.

Safe. She closed her eyes and laughed quietly to herself, embarrassed, alone as she was, by her own stupidity. Picking up the box again she hauled it into the living room and put it neatly by the stove. Then, drawing the curtains against the darkness she went back to the kitchen and put on the kettle. The phone rang as she was waiting for it to boil.

'Kate, my dear. Just checking to see that everything is all right.' It was Roger Lindsey. 'I'm afraid we've been out most of the day so I thought I would give you a quick call to make sure you have everything you need.'

'Thank you. I'm fine.' She took a deep breath, astonished at how pleased she was to hear the sound of his voice. 'I came by earlier to leave my car again so I saw you were out.'

'We were having lunch with some friends in Woodbridge. Nice people. They had read your book.'

'Nice people indeed.' She smiled wryly. 'Roger, tell me, how do I make this woodburner thing stay alight all night?'

She heard an exclamation of impatience. 'Didn't Greg show you? I'm sorry, my dear. Those things take a bit of getting used to, but once you've got the hang of it you can keep it going for months without it going out. Do you want me to come up and show you?'

She shouldn't drag him over when he was ill, when he had

been out all day and must be tired, but suddenly the thought of a visitor was very tempting. 'Would it be an awful imposition? I've got a good whisky here.'

She heard him laugh. 'I'm on my way.'

It was scarcely fifteen minutes later that she saw the headlights of the Land Rover appear from the trees. Roger climbed out. 'Greg's away for a day or two. I'll give him a good bollocking when he gets back. He was supposed to show you how everything works.'

'He must have forgotten. I had so much stuff to bring in.' She closed the door behind him and led the way into the living room. She had put the whisky bottle on the table with two glasses. She poured, then she watched as he knelt before the stove and pulled the doors open. 'Start with a good blaze, like this,' he instructed. Magically a fire appeared beneath his thin hands. 'Then put on one or two of the logs. Like so.' He pushed two huge logs into the small cavity and miraculously they fitted. Then he closed the doors. 'Now, leave it for a while with the dampers open like this. Once the fire has caught properly – about two-thirds of the way down that glass, I should say – we close them tight. The secret is to get it burning slowly and steadily and then to cut off as much air as possible. You have to stack the logs in really tight last thing – that's an art you must practise I'm afraid, but you'll soon get the hang of it. It keeps this place really snug once it's working properly.'

He took the glass she offered him and sat down in one of the armchairs, gazing round the room. 'You've made it look very comfortable.'

The tall, thin man sprawling in the chair in his shabby cords and old tweed jacket was so reassuring and normal that Kate found the wave of nervous loneliness which had hit her earlier was receding fast. 'I gather your son used to live here. I'm sorry my coming here has upset him,' she said as she sat down opposite him.

'He's no business to be upset.' For a moment a shadow passed across Roger's face. 'He knows we need the money. Sorry if that sounds crude, but it's a fact of life. And it's nice for us to have a congenial neighbour.' He smiled comfortably. 'As you've gathered, it's fairly isolated up here. And to that end, Diana has instructed me to ask if you would like to come and have some supper with us on Wednesday. We quite understand if you'd rather not because you are working, but –'

'I should love to.' She replied so quickly she surprised even herself. 'I shall look forward to it immensely.'

'Good.' His smile was expansive, deepening the network of wrinkles around his eyes. 'You'll have the pleasure or otherwise of meeting our other two children, Allie and Patrick.' Draining his glass he stood up. 'If there's nothing else I suppose I'd better go home. Di will have supper ready soon.'

Stay, she wanted to say. Please, stay and talk to me. She liked his presence in the room. It was comforting. Solid. And safe. She said nothing. Smiling, she showed him to the door. 'I'll report back on my success or otherwise with the stove when I see you.'

'Do that.'

She watched as the Land Rover backed round and headed back up the track, the headlights bucking against the trees as it slid between the ruts. In a moment it was out of sight.

Closing the door and bolting it again she walked back into the living room. As though recognising the hand of a master the woodburner had settled down to produce a satisfyingly hot glow which was already warming the room. She looked round, pleased. Although Roger had gone something of the friendliness he had brought with him had remained; basking in it, she would make herself some supper, read a little, listen to some music, have a hot bath and go to bed early. Tomorrow she would spend the day with Lord Byron.

X

In the stillness of the night the tide lapped imperceptibly higher along the beach, round the headland and slowly, oh so slowly, into the backwaters of the estuary, licking at the mud, floating strands of trailing grasses and weeds, curling round the toes of sleeping geese and ducks. Rising.

In the dune the sand had dried. It was brittle, friable, ready to fall. Beneath it, only a centimetre down now, was the clay – clay which was plastic, impervious to air or water, and in the clay was the peat which held preserved the remains of four human bodies.

XI

She had been sitting at the word processor for two hours and she had not noticed that it was getting light. Now, arms and shoulders cramped and her head throbbing from her intense concentration, Kate sat back, took off her glasses and, dropping them beside her notes, stared out of the window. The mist had receded to leave a sunrise of breathtaking clarity. The narrow vee of sea visible between the shingle banks from her carefully positioned table glittered with blinding beauty. It was more than anyone could resist; besides, she needed a break. Donning jacket, scarf and boots she pulled open the front door and emerged into an ice cold wind. Looking around she took a deep breath of pure delight. This was a place where Byron himself would have felt at home.

> Roll on, thou deep and dark blue Ocean – roll!
> Ten thousand fleets sweep over thee in vain . . .

The beach was still wet from the receding tide as she tramped northwards along it, murmuring the lines from 'Childe Harold', her head ducked against the sting of the wind and the glare, her cheeks tingling beneath the whipping strings of hair as they pulled free of her scarf. The words weren't quite right, of course. This wasn't an ocean and it was neither all that deep nor dark, but still the mood was right. It was exhilarating. She wanted to jump and run and dance, but the shingle and soft sand precluded all but the most undignified gallop. Stopping at last, exhausted, she turned and began to retrace her steps. With the wind and glare behind her she could slow down and appreciate the different colours and textures of the water: where the sand rose near the surface it was pale green, even yellow. Further out streaks of deep turquoise melded with grey and black and the intense sapphire blue of a child's painting of the sea. In the distance the shingle gave way to muddy sand and she could see dunlin and redshank at the water's edge. Save for them she appeared to be the only being alive in the world.

She came level with the cottage, appreciating from here how sheltered it was behind the shingle banks, only a narrow section of its face visible behind the waving grasses and heaps of sand. In front of her, beyond the dunes, the beach swept away around the corner. There a narrow inlet led into the shallow, muddy waters of Redall Bay with its network of small islands and tidal creeks.

By the last of the dunes she stopped. Part of it appeared to have fallen onto the sand, and in the hollow on its seaward side there were signs of recent digging. Curious, she walked towards it, her boots slipping in the deep soft mixture of stones and mud and sand. The top section, out of sight of the cottage, had had a neat transverse slice removed from it. About ten feet long and two feet deep the interlocking grasses had been sectioned away and below it the sand had been scooped loosely into piles. Jumping down into the hollow she stared at the exposed wall of the dune. The resulting scar in the sand looked too regular and neat to be the result of a child's game; and it had certainly not been caused by the tide, although further along the cut had been lengthened and randomly enlarged by a muddy landslip where tell-tale strands of weed and a scattering of whelk shells betrayed a recent high tide propelled by an easterly wind.

Intrigued, Kate ran her hand lightly over the sand face. Who had been digging here, and why? Was it something to do with sea defences? She turned and looked back at the beach. The receding tide looked gentle and benevolent now, but she was under no illusions about the force it could muster if wind and moon were right.

She was about to scramble out of the hollow to resume her walk when her eye was caught by something shiny sticking out of the sand. It looked like a piece of pottery. She picked it up and examined it, then, frowning, she looked at it more closely. It was thin, fine, red, decorated with a raised pattern and it looked very like the Samian ware she had seen in the museum only yesterday. But that was impossible. She turned and surveyed the sand face again. Was this some sort of abandoned excavation? She stared down at the piece of pottery in her hand almost guiltily. Perhaps she shouldn't have touched it. On the other hand it had been lying in the loose spoil, obviously overlooked. With another high tide it would have been buried and lost. Pulling her scarf off her hair she wrapped the piece carefully and put it reverently in her pocket, then she turned and examined the exposed sand again. It was in a very crumbly state. The lightest touch dislodged another shower of soil. A few feet to her left she spotted something dark protruding from it. Cautiously she touched it. Metal. Scraping at the sand with her fingers she tried to see what it was without disturbing it. The narrow twisted neck of metal stuck out at right angles from the sand. She must ask the Lindseys. They would know who had been excavating here, and why they had stopped. She eyed the piece of metal longingly. If she touched it and it was of archaeological interest then she might be destroying valuable evidence – on the other hand another tide might remove it even more irrevocably. As she was standing there, trying to make up her mind what to do, a small crack appeared of its own accord in the top of the dune. As she watched a lump of wet sand broke away and fell at her feet. A minute later another six-inch section fell, taking the metal object with it. She bent and picked it up. Twisted, corroded, the metal was heavy and cold in her hand. She could not begin to guess what metal it was. Not gold certainly. Bronze, perhaps, or even silver. She examined it in excitement and awe. In all probability she was the first person to touch it for over a thousand years – perhaps two, perhaps more. It was a torc.

MY LOVE

The voice in her head had spoken so loudly she thought it was real. Dropping the torc she put her hands to her ears, looking round.

There was no one there. An oystercatcher was plodding slowly along the tide line near her, dipping its beak into the sand.

She could feel her heart beginning to hammer in her ears again, as it had in the woods in the dark the night before. Taking a deep breath she bent and picked up the piece of twisted metal, then she scrambled out of the hollow. She stared round, her arm across her eyes to hold back her streaming hair, loose now she had removed the scarf. There was still no one in any direction as far as she could see. Besides the voice had been inside her own head.

Taking a deep breath she turned towards the cottage. Get a grip on yourself, Kennedy. You're imagining things, she told herself sternly. Too much fresh air, that's your trouble.

The panic had gone almost as soon as it had come. Out here in broad daylight, in the brilliant sunshine and the light, tossing wind with birds patrolling unconcerned along the tide line, her moment of terror seemed absurd. It was imagination, that was all. A visit to the museum, a new preoccupation with Boudicca and the events of nineteen hundred years ago, together with the isolated situation and already she was having hallucinations. Strong coffee would soon sort that out.

Slightly faster than she would normally have walked she retraced her steps towards the cottage. Only once did she look back. There in the dazzle off the sea a sand devil whirled in the hollow where she had been standing. She watched it for a moment. It looked almost like a figure. Then it disappeared.

Letting herself in out of the wind, she shook her hair back from her face and putting her finds down on the kitchen table she put the kettle on even before she removed her jacket and boots. While the kettle was boiling she went to the phone but there was no answer from the Lindseys.

Picking up her coffee and her two artifacts she carried them through into the living room and put them down on her work table. Automatically she turned on the word processor. Waiting for it to summon up her programme she picked up the torc and examined it again. It was large – large enough to go around the neck of a full grown man at a guess, and still heavy in spite of, or perhaps because of, its corrosion. She stared at it for a long time then carefully she placed it on the windowsill before sitting down before her keyboard.

When she next looked up it was nearly one o'clock.

This time Diana was in when she phoned. Her query about the digging on the beach was greeted by a moment of embarrassed silence. 'You were there this morning, you say?' she asked cautiously.

'I was walking on the beach.'

'Of course. I think the place you're talking about is where my daughter has been doing some digging. It's for an archaeological project at school. It's not a designated site of any kind.'

'I see.' Kate frowned. She could hear the defensiveness in the other woman's voice. 'It's just that there seemed to be signs of some kind of ancient usage –' Her eyes strayed towards the doorway into the hall. She couldn't see the windowsill where her finds were lying. 'I felt that probably someone qualified ought to take a look at it. It could be an important site.'

'I think you'll find Alison has that in hand. It's her project entirely, Kate.' Diana's voice took on an unaccustomed firmness. 'Please leave it to her.'

And keep your nose out! Kate muttered as she put down the phone. She wandered back into the sitting room and stood looking down at the metal torc. If Alison was going to inform the museum then that was fine. She would show them her two trophies at the same time. She picked up the piece of twisted metal and examined it once more. It was badly corroded and bent, but the basic design of intertwined strands of metal wire was clearly visible. She scratched at it cautiously with her fingernail. A pale gleam appeared. She hesitated, then she scratched at it again, this time harder. The faint scratch showed a distinctly silvery sparkle. It was silver. She was holding a silver torc.

I CURSE YOU, MARCUS SEVERUS, FOR WHAT YOU HAVE DONE HERE THIS DAY

The voice was so sudden and so loud she dropped the torc onto the table. Frantically she shook her head. The sound had been inside her ears; it came from her brain. From her head. From her soul. Frightened she stared round the room. Then taking a deep breath she picked up the twisted metal again. It was very cold beneath her fingers. As cold as it had been when she first picked it out of the wet sand.

'This is stupid.' She said the words out loud, and her own voice sounded light and insubstantial in the empty room. She carried the torc and the piece of pottery to the small table in the corner on which the lamp stood and pulling out the drawer she laid them both in it. Closing it firmly she turned the key.

Auditory hallucination is a condition engendered by various states of mind and various physical conditions. She had read about it in one of Anne's books. But which one of them, if any, applied to her? Picking up the bottle of Scotch she walked through into the kitchen and firmly closed the door behind her. The first thing she could do was restore her blood sugar levels to normal. Perhaps a cooked lunch would dispel whatever it was which was causing this to happen.

She was sitting at the small kitchen table, with a book propped up before her, eating baked beans on toast covered in melted cheese, when there was a loud knock at the front door. Pushing her plate away reluctantly she went to open it.

A girl stood on the doorstep, dressed in jeans and a bright blue anorak, her blonde pony-tailed hair blowing wildly in the wind.

'I've come to tell you to keep away from my dig.' The green eyes were furious, the face unsmiling. 'Mum says you've been poking around in the dune. Well don't. Just because you've rented this place it doesn't give you any right to go poking around in other people's affairs. Keep away from it.' The young face was pale and strained. Her headache had been worse this morning, too bad to go to school, too bad to get up until Diana had told her what was happening out at the dune.

'You must be Alison.' Kate raised an eyebrow but, firmly suppressing the angry response which was her automatic reaction to the girl's rudeness, she merely said, 'I'm sorry. I didn't mean to interfere in your excavation. Of course I won't go near it again if you'd rather I didn't.'

'Please don't.' Alison scowled.

'You've told the museum about your finds, I gather.'

'I'm going to soon.' The girl's chin was set determinedly. She was very like her elder brother, Kate decided suddenly. They were a good-looking family, but obviously not noted for their charm. 'I'm writing it up first and taking photos and things.'

'Good.' Kate smiled. 'That's exactly the right thing to do.' She took a step back, about to shut the door but Alison still stood there, hands in pockets, obviously wanting to say something else. 'Are you really a writer?' It came out at last.

'Yes,' Kate smiled. 'I am.'

'And you're writing about Byron, Dad said.'

'That's right.'

'So, why did you come here?'

'I wanted somewhere quiet so that I could concentrate on my work.'

'And you know about history and things.'

Kate nodded. 'A bit. I studied history at university.'

'So you know about the Romans.'

'A bit, as I said. I gather they came here.'

'And there were people here even before that.' Alison's brow wrinkled slightly. 'The Trinovantes lived in Essex before the

Romans came. That's a Roman grave.' She nodded her head in the general direction of the beach.

'A grave?' Kate frowned. 'What makes you think that?'

Marcus. The thought had come unbidden and as swiftly it had gone. Marcus Severus's grave was found in somewhere called Stanway, which, she had seen on the diagrammatic map near his statue, was on the far side of Colchester, some twenty miles away.

'I just know.'

Kate looked at the girl, disquieted. 'Alison, when you've got some time, would you show me your dig? Show me properly. Explain what you've done – the digging looks very professional – and tell me what you've found.'

'You really want to know?'

'I do. Not to interfere. I'm interested.'

'OK. Do you want to come now?'

With a moment's regretful thought about her baked beans and her book Kate nodded. 'Hold on. I'll get my jacket and boots.'

The tide had receded a long way when they stood together side by side on the edge of the hollow looking at the excavated side of the dune. The wind was whipping the sand into little eddies which whispered amongst the thin dry grasses and the sun had gone, hidden behind huge threatening clouds. 'I found some bits of pottery – shards, they're called, and some metal objects,' Alison said slowly. 'They're at home. I'll show you when you come to supper if you like.'

'I would like.' Kate glanced at the girl. She did not seem to be showing any eagerness to jump down into the hollow. 'How did you know where to dig?'

'The sea started it. Half the dune collapsed. Then I began to find things.'

'What made you think it was a Roman grave?'

'That's where you find things. In graves. There was a villa on our neighbour's farm. It's under his field, very near us, and there was a Roman road to the village and another to the other side of Redall Bay.'

'Was there?' Kate was fascinated. 'Can we go down into the hollow? It'll be out of the wind and you can show me exactly how you've been sectioning the soil.'

Alison seemed reluctant, but after a moment she jumped down into the soft sand and approached the exposed face where she had been working. 'I've been very careful not to disturb anything. The trouble is the sand just falls away. You can't stop it. The wind and the sea erode this coast all the time. Even houses fall over the edge a bit further along from here, at Redall Point.' She raised her hand gently to the sand, and then drew back without touching it. 'I've left my tools in your log shed.'

'Oh, I wondered who the spade belonged to.' Kate pushed her hair out of her eyes and reaching into her pocket for her glasses squinted more closely at the surface of the dune in front of her. 'Look, do you see? Here, and here. There's a change in texture. The sand is more glutinous. It's stronger. I think there's an outcrop of clay and peat of some sort. You may have more luck excavating that. It won't crumble so easily.'

'No.' Alison took a step forward and examined the place Kate was pointing to. Then she shivered. Her headache had returned with a vengeance. 'It's too cold to work today. I think I'll go home now.' She turned away. As they scrambled out of the hollow into the full force of the wind again Kate saw the girl glance over her shoulder at the spot where they had been standing. There was an unhappy frown on her face as if she had seen something which puzzled her.

It was only after Kate had watched Alison disappear up the track through the woods and had let herself once more into the cottage that she realised that she had not said a word about her own finds. She walked back into the kitchen and looked with regret down at her plate. Then she scraped the congealed mess into the waste bin and put the kettle on. She had wasted enough time already today. Forget Alison Lindsey and her Roman grave. This afternoon she must go back to the world of the cold, bleak Aberdeen lodgings where the young George Gordon was learning the bible, and a lot more besides, at his nurse's knee.

Her eyes glued to the screen of her lap top Kate did not notice the room growing dark. Her fingers were cramped; her arms stiff and heavy and there was a cold spot somewhere between her shoulder blades which had begun to hurt quite badly. Taking off her glasses, she stretched her hands out in front of her and wriggled her fingers painfully. The fire had died again and the room was icy. Climbing stiffly to her feet she went through the now routine acts of lighting, filling and closing the stove and stood for a moment staring down at the blackened glass of the little doors. She had done it on automatic pilot, her thoughts still with Catherine Gordon and May Grey and their volatile confusing relationships with the boy in their charge, relationships which would leave him scarred for life.

Satisfied at some subconscious level that the fire would now catch and warm her she went back to the table and, sitting down she began to read through the afternoon's work.

May the gods of all eternity curse you, Marcus Severus, and bring your putrid body and your rotten soul to judgement for what you have done here this day . . .

She stared at the words blankly. She did not remember writing them. She hadn't written them. They appeared in the text suddenly, arbitrarily, half way through a description of eighteenth-century Aberdeen.

Pushing her chair back she stood up abruptly, conscious that her hands were shaking. Turning away from the screen she went back to the stove. Opening the doors she knelt in front of it and held out her hands, trying to warm them. It's just a phrase that's been whirling round in my head. I must have read it somewhere and it's somehow lodged in my brain and I typed it out. Idiot. Idiot.

Her eyes went unwillingly to the table drawer. For several minutes she tried to resist the urge to go over to it, then, giving up, she rose and went to switch on the lamp.

Picking up the torc she took it back to the fire and, sitting down on the floor in front of the blaze she turned the piece of metal over and over in her hand. She was no expert, no archaeologist, but she knew enough to be fairly certain that this was a Celtic ornament; almost certainly silver and therefore once the property of a wealthy man; a man not a woman, judging by its weight and size. It was certainly not Roman, whatever Alison thought. So it did not belong to Marcus Severus. Had not belonged, she corrected herself at once. So, whose was it? What was it doing buried in the sand on the edge of Redall Bay? The British tribes who opposed Rome had been Celts. The Celtic world, which today is linked in the popular mind purely to Wales and Scotland and Ireland and Brittany, once covered the whole of Britain – the whole of Europe. East Anglia had been as Celtic as Gwynedd or Galloway. It had been the Saxon invasions that had overridden their traces in folk memory.

She sat back, leaning against the sofa, drawing her knees up, the metal in her hands. It was warm now. The places where she had rubbed and scratched it glinted faintly in the firelight. She closed her eyes. This part of the country – this part of Essex – had been as Alison said the land of the Trinovantes, the tribe who had joined Boudicca and the Iceni in their revolt against Rome. Disillusioned and cheated by their Roman overlords in Colchester, they had not hesitated in rising up against the foreign oppressor. Had this torc belonged to one of them? A highborn Celtic lord? A prince? Was that his burial mound out there on the beach, lashed by the winter sea?

And what had Marcus Severus Secundus to do with him?

The sound of hail rattling against the window made her look up. It had grown quite dark outside. The lamplight reflected in the glass and suddenly the room felt very cold. She glanced at the fire. With the doors open the stove had consumed the logs she had thrown on earlier. Only ash remained. Rising to her feet she put the torc back into its drawer, closed and locked it, then she went to the window and, shading her eyes against the reflection she looked out. The glass was cold against her forehead. Cold and hard. The evening was totally black. Against the rattle of the rain and the howl of the wind she thought she could hear the crash of waves on the beach. With a shudder she stepped back and drew the curtains across. Then for the third time that day she built up the fire.

She awoke in the early hours with a start. Her bedroom was very cold. The wind had risen and she could hear the sea clearly now. The waves crashing on the beach, the rush and rattle of shingle, and from the other side of the cottage – the western side – the thrash and creak of trees.

She peered across the room. She had left the landing light on – a relic of that old fear of the dark – and she could see the outline of the door, the comforting wedge shape of light. For a minute she lay there staring at it, then she reached for the bedside lamp. Propped against the pillows, huddled beneath the blankets with her book and her glasses she felt warm and safe. She half relished the battering of the storm.

A stronger than usual gust of wind flung itself against the window and she heard the groan and rattle of the glass and suddenly she was aware of the smell of wet earth. Bitter sweet, cloying, pervasive, it filled the bedroom. It was the smell of gardens, of newly-dug flower beds, of ancient woodlands.

Groping for her dressing gown she reached for her slippers and padded across the room. Opening the door fully she peered out onto the landing. It was ice cold out there and unbelievably draughty. Frowning she went towards the stairs and looked down.

The front door stood wide open.

For a moment she stood transfixed. It was the wind. It must have been the wind, but the front door was on the sheltered side of the house. She ran down the stairs and threw the door shut. She had bolted it. Surely she had bolted it the night before? Sliding the bolt hard home she turned the key in the lock as well.

The kitchen and the living room doors stood open, the rooms beyond, dark. She glanced at them with sudden misgiving. Supposing it wasn't the wind that had thrown the door open? Supposing it was a burglar?

Come on, Kennedy. Who would burgle this place? She went to the kitchen door and switched on the light. The room was empty, just as she had left it a few hours earlier, her dishes stacked in the sink, the kettle still – she put her hand on the metal and saw it cloud fractionally beneath her palm – a little warm. Switching it on she turned and went back to the hall. Immediately the smell of earth grew stronger. She paused for a moment, sniffing. The front door was shut and the smell should have lessened, but now it seemed to be coming from the living room.

It was as she put out her hand to the light switch that she realised that there was someone in the room. Her mouth went dry. She held her breath, listening, aware that the other person was doing the same thing, painfully conscious that she was standing silhouetted against the bright light of the hall.

It was a woman.

She wasn't sure how she knew; she could see no one, but suddenly her terror wasn't quite so sharp. 'Alison?' Her voice sounded ridiculously loud and shrill. 'Alison, is that you? What are you doing here?' She found the light switch, clicked it on and stared round, her heart hammering under her ribs. There was no one there. The windows were closed, the curtains drawn as she had left them the night before and the woodburner was glowing quietly in its hearth, nicely banked – this time it would last easily until morning. But if the fire was alight, and the glass behind the door of the stove glowing, why was the room so deadly cold and where was the strange smell coming from? Biting her lip, she stared round again, before going cautiously into the room and looking quickly behind the sofa, behind the chairs, in the corners, even behind the curtains. All was as it should be.

It was a last minute thought to check the drawer where she had put the torc.

The lamp was no longer central on the table. Had she pushed it to one side like that, so it overhung the edge? So that one small push would have sent it toppling to the ground? She put her hand to the handle of the drawer and then drew back. The knob was covered in earth. Wet, rain-soaked earth. Cautiously, with two fingers, she pulled open the drawer. The torc and the piece of pottery were still there. They did not appear to have been touched.

So it was Alison. She had suspected Kate's theft and come back for her treasure. She probably had a key to the cottage. Hearing Kate moving about upstairs she had lost her nerve and run away. Shaking her head angrily, Kate wiped the handle of the drawer and pushed it closed. She gave one final look around the room and walked to the door.

She was about to switch off the light when she became aware of another scent in the room beyond the smell of the wet earth. It was rich, feminine, musky. The scent a sophisticated woman would wear. She gave a wry smile. Perhaps even rude, boisterous, teenage girls showed signs from time to time of one day growing up.

XII

The decision was made; the sacrifice would be at Beltane. So would the gods be placated at last; the choice of victim to be given to them; he who took the burned bread from the basket would be the one who would die the threefold death.

Nion laughed when he heard. He was young and strong and invincible. And he was in love. His body coursed with the red blood of passion. His skin took fire each time she touched him. His eyes hungered after her body even as she turned to leave him. It was known that one of the elderly druids would take the burnt morsel; one of the old men; one of the fathers, who was ready to go willingly to meet the gods.

The bedroom at the Hyatt Hotel in New York was stiflingly hot. Jon Bevan had woken suddenly, his body bathed in sweat. With a groan he brought his wrist up close to his face and scrutinised the luminous dial of his watch with eyes that felt as though they had been rubbed in hot sand. Four in the morning. Swinging his feet to the carpet he groped his way across the bedroom to the small bathroom and felt for the light switch. The bright white light was blinding. Groaning again he went in and ran the cold tap into the basin, plunging his hands in, sweeping the water over his face and shoulders. It wasn't cold. In fact it was tepid, but it was better than nothing.

What had woken him? He passed back into the bedroom and turned on the light beside the bed. The heavy double curtains were tightly closed. It was strange how he had got used to Kate's silly, paranoid need to have the bedroom curtains open at night; now he too felt claustrophobic with them shut. He lifted one corner and peered out but he knew there would be no stars there. His bedroom looked out onto a monstrous, cavernous well, surrounded by other windows, reaching up out of sight towards the heavens. Even when he had tried to crane his neck out while

67

it was still daylight he had not been able to see the sky. He pulled up the window an inch or two. Cold air rushed into the room, and with it the smells and sounds of the city. The blast of a car horn, the distant wail of police sirens, a miasma of indistinguishable music, a shout from somewhere in the dark wall of windows in front of him, and carried on the cold air, rich and spicy and nauseating, the smell of a thousand kitchens cooking steaks and fries, burgers and beans and onions. At four in the morning, for God's sake! Pulling down the window he sat down on his bed with a groan. Last night's party at the Café des Artistes had gone on until ten. Then he and Derek had gone on to 44 where they had met up with some other writers. After that he could remember little. They had gone to Peace then on somewhere else he could no longer recall – drinking, talking philosophy which had become increasingly maudlin, composing lines of stupendous prose which they had scribbled on paper napkins and promptly lost and which by tomorrow would be forgotten, and best so. He gave a grimace, embarrassed even to remember it. And tomorrow there would be more of the same. A talk to a group of creative writing students, a signing session at Rizzoli's, lunch with ... who? He shrugged. Who cares. One of Derek's minions would turn up, usher him around, line him up, make sure his clothes were on straight and his hair brushed, present him on time – a minion who would be intense, humourless, dedicated to the art of not losing an exhausted author in New York.

With an exclamation of disgust Jon threw himself back on the bed and crossed his arms behind his head. He would never sleep now. He groped for the TV remote and pressed it at random. Seconds later he switched it off again. He was not that desperate.

The trouble was, he was missing Kate. He was missing Kate most dreadfully, and the guilt he felt about the way he had treated her had not gone away. The thought made him furious with himself. He had been small-minded, jealous, insecure, unfair. He listed his faults mercilessly. Well, at least now he had a new American contract as good as under his belt and he could begin to pay her back some of the money he owed her. He glanced at his watch again, idly computing what the time was in England. Nine? Ten? Morning anyway. He pulled the phone towards him and began to dial Bill. Somehow he would persuade him to divulge her number. He had to speak to her. He was missing her too much.

XIII

The tide had turned but the wind still piled the sea in against the north-east-facing coasts of Britain. It filled Redall Bay, all but inundating the low-lying islands which were the abode of so many birds. It washed away a huge section of cliff, six metres long, further up the coast near Wrabness, bringing two oak trees which had been clinging desperately to the edge of what had once been a wood crashing to the sand. Rolling up the beach, it flooded into the hollow near the dune, worried at the soil and began to undermine the face of the excavation.

Two of the bodies lay on top of each other, the man face down, his face pressed into the seeping wetness of the clay, his head at an angle, bent against his shoulder. The garotte was embedded deep in the strange desiccated blackness which was all that remained of his skin. He was naked save for the strip of tanned tree bark tied about his arm. It was the bark of the ash; the tree which was his totem; the tree for which he had been named – Nion.

The woman lay across him, hunched, contorted by the agony in which she had died. The fabric of her clothing was strangely intact. In one or two places the colour was still visible, though darkened by the chemical processes of clay and salts and decomposition. And by the blood. Out of sight, beneath her as she lay across the other body was a sword. It was a short sword, but sharp, corroded now to razor thin metal. One of her hands still clasped the hilt. The point was embedded between her ninth and tenth thoracic vertebrae.

XIV

Kate was stacking the dishes in the sink next morning when she happened to glance out of the window and saw Alison appear from the wood. The girl had a fluorescent green haversack over one shoulder and in her hand she carried a large red radio cassette player. Still exhausted and angry after her disturbed night Kate waited for her to approach the cottage, but Alison veered off the path and headed straight towards the shed.

Drying her hands Kate went outside. The storms of the night had passed and the day was bright and crisp with only the lightest wind blowing from the south.

'Good morning.' She stopped behind Alison as the girl groped inside the shed.

Alison jumped. She turned, her spade in her hand. 'Hi.' She did not look pleased to see her.

'I thought you might be going to drop in and say hello,' Kate said.

Alison shrugged. 'I thought I'd get on.'

'Fair enough. But first, haven't you got some explaining to do about last night?'

It had not been easy to sleep after the disturbances. Even with the front door locked and bolted and the lights on throughout the house Kate had only dropped off an hour or so before dawn and then her sleep had been restless and light.

'Last night?' Alison turned back to the shed and retrieved a trowel and a broom.

'It was you who came up to the cottage.'

'Me?' She had the girl's full attention at last. 'I didn't come up last night. What on earth would I do that for?'

Kate frowned. The wide eyes looked genuinely puzzled.

'Someone came to the cottage last night. About three in the morning and let themselves in. They must have had a key.'

70

'Weird.' Alison shook her head. 'Did they steal anything?'

'No.'

'Why did you think it was me? I'm not a thief.'

'I know.' Kate tried to lighten the mood by laughing. The sound came out tightly; it betrayed her sudden misgivings. 'You would tell me, wouldn't you, because if it wasn't you, I need to know who it was.'

'Perhaps it was Greg. He's probably still got a key.'

'No, it was a woman. And she had earth on her hands. I thought perhaps you had been digging again.'

'At three in the morning?' Alison gave her a withering look. 'If it was a burglar you'd better tell the police or something. We've never had burglars here before.' The implication in her tone was that Kate had obviously brought the trouble with her. 'You'd better ring Dad.'

'Yes, perhaps I'd better.' Kate frowned. 'In fact I'll drop in and see him when I pick up the car. I need to go into Colchester this morning.'

She wasn't sure when she had decided she needed to go back to the museum. The idea had come so firmly, so ready-formed it was as though she had had it planned all along.

'He's not there now. They've gone to Ipswich for the day.'

'Oh.' Kate felt let down. Ever since she had woken up that morning she had kept a picture of the gentle, reassuring face of Roger Lindsey firmly before her. He would know what to do. 'Are you going to be all right here by yourself?' She turned to Alison who was juggling all her tools into her arms with her ghetto blaster.

'Of course. I always come up here by myself.' The voice was jaunty, firm. It belied the moment of uncertainty in Alison's eyes.

The museum was comparatively empty as Kate threaded her way through the Bronze Age and Iron Age exhibits towards the staircase. Over on her left she could hear the video playing to itself. Someone had pressed the button, activating the sequences and then they had left, leaving the sound to echo disembodied around the deserted gallery.

Marcus Severus Secundus stared blankly at the glass cases around him from dead stone eyes. His face was stereotyped – handsome, classic, the hair formally curled. Was there any likeness there, or had the statue been purchased off the sculptor's shelf by an admirer or a descendent – his son perhaps – to stand in memoriam near his tomb? She stood staring at him for a long time, trying to get behind those blank eyes. Then, gently, aware that she was breaking museum regulations, she raised her hand and ran her fingers across his face, touching the mutilated nose, tracing the line of his cheekbones, his jaw, his shoulder.

The glass case which contained the surviving contents of his grave was close by. She stood and stared down at it with a sense of shock. She had not expected to see bones.

'In an inhumation, rare at this period, excavated on site B4 at the third Stanway burial mound were found the remains of Marcus Severus Secundus and his wife Augusta Honorata. A survivor of the Boudiccan attack on Colchester in A.D. 60, Marcus Severus was a leader of the rebuilding of the town. In the grave were found symbols of his office, jewellery and small grave goods.'

Kate stared through the glass. The bones lay in heaps, displayed in a plaster replica of the grave. Neither skeleton was complete. Had they died together then, Marcus Severus and his wife? She squatted nearer the case to see better the jewellery which was displayed there. Two rings of gold, a necklace of turquoise and amber, two brooches, one silver, one enamelled and several hairpins. Those must have been hers. And his was the heavy signet ring, mounted beneath a magnifying glass through which she could see the engraving. It showed a rearing horse. And his also, presumably, was the large silver brooch with an intricate design and long embossed pin. Consulting the information cards at the far side of the display she read: 'Exhibit 4: A curvilinear brooch of native silver, Celtic. Probably dating from the first century B.C. An unusual find in a Roman grave.' So, what was Marcus Severus of the Roman Legion doing with a Celtic cloak broach? Had he bought it? Or looted it? Or was he given it as a gift?

Leaving the museum at last she turned into the town centre. Having stocked up with fresh food, a couple of films for her camera, a large torch with two spare batteries and after treating herself to a glass of wine and a plateful of fettuccine and salad at a wine bar off the High Street she made her impulse buy – a bottle of silver polish. The weathered silver of the brooch in the glass case had given her the idea. That too must once have been a corroded unrecognisable lump of metal. It was probably wrong to

72

clean the torc herself. She should leave it to the trained restorers at the museum, but if she were gentle, and very careful – she wanted to see if she could achieve that same soft radiance. The torc itself was locked in her car. She had not wanted to leave it in the cottage, giving Alison all day to look for it. Now suddenly she wanted to get back to it, to make sure it was safe.

A cold wintery sunshine flooded across the town as she retraced her steps to the car. To reach it she walked past the theatre and through the surviving arch of the Roman Balkerne Gate. There was a wonderful view of the Roman wall here, as she walked, laden with her parcels, across the footbridge over the scar which was one of the main dual carriageways into town, towards the multi-storey car park.

The drive down the track to Redall Farmhouse was alarmingly slippery. Twice the car slid out of control sideways, where some-how it had clawed its way out this morning. Presumably other cars had made the track worse. She hoped that meant that the Lindseys had changed their minds and come home early, but there was no sign of them when she parked in the barn, trans-ferred the torc from the locked glove compartment to her shoul-der bag, unloaded all her shopping and finally changed her shoes for her heavy boots.

It took a long time to walk the half mile or so to the cottage through the mud. Several times she stopped to change arms, and rest with her heavy bags. In the slanting sunshine the wood looked beautiful. Without leaves, the trees were graceful, linear dancers in the wind and there were hidden flowers around her feet; dead nettle and winter heliotrope and speedwell with the occasional small clump of snowdrops tightly furled in bud. The scent of pine and wet vegetation and resin was sharp and exhil-arating. It was, she realised suddenly, nothing like the earthy smell which had permeated her cottage the night before.

To her relief the front door was still locked. Letting herself in she dumped her purchases on the kitchen table and went on a careful tour of the place. Nothing had been touched. The hair she had, rather shamefacedly, stuck across the drawer was still there. No one had been in. The more she had thought about it during the day, the more certain she was that Alison had somehow been responsible for last night's intrusion. Who else could it have been? With a silent apology to her young neighbour in the dune for her suspicions that she would return, she transferred the torc back to its resting place. Only then, cheerful enough to whistle as she worked, did she unload her bags and put on the kettle.

XV

Alison had stood for a long time on the edge of her excavation surveying the damage the wind and tide had wrought on her carefully exposed soil face. The dune had almost broken up. Half the wall she had left the day before had fallen. It lay, a tumble of wet sand and soil in the bottom of the declivity, strewn with tangled seaweed and shells and the rotting half-eaten corpse of a large fish. At the sight of it she pulled a face. Stacking all her equipment on the edge of the hollow she jumped in. She lifted the dead fish out on a spade and hurled it back onto the beach with a shudder. Moments later a screaming gull was circling over it, its claws outstretched for a landing.

She turned back to the shambles before her and stared round. She had already spotted several more pieces of that strange red earthenware lying around in the loose soil and there were other things too. Small round things. Black. 'Coins!' Her shriek was echoed by the gull which danced into the air for a moment before returning to gorge itself on the cold white flesh of the fish.

There were thirteen that she could find. Wrapping them carefully in pieces of soft tissue which she had optimistically brought with her for just such a purpose she stowed them in the pocket of her haversack, then she turned back to the dig.

It was the silence she hated. A silence which seemed to block out the gentle constant noise of wind and waves. It was threatening. It entered her aching head like an entity, battering against her brain. She was pretty sure that it had given her the migraines which were the reason for her missing school, but this time she had thought of a way of defeating it; of keeping the headaches at bay. Half an hour later, to the deafening sounds of The Sex Pistols, she was intently sifting through the heaps of sand with her fork and trowel, systematically separating out anything of interest, when she paused, looking down at the patch of dark sand in front of her.

The dagger was half buried still, the hilt and transverse hand-guard badly corroded, but not so badly that it was not instantly recognisable. For a long moment Alison stared down at it without moving, then she dropped to her knees and reverently she began to scrape away the surrounding sand. The dagger was some fifteen inches long, the blade two inches wide at its broadest. She sat for a long time with it in her hands, staring at it, awed, as the voice of Johnny Rotten blasted across the beach, torn by the wind and dissipated across the water. When at last she stood up, she held her trophy awkwardly aloft and she reached for her haversack again.

The blast of ice cold wind took her completely by surprise. Whipping the haversack with its precious cargo out of her hands it flung it down the beach as, blinded by flying sand, she tried desperately to catch it. Her broom fell sideways in front of her and was blown away to end up wedged into the shingle at the end of the dune and her cassette player subsided slowly into the loose soil, where it continued to blast out its music into the roar of the wind before the heavy soil depressed the switches on the top and it fell silent.

The squall had gone almost as soon as it had come. Pushing her hair out of her eyes Alison scrambled out of the hollow and stared up the beach. She could see her haversack, lying in a dayglow heap amongst the tangled seaweed, fifty yards along the tide line. Running to it she caught it to her chest, panting. Then she turned.

Above the dune the sand was still spinning crazily in a whirling spiral which extended about four feet into the air. For several seconds she watched as it spun out of the hollow and away from her down the beach towards the inlet into the bay. Then as swiftly as it had come, it disappeared.

She swallowed nervously. This place was getting to her badly. She forced herself to walk back and stared down at the spot where she had been working so peacefully only five minutes before. All her hard efforts had been undone. The sand was piled randomly once more, her broom and spade lying beneath it. Her trowel had gone. Her cassette player was half-buried and silent, her picnic – two chocolate bars and a can of Coke – had fallen into a pool of sea water.

'Shit!'

She jumped down into the hole. Salvaging her belongings she heaped them on the edge. Switching on the music again she was comforted to hear it blast forth apparently unharmed. The Cure did a great deal to restore her equilibrium. Tearing the wrapper, thankfully intact and seemingly undissolved, off a chocolate bar she began to eat it.

Two yards to her left, unnoticed and almost invisible in the clay from which it protruded, a human hand, clawed and shrivelled, began, in the cold damp air, the process of disintegration.

Behind her, a faint shadow hovered over her; when at last she looked up and saw it, it was the size and shape of a man.

XVI

Oh, she was beautiful, the mother of his son. He watched her as she lay, propped on her elbow on the far side of the low table picking idly at the figs heaped on the plate before her. Her hair was rich and thick, piled high on her head and held in heavy-plaited coils by four ivory pins. Her skin was creamy, soft; her breasts, heavy, luscious beneath the soft folds of her long tunic. He felt himself tense. They were breasts which had been touched by another man's hands; another man's lips. It was strange. The heat of his fury and bitter jealousy was contained utterly by the cloak of ice which had formed inside him. Contained and controlled but not extinguished.

If he had returned to Rome, to the house of his father, would things have been different? Had he been foolish to accept the gift of land in the first colonia in Claudius's province of Britain? Colonia Claudia Victricensis which had been Camulodunum. He chewed thoughtfully at a dried fig. The land had brought him wealth, respect, honour – the perfect conclusion to an exemplary military career. But his young wife had been dismayed. She had wanted to return to Rome. She and her sister hated Britain. One of the reasons she had wanted so much to go back had been a man. She thought he did not know, but that man had been the reason for Marcus accepting this distant posting in the first place. He smiled grimly.

It was only a few months ago that she had changed her mind about Britain, and at once he had begun to suspect.

Feeling his gaze upon her Claudia looked up at him. Her smile was empty. Cold. A sham. He returned it and he saw doubt in those lovely grey eyes. But only for a moment. She thought she was safe. She thought she was clever. Let her think it. He would bide his time. The moment had to be right. Only her lover would know the real reason for his death, for Marcus could not afford to allow the scandal which would erupt if it became public. Private grief and anger must be contained, must be subservient to the public good. Any flame which might ignite the fire of revolt

*must be extinguished quietly. There must be no explosion of hate between
the native tribes and Rome.*

*But in private . . . He breathed deeply, holding his anger in with iron
control. In private, in secret, there would be revenge.*

*And his wife's punishment, afterwards, would last a lifetime, and
then through all eternity.*

For a moment Kate had been tempted to make up a thermos of
coffee and take it out to the dig to see how things were going
but she changed her mind. She had had her morning off. This
afternoon, or what was left of it, should be spent in serious work.
Besides, Alison would, no doubt, not extend much welcome to
any intruders in her private excavation. Perhaps later, Kate would
stroll out to the beach for a little fresh air, but not now.

She had worked solidly for about half an hour when the telephone brought her back to the present. Taking off her glasses she
went through to the kitchen to answer it.

'Kate. Hi.'

'Jon?' The lift of her spirits, the excitement at the sound of his
voice after so long was a purely Pavlovian response she told herself sternly, a conditioning, from living with him and loving him.
'How did you get my number?'

'From Bill.' For a moment he sounded defensive, then meekly
he said. 'I hope you don't mind.'

She smiled. 'No. I don't mind. Of course I don't mind. How is
the tour going?'

'OK. Nearly over, thank Christ!' He sounded tired and depressed.
'How are you?'

'Fine. Getting a lot of work done.'

'Is the cottage nice?'

Was he asking out of politeness or did he really care? 'Yes, it is
as a matter of fact. Very nice.'

'Bill says it's very isolated.'

'It is. It's a good place to work.' There was a lump in her throat.
Suddenly she was missing him so badly it hurt.

'Good. The money I owe you will soon be on its way, Kate. I'm
sorry it's been so long. Look, I fly to Boston tomorrow. Perhaps I'll
try and ring you from there.' There was so much he wanted to say,
so much he wanted to tell her, but he couldn't. For some reason
he was tongue-tied. He loved her and he had blown it. 'Take care.'

That was all. He had hung up. She stared at the receiver in her hand, feeling suddenly very, very lonely.

She was too unsettled to go back to work. After only a few minutes' struggle with her conscience she stood up, threw down her specs and reached for her jacket.

The beach was deserted, side lit in the falling dusk by the last streaks of sunlight from a bruised sun, going down in a haze behind the estuary. Along the tide line the dunlin were busy, probing the sand with their bills. Far out to sea the mist was waiting, hovering on the horizon, for the dark. There was no sign of Alison.

Kate stood staring down into the excavation for a long time. The mess of tossed sand and mud, the tangled weed, the shells, all spelt out the intrusion of the sea into the girl's vision of a Roman grave. There was no sign now of her meticulous digging and brushing of the sand. The vertical lines caused by the cutting edge of her spade had been replaced by a horizontal stratum, the sand intermingled now by long pale streaks of clay and broader wedges of black, the remnants of the three-thousand-year-old peat bog which had covered the river valley here when the sea was still two miles away. Looking down at the mess Kate shivered. She could see the earthenware, lying abandoned in the trench. Alison had not thought that worth collecting for some reason; nor had she gathered up the piece of metal lying on a tussock of uprooted grasses.

Slipping and sliding Kate scrambled down into the trench herself and picked it up with a frown. It was a dagger.

She turned it over in her hands, looking thoughtfully at the pitted corroded blade. It was ice cold to the touch.

Marcus

It was a whisper in her ear. A sigh on the wind. It was her imagination. Behind her, above the wood, the stars were emerging as the sky grew dark.

Scrambling out of the hollow she turned and began to walk swiftly back towards the cottage, the dagger still held in her hand, point down towards the ground, as though it were still potentially sharp. Which it was.

Indoors she slammed the door against the swiftly coming darkness, locked and bolted it and put the dagger down on the kitchen table, then she reached for the phone.

There was no answer from Redall Farmhouse.

She let it ring for several minutes, then at last she put the receiver down. If Alison wasn't at the farmhouse, where was she? Thoughtfully she walked into the living room and switched on the table lamp. She had begun to draw the curtains when she glanced at the stove. She couldn't believe it! It was out. And there were no logs in the box.

'Damn!' She stared down at it in dismay. She didn't want to go out, even to the log shed. She did not want to open the front door again. Suddenly she was shivering and to her astonishment she found she was near to tears.

Idiot. Idiot woman. Missing Jon. Frightened of your own shadow! Come on Kennedy where's your guts? What would sister Anne think of you if she could see you now? Firmly she put her jacket back on.

In the early dusk she could just see the nearest trees, their trunks glistening from the damp as she turned resolutely towards the shed, the empty box in her arms.

Alison's tools lay in the doorway higgledy piggledy as though she had thrown them down in a great hurry. Kate groped in her pocket for her new torch and shone the beam into the darkness of the shed. It caught the trowel lying on the ground, just inside the door. She bit her lip. What had made the girl leave so suddenly that she had left possibly her best find yet lying in the grave, and the tools of her trade, at first so neatly put away, thrown haphazardly down?

Better not to think about that. She had probably grown bored on her own. With a half-smile Kate remembered the ghetto blaster. Swiftly she tidied up the tools, then she loaded the box with logs and kindling. Now that it was heavy she could not spare a hand for the torch. Reluctantly she switched it off and pushed it into her pocket. After the bright torchlight the garden seemed very dark, but after all, she could see quite clearly by the light streaming out of the kitchen window.

And the headlights.

She paused, easing the box higher into her arms, watching them coming down the track, jerking up and down as the Land Rover slithered through the woods across the clear grass area and jerked to a stop outside the front door. Invisible in the darkness Kate waited as the door opened and the driver climbed out. He went to the cottage door and pushed it open.

'Hello?'

To her disappointment the voice was a deep baritone. Not Roger. Greg.

'Hello.' Kate had the satisfaction of seeing him jump violently as she came silently round the corner of the cottage, the box in her arms. 'Good evening.'

'Christ, you frightened me!' He looked at her for a moment, then long-ingrained chivalry, drummed into him by his father over the years, prevailed over intentional boorishness as he saw the weight of her load. 'Here. Let me take that.'

She handed over the box gratefully and preceded him into the cottage. 'I've been in Colchester. The fire's out, I'm afraid.' She pushed the front door closed, making sure the latch had engaged, then she went through into the kitchen and drew the curtains, cutting off the cascade of light which shone out onto the grass. The garden sank into darkness.

'I've come up to find Alison. Is she here?'

Kate swung round and stared at him. 'You mean she's still not at home? I've been to see if she was digging out there, but there's no sign of her.'

They stared at one another, the hostility which crackled between them suddenly muted. Greg lowered the box to the ground. 'Are you sure?'

'Of course I'm sure.'

Behind Kate the phone rang from the kitchen. She turned to answer it. Greg followed.

It was Roger. 'Tell Greg she's with a friend. Silly child didn't think to leave a note. Apparently she went up through the woods to the Farnboroughs'. She's spending the night with them.'

'I knew she would be OK.' Greg shook his head in exasperation when she told him. Then he leaned across to the counter and picked up the box of matches lying there. 'Do you want me to light the fire for you while I'm here?' His voice was curt, almost as if he were offering against his will.

'Would you.' She did not allow herself to sound too grateful. 'The lighters are over there. I'll get us a whisky.'

'All done.' Greg came back moments later. 'Good lord, what's that?' He had spotted the dagger lying on the table near the coffee pot. Curiously he picked it up and examined it. 'Where did you find this?'

'In Alison's excavation.'

He frowned. 'I thought she asked you not to touch anything there.'

'She did, and I had no intention of doing so. This was lying on the ground at the edge as though she'd dropped it. Another tide and it would have been lost.' She poured the two drinks and pushed one towards him. 'I told you, I went out to see if she was still there. There's a terrible mess at the excavation.'

He raised his glass and sipped the whisky, still holding the dagger. 'I thought she was doing it carefully.'

'She was. She showed it to me only yesterday. It must have been that storm last night. It's full of seaweed, and half the side has fallen in. I expect that's how that came to light.' She nodded in the direction of the dagger.

Putting down his glass he examined it more closely.

'Is it Roman do you think?' He glanced up.

Kate missed the sudden amusement in his eyes. She shrugged. 'I don't know. I don't think so. I think it might be earlier but I'm not an archaeologist. I do think she ought to get some experts here. She could be doing irreparable damage, poking around the way she is.' She still had not mentioned the torc.

'The way you describe it the sea will do a lot worse than anything she could do. At least she's saving a few things this way.' Greg put the dagger down. 'You'd better bring it when you come to dinner tomorrow.'

'I shall.' She met his eye. For a minute they studied one another, measuring each other up.

'So. How are you liking Redall Cottage?' he said at last.

'Very much. But I'm sorry you had to leave so I could come.'

'You mean you'd like me to move back in with you?' He raised an eyebrow suggestively.

'No.' She did not flinch. 'I'm paying for my privacy.'

'And I'm interrupting it.' He put down his glass.

'Not for another thirty minutes. I allow myself the occasional break. Have another?' Picking up the bottle she gestured towards the glass. He intrigued her. Handsome, boorish, presumably talented, he was something of an enigma.

'Why not. I can hardly get done for drunk driving in that thing. No one would notice the difference.'

As Kate led the way through into the sitting room he followed

83

her. She poured his whisky then she glanced at him. 'Someone broke in here last night.'

'Broke in?' His expression was bland; politely interested. If he was surprised he didn't show it.

'They seemed to be looking for something.'

'Have you told the police?'

She shook her head. 'Whoever it was had a key.' She sat down, cradling her glass on her knee.

'Oh, I see. You think it was me.'

'No. It was a woman.'

That did surprise him. 'You saw her?'

She shrugged. 'Not quite. But I know it was a woman, and I smelt her perfume. I thought at first it was Alison messing about, but now I'm not so sure. Perhaps it was a friend of hers.' She paused. 'Or of yours.'

He did not rise to the remark. 'Is anything missing?'

'No. At least, nothing of mine.' She took a sip from her glass, not looking at him. 'Did you mean to leave those pictures up-stairs?' she asked after a moment. She sat staring at the wood-burner. The fire inside roared like a wild beast.

Greg raised his foot and kicked the damper across. 'I did. There's no more space in the farmhouse. Why, don't you like them?' He threw himself down into the chair opposite her. There was a challenge in his eyes.

'Not much.'

'Too strong for you, eh?' He looked puzzled suddenly. 'Did you mean to imply that one of them is missing?'

'No, they were all there, I think. And yes, I suppose so,' she conceded. 'They are disturbing.'

'They depict the soul of this place. The cottage. The bay. The land. The sea. The sea will drown all this one day, you know.'

'So I gather.' She refused to be rattled by the dramatic decla-mation. 'And sooner rather than later if that digging is anything to go by.'

He frowned. 'It's strange. None of us knew that was there. Allie found it a while back – the signs of the dune having been dug by men and not just being natural – then only a few weeks ago a great section split off like a ripe rotten fruit and it started spewing out all these bits and pieces.' His voice was quiet, but his choice of words was deliberate. He had not taken his eyes off her face.

'It exudes evil, this place. It's in my paintings. I'm amazed Allie can't feel it. But she's an astoundingly insensitive kid. Perhaps it's because she anaesthetises herself all the time with that noisy crap she calls music.'

Kate smiled. 'I saw the scarlet machine this morning.'

He was right. She had felt it. The evil. She gave an involuntary shudder and was furious to see that he had noticed. He smiled. Pointedly he put down his glass and, standing up, he went to the stove. Opening the doors he loaded in another log. 'Do you want me to get in touch with the police about your visitor?'

She shook her head. 'Nothing was taken. I'm sure it was a schoolgirl prank. I'll bolt the door in future.'

'And you're not worried about staying here alone?' He raised an eyebrow. 'Perhaps it wasn't a burglar at all. Perhaps the woman you saw was a ghost. I told you this place was haunted. Haunted and evil. The locals won't come near it.'

Was that it, then? Was this all a ploy to frighten her away? She laughed. 'Being a writer of history I'm happy to live with ghosts.'

'I trust you're not tempting providence with that remark,' he said. Throwing himself down in his chair again he crossed his leg, left ankle on right knee and sighed. 'I used to find it very oppressive here after a while. My paintings would change. They would grow more and more angry. Whilst I am by nature quite a sunny chap.'

She was watching him closely.

'At the farmhouse I paint differently. With more superficiality,' he went on thoughtfully. 'If I ever paint a masterpiece it will be in this cottage.' For a brief moment it was as though he was talking to himself. He had forgotten she was there; forgotten he was trying to scare her. Remembering her again he glanced at her. 'Art, it seems, must wait for commerce.'

Straight from the hip. She took it without flinching. 'Don't you sell your paintings then?'

'No.'

The reply, loaded with scorn, was succeeded by a long silence. She did not pursue the subject. Studying his face as he stared morosely into the flames she was conscious suddenly of the lines of weariness around his eyes and the realisation that Greg Lindsey was a very unhappy man. The moment of insight struck her dumb. The silence dragged out uncomfortably as she, too, stared into the flickering fire.

The crash from upstairs brought them both to their feet. 'Shit! What was that?' Greg put down his glass.

She swallowed. She had heard a crash like that before and her investigation had found nothing. 'The wind must have blown the door shut,' she said at last. 'I'd better look.' She did not move. The room seemed suddenly warm and safe. She did not want to climb the stairs.

The noise seemed to have shaken him out of his introspection. He looked at her, noting her white face and anxious eyes and was astonished at his own reaction. He should have been pleased that she was scared but his studied hostility wavered and for a brief second he felt a wave of protectiveness sweep over him. 'I'll check.'

Taking the stairs two at a time he went first into the spare room. The room was empty save for her cases and boxes, and his own pictures, standing where he had left them behind the door. He noted briefly that they still faced the wall, then he ducked out of the room and switched on the light in the main bedroom. After the stark businesslike aura of the living room downstairs with its computer and books, the bedroom – his bedroom – shocked him by its unaccustomed femininity. He glanced round. Nothing was out of place. Both doors had been open. Nothing appeared to have fallen – he checked the painting on the wall. One of his, it was uncharacteristically pretty, depicting the bluebells in Redall Wood. He scowled at it. His mother must have brought it over, for it used to hang in the spare room at the farmhouse. Having ascertained that there was no reason for the bang that he could see, his gaze travelled more slowly around the bedroom for the second time, noting her towelling bathrobe, thrown across the bed, her slippers near it, both a bright flame which would suit her rather mousy colouring. He found himself picturing her in the robe for a moment. On the chest of drawers lay a heap of silver bangles – she had been wearing them the day she arrived, he remembered – and next to them a glass filled with winter flowers she must have gathered in the wood. The naturalist in him noted periwinkle, small velvety-red dead nettles and a sprig of daphne she must have found in what was once the cottage garden. Continuing his quick perusal, he studied the small collection of cosmetics. On neither occasion that he had met her so far had she been wearing any makeup at all, but obviously when the occasion demanded she was happy to gild the lily. He turned to the low windowsill where she had put several paperbacks – poetry and social history, he saw. No reader of fiction, this author.

'Have you found anything?'

Her voice behind him in the doorway made him jump guiltily.

'Nothing. Both doors were open. Nothing seems to have fallen over. The windows are closed.'

'Could it have been outside?'

'The chimney, you mean?' He smiled. 'I think we would have noticed if it had fallen through the roof.'

'What was it then?' Her voice betrayed her irritation. From the landing she had seen him studying her things. His interest made her feel vulnerable and angry.

'Perhaps it was the ghost of Marcus. I've often heard things here.' When she did not rise to the remark, he headed back towards the stairs, glancing at his watch. 'Look, Kate, I should be going back. There's nothing here. Nothing to worry about. I'll take a look at the roof as I leave, and get a few more logs in for you. It was probably out in the trees – a branch coming off or something. Acoustics are often unaccountable.' He descended the stairs ahead of her. 'If you're worried, give us a ring and Dad or I will come back and check things for you.'

'There won't be any need. I shall be all right.'

Marcus

She shivered at the name which had floated unbidden into her head, watching as Greg pushed his feet into his boots and reached for his jacket. Half of her wanted him to go. He had been perfectly polite, but she could sense his dislike. The other half was afraid. She did not relish the idea of being alone.

Which was crazy. She had rented the cottage for six months and she wasn't planning to have any lodgers. She had to get used to being alone, and get used to whatever funny noises the countryside had to throw at her. As if to test her resolution the sharp scream of a vixen rang out as he opened the front door. He turned and studied her face. 'You know what that is, I suppose.'

The bastard! He expected her to be frightened. 'I know,' she

87

said. She managed a smile. 'I've lived most of my life in the country, Greg. Because I have, or had,' she corrected herself as she remembered yet again the full implications concomitant with moving out of Jon's flat, 'a London address, it does not make me a townie.'

She thought he had the grace to look slightly shamefaced as, with a bow and a mock touch to his forelock, he headed for the Land Rover. She did not hear his parting comment as he hauled himself behind the wheel: 'And fuck you too, Lady Muck!'

It was only after she had watched the tail lights disappear into the trees that she realised he had neither given the roof a glance as he left, nor fetched her in the promised extra logs.

'Bastard.' She said it out loud this time. She glanced at the log box. There were still a few there but not enough after the blaze he had initiated, for the night. She would have to go out again into the dark.

The torch was sitting where she had left it on the counter in the kitchen. Next to the dagger. She looked at her jacket hanging on the back of the door and she reached a decision. When the fire died she would have a bath – heated by electricity – and she would go to bed. Nothing and no one was going to get her out of the front door again until it was daylight.

With an immense feeling of relief she shot the bolt on the door and walked back into the living room. She made sure the damper was closed – make the wretched thing last as long as possible – put on an Elgar tape – the Enigma Variations – loud – and then she poured herself another whisky.

She had worked for another couple of hours on the book, and was printing up a rough copy for herself when she remembered the silver polish she had stashed away in the cupboard under the sink. Switching off the computer with a sigh of relief she stacked the pages neatly away and went to the drawer. The torc looked greenish-black as she lifted it out and examined it again in the bright kitchen light. Shaking the bottle of polish she smeared some of the mixture cautiously onto the metal and began to rub it gently with the corner of a duster. Ten minutes later she gave up. Her more and more energetic rubbing had had no effect whatsoever. Disappointed, she laid duster and metal on the counter when the phone rang.

'Hi, Kate.' Jon's voice was so strong it sounded as though he was in the next room. 'I'm in Boston. How is Lord George?'

'Going well.' She found she was smiling. 'What about your tour?'

'OK. A bit tiring. Nearly over now, thank God. I'm taking five at the hotel. English tea and muffins before I get ready to go out this evening. What are you up to?'

'I'm cleaning an ancient British torc with modern British silver polish and its having no effect whatsoever.' Leaning against the counter, the phone comfortably tucked against her ear she turned and surveyed her handiwork.

'Sounds fun.' The response from across the Atlantic was muted. 'May I ask where you got an ancient British torc?'

'It was lying on the beach.'

'I see.' She could tell he didn't believe her. 'There isn't an ancient Briton wearing it, I suppose?'

'Not at the moment, no.' She smiled to herself again. 'You'd love it, here, Jon.' It was a tentative feeler; a peace offering.

'The parties are good are they?' The irony in his tone reminded her that they were no longer supposed to be friends. Or lovers.

So, why had he rung her again?

She knew better than to ask.

'There's no one to party with, here. Just the birds and I believe there are seals round in the bay.'

'And the occasional ancient Brit.'

'You got it.' She mimicked what she hoped was an American insouciance. 'Actually the ghost is Roman.'

There was a moment's silence.

'You sounded almost serious,' Jon said cautiously.

'Did I?' She reminded herself how quick he was to pick up nuances; his sensitivity was one of the things she loved – had loved, she corrected herself sharply – about him. It made his actions over the last few weeks harder to bear.

She laughed lightly. 'How silly. Only joking.'

'I see.' He was still thoughtful. 'You are all right?'

'Yes. Fine.'

'OK. Well, enjoy yourself kiddo. I'll give you a ring in a day or two.'

For the second time he had not given her time to say goodbye. The line had gone dead and she was left staring at the receiver once again. Replacing it slowly she went thoughtfully back to the table and picked up her duster.

The blast of cold air behind her, smelling heavily of wet earth, took her completely by surprise. She whirled round. The front door must have blown open in spite of her care in locking and bolting it. She peered out into the hall. The door was as she had left it. The hall was dark and deserted.

Come on, Kennedy. Either a window has come open or the wind has blown back down the chimney. She found she was whispering to herself as she looked into the warm, dimly-lit living room. There was still a faint glow coming from the stove, though the log box was empty. The room was cooling, but the scent of earth was not coming from there. It was coming from upstairs.

Her bedroom window must be open. She frowned. She had opened it earlier to stare out at the sea, watching the mist drifting in across the still, grey water as night came in from the east. Obviously she had not latched it properly. Her hand on the stair rail she began to climb.

Both doors at the top were open. Both rooms were in darkness. Reaching the top she clicked on the light. The window in her bedroom was shut as she had known in her heart it would be, and the curtains were tightly drawn across. She sniffed. There must be a patch of damp in the house which the rain had activated somehow. Ducking out of the room she peered into the other across the landing. The smell was stronger there and the air was cold. Bitterly cold. The room had a north-facing window, she reminded herself as she went to examine it. It was closed and judging by the cobwebs welded over the catch, had not been opened for a long time.

Slowly she surveyed the walls, looking for the telltale signs of discolouration on the wallpaper. Tiny lemon yellow flowers on brown green stems romped across the uneven walls and between the oak beams without a sign of damp.

Switching off the lights she walked downstairs again, sniffing. The smell was still strong. A sweet, cold smell like a newly-turned flower bed after rain. With a shrug she walked back into the living room and turning over the tape, threw herself down in the armchair nearest the fire.

When she awoke 'In the South' had finished, the fire was out and the room was ice cold. Her head ached and for a moment

90

she was too stiff to move. Forcing herself to her feet she groaned and reached for the switch on the table lamp. Turning it off she made her way to the door. A warm bed and a heap of soft pillows to cuddle into, that was what she wanted. In the doorway she turned and surveyed the room before flicking off the light switch on the wall and plunging the room into darkness. It was as she made her way into the bathroom and reached for her toothbrush that she realised she had not had any supper. Two whiskies was not exactly a nutritious way to end the evening. Perhaps that accounted for her splitting headache. She frowned. She was beginning to drink too much. She contemplated getting herself something to eat and realised that she wasn't hungry. She also realised that she had not switched on the immersion heater so there was not enough hot water for a bath. With a sigh she bent over the basin and splashed some tepid water into her face. All she wanted was sleep. Food and bath could wait until morning. That was one of the joys of living on your own, she recognised suddenly. You could please yourself. Cook or not cook. Wash or not wash. Sleep when you wanted. And just at this moment that was all she wanted.

It was as she put her foot on the bottom step of the staircase that she saw the movement upstairs. She froze, 'Is there anyone there?' Her voice sounded thin and frightened in the silence.

There was no answer.

'Who is it?' She called again. Her desire for sleep had vanished.

She was answered by the rattle of rain on the windows as a squall of wind hurtled in from the sea.

'Christ, I'm seeing things now,' she muttered to herself. Tired eyes. Too much computer, that was the problem. It was the logical explanation but it still took an enormous effort of willpower to force her up the stairs, throwing on all the lights when she reached the top. The place was empty, the windows closed against the storm. She sniffed hard. The scent of wet earth seemed to have disappeared, though when she pushed back the curtains and stared out at the blackness she could see the rain coursing down the panes of glass.

Undressing as fast as she could she slipped between the sheets, leaving the light on the landing switched on against the dark. She lay, wide awake, clutching one of her pillows to her chest, her eyes straining out through the door to the small expanse of wall – painted a dark Suffolk pink and bisected by one pale oak beam – which she could see from the bed. And she listened to the rain.

XVII

'Are you awake, Sue?' Alison stared through the darkness of her friend's bedroom towards the bed by the far wall.

'Yes.'

They had been whispering and giggling for the last two hours. Twice Sue Farnborough's mother, Cissy, had come in and shushed them wearily and told them to go to sleep; now she had gone to bed herself and the house was in darkness. For the last twenty minutes or so the silences between the two girls had been growing longer and longer.

'Do you think I should tell them at home?'

'About what happened at the grave?'

'Of course, about what happened at the grave.'

'No. They'll interfere. Parents always do. Are you going to go back?'

Alison hesitated for only a second. 'Of course I'm going to go back. I'm going to finish the excavation.'

'By yourself?'

'You could come with me.' Alison sounded almost eager.

'No way. That's not my scene.' Sue was adamant.

'Oh, come on. You'd enjoy it. It's fun.'

'It doesn't sound fun to me.' Sue grinned maliciously in the darkness. 'You were so scared you nearly wet yourself. You told me as much.'

'I didn't.'

'You did. And why else did you come here? Running all the way through the woods instead of staying at home and waiting for your mum to get back from Colchester. You were really chicken.'

'I wasn't.'

'You were. Are you going to school tomorrow?'

'No. I'm still not feeling well.'

'You're skiving off, you mean. Well, I'm going, so shut up,

Allie. I want to get some sleep.' Sue reached in the darkness for the headphones of her Walkman and switched on the little machine beneath her pillow. The blast of Sisters of Mercy at full volume in her ears seemed an unlikely lullaby but within minutes she was asleep.

Across the room Alison lay awake, staring towards the curtained windows, listening to the rain. Beneath the borrowed duvet she had begun to shiver again.

XVIII

There was a scattering of wet, sandy earth on the kitchen table. Kate stared at it. The torc lay where she had left it, next to the duster and the jar of silver polish. She touched the soil with her finger. It was wet and cold. She sniffed. The smell was there but very faint now – the smell of a newly-turned garden.

Or a newly dug grave.

She shook her head. She had not slept well. The room had been cold and the noise of the wind and rain lashing the windows had woken her several times from her uneasy, dream-laden sleep. Her head was so heavy she could not even think straight as she walked over to the sink, filled the kettle and switched it on. Perhaps after a cup of coffee she would find an explanation for the mess on the table. There had to be a reason. Earth does not just materialise on a kitchen table. It must have fallen from the beamed ceiling, perhaps released by creeping damp and rain, or it had been swept in on a freak gust of wind under the front door or down the chimney.

She spooned Nescafé into a mug and poured in the water, watching the swirl of brown granules clinging to the blue pottery dissolving as she stirred. It scalded her tongue when she drank but the caffeine shot into her system with gratifying speed. Putting down the mug she picked up the torc and stared at it closely. There was no sign of the effort she had made to clean it. Even the scratches she had made with her nail had disappeared. The metal was as greenish-black and corroded as ever. Wrapping it carefully in the duster she carried it upstairs and through into the spare room. Only one of her suitcases boasted a key. Locking the torc inside it, she pushed it into the corner and, closing the door behind her, she made her way downstairs again. She put the polish away and going to the sink rinsed out a J cloth under the hot tap. It took only a few minutes to wipe up the earth, rinse the cloth again and put it away before she dragged out her boots and jacket and throwing open the front door went outside with her log box. It was a bright sunny morning. High, white, wisped clouds raced across a vivid blue sky from the west and behind the cottage the sea glittered blindingly.

The rain had blown into the shed and many of the logs were soaked. Rummaging in the back she found a few that were dry and carried them indoors. Three times she made the trip back and forth, until there was a satisfactory pile beside the stove. Then she brought in kindling and a final armful of logs to put in the stove itself. Satisfied that she had enough fuel for twenty-four hours at least she stared down at the stove. There was no point in lighting it now. There was one more thing she had to do before she settled down to work for the day. It had been gnawing at the back of her mind since she had cleared up the soil in the kitchen.

Locking the front door behind her she wedged the key into the pocket of her jacket, and pulling on her gloves she headed across the short grass at the back of the cottage towards the beach. A flock of tern rose and wheeled as she appeared on the shingle banks and ran slipping and sliding towards the sand. The beach was wet still from the tide and trailed with weed. A line of shells, white and pink and glabrous in the bright sunlight, marked the line of the high tide. The air was so cold it made her eyes water as she turned right and followed the line of dunes towards Alison's excavation.

For a long time she stood on the edge staring down into the declivity. Another huge chunk of the dune had broken away and she could now see clearly the different strata in the bright sand. There were pale lines of clay, different shades of sand and gravel and now, clearly visible, a thick black crumbling layer of peat.

There was a strange dryness in her mouth as she half jumped, half slid into the hollow. A spray of bladderwrack lay draped across the bottom of the trench and, half-buried in the sand, something bright red caught her attention as she peered nearer. Frowning, she kicked at the sand fall. Alison's ghetto blaster lay there beneath a pile of sea weed. Stooping she pulled it free. The 'on' button was still depressed. Alison had been back this morning early and had gone again. Putting the machine on the edge of the hollow she stared round. What could have happened to make her abandon her precious cassette player? There was no sign of the girl's tools, but perhaps they were buried in the latest sand fall. She stepped closer to the face and cautiously she drew off her glove. The peat was soft, layered, compressed. It smelt, when she withdrew her fingers, of wet garden soil. She swallowed hard. 'Alison?' Her shout was whipped up by the wind and carried only a few yards before it was dissipated and dissolved. 'Alison?' She shouted louder. Scrambling up to the edge of the hollow she put her hand to her eyes against the glare and stared round. The beach was empty.

She turned round. There could be no question of the girl being there, under the sand, but for a moment her imagination was playing the wildest of tricks. She could see where it was soft and loose, where it had fallen, and where, in the bottom of the hollow, a long mound lay compressed beneath the clay. A mound that had the shape of a human grave.

She stared at it. Alison would not have come back in the dark. She was safe at her friend's house when Diana had rung last night. Whoever – whatever, she corrected herself swiftly – lay down there, it was not a twentieth-century fifteen-year-old school-girl. Kate stepped towards the mound cautiously. It was her imagination again working overtime. From a different angle the mound was just a part of the sand, shadowed by the low sunlight. She could see the worm casts on it now, and the sprinkling of loose peat which had fallen from the sand cliff.

'What are you doing here?' Alison's voice, harsh and angry, broke into her thoughts so sharply she jumped.

'Oh thank God!' The words were out of her mouth before she could stop them. 'I thought perhaps you had had an accident –'

'You thought I was buried in there?' The note of disdain quivered a little at the end. Alison stepped white-faced from behind the edge of the dune. There were dark circles under her eyes.

Kate smiled. 'Only for a second. It was when I saw your radio.'

Alison's gaze switched to the cassette player. She did not move towards it. 'I forgot it,' she said after a moment.

'So I see. I'm afraid it was buried in the sand. I think the tide probably got it.'

'Why did you come here?' Alison's voice was markedly less aggressive as she stood looking down at Kate. She still had made no move to jump down into the hole, or to pick up her radio.

'There was something I wanted to check.' Kate scrambled up beside her. 'The different lines of strata being exposed. Do you see? The sand fall last night is revealing the line of a peat bog which is probably thousands of years old.'

Alison's eyes strayed to the dark streaks in the sand for a moment. Still she had not moved. 'Did you see anything moving?' she asked. 'When you came. Was there anything – anyone here?'

Kate looked at her sharply. 'What sort of thing?'

Alison shrugged massively. 'I don't know. Yesterday, when I was here. There was something.' She looked away evasively. 'I don't suppose it was anything. Maybe a bird-watcher or a naturalist or something . . .' Her voice trailed away.

'But you didn't see them clearly,' Kate prompted.

'No.'

'Did you smell anything strange? Wet earth.'

Alison stared at her. 'The whole place was wet.'

'True.' Kate smiled.

For a moment they both looked down at the excavation in silence. Then, 'Are you going to do some more work on it today?' Kate asked at last.

Alison shrugged. 'Might. But I've got work to do to catch up for school.' She was shifting restlessly from foot to foot. She had not wanted to come today but something had made her do it. She could not stop herself.

'That's tough. I wondered why you weren't at school,' Kate said. 'Have you been ill?'

Alison nodded, but offered no further explanation. Kate did not pursue it. 'I think it's going to rain. Better to leave any digging for another day.' For some reason she would feel much better if Alison were not here alone on the beach. The thought of the child digging away in isolation in this lonely grave appalled her. And it was a grave. Alison was right.

'You said you were going to take some photos. Would you like me to do it for you later, when the sun is right?' she asked at last.

Alison peered at her through wildly blowing wisps of hair. 'Would you?'

'Of course. I should think by about midday the light would be better. I'll come out then. I'll bring the film with me this evening and whoever goes into town next could get it developed.'

'Great.'

Was it her imagination again or was there a marked lessening of enthusiasm? 'Allie, did something frighten you yesterday?' Kate asked gently.

'No, of course not!' The flash of red in Alison's cheeks and the defiant glare belied her words.

'I just wondered.'

'Why, does it scare you?' Pitying. Disdainful.

'It does a bit. Yes.'

'Why?' Again the aggressive, derisive note. But beneath it, Kate sensed there was a plea. And she knew suddenly that she must not reinforce the girl's fears. She shrugged. 'I don't know. Perhaps it was, as your brother said, that I've grown used to living in a town. One forgets the country noises. And I've never stayed so close to the sea before.'

To her relief Alison's face cleared. 'You'll get used to it,' she replied. For the first time she smiled. 'Will you really take the photos for me?'

'Of course I will. No problem.' Kate hesitated. 'Do you want to come back to the cottage for some coffee before you go home?'

Alison's nod and the speed with which she gathered up her ruined ghetto blaster and turned away from her excavation spoke volumes. Following her, Kate turned and glanced over her shoulder only once towards the dig. A cloud of gulls hovered over the place where she and Alison had been standing. Then with a wild screaming and shrieking, they wheeled as one and flew straight out towards the sea.

'Why did you lock it? We never bother.'

Out of sight of the dunes Alison was once more her supercilious self.

'Habit, I suppose,' Kate replied easily. 'After all, someone did break in.' She pushed open the door. 'Black or white?' She walked ahead into the kitchen.

'White please.' Alison had not followed her, nor had she given any acknowledgment of Kate's comment. She had walked through into the living room. 'You've let the woodburner go out,' she called.

Kate closed her eyes for a moment and took a deep breath. 'I know, but it's laid all ready to light. Do you want to do it for me?'

She reached for the coffee jar and stopped. There was a trail of black peaty soil on the worktop.

'Oh Christ.' She didn't realise she had spoken out loud.

'What is it?' Alison appeared behind her in the doorway.

Kate took a deep breath. 'Nothing. I spilt something, that's all.'

'Where are the matches?' Alison bent and rummaged in the cupboard under the sink. She had taken off her jacket and brushed back her hair with her fingers.

'There, on the dresser.' Kate was still staring at the trail of wet earth amongst the mugs. 'Allie, don't bother to light it now, OK? When we've had our coffee, I'll walk back with you. I need to drive into Colchester this morning.' Again the thought had come unprompted. Perhaps this time it was because suddenly she didn't want to be alone in the house.

'What about the photos? You promised.'

Damn the photos!

'That's OK, I'll do them later, don't worry. In fact the later I leave it, the better the light will be. We'll get more definition. I'll still have the film for you by this evening.'

She lifted two mugs out of the earth and rinsed them under the tap before reaching for the coffee jar.

'What's all this mess on the side here?' Alison had seen it. Staring down at it critically she ran a finger through it, leaving a clean trail on the varnished wood of the worktop.

Kate shook her head. 'I'm not sure. It must have come in when I brought the logs in earlier.'

The answer seemed to satisfy Alison. Turning away she returned to the living room.

'Do you like using a computer?' Her voice came through the door as Kate waited for the kettle to boil.

'Yes, quite. It makes correlating notes and chronologies and things much simpler.' Kate carried the mugs of coffee through. Alison was standing at her table looking down at her books and notes.

'My brother Patrick is a computer wizard,' the girl said. 'Most of the time, he's a nerd, but he is tops on computers.'

'Will he be there tonight?'

'Yeah.'

'And will Greg?'

Alison shrugged. 'No one ever knows what Greg is going to do.'

'I see,' Kate said dryly. 'Well, I'm looking forward to coming to dinner with your parents. They seem so nice.'

'They are, I suppose.' Alison finished her coffee and put the mug down. 'I'm going. Do you want to come with me?'

The challenge in her eyes was hostile again and suddenly Kate was tired of the child. 'I'll be ready in about half an hour,' she said. 'If you want to wait for me, that'll be nice, if not, I'll follow you over later.'

For a moment Alison hesitated, obviously reluctant to walk back alone, then with an exaggerated sigh she flung herself down in one of the chairs. 'OK. I'll wait.'

'Thanks.' Kate smiled. She gathered up the mugs and left the girl sitting there.

The door to the spare room was open and the boxes and cases in there had been strewn all over the floor. Kate stared at the scene for a moment in dismay, then she turned and called down the stairs. 'Alison, did you do this?'

'What?' The girl's voice was puzzled.

'Do all this? For God's sake!' Her case, the case with the torc was still locked, she could see that from the doorway.

Alison ran up behind her and looked round. 'What a mess.'

'All these boxes and things. I left them tidy.'

'Oh.' Alison avoided her eye. 'Well, it wasn't me. How could it have been? I haven't been upstairs at all.'

Kate found her heart was hammering rather too loudly in her chest. There had to be an explanation. This child or her brother must have done it. Perhaps while she was on the beach Greg or the unknown computer wizard had sneaked in and messed up the place. Turning, she flung open her bedroom door. Nothing in there appeared to have been touched. Everything was as she had left it.

Seeing her white face Alison frowned. She too suspected that it must have been Greg. Last time she had seen him, he had still been planning to try to scare Kate out of the cottage. He was keen on her idea of making Kate think it was haunted. Could he have done all this? Had he already taken things this far? Staring round she felt herself shiver. If it was him, then it was working. She narrowed her eyes for a moment. Was it Greg down on the beach as well? Was he behind what had happened yesterday?

Suddenly she was furious. She turned and running down the stairs she opened the front door. 'Come on. I need to get home,' she called. 'There's nothing wrong. Let's go.'

If it was Greg she would get even, if it was the last thing she ever did. The bastard! The unmitigated, double dealing, swindling bastard! He had really scared her. And he owed her a new radio cassette player.

XIX

'You shouldn't have come.' Nion took her hands. 'You take too many risks. What if you were seen?'

She broke free and ran a few steps in front of him to the edge of the water, skipping like a child. 'Who is there to see? He's out all day. The slaves are too busy to care. The child and his nurse think I am visiting my sister.' She pirouetted, laughing. 'I've never been so happy. I can't believe this is happening. Me, a staid Roman matron, and you –' she stood in front of him, staring into his face and rested her hands for a moment on the folds of his cloak, '– you, a prince of the Trinovantes.'

Nion laughed, throwing back his head, his strong teeth white in his tanned face, the laugh lines at eyes and mouth carving deep into the square features.

Around them the dunes stretched for miles; sand, spun and blown by the wind into hollows and ridges, the shingle thick and clean as the tide drew back. Nearby, her mule waited patiently beside the horse, which stood between the shafts of his chariot, grazing listlessly on the salt sand flowers and grasses. They were alone. Quite alone. He caught her against him, burying his face in her hair.

'I want you to come away with me. One of my brothers is in the west. We could go to him there. Your husband would never find you.'

She tensed, raising her face slowly to his and he read the conflicting emotions in her eyes. Desire. Hope. Excitement. All three blazed in their sea-grey depths, but there was doubt there too. Doubt and fear. 'I can't leave the boy.'

'Then we'll take him with us.'

'No.' She shook her head sadly. 'No. He would never allow his son to go. Me –' she hesitated. 'I don't know if he would come after me, but he would search the whole earth for his son.' Her eyes brimmed with tears. 'And I could not ask you to leave this – your home.' His land, his woods, his pastures, his fields, his water, the salt pans which made him rich, all worked by the men of his people.

She shivered as she looked up again and raised her lips towards his. His gods were powerful, cruel, demanding. Sometimes she wondered if they had given their blessing to their servant's union with a daughter of Rome, or if they were jealous, biding their time, waiting to punish her for her presumption.

Behind them the sun glittered on the sea, turning it the colour of jade. As his hands moved down to release her girdle she forgot her fear; she forgot everything, drowning in the pleasure of his touch.

'We'll have to give you a season ticket at this rate!' The man in the ticket office at the museum greeted Kate with a cheery smile.

She smiled back. 'I think you might. Or a job!' She was still wondering why she was here. Was it the thought of the next book, bubbling uncontrollably in her subconscious, or was it just the fascination of that strange, half-excavated pit on the beach beside her cottage? She refused to admit that she felt a slight reluctance to stay in the cottage alone. She could not allow that. But perhaps it was a little of all three. She was feeling guilty. She shouldn't be here. She should be working with George Byron and his irritating, hysterical mother.

Retracing her steps upstairs she went to stand once more in front of the statue of Marcus Severus, gazing into his face as if somewhere there in the cold, dead eyes she would find the answer to her riddle. For he had something to do with that grave on the shore, she was sure of it. Marcus Severus Secundus and Augusta, his wife. Thoughtfully, she turned to the display case where his bones lay exposed to view. There was no answer there. Nothing but the gentle hum of the lights and in the distance, the muffled and unreal shouts and screams of the video replay of Boudicca's massacre.

As she parked the car in the barn later she glanced at Redall Farmhouse with a certain amount of longing. They were there this time; she could see smoke coming from the chimney and there were lights on in the kitchen. They were expecting her to supper; supposing she knocked and went in now? Perhaps she could help prepare it, or sit out of the way by the fire sipping tea or better still whisky, until the appropriate time. But she couldn't, of course she couldn't. She glanced at her watch. It was barely three o'clock. She had another five hours to wait before she could knock on their door.

Shouldering her bag she turned up the track into the woods. The early sunshine had gone. The sky was growing increasingly wintry and as the wind rose a quick light shower of sleet raced through the trees. She shivered. At least the fire was ready to light at home.

Home. She hadn't thought of the cottage as home before, but for now that's what it was. She could draw the curtains against the coming darkness, have tea and a hot bath and do a couple of hours work before setting out on the walk back through the dark.

Opening the door she dumped her bag on the floor and glanced round, unconsciously bracing herself against signs that anyone had been inside. There were none. The cottage was as she had left it. The kitchen was spotless, the doors and windows closed and the air smelt faintly of burned apple wood. Relieved, she unpacked her shopping and went to light the woodburner, then slowly she went upstairs.

Pulling open her cupboard she looked through the clothes she had brought with her. Since she had arrived in north Essex she had worn trousers and thick sweaters, but she wanted to change into something a little more formal tonight. More formal, but still practical, bearing in mind that she had a long walk through the muddy woods. She pulled out a woollen skirt and a full sleeved blouse and threw them on the bed.

It was then that she remembered her promise to Alison to photograph the grave. She glanced at the window. It would soon be getting dark and the sky was already heavy with cloud. Perhaps she could leave it until tomorrow. But she wanted to keep her promise. She needed to win the girl's trust, for the sake of what was left of the site. She hesitated for a moment longer, then reluctantly she went to find her camera. She loaded a new roll of film and with a wistful glance at the fire she grabbed her anorak and set out into the cold.

The beach was very bleak. Turning up her collar, she put her head down into the wind and walked as swiftly as she could back towards Alison's dig, firmly resisting the urge to glance over her shoulder at the coming darkness. The wind had blown the sand into soft ridges, rounding the sharp corners, drying the surface of the soil so the different strata were harder to see. Squinting against her hair which whipped free of its clip into her eyes she raised the camera and peered through the viewfinder. She doubted if anything would come out even with the flash, but at least she would have tried. She took the entire roll, shooting the dig from every angle, and trying, rather vainly, to get a few close-ups of the sand face itself. She did not see the dark, withered stumps which had been a man's fingers; nor the black protrusion which was his femur, broken and splintered and already crumbling back into the sand.

Safely back inside the cottage she locked the door with a sigh of relief and, taking the film out of the camera, put it into its plastic case and tucked it into her shoulder bag. She was damp and thoroughly chilled. Slotting a tape of Vaughan Williams' Fifth Symphony into her cassette player and turning it up loudly, she climbed the stairs and went back into her bedroom, pulling off her scarf and shaking out her wet hair as she began slowly to undress. Putting on her dressing gown she paused, listening, as the music downstairs grew quiet. She could hear a strange buzzing from the spare room. She frowned. For a moment she hesitated, biting her lip. What was it about this damn house which made her so jumpy? It was a fly, that was all, awoken by the morning sunshine. Taking a deep breath she flung open the door and switched on the light. The room was deserted. A quick glance showed that her cases and boxes were undisturbed; Greg's pictures stood where she had left them, face to the wall behind the door, and she was right, a couple of bluebottles were crawling across the window. As the light flicked on they buzzed angrily against the glass. Shaking her head she backed out and closed the door. Tomorrow she would deal with them.

The bathroom was very cold. With a shiver she pulled the cord to switch on the wall heater and, putting the plug in the bath, she turned on the hot tap. As the windows steamed over she closed the curtains then she tipped some foaming bath oil into the steaming jet of water and stood back, twisting her hair into a knot on the top of her head as she watched the bath fill with fragrant froth. Lying back in the warmth was ecstasy. With a groan of pleasure she submerged all but her head and closed her eyes.

She hadn't noticed the bluebottle in the corner of the window frame. As the light and warmth woke it up it crawled from beneath the curtain and buzzed angrily towards the strip light over the basin. She opened her eyes and watched it, irritated. The discordant buzzing spoiled her mood. After dashing itself several times against the mirror it took off and made a low swift circuit of the bathroom. Involuntarily she ducked as it swooped over her head. 'Damn and blast!' She flicked foam at it. She would not let it spoil her bath.

As the water began to cool she turned on the hot tap hopefully, knowing before she did it that the tank would not yet have heated up again. As she expected it was cold. Heaving herself to her feet she stepped out onto the bath mat and wrapped a towel around herself. Wiping the steam from the mirror she peered at her face. Out of the corner of her eye she could see the bluebottle on the frame of the mirror. She flipped at it with her hand and it took off, swooping up to the light. It was then the phone rang. Wrapped in the towel she picked it up in the kitchen.

'Kate, I was worried. Are you OK?'

'Jon?' Her heart leaped as she sat down, shivering. 'God, I wish you were here.'

'I thought so. Something is wrong isn't it? I could hear it in your voice yesterday.'

She could have bitten out her tongue. Why had she said it? It was over between them. Anyway, what was the use of worrying him when he was so far away? 'Nothing is wrong,' she said hastily. 'I just meant you'd like it here. The big skies, the sea, the silence. They would appeal to you.'

'Perhaps I'll come and see you when I get back.' There was an echo on the line this time – a pause between each sentence; it made them both sound awkward and they didn't talk for long. After she put the phone down she sat looking at it thoughtfully for several seconds. If it was all over between them, why did he keep ringing?

At a quarter to eight she switched off her computer and the desk lamp and standing up, she stretched. As she worked she had been conscious of the wind rising outside the cottage. It rattled the windows and from time to time she heard the spatter of rain against the glass.

Carefully she built up the fire and shut the doors as tightly as she could, closing the dampers right down so the stove would be snug and still alight when she came home later, then reluctantly she began to pull on her jacket and boots. With one glance

107

behind her into the living room where she had left the single lamp on the side table burning to welcome her home, she stepped out into the night and pulling the front door shut behind her, she turned the key in the lock. For the last hour, she realised, she had been hoping that the phone would ring and Roger would suggest he came to fetch her. It would only take him ten minutes in the Land Rover. She sighed. Clutching her torch firmly she switched it on and directed the beam up the muddy track into the trees.

It took her half an hour to walk the half mile through the wood. The track was muddy and slippery and the wind had scattered the springy resinous branches of the pine trees on the ground, making the path treacherous in the unsteady torchlight. Several times she stopped and glanced around, shining the torch into the trees. The narrow beam showed only wet, black trunks, deep shadows and a tangle of matted undergrowth.

Diana opened the door with an exclamation of surprise. 'Kate, my dear, you haven't walked! Greg said he was going over to pick you up half an hour ago.'

Greg, she thought. I might have guessed. She smiled, realising suddenly that her face was so cold it was hard to make her muscles work. 'I wish I'd known, I would have waited for him,' she said. She followed Diana inside, shed her wet outer garments and found herself ushered towards the dreamed of inglenook. Within minutes she had been settled into the warmest corner of the sofa with a whisky in her hand and a cat on her knee.

The room smelled gloriously of burning apple logs, and cooking; she sniffed in anticipation; garlic, oregano, tomatoes – something Italian then. Lying back with her head against the cushions she smiled at Roger who had seated himself opposite her. 'This is heaven. It's not worth cooking for myself. I've been living on baked beans and tinned soup for the last few days.'

'So, how is your book going?' Roger smiled. At the Aga Diana had lifted the lid off a pan and was stirring gently.

Kate took a sip of her whisky, feeling the warmth flowing through her veins. 'Quite well. From the work point of view coming here was a good move. It's given me the time to concentrate.'

'Not much else to do over there, eh?' Roger smiled. He cocked an eye at the door as it opened and Greg appeared. 'I thought you were supposed to be fetching our guest,' he said sharply.

Greg grimaced. 'I'm sorry. I didn't realise the time. I was on my way out now to get you.'

Kate eyed him cryptically. She did not believe it. He had meant to leave it so late that she had to walk. She said nothing, however. She did not want to spoil the mood of the evening. 'Don't worry,' she said easily. 'No harm done. I enjoyed the walk.'

'Well, you can be sure he will drive you back after supper,' Roger put in quietly, and hearing the note of steel in his voice Kate realised that Greg's father was as aware as she was that his omission was deliberate. She relaxed back in the cushions further with a sigh of pleasure, her hand gently stroking Serendipity Smith into a state of ecstasy, surprised to acknowledge how relieved she felt that she would not have to face the cold wet trees alone again that night.

It was when Alison and Patrick appeared that Greg, who had been morosely drinking beer in the corner chair, looked up. 'Did you remember to bring the dagger you found in Alison's dig?' he asked. Though his voice was quiet there was a hostile edge to it that Kate picked up immediately.

She frowned. 'I did indeed.' Carefully, so as not to disturb the cat she leaned down to the soft leather shoulder bag which lay at her feet and rummaged inside it. The iron dagger was wrapped in a piece of newspaper. Lifting it out she held it up to Alison. 'I found it lying on the sand,' she said. 'I only moved it because the tide was coming in. It would have been lost.'

For a moment Alison hesitated. She took the newspaper packet with obvious reluctance. 'Thanks.' She put it down without opening it. 'I had put it in my haversack. It must have fallen out.'

Kate raised an eyebrow. 'Aren't you going to look at it?'

'Later.'

'What's wrong, Allie? Lost interest already?' Greg's challenge brought a flush of angry pink to Alison's face.

'Of course not.'

'You weren't there today.'

'I was.' The retort was flashed at him furiously. 'That just shows all you know. *She* saw me. Didn't you?'

'I did,' Kate acknowledged.

'So, what do you think of Allie's dig?' Roger interposed quietly, long used to stepping into the quarrels of his children.

'Remarkable.' Kate sat forward. 'I hope Alison is going to get some experts up here soon. The tide is taking away the sand very fast. If she's not careful the whole thing will have disappeared before it's properly recorded.'

'Did you remember to photograph it?' Alison's question stemmed not so much from interest, Kate sensed, as the desire to catch her out. It was with some satisfaction that she nodded. She reached again into her bag and produced the roll of film.

'I'm afraid the light wasn't as good as I'd hoped. It may not have come out, but it's better than nothing.'

Alison took the film and threw it down on the table near her. 'Thanks,' she said again.

'It was very good of you to take them for her,' Roger put in. He had been watching his daughter with a frown. 'Alison, have you told anyone yet about your finds? Kate is right. Someone expert on these matters needs to come and see it soon.'

'She'll do it when she's ready,' Diana put in from the kitchen. 'Don't pester the child. Give her a chance to write up her project on her own first, if that's what she wants.'

Kate turned in her seat, resting her arm along the back of the sofa so she could see Diana who was grating parmesan at the kitchen table. 'It really is getting quite urgent,' she said almost apologetically. 'A few more high tides and the tumulus will have gone.'

'So that's what it is. A tumulus,' Greg put in. 'It seems to me we have our own expert here on the premises.'

'I'm not an expert,' Kate turned back, conscious that the cat on her knee was becoming increasingly irritated by her apparent inability to sit still. 'Far from it. But I do think it could be important.'

MARCUS!

The voice seemed to echo round the room.

Digging its claws into her knee the cat leaped off her lap and streaked out of sight up the stairs.

The others looked at it in astonishment.

'Sorry. I hope he didn't scratch you,' Roger said with a puzzled smile. 'I can't think why he did that. He seemed to like you.'

'It's probably the smell of mum's cooking,' Patrick put in his first comment of the evening.

Had none of them heard it then, apart from the cat? The pain of the voice which seemed to ring round the room had rung so loudly in her ears. The anguish. The fear.

Completely disorientated, Kate realised that Greg was watching her closely. 'Perhaps you don't really like cats,' he put in softly. 'They often go and sit on people who don't like them out of sheer perversity.'

'Of course I like them,' she snapped. Her hands were clenched tightly around her empty glass. Noticing, Roger levered himself to his feet. 'Here, let me get you another one, Kate. Forget the moggy. He's a damn nuisance.' His voice was soothing. 'So, tell me, how do you like Redall Cottage?'

'Did you see the ghost again last night?'

Greg's question floated into the conversation before she had time to answer Roger's.

'What ghost?' Diana asked. 'There's no ghost there, Kate. Take no notice of my son. He's trying to wind you up.'

'Would I?' Greg smiled. 'Of course there's a ghost there. Kate and I were discussing the unpleasant atmosphere at the cottage when I was up there last night. Weren't we? And she told me she'd seen it.' He appealed to her to substantiate his claim. 'We both believe it has something to do with that grave on the beach.'

Alison had gone white. 'Shut up Greg.'

Her brother looked at her. As their eyes met, he raised an eyebrow very slightly. Guiltily Alison looked away. He had explained it all to her an hour ago, when she had challenged him on the subject, how he was going to drive Lady Muck out of the cottage; how she was already nervous of being on her own out there; how it would take only one or two small things – noises perhaps, or strange happenings in the cottage – to send her screaming into the night. But he hadn't mentioned the grave.

Kate was watching Greg closely. He was a handsome man, with, at first glance anyway, an honest face and guileless eyes. She had noticed how he could hold her gaze with his own, steadily, the humour and challenge trembling just behind the mask. But it was a mask. He was playing with her.

'If it is a ghost it is a nice one.' She smiled at him. 'And it wore a beautiful scent.'

Alison bit her lip. 'Stop joking about it. It's silly.' Her voice had risen in something like panic. 'When's supper going to be ready? I'm starving.'

111

From the far end of the room where she was laying the kitchen table Diana looked up and smiled. She had been listening to the exchange and had half guessed what Greg was up to. 'It's ready now. Come and finish this for me, Allie. Then we can eat. Greg, come and pour the wine. And Roger and Patrick, sit where you are till I call you. I know you both. The moment you think I'm about to announce the meal you will disappear on some urgent errand and I shan't see you for hours.' She turned to drain the pasta.

The room was busy, bustling, warm. Kate took another sip of her whisky. She was beginning to feel lightheaded. Had none of them heard it? Or had the voice, somehow, come from Greg?

Suddenly she realised that he was standing in front of her. He put out his hand for her glass. 'Come. Let me take you in to dinner,' he said, extending his arm.

She scrambled to her feet. 'Thank you.' He was about her height, broadly built and solid; she could smell his aftershave. With a sudden feeling of shock she realised he was really a very attractive man. Strangely conscious of the firm touch of his hand beneath her elbow she let him escort her to the table, where she found herself seated between him and his father.

'If there are ghosts, then there are two of them.' Kate was enjoying herself. 'And they are Roman,' she added as Diana laid a dish of paté on the table in front of her. 'One would be your Marcus Severus Secundus, and the other, the one I think I saw, might have been – perhaps – his wife, Augusta.'

Roger laughed. He dug his knife into the butter and carved himself off an unfashionably large corner. 'Good lord! How on earth have you come to that conclusion?'

Kate turned to Greg. 'You said Marcus haunted Redall Cottage,' she said. 'I went to the museum and saw the exhibits about him and his wife. That is how I know her name.'

Greg grinned. He reached for the butter himself. 'I think there must have been a beautiful villa here in their day. It's strange. You make him sound almost approachable. I can't say I've ever been on first name terms with him. I don't think he was at all a pleasant character.'

'Why do you say that?' Kate hadn't taken her eyes off Greg's face, trying to read his expression.

'Greg.' Diana reproved her son from the end of the table.

'I'm sorry, Ma, but I think Kate should be warned. She is, in a way, Marcus's guest, after all. And if he and his wife have introduced themselves, it would seem that they are going to seek a closer acquaintance with her.'

There was a moment's silence.

'The dagger belonged to him,' Alison put in softly. 'He used it to kill people.'

Kate glanced at her, in spite of herself giving a little shiver of apprehension. Alison was staring down at her plate. Her headache had come back.

'I'm glad to be rid of it then,' Kate said. She forced herself to sound cheerful. 'It will be safer here out of his reach with you looking after it. I was talking to a friend in the States on the phone this evening and telling him about it,' she went on, determined to show that she was in no way upset by the sudden atmosphere in the room. 'They don't have Roman ghosts in America. He was quite jealous.' Were they in it together, Greg and Alison? Were they all having a good laugh at her expense? 'In what way is he unpleasant?' she pressed Greg. She watched him closely. If he told her at least she would know what to expect.

He shrugged. 'They say that on certain nights, when the tide is high and the moon is full, you can hear the screams of his victims –'

'Greg, that is enough!' his father put in abruptly. 'You are frightening your sister.'

'Rubbish. Allie's as tough as old boots. It would take more than that to frighten her,' Greg retorted. He turned to Kate. 'And I'm sure our lady historian is not frightened by ghosts. They are, after all, her stock in trade. She should be very pleased to be able to rent a couple so reasonably.'

So there you had it. The barb which had betrayed him. Kate smiled. Suddenly she felt more cheerful. She could handle Greg Lindsey. Taking another mouthful of Diana's delectable home made paté she turned back to him. 'Why should they haunt the grave on the beach? They weren't buried there, and I'm fairly certain that it's not a Roman burial.'

'How do you know it's a burial at all?' Patrick put in another of his rare remarks. 'Allie hasn't found a body has she?'

'No, I haven't!' Again the panic. Unexplained. Sudden. Overwhelming. Alison clenched her fists against the sudden pounding behind her eyes.

113

'And she probably won't. The sand dissolves bodies,' Kate put in. She hadn't looked at Alison. 'Like at Sutton Hoo. Although that is a Saxon burial and therefore probably much later, it must be the same principle. The salts in the sand dissolve everything except the shadow. And archaeologists can only find that if the site has been undisturbed.' She caught site of Alison's strained look and hastened to add: 'The trouble with Redall beach is that now it is right on the edge of the sea. The tide and the wind have already damaged the site beyond any hope of finding that kind of evidence.'

The peat. The peat strata in the dune. The words floated into her mind as she stared down at the paté on her plate. The peat was newly exposed, only the edge was crumbling, smelling of sweet garden earth . . .

She dropped her fork. The others were looking at her. 'I'm sorry.' She smiled, scrabbling for it. 'It's all this talk of ghosts. I think you are at last making me nervous.'

'And that is unforgivable,' Diana put in firmly. 'I'll have no more of this nonsense. I have known that cottage for most of my life. It is not haunted. It has never been haunted and we will not discuss it any more.'

Kate stole a glance at Greg. He had meekly turned his attention to his plate.

At the end of the meal as the others made their way back to the fire Diana put a hand on Kate's arm. 'Stay and help me make the coffee. I haven't had the chance to talk to you properly yet.' She smiled as she lifted the kettle from the hob and carried it to the sink. Neither woman spoke as the water ran into the kettle, then with a glance over her shoulder Diana beckoned Kate nearer to the stove. There was a hiss of steam as she put the dripping kettle onto the hot plate. 'I think you have gathered that Greg is trying to scare you away from Redall Cottage,' she said quietly. 'I am so sorry he has decided to be childish like this. He can't forgive me for making him move out. It's got nothing to do with you. It is me he is angry with.'

Kate turned to the table and began to stack the plates. She glanced at the far end of the room where Roger was choosing a CD from the pile on the stereo. Greg was bending over the fire, coaxing some fresh logs into a blaze.

'I had guessed that was what was going on,' she said after a moment. 'He and Alison are both in it, I think. Don't worry, I can handle it.'

'You're sure?' Diana frowned. 'It seems so feeble to say I can't do anything about it, but whatever I say to them, they will go on if they think it's working.' She banged two of her dishes together crossly and carried them over to the sink. 'I hate to think of you out there on your own. It's so far from anywhere.'

'You don't think they would harm me?' Kate looked at her in astonishment.

'No. No. Of course I don't think that. Neither of them would hurt a fly. But they might think it amusing to frighten you.' She shook her head. 'Oh, my dear, I am so sorry. I feel dreadful about this. Greg is not an easy person . . .' Her voice trailed away helplessly.

Kate felt a surge of anger. Impulsively she put her hand on Diana's arm. 'Please, don't upset yourself. I told you, I can cope.' She grinned. 'It was real ghosts I wasn't sure about. I can deal with imposters. I expect I can play them at their own game.' Diana looked at her gratefully and Kate smiled again. 'Just so long as I know it's them. And just so long as I know you and Roger are there – a touch of sanity at the end of the phone.'

'You can be sure of that.'

'Then there's no problem.' She picked up the coffee jug and carrying it to the sink ran some hot water into it to warm it. Greg and his father were sitting down now, one of either side of the inglenook. The two younger Lindseys had vanished. Quietly, the sound of music floated through the long, low-ceilinged room.

It was nearly midnight when reluctantly Kate climbed to her feet and announced that she ought to go home. Roger had been asleep in his chair for the last twenty minutes and Diana, for all her animated conversation, looked exhausted.

Greg stood up immediately. 'I'll drive you back. You don't want to walk up through those woods on your own at this time of night.' He grinned.

Kate glanced at Diana and she smiled. The implication was clear. More ghosts. 'Thanks. I wouldn't say no to a lift. It's surprising how long that path can be when you're tired.'

The sky had cleared. It blazed with stars and there was a fine layer of frost on the windscreen. Greg opened the door for her

115

then he fumbled about under the driver's seat for a scraper. 'It won't take a moment. Did you leave the stove banked up?'

She smiled. 'I think I'm getting the hang of that beast at last. It's voracious in its appetite for attention, isn't it?'

'It is indeed.' A small circle cleared in the frost – apparently all he required to see the narrow track – he climbed in beside her and slammed the door. The engine started reluctantly, revving deafeningly in the silent darkness. Shoving the gearstick forward Greg turned the vehicle around and headed for the trees. A sheen of frost lay on the damp ground and the spinning wheels shattered crazy patterns into the thin veneer of ice on the puddles between the ruts.

Kate hung on grimly as the Land Rover slithered around.

'The friend you mentioned in the States,' Greg said suddenly, out of the silence. 'Your boyfriend?'

'He was.'

'What happened?' He hauled at the gear lever as the tyres spun.

'People grow apart.'

'But you keep in touch.'

She looked sideways at the handsome profile, trying to interpret the cryptic tone and she felt a small shiver of excitement. 'Yes,' she said firmly. 'We keep in touch.'

To her surprise he did not speak again until they arrived. Jumping down from the high seat she leaned in to thank him, but he was already climbing out.

'You'd better let me check everything is all right,' he said. 'The least I can do.'

'There's no need. I'm sure the ghosts have gone.' She smiled at him, but she gave him her key. Buoyed up with the knowledge that Diana and Roger were on her side she was curious to know what he would do next.

The lamp in the living room was still alight as they went in, and so, to Kate's relief, was the woodburner. Greg glanced at it almost approvingly and she saw him take note of the huge pile of logs next to it. If he was amused by her foresight he gave no sign. 'It all looks OK to me. Do you want me to check upstairs?'

'No need. Thanks, but I'll be fine. I'm not afraid.' She hadn't taken off her coat, waiting pointedly by the door. He gave a final glance around. 'OK then. I'll see you around.'

'Thanks for bringing me home. And thank your parents again for me, for a lovely evening. I really enjoyed it.'

'Good.' For a moment he paused, looking at her. It was there again, the humour, just behind the sober, almost stern exterior and for a moment she thought he was going to stoop and kiss her cheek as his father had done. If he was, he changed his mind. He gave a curt half-bow – the Englishman's salute – and turned away.

For a moment she stood watching as he climbed back into his vehicle and, flooding the darkness again with the arcing headlights, turned it and headed back into the trees. Closing the door she gave a sigh of relief. The cottage was warm and safe. The fire was lit, the water hot – she had left the immersion heater on to be sure – the door was locked, and she had allies. Marcus was a trick. A figment of someone else's imagination.

XX

Switching out the lamp she turned towards the kitchen. A cloud of angry flies rose and buzzed around the light, hitting the ceiling, banging against the walls as she stared at them in disgust. Where were they coming from? She glanced round. She had left no food out, nothing to tempt them. Besides, it was winter. She walked over to the dresser, and then she stopped. A trail of wet peat lay over the pale wood surface. There was more on the floor in front of the cupboards and more again in the sink. She stared down into the stainless steel bowl and felt her stomach lurch as she saw maggots in the filth that lay there. The room, she realised suddenly, was once again full of that sweet, intense odour of rich earth. A smell which she had not noticed at all as she opened the door.

She clenched her fists. Greg. This was something to do with Greg. Somehow he had arranged all this while she was out. One of his friends must have come to the cottage, using his key, while they knew she was safely at the farmhouse and had had all the time in the world to prepare a little surprise for her.

Furious, she turned both taps on full, watching the black soil and maggots swirl away down the drain. Then she set about clearing up the rest of the mess. About the flies she could do nothing. Several energetic minutes with a rolled up newspaper only bagged a couple. Tomorrow she would buy a spray.

Turning off the light at last and closing the door firmly behind her she paused at the foot of the stairs, looking up. Her mouth had suddenly gone dry. What had they done up there? Cross and very tired she walked firmly up, and turning on the light in her bedroom she stood in the doorway and stared round, holding her breath. As far as she could see there was nothing wrong. With a sigh of relief she went in and going to the bed she pulled back the lace cover. The sheets were undisturbed. Relieved that they had not succumbed to a childish urge to defile her bed in some way she looked round carefully, searching for any signs of intruders, but there were none. The room was as she had left it. The only smell in there was from the sweet-scented stems of daphne in the glass on the table by the window. Walking over to the window she drew back the curtain, and opening it she leaned out. The night was clear as crystal. The starlight was so bright she could see every detail of the garden and the hedge and across the dunes towards the sea which lay luminous and still, the movement of the waves on the beach dulled into a slow, heavy, rhythmic beat like the steady breath of a sleeping animal. She stood for a long time, her elbows on the ice-cold sill, then at last, shivering, she closed the window and turned back towards the bed.

The creak of the door on the landing made her jump out of her skin. She spun to face it, her heart thundering beneath her ribs. There was someone there; someone hiding in the spare room. Taking a deep breath she glanced round for some kind of a weapon to defend herself with. There was nothing that she could see save a wire coat hanger lying on the chair. Picking it up she held it out in front of her as, white knuckled, she tiptoed to the door. She had not quite shut it and it was easy to creep into position behind it and from there peer round onto the dark landing. She frowned. In the narrow stream of light which fell from her bedroom across the rush mat and up onto the wall on the far side, she could see the door of the other room was still open. The room beyond it lay in darkness. For a moment she was tempted to slam her own door closed and jump into her bed, putting her head under the pillow and praying that whoever it was would go away. But that was impossible.

'Greg?' Her voice came out as a squeak. She cleared her throat and tried again. 'Greg? Come on. I know there's someone there.' Flinging her own door back against the wall she walked openly onto the landing and pushed open the door opposite. 'For God's sake, stop messing about. It's one o'clock in the morning. Come on. The joke's over!' She flicked on the light and peered round. For a moment she was too horrified by what she saw to react.

Her boxes and cases had been strewn all over the place; Greg's pictures had been thrown over, the stretchers broken, the canvas slashed and all round the room was a dusting of black earth. The smell of it was overpowering, sweet, rich, cloying. Clutching the door, leaning against it for support she found she had begun to shake; her knees were on the point of giving way. She could feel the bile rising in her throat. Whoever had done this, whoever had been there had wrecked everything in the room. Her eyes strayed to her locked suitcase. It had been torn apart at the hinges. The duster in which the torc had been wrapped was shredded and the pieces lay scattered across the floor. As far as she could see the torc itself had gone.

'Oh God!' Her lips were dry, her palms wet.

Turning, she peered down into the darkness of the stairwell.

'Where the hell are you?' she screamed. She ran down the stairs and flung on the lights in the hall. 'Where are you?' The front door was still locked and bolted as she had left it – the key lying in the dish on the hall table. She ran into the living room. It, too was as she had left it, the windows closed. The kitchen was deserted too, save for a cloud of bluebottles which rose as she turned on the light and homed in at once in their endless circling of the ceiling.

She picked up the phone. It rang for a long time before Diana answered, her voice muzzy with sleep.

'Diana, I'm sorry to ring so late.' Kate was unaware of how her voice shook. 'Can I speak to Greg. You warned me. You warned me and I thought I could cope but this is too much. He's got to come and clear all this up now!'

'Kate, what's happened?' Diana, sitting up in bed at the farmhouse reached for the bedside light. Beside her Roger groaned and opened his eyes.

'The place has been smashed up. My cases – his pictures – his own pictures – have been shredded!' Kate swallowed hard, trying to make herself breathe more slowly; trying to regain a little calm. 'Please, just tell him to get here!' She slammed down the phone and turned to survey the kitchen. At first she had thought it was all right – clean – but now she could see that she had missed a patch of earth on the dresser behind a pile of oddments – a kitchen timer, a couple of books, a pen. She stared. A maggot was wriggling across a shopping receipt she had tossed down when she came back from Colchester, its white gelatinous body dotted with grains of fibrous peat. For a moment she thought she was going to vomit where she stood. She closed her eyes and took a deep breath, feeling the chill of sweat on her face. Slowly she backed away from the dresser. Slamming the door on the kitchen she went to open the stove. She stood over it, holding out her hands, waiting for the sound of the Land Rover. It was a full twenty minutes before she heard the engine and saw the reflection of the headlights through the curtains.

Her legs were so weak she could hardly reach the front door. Fumbling she inserted the key and pulled back the bolts to let Diana and Roger and Greg into the hall.

'What's happened?' Diana put her arm round her. 'Oh, my dear, what's happened?'

'Ask him.' Kate nodded at Greg, ashamed to find she was near to tears.

'I don't know what the hell you think I've done,' Greg retorted sharply. He walked into the living room and peered round. 'What has happened?'

'Upstairs.' Kate pulled herself together with difficulty. 'The spare room.'

She and Diana remained in the hall while Greg ran up the stairs two at a time followed more slowly by his father. For a moment there was silence, then they both heard Greg's string of expletives.

'Would he really do that?' Kate asked. 'Destroy his own paintings?'

Diana looked at her with a frown. Releasing Kate she climbed up after the men.

Greg was standing in the middle of the room, one of his canvasses in his hand.

He spun round as Diana came in closely followed by Kate. 'Who did this?' His lips were white.

'I thought you would be able to tell me that,' Kate retorted. 'It was your plan, wasn't it? To scare me witless so that I would leave and you could come back here.'

'Do you think I'd destroy my own paintings?' He shouted. 'Do you think I would do this? Christ Almighty! This was one of my best pieces.'

It was the picture of the cottage under the sea.

'Why did you leave it here then?' Kate flashed at him. 'If it was so precious, why not take it with you?'

'Because – because it belonged here.' He glared at her. 'Because I had meant to have it framed to hang here.' He looked down at the torn, bent remnant in his hands.

'Obviously your bully boys got their orders wrong.'

'What the hell do you mean?' he shouted. 'Where have you got this idea from? Ma, I suppose?'

'You can't deny you meant to scare Kate away,' Roger put in. 'I could not believe anything so childish of you when your mother said she thought that was what you were up to. But she was right. I saw it tonight at dinner.' He leaned against the wall, his hand going surreptitiously to his chest beneath his jacket. His face was grey with exhaustion.

Greg stroked the painting in his hand with a gentle forefinger. 'I don't deny Allie and I were going to have a bit of fun, talking about ghosts and that. It was going to be worth it.' He flashed a grimly defiant look at Kate. 'But this – no.'

'Then who did it?' Kate whispered.

They looked at each other.

'Vandals?' Diana took a few steps forward, and stooping, picked up a small sketch which had been torn free of a book which had rested with the paintings against the wall. She looked down at it sadly.

'Vandals would not have contented themselves with one room, surely,' Kate said. 'And nothing has been stolen as far as I can see.' She stopped. The torc. The torc had gone. Unless it was lying with the rest of the rubbish buried somewhere in the debris.

Roger was watching her face. 'Is something missing?' he asked.

'Maybe. Something I found on the beach. I had locked it in that suitcase.'

'Something from the dig?' Greg turned on her accusingly.

She shrugged. 'I was going to take it to the museum. I was pretty sure Alison wasn't going to bother and that site is too important for a child to be playing about destroying what is left of it. I'm sorry, but I really felt that. It was a torc. It was important.'

She walked into the room and picking up the suitcase tossed it aside, pushing at the drift of papers underneath with her foot. A clot of peaty soil fell off the case at her feet. Something was wriggling about in it. She stared at it for a moment then she turned away.

'Oh God!' Diana covered her eyes in disgust.

'I think we'd better call the police.' Roger sighed. 'If Greg had nothing to do with this, and I don't believe in a million years he did, then obviously it is a matter for them.'

'But no one broke in,' Kate said quietly. 'The door was locked. The windows were all closed.'

'They were. I checked downstairs.' Greg threw his damaged painting into the corner with some force. 'What a pity you didn't let me check upstairs too. I might have saved you some of the shock. I'll ring the police, Dad.' Forcing his way past them he disappeared.

Diana reached for Kate's hand. 'You must come back and stay with us, my dear. You can't possibly stay here alone after this.'

Kate didn't argue. Following the others down the narrow staircase she ducked into the kitchen long enough to retrieve four tumblers and the bottle of whisky then she followed them into the living room, where Greg, having rung the police, was stoking up the fire. 'They'll be here as soon as possible,' he said. He straightened and faced Kate. 'I owe you an apology. Dad was right. It was unspeakably childish of me to try and frighten you away, but I swear to you, I had nothing to do with this.' His shoulders slumped slightly as he accepted a glass of whisky from her. She had added no water to any of them. 'I may have been offhand about my paintings up there, but some of those were very special. To me, at any rate. I would not have damaged them.'

She gave him a watery grin. 'I believe you.'

'Kate dear.' Roger sat down in the armchair near the fire. 'I think perhaps you should check all your belongings. Make sure nothing else is missing.' He glanced across at the table where her laptop computer and the printer sat amongst a litter of books. 'Though I can't believe anyone would have broken in and missed that. That of all things they would have taken, surely.'

Kate nodded. 'Thank God they didn't. But you're right. I'll check. I had some silver bangles and rings in the bedroom. I didn't notice if they were still there.' She moved towards the door, then she hesitated. Upstairs was suddenly somewhere hostile.

Without saying anything Greg followed her. 'I'll go first,' he said.

Nothing in her bedroom had been touched. There was no sign that anyone had been there at all. They searched carefully, then ventured once more into the spare room. 'I was going to look for the torc,' Greg said. 'But perhaps we'd better not touch anything else. They will probably want to fingerprint everything in here.'

She stared round. The bluebottles were still here as well, their angry buzz vibrating in the silence as they divebombed the single light bulb in the centre of the ceiling. She shook her head. 'I don't understand. I just don't understand,' she said.

He shrugged. 'Who can tell why people do things. There are so many reasons. I think this person was angry. For some reason he was angry.'

'He was searching for something he couldn't find perhaps.'

'But what. Money?'

'If it was money he would have looked in the bedroom. Under the chair seats. Up the chimney.' She gave a weak smile. 'I remember when my sister's flat was burgled. That was what they did. No. It was something in here, he wanted. Something specific.'

'The torc?'

'But how would he have known it was here. I was the only person who knew about it.'

They looked at each other.

Marcus

The word had not been spoken out loud, but it was there, hanging in the air between them. Kate shook her head. Marcus as a personality was an invention; an invention she and Greg and Alison had thought up between them in a strange spontaneous way; the creation of a fertile mind, hers, fed by the promptings of two devious ones, theirs.

'So, who else knew about it?' Greg prompted softly. 'You thought of someone, just then.'

'Only Marcus,' she said.

XXI

The police spent a long time searching the spare room at the cottage and it was after four before the tired men climbed into their vehicle and drove along the bumpy track back to Redall Farmhouse followed by the Lindseys' Land Rover. Kate stood for a moment watching the taillights of the police vehicle as it disappeared away into the woods, then she followed the others back inside. Her head was spinning and she was exhausted. She had grown to love Redall Cottage, she realised, in the short time she had been there, in spite of her occasional nervousness, and suddenly what confidence she had in the place had been smashed. It was as if a new friend had turned round and kicked her in the teeth.

Diana had paused to wait for her in the entrance hall. 'You can sleep in Greg's room, Kate. He's gone straight upstairs to make up the bed for you.'

'But what about him?' Kate followed her into the warm familiar room. The fire had died to ash but it was still cosy, still redolent with coffee and wine and the faintest suspicion of oregano and garlic from their supper so many hours before.

'He will be perfectly all right,' Roger put in sternly. 'He has appropriated my study through there as his studio.' He indicated a room off the entrance hall which she had not so far seen. 'He can camp in there. You look completely exhausted, my dear. I suggest you go straight upstairs and sleep. We'll talk in the morning.'

In spite of her tiredness Kate found herself staring around Greg's bedroom as she sat wearily down on the bed, but if she was looking for some clue to his personality amongst his belongings she was disappointed. The room had obviously been – and still looked like – the spare room of the house. The furnishings, though comfortable and charming, had that strange air of not belonging to anyone in particular which spare rooms acquire. The style was too feminine to be Greg's; too masculine to be a woman's room. She looked down at his things on the table by the window. In front of the small, square Edwardian dressing mirror lay a scattering of belongings. Besides the obvious brush and a comb there were cufflinks – so, he dressed up formally when he wanted to – somehow she couldn't quite picture it. There was a paintbrush, seemingly unused, several pencils of differing hardness, a pile of small change, a crumpled train ticket issued at Liverpool Street, a chain of paper clips, some Polo mints in a scruffy remnant of silver paper and an exquisite enamelled snuff box. She picked the latter up and stared at it for a moment, enchanted, then she continued her weary scrutiny of the room. The walls were covered with a pretty flowered wallpaper and criss-crossed with beams, the ceiling was low, the furniture mainly Victorian. It was small and comfortable and safe.

It took her only two minutes to undress, donning the cotton nightshirt she had stuffed into her shoulder bag with her tooth-brush, and slide gratefully into the bed.

Pulling the duvet up over her head Kate closed her eyes. Minutes later she opened them again. She was too tired, too stressed, her brain too active to sleep. Hugging the pillow she lay looking towards the window at the blackness of the sky and the tears began to run down her cheeks. Outside, across the grass, the mud gleamed in the starlight as slowly the tide crawled in across the saltings.

It was daylight when she fell at last into a fitful doze and well after eleven before she awoke, rocketed out of her uneasy dream by the sound of loud pop music from the room next door. Sitting up slowly she swung her feet to the floor, rubbing her face wearily in her hands. From downstairs, as Johnny Rotten paused momentarily to draw breath, she could hear the sound of a vacuum cleaner.

Ten minutes later, her face washed in cold water, her hair brushed and fully dressed in her skirt and blouse of the night before, she ran downstairs. The sitting room half of the large living area was deserted – even the cats were missing. Peering through the oak studs which divided the room she saw that Roger sat alone at the kitchen table. He was reading *The Times*. The sound of the vacuum had shifted to the furthest recesses of the house as he looked up and saw her. He smiled. 'Coffee is on. Come and have a cup. You look as though you could do with one.'

'Thank you.' She sat down opposite him. She wondered for a minute how he had managed to get hold of a newspaper so early – surely they weren't delivered out here – then she remembered the time. It was already nearly midday. Time and plenty for any of her hosts to have gone out, half way round the county and returned if they had wanted to.

He pushed a cup towards her before folding his paper and setting it neatly beside his plate and leaning forward on his elbows. 'I had a long talk with the police this morning on the phone. After due reflection overnight they seem to think as you did that Greg probably did it himself, or at least that he was responsible. There was absolutely no sign of a break in and he is the only person besides Di and myself, and you of course, to have a key to the cottage.'

Kate stared at him. 'But surely, he wouldn't destroy his own pictures.'

Roger sighed. 'It's difficult to tell sometimes what is going on in my son's mind, Kate. I often think he hates his talent.' He poured some more coffee into his own cup. 'My dear –' he paused, searching for the right words. 'I would of course under-stand if you decided that you wanted to leave, and I would be more than happy to return your rent. All of it. I am extremely embarrassed by everything that has occurred. But if you still want to stay –' He hesitated. 'If you still want to stay at the cottage I shall get someone over there today to change the locks, and I will see to it myself that no one has a key but you for the rest of your tenancy. I can't apologise enough for all the distress this must have caused you.' He smiled. He looked exhausted. His face, beneath dry, paper-thin skin was drained of colour.

Impulsively Kate reached over and put her hand over his. In the daylight her fear had evaporated. 'I think I would like to stay. It's so lovely here and my book is going so well.' She glanced at the window, framed in blue gingham curtains. 'Of course, it's easy to say that now, with the sun shining outside and the house busy with people.' She looked down into the depths of her coffee. 'I'm not sure how I will feel in the dark, on my own.' She shrugged apologetically.

'Give it a try.' He turned his hand over to take hers for a moment. 'You can change your mind any time. And if you're nervous, you know we can be there very quickly. One of us will always come if you call, I promise.' He stood up. 'Greg is out. Come and look at his pictures.'

She followed him towards the study and paused in the doorway looking round as Roger made his way towards his chair behind the desk and threw himself down in it. 'He has talent,' he said tiredly. 'It does not excuse him, but maybe it helps us to understand him a little.'

Kate walked slowly round the room. She had already formed a view of Greg's talent from the paintings at the cottage, but this selection reinforced it tenfold. He was very good indeed. 'Who is this woman?' Curious, she held out a small portrait. It was one of several of the same subject.

Roger shrugged. 'I don't recognise her. They are all recent, though.'

Kate stared down at her. The woman had large, oval, grey eyes, too large for her face – they were the same in each painting – and looped chestnut hair. In every case she was dressed in blue, but there was no detail of what she was wearing, just a blur, a hint of shoulders, arms, no more. She shivered and put the painting down. 'He's good.'

Roger nodded. He gave a small conspiratorial smile. 'Don't tell him I showed you. Come on. We'll start on the potatoes and after lunch we'll take you back to the cottage.'

She couldn't help a feeling of slight trepidation as she let herself into the cottage later, but the presence of both Roger and Diana at her heels reassured her, as did the arrival twenty minutes later of the locksmith. While he fixed the door, the others worked upstairs with her, tidying the spare room and cleaning it.

Roger checked the two windows. 'Do you want him to fit window locks while he's here?' he asked doubtfully examining the window frame. There was no sign of a forced entry anywhere in the house.

Kate shrugged. 'It seems a bit like overkill –'

'Perhaps they could be screwed down. It would be less expensive,' Diana interrupted. 'I think we should take every precaution. And there should be a larger bolt on the front door as well as a dead lock.'

It was nearly dark by the time they had all gone. Kate looked round. Strangely she was relieved to see them go. Comforted that the house was now defended like Fort Knox and reassured that her strange experiences were in some way due to Greg she had found herself longing for them to leave; after twenty-four hours without writing she was suffering from withdrawal symptoms.

Taking a cup of coffee to her desk she sat down and pulled the pile of typescript towards her. Pen in hand she began to read.

Outside, the winter day had sunk into a cold sullen night. Once or twice she looked up towards the windows, listening. She had decided against having them screwed shut in the end. It seemed so sad to have to lose the reassuring noise of the sea and the fresh air.

At this moment however there was no sound from outside at all. No wind, no sea. A total silence enveloped the cottage, broken only by the quiet hum of her computer and the pattering of the keys beneath her fingers. The shrill ring of the phone from the kitchen made her jump violently.

It was Jon. His voice was light and sociable again, casual, as though he had no real reason to make a transatlantic call to her at all. 'How are you?'

'So, so,' she replied. She sat down on the high stool. 'Actually, not so good. I've had a burglary.'

'You're not serious. Oh my God, Kate, are you OK?' The real concern in his voice made her wish for the second time that she hadn't told him her news.

'Yes, I'm fine. They didn't take anything except –' she paused, '– do you remember last time you phoned I was cleaning a torc?'

'Belonging to an ancient Brit?' Superficially light-hearted though the words were, she could still hear the worry in his voice.

'They took that. And they smashed up some paintings.'

'Kate, you can't stay there –'

'No. No. I'm fine. I have the phone, and they've changed all the locks. I am bolted and barred like someone in Holloway, except that I am the only one with a key. It was probably local kids who thought the cottage was empty. I don't suppose they will be back.'

'Have the police been? Are you sure you're all right? Oh God, Kate, I wish I were closer.' The warmth of his voice filled the kitchen. 'Take care, my darling, won't you.'

She hung up thoughtfully. My darling, he had called her. My darling. He still loved her.

She was aware suddenly that the wind was getting up outside. She could hear the soft moaning of the tree branches from the wood, but it didn't matter. Suddenly nothing mattered any more. Feeling unaccountably happy, snug, knowing there was a good supply of firewood in her box, and with a brand new lock and a bolt top and bottom on the front door, she smiled. The sound made her feel all the more secure and cosy.

She went back to her book. It was hard to concentrate; her mind kept wandering back to Jon, but eventually the narrative captured her again and she was drawn back to the childhood of her poet. Catherine Gordon was something of an enigma in her relationship with her son, her love as twisted and deformed as the poor club foot of her child. Kate leaned back in her chair, chewing the end of her ballpoint. A squall of wind hit the cottage. She felt the walls shudder and heard the sudden crack of rain against the window as she sat forward, her hands on the keys and began writing again. A minute later she stared at the screen in horror.

May the gods of all eternity curse you, Marcus Severus, and bring your putrid body and your rotten soul to judgement for what you have done here this day . . .

Christ! she whispered. *Oh Christ!*

Another squall hit the windows and she flinched as though the wind and rain had hit her. Quickly, as though afraid it would burn her, she switched off the computer and pushed back her chair. Her hands were shaking.

I didn't write that.

But she had, like some robotic amanuensis, taking down dictation. She stared round the room. It was very still. The squall had retreated as fast as it had come and the night outside was silent once again. All she could hear was the pumping of her pulse in her ears. She grabbed her cassette player and inserting a cassette with trembling hands, she switched it on. The sound of Sibelius filled the room as taking a deep breath, she moved over to the stove and bending down, opened the doors to stare at the warm glow of the smouldering logs.

'I am tired, that's all,' she whispered to herself. 'It's been a long day. I need sleep. A lot of sleep.' She poured herself a small whisky with a hand that was still far from steady. Sipping it slowly she stood for several minutes in front of the stove.

Only very gradually did she become aware that there was someone standing behind her. Her knuckles white on the glass, the hairs on the back of her neck prickling with fear she held her breath, not daring to move. 'Alison?' Her voice was hoarse with tension. It was a woman. She was certain it was a woman. 'Alison, is that you?' Slowly she turned round.

The room was empty. She stared at the closed door. It had warped slightly over the years and already she had learned the sound of its squeak as it opened or shut. It was distinctive; loud. And she had not heard it.

'Come on, Kennedy. Pull yourself together.' She took a gulp of the whisky, feeling the heat of it burning her throat and creeping through her veins. It gave her the courage to walk over to the door and pull it open. Outside, the hall was deserted. The front door was still barred and bolted as she had known it must be. There was no one there. Resolutely, her glass still in her hand she climbed the stairs and flicking on the lights she peered into her bedroom. It was empty. The room was tidy. For a moment she hesitated in front of the spare room, then taking a deep breath, she flung the door open and switched on the light. The room was as they had left it earlier. Tidy, neat, almost empty, her cases stacked against the wall. The remnants of Greg's paintings were gone – retrieved to the makeshift studio in his father's study. Both windows were shut. The bluebottles had disappeared. Of the torc there was still no sign.

With a sigh of relief she went heavily back downstairs and into the living room.

Oh God, it was there again! The smell of earth and with it that sweet, indefinable scent. Shaking her head wearily she went over to the stove, piled in as many logs as she could and slammed the doors shut.

'Go to hell, Marcus, wherever you are, and leave me in peace!' she said out loud.

She turned round to switch off the desk lamp and let out a scream, knocking her empty glass to the ground.

A woman was standing in the corner of the room.

In the fraction of a second that she was there Kate saw her auburn hair, her stained, torn, long blue gown, and she knew that somehow, somewhere, she had seen this person before. And then she was gone, leaving only the scent of earth and with it the cloying, flowery perfume.

A taste of acid in her mouth, Kate backed towards the door. She reached it and backed into the hall, her eyes on the spot where the woman had stood. She didn't believe in ghosts. No one sane believed in ghosts. Only to joke with the Lindseys. It was her imagination; she was too conscious of the black stormy night outside the windows and it had created this vision inside her head. That was it. Who was it who had said we are all mad at night? Was it Mark Twain? She shook her head. Whoever it was was right.

Or it might be the whisky. Perhaps she had been drinking too much. And the rest of the bottle was in the living room where – it – had been standing. Too bad. She could do without it. She took the stairs two at a time and running into her bedroom she slammed the door. She was still shaking, but not so much she couldn't drag the Victorian chair, heavy for all its neat smallness, across the room and wedge it under the handle. Why, oh why hadn't she insisted on having a bolt fitted to her bedroom door as well while the locksmith was about it this afternoon?

It was only as she pulled off her clothes and dived into bed, pulling the covers up over her head, that she remembered that ghosts can walk through walls.

XXII

In his bedroom Patrick frowned. The mathematical formula he had been working on wasn't going to come out. Somehow he had to try it another way. He paused for a minute, staring into space. He could hear the music from Allie's bedroom blaring down the passage. Even with two doors closed in between it was deafening. He sighed. Yelling would do no good. If anything it would make her turn it up louder. He frowned for a minute pondering on how she had persuaded Greg to fork out for a new radio cassette. Their father had said that the insurance would probably pay in the end, but why had Greg put his hand in his pocket so fast? He puzzled over it for a few minutes more but already his mind was going back to the figures on his screen.

Around him his books, their spines all neatly aligned, were gleaming, friendly companions in the semi-darkness. The only light in his room came from the anglepoise lamp on his desk and from the screen of the computer.

He thumped the enter key a couple of times and tried again, conscious suddenly of the sound of the sea in the distance and the whine of the east wind and the patter of rain on the window.

Before him the screen shivered. He frowned and rubbed his eyes. A letter had dropped from the top of the screen to the bottom. Then another, then another.

'Oh, no! Oh fucking hell!' He stared at it in disbelief. 'Not a virus! Not a fucking virus!'

Holding his breath he tapped at the keys frantically, trying to save what he had been doing, but already the screen was blank and the cursor was moving purposefully up to the top left hand side once more. Slowly a message appeared.

May the gods of all eternity curse you, Marcus Severus Secundus and bring your putrid body and your rotten soul to judgement for what you have done here this day . . .

133

Patrick stared, clutching at the wooden arms of his chair. For a moment he sat without moving, reading the message through and through again, then he stood up with such violence that his chair fell onto the floor behind him.

'Allie! Allie! I'm going to wring your bloody neck!' He hurled himself at the door. 'What have you done to my computer, you stupid, silly cow?'

He pounded the six short strides down the passage and threw open her bedroom door.

After the comparative darkness of his room, hers was a shock. At least six light bulbs blazed in there – two spotlights, a ceiling light and three desk lamps, sitting at strategic angles on the floor. No wonder she had migraines!

His sister was lying on her bed, still fully dressed, a dazed look on her face as she listened to her Sisters of Mercy tape for the thousandth time.

Patrick flung himself on the machine and pulled out the cable. 'You cow! Do you realise what you've done? You've only fucked up my project, that's what!'

'What?' She stared at him blankly. The sudden silence after the blare of music was strangely shocking.

'The message on my computer. Very funny! Very droll! Let's all have a good giggle!' He was almost spitting with fury.

'What message?' She lay back again and put her arm across her eyes. 'I haven't touched your silly computer.'

'Then who has?'

'I don't know and I don't care. Get out of my room.'

'Allie.' His voice was suddenly very quiet. 'I am warning you.'

'I told you, I don't know anything about it,' she repeated. 'Get out.'

He leaned forward and seized her arm. 'Come with me.'

'No!'

'Come with me!' He dragged her off the bed.

'Paddy! You're hurting me!' she wailed as she followed him unwillingly down the passage and into the womblike darkness of his room.

'There. Explain that!' He flung his arm out in the direction of the screen.

She leaned closer and peered at it.

'It looks like maths,' she said. 'I haven't a clue what it is.'

134

'Maths?' He pushed her aside. The screen was neatly ordered, the formula complete. Nothing flickered. He stared at it in disbelief. 'But it all fell off. There was a message – a curse –'

'Bullshit!' she said rudely. 'Can I go now?'

He didn't hear her. He was running his finger over the screen. 'I saw it. A message. A curse –'

But Allie had gone, slamming the door behind her.

XXIII

'I hope it doesn't snow too hard. I'd hate for you to miss your last talk,' Sam Wannaburger, Jon's American editor, said apologetically as he hefted up the heavy case. 'I'm just so glad you agreed to come out and see us.' He had collected Jon from his hotel in a pickup the size of a pantechnicon and driven him in the general direction of south-west. They had stopped at last at a white-painted clapboard house set back from the main street in a small town somewhere in deepest Massachusetts. The floodlights had been switched on, illuminating the graceful lines of the house and its surrounding fir trees, making it look ethereal, floating in a sea of whiteness – for here the grass and the sidewalks were already covered in two or three inches of soft white fluffy snow. 'Anyway, it's too late to worry about it now. We'll have good booze, good talk, good food. It won't matter how hard it snows! And if we can't get back to the big city in the pickup we'll leave it to AmTrak to get us there!' Sam clapped Jon on the back and pushed him none too gently up the path towards the front door.

It was a wonderful house. Huge, converted, so Sam told him proudly, from an early-nineteenth-century carriage house. The fireplace alone was about twelve feet across, the logs burning in it cut to scale; the huge, soft sofas and chairs around it built obviously for seven-foot Americans. The house smelled of hot-house flowers and – Jon hid a smile as he raised his head and sniffed surreptitiously like a pointer – could that really be apple pie?

Sam's wife was thin to the point of emaciation, and so elegant she looked as though she would break if she moved too fast. Her hand in Jon's was dry and twiglike, her life force, he thought vaguely as he smiled into her bright birdlike eyes, hovering barely above zero. She was one of those Americans who filled him with sadness – dieted, corseted, facelifted and encased in slub silk which must have cost old Sam a few thousand bucks, and looking so uncomfortable that he hurt for her. It was so incredibly sad that, for all her efforts – perhaps because of them – she looked years older than dear old rumpled, slobby Sam with his beer belly and his balding scalp and his huge irrepressible grin. I wonder, he thought idly as he saw her stand on tiptoe and present her rouged cheek to her husband for kissing – a kiss which left a good two inches of cold air between them – if she ever kicks off her shoes and has a good giggle. The thought reminded him of Kate and he frowned. Worried about the burglary he had tried to ring her three times from Boston after his last quick call and on none of them had she picked up the phone. Automatically he glanced at his watch and did the calculation. Six p.m. in Boston meant it was eleven or so in the evening at home. He glanced at Sam. 'Could I try and call Kate one last time. It's eleven over there. I'm sure she'll be at home by now.'

'Sure.' Sam beamed. 'Let me show you your room. You've your own phone in there.' He lifted Jon's case and led the way up a broad flight of open stairs which swung gracefully from the main living room up to a corridor as wide as a six-lane motorway. Jon's bedroom was not as large as he had feared but it was luxurious beyond his wildest dreams – bed, chairs, drapes, carpet, toning, matching, blending greens, until he had the feeling he was walking in a woodland womb. He smiled to himself at the metaphor. Ludicrous. Overblown. Outrageous. Like the room. Like his host. And wonderfully welcoming. He sat on the bed as Sam left him and pulled the phone towards him.

Twenty minutes later, showered and dressed in a clean shirt and a cashmere sweater Kate had given him for his birthday last year, Jon ran downstairs and accepted a large whisky mac from his host. His call had been a dead loss. After a great deal of hassle and toing and froing between the ladies of AT&T and the British exchange, they had established that the phone at Redall Cottage had gone suddenly and totally dead.

XXIV

The priests had walked in solemn procession to the sacred place in the circle of trees on the ridge above the marsh. Nion was not senior among them – he was young – but his royal blood gave him a certain precedence as they made their way, robed and solemn, to their appointed places in the circle.

Nion glanced round. The faces of his teachers, his friends, his colleagues, were taut, their thoughts turned inwards, their bodies bathed and dedicated to their purpose. He grimaced, trying to turn his own mind to prayer and meditation. The choosing of the sacrifice was a ceremony he had taken part in only once before. On that occasion the sacred bread had been baked on the flame and broken as laid down by tradition centuries old. The scorched piece, the piece which belonged to the gods, had been chosen by an old druid of four score summers or more – a man dedicated and ready for whatever the gods decreed. But even he, when he drew out the burned portion and knew that he was to die, had betrayed for a brief moment a flash of terror, before he had bowed his head in acceptance.

The ceremony was strictly ordained. The man was honoured by his colleagues, crowned with gold. In the hours that remained he would bid farewell to his family, order his affairs and at the last divest himself of all his raiment, bathe in waters sanctified with herbs and spices, then, drinking the sacred, drugged wine of death he would kneel willingly for the sacrifice: the garotte if his death was dedicated to the gods of the earth, the rope if to the gods of the sky, and the third death, the death by water if to the gods of the rivers and seas.

Now Nion watched, his head covered, as were those of the others, as the bakestone was blessed and heated. His mouth was dry with apprehension, even though the choice was preordained. He stole a glance at the oldest druid there, a man as frail as a windblown reed, his bald pate beneath the linen veil wrinkled as an old, dead leaf. Almost certainly he would be chosen, the bread passed in such a way that his would be the *burned piece. How did he feel, knowing that by the next dawn he would be dead?*

Nion closed his eyes and tried to concentrate on prayer, but at noon he was to meet Claudia. His body, strong, vigorous, lusty, quivered at the thought. Sternly he reprimanded himself, and brought his thoughts back to the scene before him.

The bread was cooking now, the fragrance sharp on the morning air. His nostrils picked up the acrid smell of scorching and he swallowed nervously, his eyes going once more automatically to the old man who had blanched to an unhealthy shade of buttermilk.

He watched, arms folded beneath his cloak, as the bread was allowed to cool and broken into small pieces – twenty-one, seven times three – one for each of them, and put into the basket. Slowly it was carried round the circle. Slowly. Slowly. One by one the hands went in. The choice was made. The hands came out. One by one the faces relaxed into relief and the portion was eaten. The old one's turn came. He put in his hand, shaking visibly, and withdrew it. Nion saw him turn the fragment over and over in disbelief. Then his face relaxed into a toothless smile. So, the gods had rejected an old, frail man. In the face of the threat from Rome such a sacrifice was not enough.

Nion's stomach knotted sharply in fear. He noticed suddenly that several men were watching him surreptitiously from beneath their head-dresses.

The woven bowl was coming closer. His hands were sweating. Only five more portions remained. Then it was before him, held in the hands of the archdruid who had baked the bread and taken the first piece himself. For a moment Nion hesitated. He raised his eyes to the other man's face and read his fate even before he had put his hand in the basket.

The bread fragment he took was crumbling, still warm from the bakestone, and it was burned black.

The tide was high at six in the morning and the wind was from the north-east, crossing the Urals, dripping ice across the continents, whipping the sea into angry peaks of foam.

Tossing in her bed, Alison was dreaming uneasily. All around her the cold wet earth was pressing down, clogging her nostrils, crumbling into her eyes, filling her ears so she could no longer hear, weighing her into the damp sedge. Hiding her. Hiding the truth. The truth which must be told. With a cry of panic she sat up, untangling herself from the duvet. She stared round the room. It was pitch dark and she could hear the rain pouring down in the garden outside. When it grew light there would be a puddle on the windowsill.

Still dazed by her dream, she stood up and reached for her clothes. There was something she had to do; something urgent. The pounding behind her eyes was insistent, like the beat of the tide upon the shore, driving her, pushing her against her will. Opening the door she stood for a moment on the landing, listening. The house was silent. Her parents slept at the far end in a bedroom which looked out across the woods. Next to her, Greg and beyond him, Patrick, always slept like the dead until they were awakened. She shivered violently. Today was a day for awakening the dead.

Scarcely knowing what she was doing she hauled on her waterproof jacket and forcing her feet into her boots she opened the door and peered out into the icy morning. The wind was roaring in from the north-east full in her face as she pulled the door shut with difficulty behind her and set off in the darkness towards the track through the woods. All she knew was that she had to get to the grave; she had to get there before the tide washed it away.

She had to save it.

XXV

Kate had slept in the end, too exhausted to do anything else, but she too had awoken at six to the sound of rain against the windows. It was steady rain this time, hard and unrelenting and behind the sound of it she could hear the wind.

She didn't want to get up. There was something frightening downstairs, something which when daylight came she would have to confront, but until then she was going to stay where she was, safely tucked up in her bed with the lights on. Wearily she reached for her book and lay back huddled against the pillows.

When she dragged herself out of bed an hour later and pulled back the curtains all she could see was blackness, alleviated only by the streaks of rain sliding down the glass. But she couldn't go back to bed. She was too conscious of the silence outside her door.

Pulling on a pair of jeans and a thick sweater she went out onto the landing and peered down. All seemed as usual down there. She stood for several seconds, then taking a deep breath she ran down and flung open the living room door. The room was empty. The woodburner still glowed quietly. All was as it should be. Lights burned in every room – God knows what her electricity bill would be when she left – but all was quiet. There were no strange smells, no figures lurking in the shadows.

Her face doused in cold water and a mug of strong coffee at her elbow she poured some muesli into a bowl and reached into the fridge for some milk. She was a first class prize idiot with a powerful five-star imagination – how else could she be a successful writer – and a bad dose of nervous collywobbles. All she needed was food, coffee – both being attended to – and then a bracing walk in the rain to clear her head. Then in the cold light of day, probably with more coffee, she would switch on the computer again and get back to young George and his mother.

The knock on the front door took her completely by surprise. Greg stood outside, his collar pulled up around his ears, rain pouring off his Barbour jacket. His hands were firmly pushed into his pockets.

'You see. No key. I had to knock,' he said grimly. The wind snatched the words from his lips and whirled them away with the rain. 'May I come in, or am I too dangerous to allow over the threshold?'

'Of course you can come in!' Kate stood back to let him pass and then forced the door closed behind him. 'Why the sarcasm?'

'The sarcasm, as you call it, was perhaps engendered by two hours of questioning by the police last night who seem under the impression that you still think I robbed the cottage.' He pulled off his jacket and hanging it on the knob at the bottom of the bannisters, shook himself like a dog. 'I just thought I would come and thank you in person for your vote of confidence and, incidentally, collect one or two of my things which I would rather not leave here any longer.'

Kate could feel her antagonism rising to match his. 'I assure you, I didn't tell the police it was you. If they thought so they must have got the idea somewhere else,' she said furiously. 'And I must say, I wonder if they aren't right. It seems the sort of half-baked stupid thing you would do to try and get me out. That was the idea, I take it? To get me out.'

'It would be wonderful to get you out.' He folded his arms. 'As it happens, I think the wind and the weather will do it for me. Now, if you don't mind, I should like to collect my property and then I shall leave you to your triumph behind your locked doors.'

'What property exactly have you left behind?' They were facing each other in the hall like a couple of cats squaring up for a fight. 'It seems to me you cleared everything out on Wednesday night.'

'The torn paintings, yes. There are two more here. On the walls.' He strode past her into the living room. There in the corner, hanging near the window, was a small portrait sketch of a woman. Kate had hardly noticed it. He took it down and laid it on the table. 'There is another upstairs. If you will permit me.' Still unsmiling, he turned away and ran up the stairs two at a time.

Kate shrugged. How petty could you get! In spite of herself she walked across to the picture and looked down at it. It was the woman whose portrait she had seen over and over again in the study at Redall Farmhouse, but in this version her figure was full length, her garment clearly drawn.

He had come back into the room again in time to hear her gasp. 'What is it?'

She looked up at him, her face white. 'You've seen her. You've see her here.' She was accusing, taut with shock.

'Who?' In his hand he held the small picture of the bluebells which had been hanging in her bedroom. She glanced at it regretfully. It was so unlike his usual style. She had really rather liked that one.

'The woman in the picture. I saw her. Last night.'

He frowned. 'You can't have. I made her up. She came out of my head. She's a pastiche of styles – something I was doing for fun. A doodle.' A doodle of a face which had come without his bidding and which had tormented him.

'A doodle of so much importance that you can't leave her here with me.' Kate spoke so softly he had to strain to hear.

'That's right,' he said. His voice was aggressive. 'What do you mean you saw her last night? You had a visitor, did you? Are you sure she wasn't a burglar or a vandal?'

'She was a ghost.'

She said it so flatly that he wasn't sure he had heard her correctly. For a moment he stared at her. He was the one who was supposed to be doing the frightening; the one who had decided to use ghosts to scare her away, and yet, with that one small sentence she had sent a shiver down his spine, a shiver which had raised the hairs on the back of his neck.

A moment later he shook his head. She was trying to play him at his own game. Fine, if that was the way she wanted it. 'Where did you see her?'

'There. Almost where you are standing. Your sketch is monochrome, but her dress was blue, like the other pictures you've done of her, the ribbons and combs in her hair were black.'

Greg had to fight very hard the urge to move to another part of the room. 'Supposing I admit that I have seen her.' In his dreams; in his head; even in his heart. 'Doesn't it frighten you, sharing the house with a ghost?'

For a moment she paused, as if she were considering. She looked him in the eye. 'I suppose, if I'm honest it does, yes.'

'But you're going to stay, just to spite me.'

143

'If you don't mind my saying so, you have a very inflated idea of the importance you hold for me,' she said seriously. 'I'm staying because I came here to write a book; because this is my home for the next few months and because –' she hadn't meant to add this, but it came out anyway '– I have nowhere else to go. I can't afford London rents at the moment.' None of his business why.

'So, you're staying.'

'So, I'm staying.' She glanced at the painting under his arm. 'I'm sorry you're taking that. I liked it.' The remark was a concession.

He did not rise to it. It was a trifle, a pretty sketch of which he was not proud. 'I am sure you can buy yourself a print if you need bluebells on your walls.'

She narrowed her eyes. 'I don't think I'll bother,' she said dryly. 'Now, if there is nothing else, I would like to get back to work and I expect you have to report to a police station somewhere.' She smiled sweetly and was rewarded with a scowl.

'No, I am sorry to disappoint you but they did not arrest me. Nor any of my friends.'

'I'm sure it is only a matter of time.' She stepped past him and went towards the front door.

The wind had changed slightly and as she opened the door, rain swept into the hall, icy, harsh, cruel. She stood back and he walked out without a backward glance. By the time he had climbed up into the Land Rover she had closed the door and walked back into the kitchen.

She was thoughtful. Every shred of intuition told her that he was not lying; that the break-in had had nothing to do with him. But the picture? What did the picture of the woman mean?

She waited until he was safely out of sight before donning her weatherproof jacket and her scarf. Her enthusiasm had gone but she was determined to go out anyway, to clear her head, to get rid of the terrible throbbing behind her temples and, dragging her mind back to the book, to straighten out her thoughts about the next chapter. Somehow she had to rid herself of the images of the last few days. The cottage had ceased to be an impersonal place to work and think. It had become tied up with personalities: with Greg and Alison; with Roger and Diana – and, God help her, with Marcus and the lady in a blue gown.

The grass clung wetly to her legs above her boots, soaking her trousers. Then she was on the short turf and then the sand. The tide was on the ebb, but the angry white-topped waves still lashed the beach, sucking at the stranded weed, filling the air with the sharp, cold smell of far-off ice.

Turning her back doggedly on the dig Kate walked into the wind, her hands pushed firmly to the bottom of her pockets. The cold was so fierce it stung her face, it hurt to breathe. She clamped her lips tight across her teeth and, head down, walked firmly forward, scarcely aware of the beauty of the sea beyond the beach where the air was crystalline, the colour of mother-of-pearl, and the heaving mass of water had the solid shine of polished pewter. Somewhere nearby a gull screamed. She looked up and saw it weaving and circling effortlessly on the wind, part of the fearsome force of it.

> There is a pleasure in the pathless woods
> There is a rapture on the lonely shore,
> There is a society, where none intrudes,
> By the deep sea and music in its roar . . .

It was elemental; wonderful. As always, Byron had the words to convey the power of the scene; if only she in her turn could bring his images into her book . . .

The sand whirled around her feet in eddies, loosened by the sleet. Ahead she could see the body of another gull, one which had lost the battle with the elements, lying wet and bedraggled on a patch of wet shingle. A tangle of weed lay near it, and it was not until she was close, staring down sadly as she compared it with the beautiful wild beauty of its colleague above her head that she saw the cruel pull of nylon fishing line around its legs. Overwhelmed by anger at the thoughtless, careless arrogance of man she stooped to touch the mottled grey brown feathers. It wasn't even an adult bird. This must have been its first winter, its first joyous tussle with the elements. The bird's body was cold and hard, the feathers clamped scalelike against its body. Shivering, she straightened and walked on.

She did not walk for very long. The opaque mist on the horizon was drawing closer; the wind strengthening. She could see a faint shadowing across the waves which was a shower of hail sweeping down the coast and towards Redall Bay. Turning, she walked briskly back, more comfortable now that the wind was behind her.

She had not intended to walk as far as the grave, but somehow she could not resist it. One glance, to see if it were still there. Each tide now was a threat. Each storm, each wind.

Her shoes sliding on the side of the dune she was nearly there when the first shower of hail hit her. Sharp, biting, the ice cut her hands and face, tearing at her scarf as she scrambled the last few feet and stood looking down into the hollow below the exposed face of the dune to find that she was not the first person there. Alison was kneeling on the sand, her hands ungloved, hanging at her sides, her eyes fixed on the exposed face of the working. One glance at the trail of wet weed and shells showed Kate that the early morning tide had come nowhere near the edge of the excavation this time. It was still safe.

She hesitated, unsure whether to creep away, not wanting to intrude and risk a mouthful of abuse. The girl was unmoving. Kate frowned. She took a step closer. There was no sign of any spades or trowels, no ghetto blaster, no tools of any kind. Still Alison had not moved. Her hair whipped wildly around her head; her jacket flapped, unzipped, around her body.

'Alison?' she called, uneasily. She paused, waiting for the girl to turn and swear at her for intruding upon her private thoughts, but Alison didn't stir.

'Alison!' she called again, more sharply this time, and she began sliding down the side of the hollow. 'Alison? Are you all right?'

Alison gave no sign that she had heard. She was staring at the sand and peat face of the dune.

'Alison?' Her voice rising in alarm Kate put her arm around the girl's shoulders. 'Alison, can you hear me?' She shook her gently. The girl's body was rigid and cold beneath the flapping parka, clad, beneath it, in only a tee shirt and thin sweater. 'Alison, what's the matter?'

Behind them another shower of hail swept in from the sea. The hailstones rattled against the wiry grass, shushing into the sand, battering their faces. To Kate's horror she saw that Alison neither blinked nor moved as the hail hurled itself against her face and slid down her cheeks. 'Oh God!' She glanced round wildly, half hoping that there would be someone else around, someone who could help, but knowing already that there was no one on the beach at all. 'Alison, you must listen to me!' She grabbed the girl's hand which was ice-cold and began to chafe it vigorously. 'Alison, you've got to stand up. Come on. You can't stay here. You'll catch pneumonia. Come on. Stand up.'

Alison gave no sign of hearing her. She stayed totally rigid except for the hand which Kate was tugging which was limp and cold as death.

Kate stared round, her hair tangling across her eyes, her own face ice-cold with sleet. In only a few moments the sea had changed from pewter to the colour of black ink; opaque, thick, sinister in its uneasy movement. Far out there was no distinction now between sky and water. All were black and threatening.

'Alison, come on. The weather is getting worse.'

Dropping the girl's hand Kate moved in front of her. Alison's face was frozen into immobility, the eyes staring straight ahead, not reacting when Kate brought her hand sharply towards them. 'Right.' Kate spoke with some force. 'I'm sorry to have to do this.' She pulled back her hand and gave Alison a sharp slap. The girl did not react. She did not even blink. Behind them another curtain of hail raced across the sea, embedding itself in the sand, turning the beach a glittering white.

Kate stared at her in despair, then dragging off her own jacket, she pulled it roughly around Alison's shoulders. Without the padded, fleece-lined protection, the cold enveloped her like a curtain, wrapping itself around her, embedding itself in her lungs, clawing at her bones, but she ignored it. She pulled Alison's arm around her neck and heaved at her, trying vainly to raise her off her knees. 'Stand up, blast you. Stand up,' she cried through gritted teeth. 'You've got to move, Alison, or you're going to die of cold.' She struggled desperately against the dead weight of the girl. Alison was barely two inches shorter than she was, and although not plump she was solidly built. Nothing Kate could do seemed to shift her from her knees.

'Please.' Stopping her futile effort Kate stood back, wiping the streaming sleet from her face, feeling the ice soaking through her own sweater. 'Please, Allie, you must try. Stand up. I'll help you. Then we'll go to the cottage. It's warm there. Warm and safe.' In spite of herself she glanced at the streaming sand around them. Just at this moment she was not prepared to think what could have sent Alison into this state. She did not dare.

Taking a deep breath she pulled the girl's arm around her shoulder once more, and putting her own around Alison's waist, she heaved at her, rocking her sideways slightly to try and gain some momentum. As though sensing the movement for the first time, Alison stirred. 'That's it. Help me. Try and stand up.' Kate was elated. Taking another deep breath she renewed her efforts with the last of her strength and this time Alison tried feebly to scramble up. 'Good. And another step. Good girl.' Kate pushed her frantically, terrified she would fall again as, unsteadily, Alison rose to her feet, leaning heavily against her. 'Good, that's it. Now, we've got to get you out of here. One step at a time. Steady. That's it.' Sweat was pouring off her face in spite of the icy downpour as, somehow, Kate half guided half pushed Alison up the bank and onto the beach. Still the girl's eyes hadn't moved; still she did not appear to register anything going on around her, but she was stumbling forward, guided by Kate's desperate tight grip around her waist, hanging from Kate's shoulders like a giant rag doll.

Twice they had to stop while Kate fought to regain her breath but slowly they drew nearer to the cottage. Somehow Kate managed to prop the girl up against the wall as she groped for her new, shiny keys then at last the door was open and they were inside out of the hail. Slamming the door closed with her foot, Kate half carried, half dragged Alison into the living room and unceremoniously tipped her onto the sofa. Gasping as she tried to regain her own breath she ran upstairs to her bedroom and dragged a blanket off her bed. Gathering up her dressing gown on her way out of the room she ran downstairs again. Alison lay where she had left her, half on the sofa, her legs still trailing across the floor.

'Right, let's get you out of those wet clothes.' Awkwardly Kate bundled the girl back against the cushions and began to pull off the soaking sweater and tee shirt. Then the slip of cotton which was her bra. Somehow she forced the cold unbending limbs into her towelling dressing gown, trying to rub some warmth into the wet slippery skin which reminded her horribly of the feathers of the dead gull. She pulled off the girl's boots and then her jeans and socks, and somehow lifting her legs onto the sofa, tucked her up in the blanket, making a cocoon out of which the girl's head, with its straggly wet hair, poked like the head of a startled doll.

'Phone.' Aware that her own teeth were chattering Kate turned towards the kitchen. Shaking, she waited for the number to connect her to Redall Farmhouse. It was only as she tried for the second time that she realised that there was no dialling tone. The line was not dead – she could hear it alive, hissing slightly, resonating as though there were someone at the other end. But the number made no impression on the echoing silence. 'Oh, no. Please.' It was a sob of desperation. She took a deep breath and punched nine nine nine. The line remained silent, expectant, as though someone at the other end were listening as desperately as she was. 'Hello?' She shook the receiver. 'Hello, can you hear me? Is someone there?' But no one answered. A fresh wave of ice hit the kitchen window. Slowly she hung up. She had never felt more alone.

She went back to the living room and stood looking down at Alison. The girl's face was unchanged, her muscles somehow frozen in the same look of astonished terror. She was not blinking. Her pupils did not appear to be reacting to the dim light of the sitting room. They were still pinpoint small, staring. Reaching into the blankets Kate felt her hand. Was it marginally warmer? She thought so. What was one supposed to do with cases of hypothermia? No alcohol. Wasn't that what they said? Hot water bottles. She had no hot water bottle and she was pretty sure that she would have seen one if there was one in the house. Somehow she did not think it was something that Greg, or even his parents would consider a necessity. So, what else could she use? A hot brick. Wasn't that what people used in the old days? A hot brick wrapped in flannel. She gave a grim smile. There was neither brick nor flannel in the cottage that she had seen. Then she remembered the stones outside, edging what had once been the drive. Large smooth stones, pebble shaped, perhaps off the beach. One of those would do, surely, wrapped in a towel. She turned and ran back to the front door. Pulling it open she stared out at the storm. The clear morning had turned into a vicious darkness lashed by squalls of hail and sleet which tore at her clothes, reminding her that she, too, was chilled to the marrow and wet through. She dived out and heaved at one of the stones. About ten inches long and shaped like a pillow, for a moment she thought it was stuck fast. Then it came up out of the icy ground with a small sucking noise and she carried it back inside, staggering under its surprising weight. She laid it gently on top of the woodburner, and opening the doors, stacked in some more logs. 'Not long, now,' she said over her shoulder. 'I'm getting something to warm your feet. Would you like a hot drink?' She glanced round at the girl. 'You're safe now, Allie. Come on. Try and wake up.' Sitting down on the edge of the sofa she put her hand on Alison's shoulder. The girl flinched. The movement was so sudden and so violent that Kate jumped. She frowned. 'You're safe, Allie,' she repeated gently. 'There's nothing to be afraid of.' She found herself looking towards the window. Outside, beyond the streaming sleet as it slid down the glass, she could see nothing. What had happened out there in the dune? She wished fervently that Greg was still around. Or that he would remember something and come hurtling back in his Land Rover. Perhaps she should try the phone again.

As she stood up Alison grabbed her wrist. Kate gave a little cry of fright. The girl was staring at her now, her eyes suddenly fully focussed in her white face. 'Don't leave me.' Her voice was hoarse, barely audible.

Kate breathed a sigh of relief. 'You're all right. You're safe.'

'No.' Alison shook her head. The movement seemed to hurt her and she flopped back, her eyes closed for a second. Kate frowned. She was relieved that the awful horrified stare had gone, but the monosyllabic answer had chilled her. 'Why are you not safe?' she asked softly. 'What happened? Do you want to tell me?'

For a moment she thought Alison had not heard her but slowly the girl's eyes opened. 'They're free,' she whispered. Her fingers clutched with surprising strength at Kate's hand. They were still ice-cold. 'I've released them.' Her words were slurred, as though she were slightly drunk. 'They've been waiting. Claudia. Claudia wants her revenge.'

'Claudia?' Kate stared down at the white, pinched face, puzzled. 'Who is Claudia?'

Alison smiled shakily, but her voice when it came out was surprisingly strong. 'Claudia is a whore; a traitor. She's an animal. She deserved to die.'

Kate stared at her in horror. 'Alison, do you know where you are?'

The green eyes opened. They roamed the room unsteadily then they focussed on Kate. For a moment the girl said nothing, then abruptly she burst into tears.

150

'Oh, Allie, love, don't. I told you, you're safe.' Kate was astonished at the strength of the wave of compassion which swept through her. Leaning forward she put her arms around Alison and held her close. The girl suddenly seemed as frail as a bird, every bone sticking out beneath the warmth of the dressing gown, her body still radiating a terrible chill. 'Listen, let me go upstairs to fetch a towel. I've heated a stone up for you. I can put it near your feet to warm you up once I've wrapped it.' Glancing at the stove Kate began to rise.

'No!' Alison clutched at her again. 'Don't leave me.'

Kate subsided onto the sofa beside her again. 'There is nothing here to frighten you, Alison,' she repeated gently. 'You're safe.'

As though to emphasise her words an extra loud gust of wind shook the cottage. A puff of smoke blew out of the open stove into the room, bringing with it the pungent aroma of burning oak and apple. Kate glanced at the window, wondering for a moment if it would hold against the force of the storm. Something moving on the sill caught her eye. Water. There was water on the sill. The window was leaking. She moved slightly, without letting go of Alison's hand and craned sideways to see better. Sure enough, a puddle had formed on the wood. She stared. Floating in the puddle were bits of leaf and soil and there, wriggling around the edge were several maggots.

For a moment she thought she was going to be sick.

'What is it? What's happened?' Her voice rising shrilly in panic Alison clutched at her harder. 'What have you seen?'

'Nothing. Nothing at all.' Wincing at the pain of the girl's clawed fingers Kate tried to free herself. 'Some rain leaking in, that's all. It's hardly surprising, the wind's so strong.' Somehow she forced herself to sound calm. 'Listen, I must go and get something to mop it up. I'll stick a towel on the sill. There must be a leak in the window frame. Then why don't I make us a hot drink. I'm sure you'd like something, wouldn't you?' How she kept her voice steady, she didn't know. Firmly she tried to unfasten Alison's fingers. She was like a child, clutching desperately at her mother's skirt. The moment Kate managed to dislodge one hand the other grabbed at her again. 'Allie, there's nothing to be frightened of,' she repeated.

Allie nodded frantically. 'There is. There is, don't you understand? Claudia is free. Claudia and . . .' she hesitated, frowning,

151

her head suddenly cocked to one side as though trying to hear something from far off, in another room. 'Claudia and . . . and . . . Claudia and . . .' Her voice was fading. A look of puzzlement appeared on her face. 'What was I saying?'

'Nothing, Allie. Nothing at all.' Kate forced her voice to a calmness she did not feel. The child was hallucinating. Was that a symptom of hypothermia? She did not know. The vagueness, the fear, were they all part of it? Oh God, they needed a doctor. 'Allie, I want to go and ring your mother. You'll be quite safe here. I'll only be in the kitchen. Look if I leave both doors open you'll be able to see me all the time –'

'No!' Alison's voice slid up into a scream. The sound made Kate's skin crawl.

Alison was fighting with the blankets. 'I'll come with you. I don't like it here. That window. She is going to come through that window.' She flung out her arm. Kate looked where she was pointing. There was more earth in the puddle now. Earth and peat and – she could feel the bile rising in her throat as she saw a movement at the edge of her vision.

Suddenly her mind was made up. 'OK. Let's go into the kitchen. Come on. I'll help you. We'll make a hot drink and I'll try and phone.'

Please let it work. Please God, let the phone work.

Her arm around Alison, she helped the girl shuffle through to the kitchen and sat her, still cocooned in the blanket, on a stool.

Quietly, she closed the door and turned the key, then, her hand shaking with fear, she picked up the phone.

The line was still dead.

XXVI

Defiantly leaving his car in a parking space reserved for the disabled right next to the castle gates Greg strode towards the entrance. He glanced at the sky. Snow and sleet showers, they had forecast, turning to unseasonably heavy snow later. That probably meant sleet out at Redall Bay, but you never knew. Sometimes it settled. Whatever happened it would be worse in Colchester. It always seemed to snow heavily there.

It was a long time since he had been in the museum. He stared round, confused. The huge hall with its peripheral exhibits had vanished. Instead it was sectioned, partitioned, intimate, the lighting low and seductive and from some distant corner he could hear the tinny insistent blare of videoed commentary. He frowned. Why couldn't the buggers leave things alone? He could have found his way to Marcus blindfold before. Now, God knows where he was.

He was upstairs, near yet more video crap. With an impatient glare at the booth from which sounds of massacre were emerging, Greg stood in front of the statue and stared long and hard at its face. Then he, as Kate had done, moved to the exhibit and looked down at the man's skeleton. She had been right. It was not Marcus himself who was buried at Redall. So who was it? His eyes strayed to the other remains. Smaller, though not significantly so; Marcus's wife had strong, well-formed bones. His art school study of the skeletal form had been fairly rudimentary, but it was thorough enough for him to give an educated guess that she had been young when she died. How, he wondered. Illness? Injury? Childbirth? He glanced at the inscription. There was no clue there, no notes beyond the bare minimum. He stared down at what was left of Marcus's skull. Was his story written there, in the imprint of his bones? His loves, his hates, his triumphs, his disasters? He brought up his hands and rested them against the cold glass of the display case. 'Come on, you bastard, cough.' He hadn't realised he had spoken out loud until he saw a woman near him turn and stare. She caught his eye and hurriedly turned away. He grinned absent-mindedly but already his attention was back on Marcus. Rich, successful Marcus who had made good after the Boudiccan defeat; who had returned to Colchester and to Redall and bought land, probably when prices were rock bottom, like today – he grimaced – was that how it had been? Or had he just helped himself to some property he fancied and marched in? Had Redall's former owner died in the rebellion, leaving his lands wasted and deserted, or did he sell at a profit? He leaned closer to the glass, resting his forehead against it and closed his eyes.

HATE

ANGER

FEAR

FURY

The emotions sweeping through him obliterated every other thought in his head. They swirled round him, shimmering with colour: Red! Black! A vicious violent orange! He was spitting, shouting, tearing at the air, aware in some distant part of himself that there was foam at the corners of his mouth, hearing howls of anguish in his ears and realising they were his own.

Then, as suddenly as they had come, the noise and the colour and the pain were gone and he was conscious of a sudden total silence around him.

Christ, had that been him? Had he really screamed out loud, or had it all been inside his head? The tape in the booth had reached its end and was silent for a few minutes before it marshalled itself for yet another enactment of the conversation between two Romans as the hordes closed in. The hall echoed with silence and cold.

The quick, anxious tap of heels on the floor did not intrude on his shock and terror until he felt a timid hand on his arm. 'Are you all right? Would you like me to fetch someone?' The woman who had been watching him was staring anxiously into his face. 'I saw you staggering about. I thought perhaps –' She faltered as he stared at her, blankly. 'I don't know, but I wondered if you were epileptic or something . . . ?' Her anxiety petered out and she blushed crimson. 'I'm so sorry.'

He gazed at her vaguely. 'I'm all right. Thanks. It must be the heat in here.' He stared round, confused. The hall was cold. Very, very cold.

Slowly she was backing away. She would hurry as soon as she was out of sight and run downstairs and perhaps send up one of the attendants. Well, when they came, whoever they were, they would find that he wasn't pissed. In fact he had never been more sober.

He reached out a hand towards the glass case and then withdrew it quickly as though it had stung him. Whatever had attacked him, overwhelming him with its vile emotions, had come from behind that glass.

XXVII

There was no escort, no guard to watch over him. They trusted him absolutely. The gods had spoken; there was no question but that he would obey. Last minute private farewells were common; what more natural than that a man should say goodbye to the world.

'NO!'

Her scream of agony echoed across the dunes and marshes, the sound rising and falling across the land and the sea until it was lost in the clouds beyond the horizon.

'Claudia – my love –'

'No! I won't let them! What kind of barbaric gods do you worship that they can do this? You can't go back to them. You can't! You can't . . .' She burst into tears.

'Claudia. I have to. The gods have chosen me.' His voice was firm, his strength surprising, even to himself.

'I hate your gods!'

'You mustn't. You must honour them as I do. And obey. To be chosen for the Great Sacrifice is the highest honour possible.'

'Honour! I thought your people sacrificed their prisoners! Their slaves! What kind of honour is it to die like them?' The tears were running down her face, streaking the saffron eyeshadow she had so cheerfully applied before she left home.

'The greatest. The gods have demanded the blood of a prince.' He spoke calmly, his need to reassure her in some strange way giving him courage. 'Maybe we offended them, my dearest, with our love,' he said gently, touching her face with the tip of his finger as though trying to memorise the position of her nose, her mouth, her eyes for all eternity. 'Perhaps it is best like this. Your gods too, I hope, will be appeased and honoured by my death.'

'No.' She shook her head blindly. 'No. I worship Fortuna. She does not demand the death of her followers. She wants them to live, and be happy. No, I won't let you die. If you die I want to die too.'

156

'No!' He took her shoulders and shook her gently. 'Claudia, you must live. For your son's sake. You can't leave him. And for my sake. To carry my memory in your heart. You must be strong. You are a daughter of Rome, remember?' It was something she took such pride in, her noble breeding. As he hoped, the words reached her.

She straightened her shoulders a little and raised her head, though tears still streamed down her face. 'You're not afraid?'

'Of course I'm not afraid.' He smiled sternly. 'I am a prince and I am a priest. Why should I be afraid to meet my gods?' He reached up to the heavy silver brooch which fastened his cloak. 'I want you to have this. Wear it for me and don't grieve too much.'

She took it with a shaking hand and pressed it to her lips. 'When . . . when will it happen?'

'At dawn. As the sun shows over the eastern edge of the world.'

'Where – ?' It was barely a whisper.

'At the sacred marsh.' He smiled sadly. 'On the land that belonged to my fathers and my fathers' fathers. In the place where the gods congregate and this world and the next run side by side.' He took a deep breath. 'You must go now.'

'Not yet.' Her voice slid up in agony.

'Please, Claudia Honorata. I wish to bid you farewell without tears. I want you to be as full of honour and courage and pride as you would have been had you been my wife.' His voice was stern.

She closed her eyes for a moment and took a deep breath. 'If that is your wish, husband of my heart.' She forced a tight, meaningless smile and, raising her face, she kissed him on the cheek. He took her hands and pressed them to his lips, then, unable to trust himself further he turned away and ran towards his chariot.

The phone was still not working. Three times she dialled, her hand sweating, slipping on the receiver, and three times she was greeted with the strange echoing silence, the conviction that at the other end someone was listening to her heavy breathing.

'What's wrong?' Alison was shaking visibly.

'The phone doesn't seem to be working.'

'You mean we're cut off?' The girl's voice slid into a squeak.

'It's all right, Allie. It doesn't matter. You're safe here. Safe and warm.' Kate forced herself to smile reassuringly. 'I'll make that hot drink now. What would you like?' She glanced at Alison, who shrugged.

Picking up the kettle Kate walked across to the sink to fill it, staring out of the window as she did so. The trees in the wood, only just visible through the streaming sleet, were bent double before the force of the wind. There was a strange darkness in the sky which was heavy with brownish cloud. Snow. It was snow cloud.

She turned on the tap. There was sand in the sink. Sand and peat and – with a shudder she snatched the kettle away, letting the stream of water swish round the sink to wash the maggots and soil away. She glanced at Allie, hoping she had noticed nothing. The girl's eyes were closed and she was swaying slightly on her stool.

With a grimace Kate filled the kettle and went to plug it in. 'Do you want to go back by the fire next door?' she asked gently. 'You can lie on the sofa and have a snooze.'

'No.' Allie shook her head. 'I want to stay with you.'

'OK.' Kate reached down two mugs. Her hand hovered over the coffee jar then moved on to an unopened tin of drinking chocolate. Diana must have put it there when she stocked up the cottage with groceries. Chocolate was rich, soothing, comforting. It would do them both good. She levered off the lid with a spoon and tore back the paper seal. The tin was full of earth. A fat white maggot wriggled indignantly at the sudden light. With a scream Kate hurled the tin across the room and it hit the wall with a crash.

Alison jerked upright. 'What is it?' She stared at the red tin which had rolled into the corner leaving a trail of powdered chocolate across the floor.

Kate rubbed her eyes. She was shaking like a leaf. 'I'm sorry. It slipped out of my hand. How silly . . .'

Somehow she forced herself to pick it up. She sniffed the remaining contents cautiously. It smelt good; rich, sweet and clean. 'Luckily there's enough left to make us a drink.' She was imagining things. Stupid. She had to be calm and strong for Alison's sake. She took a deep breath. 'Allie, who is Claudia?'

'Claudia?' Alison turned towards her. The colour had returned to the girl's face a little now and she seemed more alert but there was a strange blankness somewhere behind her eyes which made Kate uneasy. 'I don't know anyone called Claudia. Why?'

'I thought you said –' She stopped with a sigh. 'No. Perhaps I

158

heard you wrong. It doesn't matter. Look, the drink is ready. Let's both go next door and sit by the stove.'

The sleet was lashing the panes and she could see the puddle on the sill was larger now. It had begun to drip onto the floor. Putting down the chocolate she went back into the kitchen for a cloth. Alison was still perched on her stool. 'Come on. I'll put some more logs on. Do you want me to help you?'

Alison shook her head. 'Is it . . . is it all right in there?'

'Of course it's all right. The window is leaking a bit that's all.' She reached for the cloth. 'I'll mop it up and then I'll stoke up the stove.'

She approached the window cautiously, peering at the sill. There were still flecks of soil floating in the water, but the maggots had disappeared. With a sigh of relief she mopped up the water and wedged a clean drying-up cloth into the angle between the sill and the window frame to catch the melted sleet as it seeped through, then she turned to the stove. There were only three logs left in the box. She opened the door and wedged one of them into the stove, and opening the dampers roared it up a little, then she plumped up the cushions on the sofa. Behind her Alison had shuffled as far as the doorway. She was peering into the room.

'Has she gone?' she said.

'Who?' Kate swung round.

' – ' Alison's deep breath was cut off short and her shoulders slumped. 'I don't know. There was someone here . . . or was she on the beach . . . ?'

Kate walked over to her and put her arm round her shoulders. 'There's no one here, Allie,' she said softly. 'And there's nothing to be afraid of. You got very cold on the beach and I think you've had a touch of hypothermia. That sometimes makes people imagine things. Come and sit down and put your feet up then have a drink. You'll feel better soon, I promise.' She would not look at the corner where she had seen the figure of the woman. That, too, was imagination. 'I'll tell you what, why don't we have some music.' She went to her pile of cassettes and shuffled through them with a small half-smile at the thought of what Alison was going to think of Vaughan Williams or Sibelius or Bach when her tastes were so demonstrably different. Her hand hovered over the tapes. Fauré's Requiem. How had that got there? It was Jon's. She stared at it for a moment, then she opened its box and took it out. Was it some atavistic need for prayer that made her choose it? Whatever it was it would do no harm. As she slotted it into the cassette player her eye was caught by the pile of typescript on her desk. She shrugged. Now was not the time to worry about work. Perhaps if Alison fell asleep she would be able to do some writing. It was obvious at the moment that the girl could not walk anywhere, so there was nothing she could do but keep her warm and wait. But later, when Alison was better, should they try and walk back to the farmhouse, or should they wait for Roger and Diana to miss the girl and come looking for her? She felt so alone without a telephone; so thrown back on her own resources.

As the ethereal strains of the *Introit* and *Kyrie* filled the room Alison sank back without protest and closed her eyes. Kate watched her surreptitiously from the chair opposite. The log was burning well. Soon she would have to put on another. Then there would be only one left. Her gaze turned to the window sill. The tea towel was still dry and there was no sign of any movement there.

The tentative knock on the front door was almost lost in the strains of music but at the sound of it a shot of adrenalin propelled Kate out of her chair in a panic, every nerve stretched. She looked at Alison, but the girl didn't seem to have heard it.

Patrick stood on the doorstep, a yellow cycling mac over his thick jacket, his hair plastered to his head, his cheeks pink with the effort of bicycling down the wet muddy track.

'Hi. Mum wondered if Allie was here. Your phone's out of order, did you know?'

'Yes, I did and yes, she is.' Kate pulled him into the hall and closed the door. 'Thank God you've come!' She glanced over her shoulder into the living room. Alison still appeared to have heard nothing. Her eyes were closed and her face had relaxed into sleep. 'Come into the kitchen where we can talk.' Kate led the way and closed the door silently behind them. To her shame she found that her hands were still shaking. 'Listen, something very odd has been happening. I found Alison out in the dunes, kneeling in the excavation in some sort of trance. You've got to fetch your parents and the Land Rover to take her home. She's OK, more or less, but she's not well enough to walk. I think she ought to see a doctor.'

'Oh hell.' Patrick's thin face was a picture of worry. 'The reason I came on the bike was because Greg's taken the Land Rover. No one knows where he's gone. The Volvo won't make it through the woods. It's a quagmire. And there's been a severe weather warning on the radio. It's going to snow hard.'

'Damn!' Kate gnawed at her thumbnail.

'What's wrong with Allie? What was she doing out at the dig in this weather?' Patrick asked thoughtfully.

'I don't know. She had no spades with her or anything. She seemed to be in a state of shock.' Kate eyed him. She had barely spoken to this intense young man before, but what she had seen she liked. He appeared to be steadier and calmer than either his brother or his sister – far more like his father in fact. 'Something happened to her out there, Patrick. I don't know what it was, but it scared the hell out of her. She's still frightened. And so am I.' She hadn't meant to add that last bit.

Patrick was eyeing her warily. 'She started something when she messed about with that grave, didn't she?' he said. His voice was pleasant, light, calm. 'She's stirred something up.'

Kate swallowed. 'I suppose it's possible,' she said cautiously.

'Do you think it's Marcus's grave?'

Kate shook her head. 'I don't see how it can be. They found his grave near Colchester somewhere.' She hesitated. 'I think it's a woman's grave.'

'I see.' He frowned. He seemed unsurprised. He didn't ask her how she knew. He was more concerned with turning over this new set of possibilities in his mind. 'You mean the ghost is not a joke. A woman really does haunt this cottage. Do you think Allie saw her?'

Kate nodded. 'Her name is Claudia.'

Patrick's eyebrows shot up. 'How do you know that?'

'Allie was muttering about her. She doesn't remember now, but she said the name several times.'

'Wow.' Patrick looked awestruck. 'Oh, Jeez. I wish Mum and Dad were here.' He glanced up and swatted exasperatedly in the air as a bluebottle divebombed the light near him. Kate stared at it. Something cold had lodged in the pit of her stomach. Where were they coming from, the bluebottles – and the maggots?

As if reading her thoughts Patrick grinned. 'You often get

them in old houses in the winter,' he said comfortably. 'They hibernate or something. There are probably dead mice under the floorboards. You've heated the place up a lot so they've woken up.'

He was right of course. Kate shuddered. Had she really begun to wonder, deep down in the innermost part of herself, if the maggots and the soil and the flies had somehow come out of the grave? She gave a feeble grin. 'I was beginning to think the worst.'

'Have you really seen her? Claudia?' Patrick's eyes were like his brother's. They were deep grey-green, all-seeing, but unlike Greg's they were sleepy, gentle. Misleading. She could feel them boring into her soul.

'Yes, I've seen her.'

Once again he seemed to accept her answer without surprise. There was no mockery or disbelief in his voice when he asked his next question:

'Do you think she smashed up the house?' He held her gaze.

She shrugged. 'I've never really thought about the idea of whether or not I believe in ghosts, before. They seemed a nice idea – at a safe distance.'

'Scientifically, the idea is untenable, of course.'

She smiled. 'Is it? I wonder.'

'Psychokinetic energy is something that is measurable, I believe, and has been shown to be capable of hurling things about a bit. That is what poltergeists are. They are often connected with the presence of a teenager. All our frustrated angst.' He smiled and Kate found herself thinking with a certain wry amusement how very much more mature this intense boy was than his elder brother.

'Allie is a bit of a prat,' he went on, 'but she's a nice kid. There's nothing malicious about her. She wouldn't do this on purpose.' He was speaking from the safe platform of two years' superiority. He glanced up as an unusually strong gust of wind hurled a shower of hail against the window and he shuddered. 'Can I see the room where it happened before I go?'

'Help yourself. On the left at the top of the stairs.' She stayed in the kitchen as he ran up, listening to the sound of his feet overhead. A couple of minutes later he came down again. 'It's all tidy.'

162

'She got what she wanted.'

'Allie?'

'No. Not Allie.'

His eyes widened. 'I didn't realise that something was missing? I thought Mum said they hadn't taken anything.'

'They – she – took the silver torc which I found in the grave.'

'Wow.' There was a pause as he thought this over. Then, 'It can't have been a ghost. It must have been a real thief after all.' He sounded disappointed. 'Ghosts can't steal things.'

'They can.' Unnoticed by either of them Alison had appeared in the doorway. She was clutching the blanket around her shoulders like a cloak. Her face was transparent in its whiteness. She walked uncertainly to the stool and dragged herself up onto it. 'She wanted the torc because it was his.'

'Whose?' Patrick stared at his sister.

'– '

Again she had begun to speak and stopped without uttering a word as though the word – the name – had been snatched from her lips. 'I don't know. But she loved him.'

Patrick shot a quick look at Kate. It seemed to be a plea for understanding. 'Listen, Allie. I'm going to go home and get Mum and Dad. You ought to be in bed or something.'

'I'm OK.' Belying her words, Allie's body gave an involuntary shudder.

'Will you bring them back as soon as you can?' Kate asked quietly as she went with Patrick to the door. 'Please. I don't think we – she – should be here alone.'

She watched as he pulled on his bright yellow cycling mac. She didn't want him to go. She wanted to catch at his sleeve and shout at him to stay. She wanted him to barricade himself inside with them. Stupid. What was there to be afraid of?

'She needs a doctor, Patrick. She's OK I think, as long as she keeps warm, but I don't know about these things. I'd feel much happier if someone took a look at her.'

He nodded. 'Don't worry. Mum used to be a nurse. She'll know what to do. I'll be home in ten minutes. If Greg's not back with the Land Rover we can ring Bob Farnborough up on the main road. He's got a four wheel drive which will do.' He turned away into the sleet then he stopped. 'It will be OK. Don't worry. Just keep the door locked.'

She stared at him. As their eyes met she realised he was scared too and that he was as aware as she was that doors would not keep Claudia, if it was Claudia, out.

XXVIII

At the bottom of the hollow the sand was stained by the peat as it leached out of the exposed face of the dune and dispersed in the icy puddles. The rain and hail washed at the leathery skin, keeping it moist, preserving it momentarily from the air, rendering it supple again. Strands of hair, long, coppery, still silken after more than nineteen hundred years washed across the blind face which stared up at the darkness. Her arm, lying across his chest was twisted, broken, the fingers outstretched. As the cold air touched them they drooped and grew supple again, caressing his shoulder, skin melting into skin, lips into lips, dry brittle bone crumbling to become one with the sand.

A squall from the sea, hitting the dune face, brought down more sand. The soft, wet mixture of peat and soil swirled in the icy water and slowly the silver torc which lay in the loose grip of Nion's fleshless fingers sank out of sight once more.

XXIX

Standing at the window looking down into the street Bill sighed. He hated London in the rain and this cold, blustery hail was the worst kind of rain. It was too wet to turn to snow and settle, too cold to bear against the face, suitable only for turning the muck and leaves and litter which blew in the gutters into a disgusting soup. He could hear the rainwater gurgling down the gutter near the window. It sounded like a bath emptying and was extremely depressing. He was trying to make up his mind about going to the cottage. He had been looking forward to a break all week. After careful manipulation of his diary he had managed to clear all Monday and half of Tuesday so it could be a long weekend. The best kind. But now the weather looked as though it was doing its best to screw the whole plan. He walked back to his desk and picked up the glass of wine from his blotter – a remnant of yesterday's party, the bottle retrieved from a fridge on the next floor. It was up to him. He had only himself to please. Did he really want to go flogging up the A12, taking a risk on whether this cold wet rain would turn to snow when he left the outskirts of London? Of course that in itself was tempting. He could think of worse places to be marooned than Redall Farm Cottage in the run up to Christmas, and if he took enough food and booze he could disappear there for several days happily. He walked back to the window, battling with his conscience. He had a tight schedule in the second half of next week. Christmas was getting close and he couldn't really take the risk of missing any time in the office. He watched two London buses inch past beneath his window, their domed scarlet roofs slick with sleet which for a fraction of a second remained unmelted then turned to water before his eyes and ran in streams down the windows.

Behind him the phone rang. He paused to drain his glass before going to the desk and lifting the receiver.

'Bill, it's Jon Bevan.'

Bill eased himself into his chair with a raised eyebrow. 'Hi. When did you get back?'

'I'm not back. I fly home tomorrow. Bill, I'm a bit worried. I can't raise Kate. Her phone is out of order. Do you have the number for the people at the farmhouse?'

'Sure.' Bill reached for a bulging, shabby filofax, something he was comfortable with only now that they were truly out of fashion. 'How is it going out there?'

'Not bad. I wanted to check if I would be welcome at Redall.'

'Can't help you there. I haven't spoken to anyone there this week.'

'So, you don't know about the burglary?'

'Burglary!' Bill frowned, shocked. 'At the farmhouse?'

'No, at Kate's cottage. She sounded edgy when I last spoke to her. Almost frightened. It's been worrying me.'

'Frightened?' Bill stared at the agitated, circular doodle he had been sketching on the pad in front of him. He added a couple of swirls, and then an eye. 'I should think so, if she was burgled. Did they take much?'

'I don't think so. Something she dug up in the sand, that's all. I'm sure she's all right. I'm sure there's nothing to worry about.'

Bill laughed. 'I'm sure there isn't but I'll give the Lindseys a ring and check. I was wondering whether I should drive up this evening, funnily enough. I'm not sure though. The weather is pretty bad over here.'

'It's bad here too.' In Massachusetts Jon glanced out of his bedroom window at the thick, white snow which whirled across the garden blotting out the view of the maples on the far side of the lawn. 'I think you should go, Bill. Look, if you do, will you ring me when you've seen her? Or get her to ring me from somewhere. Hang on. Let me give you the number here.'

Bill copied it down. 'I'll get back to you as soon as I've spoken to Diana, OK? Don't worry, old son, I'm sure Kate is all right.'

He tried her number first. It was, as Jon had said, dead. Then he rang the farmhouse. It was some time before someone picked up the phone.

'Greg?' Bill had been about to hang up. 'It's Bill Norcross. Can I speak to Diana?'

'Sorry. They all appear to be out.' Greg's voice was distant. 'What can I do for you?'

'I just wanted to check what the weather was like your end. I was planning on coming down today.'

'It's windy and hailing and the forecast is lousy. I should stay tucked up by your fire in London if I were you.'

'Have you seen Kate at all?'

'I have indeed.' Greg's voice became even colder.

'Is she all right? Her phone is out of order.'

'She seemed admirably well when last I saw her. Fighting fit, you might say. Did you report it?'

'I'm about to.'

'Good. Well, as soon as it is mended you can ring her and ask her for a weather forecast on the hour, can't you?'

Bill frowned. 'I'll do that. Thanks, Greg.' He hung up. The pencil with which he had been doodling snapped in two. He stared down at it in surprise. 'Bastard,' he murmured to himself. 'Bastard.'

It was nearly two hours after Patrick had left Kate and Alison on their own that Kate, glancing out of the front window saw an ancient vehicle slither to a stop outside. It was driven by a stranger but she saw Diana and Roger climbing out, closely followed by Patrick.

'Thank God,' she murmured. Alison was lying, wrapped in blankets once more, on the sofa. The girl appeared to be asleep.

Running to the door Kate pulled it open.

'Where is she?' Diana's face was white with strain. She pushed past Kate and went into the living room.

'Hi Mum.' Alison opened her eyes.

'What happened exactly? Roger paused in the hall and caught Kate's arm. 'Sorry, let me introduce you. This is Joe Farnborough. He kindly drove us up here.'

Kate glanced at the tall, white-haired man who was staring down at her with undisguised curiosity. Catching her eye he grinned, his eyes silver in a tanned weather-beaten face. 'Young Allie got herself in a spot of bother, has she?' He asked.

She shrugged. 'I think she'll be fine. But she ought to be at home.' They followed Diana and Roger in to the living room and found them bending over Alison. Diana was holding her hand. 'I'm OK, Mum. Honestly.' The girl looked white and strained but her voice had regained some of its strength and with it its peevishness. 'Don't fuss. Just take me home.'

'But what happened, Allie?' Roger sat down, pushing the blankets aside. 'Come on, you must tell us.'

Alison shook her head. 'I'm not sure. I went out to the grave. I wanted to see it. It was early. It was still dark.'

'You went out when it was still dark!' Diana repeated, shocked.

Alison nodded. 'I don't know why. It was just something I had to do. I took a torch. The woods were wet and cold and it was very dark and I was scared.' Her voice trembled. 'When I got to the cottage I saw that all the lights were on. That made me feel better. I thought I would knock and ask Kate to come with me. But I couldn't.' She burst into tears. 'I wanted to, and I couldn't.'

Kate stared at her, appalled. 'Allie, why not? I would have gone with you.'

'I don't mean I couldn't because I didn't want to. I wanted to, but she wouldn't let me.'

There was a moment's silence. Kate met Roger's gaze. It was thoughtful; she guessed that Patrick had already told them about Claudia.

'Who wouldn't let you, Kate?' Diana asked gently.

'Someone. Her. I don't know. He wants to stop me, but she wants to tell me something. They're fighting in my head.' She put the heels of her hands to her temples, still crying. 'She wants me to know.'

'She wants you to stop digging up her grave?' Patrick put in from the doorway. 'That's it, isn't it?'

'No.' Allie sat up. 'No, that's the point. She wants me to. She wants me there. She wants me to find . . . something.' She lay back again.

'Well, whatever it was that happened, I suggest we get you back home, young lady,' put in Joe Farnborough from the doorway. 'I don't want to hurry you folks, but I must get into town and collect some stuff before this weather gets any worse.'

'Of course, Joe. I'm sorry. It was so good of you to come like this,' Diana started to bustle. 'Roger, can you carry her?'

'No need, Mum. I can walk.' Sniffing miserably, Alison swung her legs over the side of the sofa and stood up.

Kate watched as she was ushered out of the door and into the back of the Land Rover – a model even more ancient and muddy

169

than the Lindseys' own. It was Patrick who turned and looked at her. 'Dad. Can Kate come with us? I don't think she ought to stay here alone.'

Roger swung back towards her. 'Of course. That goes without saying. You must come with us, Kate, my dear. We have got to discuss all this very seriously. And if nothing else, we've got to report your phone out of order and get it fixed before you can stay here alone.' He unhooked her jacket from behind the door and held it out to her.

Kate closed her eyes in relief. For a moment she had thought they were going off without her and she had known she would not have the strength of will to call after them. The urge to stay in the cottage was as strong as the urge to leave it. Turning back into the room she began to switch off the lights. She closed the doors on the stove and glanced round. The water had begun to seep back across the windowsill under the cloth. At the edge of it she could see a few dark specks of soil and there, in the shadows, something small and white wriggled purposefully towards the edge of the sill. She turned away sharply and grabbed her shoulder bag. As an afterthought she picked up the pile of typescript that sat on her desk, and with it the diskette from her computer. Then she followed Roger outside and banged the front door closed behind her.

XXX

Diana had gone downstairs. Alison slid down in her bed. Beside her, out of sight under the duvet was an old, well-worn teddy bear with one ear. All the lights in the room were on.

A couple of minutes later Greg appeared in the doorway. 'Are you awake, Allie?'

She pushed the teddy bear even further down the bed. 'What?'

'Look. We ought to talk.' He came in properly and shut the door. Sitting down on the edge of her bed he folded his arms. 'I know I said we ought to scare her off. Kate, I mean. I know I said a lot of things about her being in the way. And I meant it. She's a pain.' He lapsed into silence for a minute, staring thoughtfully down at his feet.

'She was nice to me,' Alison put in at last. There was none of the usual stridency in her voice.

'What really happened, Allie?' He looked at her again. 'Out there. You weren't just trying to scare her, were you.'

'No.' Her voice was very small.

'So. What happened?'

'Nothing.'

'It can't have been nothing.' He put his hand for a moment on the hump of her shoulder beneath the duvet. 'Come on. You can tell me.'

'It's the truth. Nothing happened. I didn't see anything. It was just feelings.' Her mouth began to tremble. She sat up and defiantly retrieved the teddy, hugging it tightly against her chest. In her dayglo green nightshirt, with her hair all over her face, she looked about six.

Greg was astonished by the wave of affection which swept over him. 'What sort of feelings?' he asked gently.

She frowned. 'Fear. Anger. Hate. They all sort of hit me, all

171

jumbled up inside my head in a sort of red whirl. It hurt.' Her eyes flooded with tears.

He stared at her but he wasn't seeing her. He was seeing a short, grey-haired woman in a pale blue puffa jacket which went ill with her high heels. 'I saw you staggering about . . . I wondered if you were epileptic or something . . .' the voice echoed in his head.

Under the thick layers of Viyella shirt, lambswool sweater and ancient tweed jacket he could feel the tiptoe of goose flesh up his arms. His mouth had gone dry.

'What is it?' Her eyes were huge and round, the pupils dilated. 'What's wrong?'

'Nothing. Nothing's wrong, sweetheart.' He never called her that. The endearment frightened her even more than the strange preoccupation on his face had done.

He stood up. 'Listen, Allie. You must get some sleep. OK? Lie down again and I'll tuck you in.' He leaned over as she slid down on the pillows, pulling the duvet up to her chin and patting it with awkward, unaccustomed tenderness. 'Shall I turn out the lights?'

'No!'

He glanced at her sharply. The muffled word, filtered through the threadbare fur of the teddy bear, held a note of real terror.

'OK. No sweat.' He tried to smile. 'Sleep well, prat.' That was more like it. More normal. Sort of.

Downstairs the others were sitting around the fire with mugs of steaming tea. Greg took up position with his back to the inglenook – a speaker addressing a meeting. 'We have to fill in that excavation. Alison must not go up there again, and I think, personally, that Kate ought to move out of the cottage.'

'So that you can move back in.' Kate's words were mild enough, but he saw a hardness in her face which spoke a great deal about her determination to stay, and did he but know it, of her increasing unease in his company.

He sighed. 'No. As a matter of fact I have no desire to move back in at the moment. But do you really want to stay there? After everything that has happened? I can't believe you are getting much work done if you keep being interrupted.'

'As a matter of fact, I am working very well at the moment, thank you,' Kate retorted. 'And it would be very small-minded

172

of me to resent the time I've spent with Alison. She's a nice, intelligent girl. I'm getting fond of her. I don't know why she stayed out at the dig like that – I'm sure she will explain when she feels better – but it has not put me off staying at Redall Cottage in any way. Those locks you have put on for me make me feel as though I were living in Fort Knox.'

'I agree about filling in the excavation,' Roger put in. He leaned back on the sofa comfortably. 'There has been nothing but trouble since Allie found that place. I suggest we get Joe up there with a bulldozer to flatten it.'

'No!'

Kate hadn't realised the word came from her own mouth until she saw everyone staring at her. 'No,' she repeated more softly. 'I don't think we should do that. It's an important site. Much better we get in touch with the local archaeological society or the museum or someone quickly and get them out here to see what is really there.'

'I don't think we want to know what is really there,' Greg said abruptly. 'Don't you agree, Dad? Allie is upset enough as it is.'

'She's not upset at the idea of it being a grave,' Kate retorted.

'Excuse me, but I think she is. She may be a brash, tiresome kid on the outside, and she certainly has loads of guts, but inside she is hurting. This whole thing is upsetting her a lot. You've seen yourself how it's stimulated her imagination. It's bad for her. Ma,' he appealed to his mother, 'you must back me up.'

Diana frowned. She had been listening to the whole exchange in silence. 'You're both right in a way. She is obsessed by that place and I don't think that is good for her, but I don't think the right answer is to try and bury it. It would still be there and she would know it.'

Kate nodded. 'Better to get it excavated properly – a rescue dig can be arranged very quickly, you know. Then we'll all know the truth.'

'The truth about what?' Greg's voice was very quiet. 'What is it that's so important we know? I don't think there is anything there that we need to know about. Nothing at all.'

XXXI

The light was strangely cold. In the cool dawn before the sunrise the marsh was laved with a pale veiling of mist which lapped across the grasses and reeds in a silent, muffling shroud.

Nion stood at the edge of the pool. Bathed, dressed in his finest array, he was ready. Behind him the two priests stood, the tools of their trade openly displayed before them on a wooden altar – a rope, a knife. They waited now, in prayer, respectfully watching his preparations. When the moment came he would tell them.

He frowned. Why only two priests? He had expected them all, a circle of attendants, not this quiet, almost shabby affair unwitnessed and unsung. Slowly he began the business of preparation. Around his neck he wore two torcs. The great twisted golden torc, the symbol of his royal blood and priesthood, and below it one of carved silver which Claudia herself had given him. He took off the first, pulling the heavy gold over his warm skin, feeling the constriction, swallowing, closing his mind to what was to come. He took the torc in his hands, gently running his fingers across the intricate design on the metal, admiring it for the last time. It was truly a worthy gift to the gods. He held it up above his head, half expecting an early stray beam from the still-hidden sun to catch the gleaming metal. None came. He murmured the words of offering and then hurled it with all his might into the mist-covered water. It was gone before him to the world beyond. Next came the silver. Pulling it from his neck he touched it to his lips, then he hurled it after the first. He turned and gathered up his weapons. Sword, spear, dagger. One by one he raised them in offering, balanced across his palms, and threw them. Beneath the curling white of the mist they sank into the cold brown water and began to settle inexorably into the mud.

His clothes next. He unfastened his cloak, folding it carefully into as small a bundle as possible, doing it slowly, meticulously, perhaps stretching out the last few moments before the rim of the sun showed above the sea. Pinning the bundle with his cloak pin he hurled it after his weapons. Next came the bag of coins, his leather belt, his armlets, his tunic. Finally he was naked, save for the strip of woven ash bark around his arm, his birthright and his name sign. The cold air played across his skin. He frowned. He would not want the priests to think that his shiver was one of fear. Imperceptibly he straightened his shoulders, his eyes, like theirs, upon the eastern horizon which with every second grew brighter. Behind him he was conscious suddenly that one of the priests had reached to the altar and taken up the garotte. He was winding it onto his hands.

Nion clenched his fists. The sun had still not appeared but out there, beyond the cold waters, hidden by the mists, the gods were waiting.

The phone at Redall Cottage was working again by late afternoon. Roger drove Kate back there in the Land Rover through the heavy sleet and slush and toured the cottage with her room by room. 'It all looks all right,' he said at last. He had insisted on lighting the stove and carrying in a new supply of logs. 'Are you really quite sure you feel happy about staying here?' On the kitchen table stood a cardboard box full of tins of food, a jar of coffee, a bottle of Scotch, some matches and several other things that Diana had extricated from her own larder. 'Just in case you get trapped by this awful weather they're forecasting,' she had said to Kate. Taking her aside she too had asked her yet again if she wanted to stay with them, but Kate was adamant. 'I must work. Really.'

Roger looked round, seemingly reluctant to leave. 'Are you sure you're happy about this?' he asked again.

'Perfectly happy.' She grinned at him. 'Really. I want to get back to work.'

'Good.' He gave a gentle smile. 'Well, you know where we are if you want anything.'

She stood at the door to watch him drive away into the woods, then she turned back to the house. Nothing had been decided about the excavation. Greg had wanted it buried deep beneath the sand; Roger and she had wanted to call the Colchester archaeological people and Alison, when at last she had woken up had become totally hysterical at the thought of anyone touching it at all. In deference to her tears Diana had vetoed any action at least for a day or two and reluctantly, Kate had had to acquiesce. It was after all their land; their dune.

She glanced at her watch. It was nearly four. She put on the

175

kettle and then hauling herself onto the stool, she reached for the phone. Anne was in.

'Hi, stranger. I was wondering how you'd been getting on.' Her sister's voice was cheerful.

'I'm fine. How's Edinburgh?'

'Wonderful. Better than I had hoped even. The job is quite fascinating and I love the city and C.J. loves the flat. It's huge compared with our old one, and there's a walled garden at the back. He's in seventh heaven. At least he was until the snow started.' She laughed. 'So tell me about the wilder shores of East Anglia.'

'A bit strange, actually.' Kate paused, watching the steam begin to rise from the kettle spout. 'Anne. Are there such things as poltergeists?'

There was a moment's silence the other end of the line. 'Now there's a fascinating question. Why do you ask?'

'Various reasons.' Kate smiled wryly. There would be no turning back now until Anne had wormed the last tiny detail out of her. She took a deep breath. 'Let me tell you the story then you give me your opinion . . .'

It took a surprisingly long time to tell. Anne listened in silence, clicking her fingers once at Carl Gustav as he flexed his claws provocatively against the back of an armchair. He beamed at her and leapt onto her lap, cuddling down for a long stay.

'From what you say and your initial question you suspect the activity is centred around Alison, am I right?' she said at last.

'That's how it works, doesn't it? Teenage angst and all that. Frustrated energy.'

'That's how it works.' Kate could hear the smile in Anne's voice. 'If it works. The bangs you have described sound to me as though they could just be wood splitting. You've probably heated up the cottage more than anyone in ages and it's falling apart. Had you thought of that? I suppose it could be explosions of psychic energy if one believes in such things. I've certainly read about them. But the rest. The soil. The maggots. Ugh. That doesn't sound like poltergeist activity either, to be honest. More like a horror novel.'

Kate pursed her lips. 'Anne, this is not a novel! Come on. I want your help.'

'Well, then, perhaps the sudden heat has woken them up.

Wasn't that what someone suggested to you? That sounds more realistic. But even more likely it sounds to me like some kind of practical joke, Katie, love, and if the brother – Greg, did you say his name was? – is anything like as angry as you say, I should look no further than him. He sounds a very unhappy and frustrated man.'

'You don't think any of this could be supernatural then?'

'I think it's unlikely. Even the ghost you think you saw. You were tired; you could have imagined it. The smells are easily explained. They hang around for months, even years in houses sometimes. And maggots for God's sake! What are you supposed to think? That they are coming from a two-thousand-year-old grave? How long do you think the flesh lasts on bones? How long do you think any organic matter survives at all? Besides, how would they have got into your cottage?' Anne fondled Carl Gustav's ears. Kate could hear his purr down the telephone. It made her feel suddenly terribly lonely.

'How do I handle it, big sister? I don't want to leave this cottage. It's wonderful. I love it and I'm working well.'

'Has anything happened since you had the locks changed?'

'Yes.'

'And you don't believe the maggots are breeding on something terribly dead beneath the floorboards?'

'No.' Kate looked down at her feet. The cottage floors, she had established, were uncompromisingly concrete.

'And you don't think Alison could have slipped a matchboxfull onto the windowsill while you were out of the room?'

'No. I don't.'

'I think I'm going to need notice of this one. It's tricky.' Anne laughed out loud. 'Intriguing but tricky. You're not scared?'

'I don't think so.'

'You don't sound very certain.'

'Well, would you? In the middle of nowhere? It's beginning to get dark. There's a bluebottle in here now.' It hadn't been there a few minutes ago, she was sure, and yet there it was, circling the light.

'Well, take comfort that there is nothing supernatural about bluebottles. You may not find out where they are coming from, but as sure as eggs is eggs, they are coming from the maggots who in turn are coming from some source of putrid flesh –'

'What did you say?' Kate interrupted her, her voice tight with fear.

'I said putrid flesh.'

'"Your putrid body and your rotten soul,"' Kate quoted slowly. 'Those are the words which keep going round and round in my head.' She was suddenly very scared.

'It's a coincidence. Have you never heard of synchronicity?' Hearing the fear in her sister's voice, Anne was immediately reassuring. 'Besides, it's hardly a coincidence when one is talking of maggots. Listen, love, I have got someone coming to supper. I really ought to get on or they will be having sardines on toast. Can we talk again tomorrow? I'll look up something about poltergeists and teenage werewolves to give you some ammunition to throw at young Alison, but if I were you I should have a stiff drink, bolt every door, check for matchboxes of maggots under the sideboard and lose yourself in the book. And if you're really, really scared I want you to ring me at once. Any time. Understand? Must go.'

She had hung up before Kate had a chance to say goodbye.

'Anne. Anne?' She shook the receiver. Anne had gone but the line still sounded as though it were open. She listened for a moment longer. 'Oh no. Not again.' She felt a moment of quite irrational panic as she jiggled the phone, hung up and lifted the receiver again. The line had not disconnected. It was live. There was no dialling tone. She put it down again and lifted it a second time. The same thing happened.

In Edinburgh Anne stared at the phone on the table in front of her and bit her lip. It was unlike Kate to be afraid of anything; very unlike her. To hell with the guests. Kate was more important than a perfect soufflé. She reached for the receiver again and dialled Kate's number.

The line was dead.

Bleakly Kate stared round the kitchen. Damn and blast it. It didn't matter, of course. Tomorrow she would walk up through the woods to the farmhouse and report the phone once again. There was no reason she should want to phone anyone again tonight. As Anne had said she should have a drink, check for maggots, and then go back to work.

It was a quarter to midnight when at last she turned off her computer, stretched and stood up. Her eyes were weary and her brain felt scrambled. She stared down at the pile of printed pages on the desk then she picked up her glasses and put them on again, reading through the last section one more time. It was good. It was exciting, alive, tremendous. Exhilarated, she stood up and wandered through to the kitchen and reached for the new bottle of whisky. The Lindseys, it appeared, drank Johnnie Walker. She poured herself half an inch and went back into the living room. Damn it, with the phone cut off no one could ring her either and she had, she realised suddenly, been hoping for another call from Jon. She sighed. She missed him so much.

The sharp bang above her head hardly made her jump at all. She stared up at the ceiling again and slowly she leaned forward to the table and reached for the bottle. 'Sod off, Marcus,' she murmured. 'You're either psychic energy or you're a splitting beam. Either way you are not my problem.'

XXXII

Greg found Allie in the kitchen next morning. She was sitting at the table, still wearing her dressing gown. Her face was pale and strained. He sat down opposite her and reached for the coffee pot. 'How are you feeling, prat?' he asked.

She glared at him. 'Awful.'

'Did Ma say you ought to see the doctor?'

'No. She thinks I'm all right. Just tired.'

'Didn't you sleep?'

'What do you think.' She put her arms on the table and rested her head on them.

'We are going to ring Joe today and ask him to bring a tractor up to flatten the dune,' he said gently. 'Dad agrees that that would be best. It's only a matter of days anyway before the sea takes the whole lot away.'

'You can't.' She stared up at him aghast, her fair hair flopping across her eyes. 'You can't do that. It's an archaeological site. You won't be allowed to.'

'No one is going to know. I'm sorry, Allie, but my mind is made up. There are things there which are best left untouched. If you think about it you'll agree.'

'No!' She jumped up, scraping the chair legs across the stone slabs. 'No. I won't let you! You can't. You mustn't!'

'Allie –'

'No.' Her voice had risen to a shriek. 'Don't you see. People have got to know. They must know the truth!'

'The truth about what?' He frowned.

'The truth about –' She shrugged, subsiding once more. 'The truth about what is in the grave. The truth about what happened there. The truth about –' She stopped dead. It was as though the name on her lips had been snatched from her. 'The truth about whose grave it is,' she improvised. 'You must not touch it. No way.

180

If you even think about ringing Joe I shall phone the museum and tell them. They will put a preservation order or something on it.'

'What on earth do you know about preservation orders?' Greg asked. He could feel his anger rising. He had been a fool to tell her. He should have rung Joe and they could have gone ahead with it without telling her. After the event it would be too late to stop it.

'I don't know anything about them, but I know you can get them. You can get them to stop farmers ploughing up their fields when there are special things on them.'

'Well, there is nothing special about this. A few old bits of pottery and stuff in a dune on the edge of the sea. Big deal. It's better forgotten.'

'No.' Her eyes narrowed. She looked like Serendipity when he had a mouse or a bird and he thought someone was going to try to take it from him. 'No. You are not to touch it. The truth has to come out.'

Greg stood up, picked up his cup of coffee and found the cup was rattling on its saucer. 'Please yourself.' He wandered through towards the sofa and sat down next to the cats who were ensconced firmly in a manner which denoted profound rejection of an outside world where the sleet slanted out of a slate sky and the wind knifed round corners and through unresisting flesh. He felt extraordinarily upset. Adrenalin flooded through his body; he felt a dry sickness in his throat. His hands, clenched around the cup were shaking slightly and he was angrier than he had ever been. He took a deep breath trying to steady his breathing. What on earth was the matter with him? He didn't care one way or the other about the damn grave and being tactically defeated by Alison was no big deal. She did it all the time and mostly he tolerated it. He took a swig of the coffee and leaned back, closing his eyes.

Behind him she was still sitting at the table. She sniffed, surreptitiously wiping the back of her hand across her eyes. Her head was throbbing and her face felt puffy from lack of sleep. There was still something she had to do but she could not remember what it was. She stared at the window wearily as a gust of wind threw more hail at the glass. The kitchen was cold. She glanced at the Aga. It was lit. The kettle on the hot plate was steaming gently, so why was it she could not stop shivering? Standing up shakily she went to where her brother was sitting and perched on the arm of the sofa. 'I'm going to ring the archaeological people.'

He glanced up at her. 'You're a fool. They won't want to know. Anyway, what the hell could they do in this weather?' As if to reinforce his remark another gust of wind shook the house. The fire flared up. Several sparks shot out onto the hearthrug. Automatically Alison got up and stood on them one by one. 'They will want to know.'

'They will not want to know. Anyway, by the time they get here there will be nothing to see. I expect the sea will have done all the excavating for you.' He drained his cup, watching as she tramped methodically over the carpet to make sure she had extinguished the last spark. She turned towards the door.

'Where are you going?'

'To phone.'

'Now?' He sat up.

'Yes, now.'

'Allie, you mustn't.'

'Why not?' She swung round to face him, her hair hanging in curtains across her face. 'Just why are you so against it?'

'Because I think it will only cause more trouble.'

'What kind of trouble?' She raised her chin slightly in the defiance which was more natural to her than this haggard exhaustion.

He stood up. 'Leave it alone, Allie. Please. Look let's wait at least until Monday. With the weather like this they won't be able to get here anyway. Even better, leave it until the spring. Then they can come and see if it's still here.'

'That's the whole point.' She stamped her foot. 'Don't you see? They must get to it before it is washed away. They have to find out who is buried there, and why.'

'No.' His face had closed, his voice was harsh. 'No. No one must ever find out.'

'Why on earth not?' She stared at him in astonishment and was frightened to see the implacable rage in her brother's face. 'Greg, what is it? I don't understand.' His eyes were hard, the pupils contracted to tiny pinpoints although the light in the room was low. Behind him the two cats leaped from the sofa of one accord and vanished behind the Aga.

'Greg?' Her voice was pleading. 'What is it? You're frightening me.'

For a moment he went on staring at her, as though his hatred of her were too great to contain, then visibly he seemed to shake himself free of whatever strange emotion had gripped him. 'I'm sorry. I don't know what's wrong. I don't give a screw what you do about your stupid grave, Allie. Do what you like.'

He was shaken. It had happened again, the strange feeling that there was some kind of alien being inside his head, battering at his skull – an alien with terrible, raging emotions. Leaning back against the cushion with a groan he put his hand over his eyes.

With a nervous glance at him Alison escaped thankfully into her father's study. The telephone books were piled on the floor by his desk. She pulled up the swivelling chair and sat down, reaching for the local directory. All round her her brother's paintings were stacked against the walls, and on the easel. The room smelt strange, its own comfortable familiar smell eclipsed by oil and turpentine and wonderful arcane scents of varnish and paint and linseed. She flipped open the book and began to look for the number under Archaeology. There was nothing there. She tried again under Colchester. It was several moments before she found it. Holding her finger under the number she reached for the phone, aware that Greg had come into the room and was standing in the doorway watching her.

Her fingers tightened on the receiver. Ignoring him she began to dial. She listened for several minutes, frowning, then she jiggled the rest and dialled again.

'What is it. Is something wrong?' Greg's voice from the doorway was almost mocking.

'I can't get a dialling noise.' She shook the receiver and tried again. 'It sounds as if there is a crossed line. As if someone is listening on the other end.'

He smiled. 'Perhaps they are,' he said quietly.

XXXIII

Bill leaned forward and stared through the windscreen. He was bitterly regretting having set out for the cottage. Just as he was leaving the office the afternoon before, someone had come in and talked to him for hours. By the time they had gone it was getting dark and he had decided to postpone his decision until the morning.

A desultory sun was shining when he woke up at nine. He stared thoughtfully out of the window at the distant view of Hampstead Heath and then back at his bedroom which was untidy and smelled frowsty. He glared at the socks he had taken off the night before and thrown into the corner. Perhaps a weekend in the clean, bracing East-Anglian air would do him good.

The sun had disappeared almost as soon as he had joined the A1. By the time he was on the M25 the sky was overcast, deep, brown-bellied clouds massing overhead. When he got to Chelmsford it began to snow. Wet, sleety snow which swished beneath the tyres and clogged the windscreen wipers. The traffic was slow – not because there was a lot of it; unusually for a Saturday morning it was light, but because the visibility was appalling. Silently Bill cursed himself for his stupidity in setting out at all. He leaned forward and pressed a cassette into the deck, not taking his eye off the sleety road. He would drive as far as Colchester, park the car, give himself a drink and a meal at The George and then make the decision whether to go on or go back.

XXXIV

Kate dreamt again that night. In the midnight shadows on the beach something threatening stalked the darkness. She ran, glancing behind her over her shoulder, aware that the threat was growing closer and closer all the time. She could hear herself sobbing out loud as she tried to draw breath, pushing herself with the last of her strength as she felt the sand slip and lurch beneath her shoes. She was going to make it. She stretched out her hand, hearing the footsteps pounding ever closer behind her on the sand. She was home.

She reached out to the door and became aware suddenly that someone was standing in the doorway, holding out his hand to her. It was Jon. She saw his smile, saw his hand, felt the brush of his fingertips and then she stumbled. Her hand grasped at the thin air and the door began to close, with her still outside in the darkness, alone . . .

Kate awoke with a groan, her face wet with tears. Her head was hammering like a water pipe and her mouth was dry. She tried to sit up, groaned again and lay back on the pillow wishing she were dead. She lay still for several minutes then she realised she was going to have to get up to go and have a pee. Staggering a little, she managed to grope her way downstairs. The chill in the cottage told her at once that she had forgotten to stoke up the woodburner. Her face washed, her teeth brushed, and her hair combed, she felt only marginally better. She put the kettle on and then went through into the living room. Drawing back the curtains she found it was daylight outside – but only just. The sleet which sheeted down out of the east was backdropped by clouds the colour of pewter; she could feel the beat and push of the wind against the cold windowpane. She glanced down at the sill. The surface was quite dry. There was no sign of anything untoward lurking there.

Back in the kitchen she made herself a cup of black coffee. As she sipped it she lifted the phone and listened. Still no dialling tone. Still nothing but the strange interplanetary echo. Slamming it down, she winced slightly as the crash reverberated up her arm and through her skull.

She forced herself to get dressed, donning a shirt and thick sweater over trousers and two pairs of socks. Then she dragged on her jacket, scarf and gloves. Her boots were by the front door. Before she left she relit the stove and left it burning nicely in the hope of having a warm cottage to come back to. With a bit of luck someone would give her a lift back from the farmhouse.

Patrick opened the door to her. 'Hi.' He smiled, his face lighting up at the sight of her. 'Come in.'

The thought that he was pleased to see her warmed her. 'How's Allie?' She followed him into the hall and pulled off her boots.

'She's all right. A bit weird, but she'll live.'

For a moment she wondered whether to ask him to expand on this rather cryptic reply but she thought better of it. 'Patrick, could I possibly use your phone? Mine has gone on the blink again.'

'Sure. There's one in the study.' He indicated the door on his right. 'Phone away then come into the kitchen. The others are there. I'll tell them to pour you a coffee.'

With a grateful smile at him she opened the door into Roger's study. The phone was on the desk. Shaking her head free of her woollen scarf she made for it.

'Can I help you?' The quiet voice nearly scared her out of her wits. She swung round. 'Greg! I'm sorry. I didn't realise that there was anyone here.'

'So I gather.' He was sitting on the arm of a comfortable, shabby old armchair near the window, a sketchpad in one hand, a pencil in the other, the pale paper illuminated by one of the shaded wall lights. She couldn't see his face in the shadow.

'I wanted to borrow the phone.'

'So. You don't trust us, eh? Going to ring the museum yourself, were you?' His voice was harshly sarcastic.

'No, I wasn't.' Indignantly she glared at him. 'I said I would do nothing until we had discussed it further, and I meant it. Besides, if I was going to phone someone about the grave I would hardly walk all the way over here through this foul weather in order to do so. I have in fact come to report my phone out of order again.'

'I see.' He gave her an amicable grin. 'Well, I'm afraid you are out of luck. This one is kaput also.'

She was astonished at the sudden wave of fear which swept through her. For a moment she thought her legs were going to give way. She leaned on the desk. 'Are you sure?'

'See for yourself.' He half turned away from her, going back to his drawing.

She picked up the receiver and listened. The sound was the same. That strange echoing silence which seemed to connect to distant spheres. Putting it down she found the palm of her hand was slick with icy sweat. 'Have you reported it?'

'I believe Dad is driving up to the village later. He will no doubt do so then.' He glanced up. Her face, which had been pink and shiny from the wind and rain had gone white. 'Are you all right?'

'Yes, of course.'

'It worries you that much? Not having a phone?'

'Yes.' She forced herself to smile.

'You're scared, out there on your own, aren't you?' His voice was very soft.

'No. Not scared.' She took a deep breath. 'But I am inconvenienced. I need the phone for my work. I need to speak to my editor; and I need it for research.'

'Busy lady.' He put down the sketchpad and stood up slowly. 'And of course you want to phone the man in America. Well, I'm sure it will be mended soon. The wiring is old. They are always having trouble with phones round here. Next year, I gather, our exchange will be updated to the space age. Heaven knows what will happen then. If they keep the same old telegraph posts and fraying wires it will still go off if it rains.' He paused, eyeing her thoughtfully. 'So, how is your book progressing?'

'Do you really want to know?'

'I would not waste time asking unless I wanted to know.' He shaded in part of his drawing, the strokes of his pencil sure and firm.

'Then thank you. The book is going well.'

'Good.' He glanced up. 'Kate. You saw Allie, yesterday. You know the state she was in. Please use your influence to dissuade her from going on with this archaeological plan of hers. It's upsetting her too much. She's having nightmares – all kinds of horrors. She's imagining god-knows-what monsters climbing out of the grave. You must see how bad it is for her. It's like some awful horror movie.'

Thoughtfully Kate moved round the desk and took Roger's chair. She leaned forward, her chin on her elbows. 'It's not knowing what's there that is worrying her, Greg. If you cover it up and bulldoze it all into the sea the effect will be the same. It, whatever "it" is, will still be there because it's inside her head. It would be much better to get some professionals in to look at it. They may say "Look this is all nonsense. This is no more than a spoil pit. There was no grave here," or they may say, "Yes, this was a grave, an Iron Age cremation perhaps. Look. It's all gone. There's nothing left except a few shards and some metalwork". Her worst fears would be laid to rest. And I am sure they would enlist her help. Help her with her project. Encourage her. Talk about it. That's the best course of action, I really do believe it. The worst thing you could do is pretend that there is nothing there.'

'Quite the psychologist, aren't we.'

She refused to let herself be roused by his deliberately mocking tone. 'No. I think it's common sense.' She stood up. 'Patrick said there would be some coffee in the kitchen. Are you coming through to get some?'

He shook his head, not raising his eyes from his sketchpad.

'Then, if you'll excuse me, I think I will. It was a long walk through the woods and I'm very chilled –'

'Kate.' He had put down his pad. 'Tell me something. Do you think it's all her imagination?'

She held his gaze for a full half-minute. 'Not completely. No.'

'That's a little ambiguous, if I may say so. Do I gather you still suspect me?'

'There is a particularly irritating phrase which is in this case I think suitable. If the cap fits.'

'Obviously you think it does.'

Walking towards the door she shrugged. 'I find it hard to make up my mind, Greg. Put it this way. If it isn't you, then I think that maybe we should all be worrying with Allie.'

'Let me show you something before you go and get your coffee.' Greg stood up. He went across to the desk and rummaged in the bottom drawer under a pile of notebooks of his father's. Bringing out a photograph wallet he laid it on the desk. 'I had your pictures developed at Boots.'

She glanced up at his face then she felt in the pocket of her jeans for her spectacles. Reaching for the wallet she flipped it open and pulled the photos out. The room was silent as she studied them. When she looked up at him again her face was even whiter than before. 'You could have faked these.'

'Oh come on. I would hardly bother to go that far.'

'Have you shown them to Allie?'

'Obviously not.'

She looked down at them again. They had come out well in spite of the strange light. Every grain of sand was visible, every line of strata, every trail of weed and every shell. In three of them there was, clearly visible, something else, something which she had not seen when she took the pictures.

'What do you think it is?'

Greg was leaning over the desk beside her. He pointed to one of the pictures. 'It looks like something spinning: a dust devil; a whirlwind perhaps. What did it look like when you took the pictures?'

She shook her head mutely. 'I didn't see it. I didn't see anything odd at all.' She gave an involuntary shiver. 'The light wasn't very good. To be honest I didn't think they would come out.' His head was very near hers as they leaned towards the desk. She was surprised to feel a strange tingle of something like excitement as his shoulder brushed hers. Cross with herself, she moved away sharply. Taking one of the photos she carried it to the lamp where he had been sitting. The entire periphery of the photo was clear and fully in focus but about one third of the way down, slightly to the left of centre was a strange, swirling, bright mass. 'Do you think my camera was letting in the light somehow?' she said slowly. She held the photo closer to the lamp.

'I don't think so. The whole picture would have been spoiled. If you look at the edges of that thing you can see everything completely clearly. Here. Try this.' He picked up a magnifying glass which had been lying on the desk. 'You see, the thing, whatever it is, is clearly superimposed on the background. It was in front of it, blocking it off.'

Taking the glass from him she squinted through it. 'What is your theory?'

'I think it's an energy field.'

'And where do you think the energy is coming from?' Her question was guarded.

'The way I see it, there are only three possibilities. The first is a human source. You.' He glanced up at her. 'Could you have been projecting some kind of force field? Repressed anger, perhaps? Indignation? Frustration?' He grinned. 'I should imagine you've been feeling all three since you arrived at the cottage.'

'Very probably,' she retorted tartly. 'But not in sufficient quantities I think, to create a whirlwind.' He was standing very close to her again, staring down at the picture in her hand. This time she did not move away. 'What are your other two suggestions?' she asked.

'That it was just that, a whirlwind, and somehow you missed seeing it. Or the energy came from the earth.'

'The former is out of the question.' She hoped he hadn't noticed the sudden tremor in her voice.

'And the latter?'

'Earth energy? Like ley lines, you mean?'

'That or perhaps from some external source in the ground.'

There was a long silence as she digested his words. 'Greg. What are you trying to say?' When she looked up at him his face was very close to hers. He was, she noticed for the first time, unshaven. The shadow of beard was a rich golden colour, far brighter than his hair.

He shrugged. 'I'm just wondering whether perhaps it could come from something that is buried there.'

'Something or someone?'

'It is someone, I'm afraid.'

'But we can't be sure. And surely it is the best reason to try and find out.' Again the slight tingle of excitement as his hand brushed her shoulder.

He reached for the photo. 'I think we can be sure, Kate. Look at this other one. See what you think.' He turned to the desk and shuffled through the prints. 'Here. Look at that corner. On the sand face.' His forefinger was smudged with a grainy smear of cobalt blue. Taking the print her hand accidentally touched his. He did not move away.

She stared through the magnifying glass, angry to find her hand was shaking suddenly. 'What am I supposed to be looking at? There's no sand devil on this one.'

190

'There. Wait, let me point with a pencil. Look.' The fine point also trembled slightly, she noticed. She screwed up her eyes, staring at the fine definition of the photo. The sand, the lines of peat, the shells, all were startlingly clear, and there, at the edge of the photo was something protruding from the sand face.

'Dear God!' she whispered.

'It's part of a hand, isn't it,' Greg said softly.

She looked him straight in the eye. 'Did you put it there?' Their faces were only eighteen inches apart.

'No.'

This time she believed him. Suddenly there wasn't a shadow of doubt in her mind. She could feel the fine hairs on the back of her wrist standing on end as it held the photo. 'We have to go out there and see.'

'Yes.'

'What did you tell Allie about the photos?'

'That I put them in too late for the one-hour service so they would be a couple of days. She seemed quite relieved.'

'She's terrified of the place. She wants nothing to do with it anymore,' she said thoughtfully. 'And yet she still wants it excavated. That's strange. Dangerous.'

He nodded. 'So, we are on the same side.'

'Is it a question of sides?' She shook her head thoughtfully. 'No, Greg. The grave must be investigated, surely you can see that. If there is a body on the beach, a coroner has to be informed for a start, however old it is. Probably the police too, for all I know.'

'It's hardly a murder enquiry!'

He had said the words laughingly. Throwing back his head he took the print from her, all the anger gone, his thoughts a delicious mixture of clandestine intrigue with a bulldozer, coffee in the kitchen and the woman standing so near to him. She was, he realised suddenly, really very beautiful when she wasn't being so stroppy.

The sudden drop in temperature took them both by surprise. It was as though someone had opened a freezer door nearby. For a second the atmosphere in the room was electric.

'*Marcus*.'

The whisper came from Kate's mouth. Without realising it she had clutched at his arm. 'Oh, sweet Jesus, Greg, what is it?'

He shook his head. 'God knows. Come on. Obviously we've touched a chord somewhere. Let's get out of here. And not a word to the others. Not yet. Not until I've had a chance to think.' Dropping her arm, he opened the door and ushered her through it into the hall.

She followed him, glancing back over her shoulder as she did so. The room looked perfectly normal. There was nothing there to frighten them; nothing out of the usual at all. The temperature, she realised as she closed the door behind her, was as warm as it had been before. Only one thing was different. The smell of paint and varnish and linseed oil had been eclipsed totally by an all-pervading smell of wet, cold earth.

XXXV

Her eyes were blinded by tears as she parted the clump of elder with a shaking hand and peered through. She could see him standing only a few yards from her, naked now, his arms raised in salute towards the eastern sky, his fists clenched against the crimson clouds. Behind him the priests were waiting. She saw the golden knife, the ligature, the bowl which contained the sacred mead. As she watched, he turned. For a moment she saw his face. His expression was closed, cold, impassive, as though his spirit had already fled.

The priest stepped forward with the bowl. With a bow he handed it to Nion. The young man turned back towards the east. He raised the bowl towards the red clouds. On the distant horizon, two miles away, where sea met sky, crimson colour bled upwards from below the rim of the earth. Behind him the priest raised his knife. They all waited, motion suspended, their eyes on the distance where the sun would appear.

Claudia bit back her tears. She clenched her fists. He would not see her, or hear her pain. Her eyes, too, went to the horizon. As she watched, the smallest segment of scarlet appeared out of the crimson mist.

Nion tensed. His knuckles whitened on the rim of the bowl. For a fraction of a second he seemed to thrust it further towards the sun, then he threw back his head and began to drink. She saw the movement of his throat; she saw the golden liquid spill over the side of the bowl, onto his chin, run down his arms and splash onto his chest. He drained the bowl to the dregs and flung it into the marsh, then he crossed his arms on his breast and knelt.

Behind him the two priests stepped forward. She saw the red reflection of the sun glinting on the knife blade as it was raised. And she saw the garotte as it was slipped swiftly and dextrously about his throat.

The meal had been excellent. Bill sat for a long time over his coffee. At his side *The Times* lay beside his cup, neatly folded to expose the crossword. In the last hour he had managed only two clues and he was feeling discouraged. He glanced up at the window. Outside the sleet appeared to have stopped. A slash of palest stone-washed denim blue had appeared between the clouds. Staring up at it he felt a sudden uplift of his spirits. Damn it, it was only twenty miles or so further.

Slotting a couple of carriers full of Marks and Spencer food into the boot of his car he tucked four bottles of wine in beside them and slid into the driver's seat.

He had no problems until he reached the track down through the Redall woods where the slush and rain had turned it into a quagmire. Parking on the side of the road he climbed out. Behind him a tractor was lumbering along the road. It drew to a halt behind his car. Bill walked up to it. 'Hello, Joe. Do you think I'd be mad to take the car down to the cottage?'

Joe laughed. He scratched his head. 'I reckon you were mad to come at all,' he shouted over the clatter of the engine. 'I tell you what. You come and leave your car up at the farm and I'll run you down to yours. Best that way.'

Bill gave up the effort of competing with the huge engine. With a grin he gave a thumbs up sign and turned back to his car. At least this way he wouldn't get trapped by the weather.

It was an hour later that Joe delivered him to his door. Waving his good Samaritan off he inserted his key in the door and pushed it open with his shoulder. The smell of cold and damp assailed him at once and he grimaced. 'Bloody fool.' He meant himself.

The front door led straight into the living room. The furnishings were shabby and not very pretty – good enough for weekends, but not so good they would get nicked. It always depressed him a little when he arrived, but he knew from long experience that once he had put a match to the fire – a resolution he had never once broken was to leave it laid ready when he left for London at the end of each trip – and turned on the lights and the radio the little house would spring to life. He found he was humming as he walked through into the kitchen – basic with an old, deep sink, a barely functional electric cooker and a pine table and chairs which were probably by now worth a fortune as antiques. Once he was settled he would dig out his wellies and stride out through the mud to visit Kate.

It had never crossed his mind that she wouldn't be at home. He peered through the windows of her cottage. The woodburner was alight. He could see the glow of the fire through the closed doors. He shaded his eyes as he leaned closer. Her desk was untidy, as though she had got up and left it in the middle of some work. And the lamp on the table in the corner was switched on. He glanced over his shoulder towards the beach. Perhaps she had gone for a walk.

His wellingtons sliding wetly on the sand and shingle, he made his way down towards the sea, standing on the foreshore at last, shading his eyes as he stared up and down the beach. The rain and sleet had drifted inland. Overhead the cloud was still thick, but it was higher now, and there was still the odd patch of blue. His hands wedged firmly into his pockets he threw his shoulders back and inhaled deeply. It was a rash move and led to a spasm of coughing, but at least he was getting the desired fresh air. He chuckled to himself, and turning north up the beach began to walk briskly over the sand. The sea was sullen, heaving menacingly on the horizon, a shifting solid mass of seemingly waveless water. The tide was midway up, he guessed, creeping nearer half-heartedly, dribbling each progression of weed and shells onto the beach before sliding back into the black depths to gather itself for another inroad onto the sand.

He didn't walk far. The wind in his face was not strong but it was bitingly cold. Turning, he glanced back the way he had come. There was no sign anywhere of Kate. No footprints on the sand to show where she had passed. Disappointed, he retraced his steps. Blow fresh air. You could get too much of that. He walked down the beach as far as the end of the dunes and climbed up to get a view across the estuary. It was alive with geese. Bustling with activity. He could hear them now, gossiping, squabbling, murmuring to each other as they spread out across the still water onto the low-lying islands and the saltings. He grinned to himself. He liked the geese. They were jolly chaps, and with them there it wasn't possible to feel lonely. He couldn't understand why people had to shoot them. But then some people would kill anything that moved, given half a chance. Shrugging himself deeper into his thick quilted jacket he turned away and pulled up short. There was a woman standing in the distance on one of the other dunes. His heart leapt. 'Kate!' he shouted. 'Over here.' He waved.

She had her back to him. He could see she was huddled into some long garment. Her hair was tearing free of its fastenings.

'Kate!' He put his hands to his mouth and bellowed. The trouble was the wind was blowing from her to him, carrying his voice away. Behind him some of the geese looked up from their grazing and he heard a volley of anxious alarm notes. He leaped off the dune and ran back through the deep, soft sand towards her, feeling the sweat break out on his body beneath the heavy jacket. Puffing, convinced he was about to have a heart attack, he scrambled up the dune where she had been standing. She was nowhere to be seen. He stared down. Half the dune had fallen away onto the beach. He could see where the tide had washed the sand into mounds of weed-covered spoil. A dead crab lay on its back amongst the debris. He wrinkled his nose. Slithering and jumping he made his way back onto the beach, staring round. Where the hell had she gone? Out at sea the evening was beginning to draw in. He could see the mist which preceded the coming darkness hovering on the horizon.

Crossly, he made his way back towards her cottage. Obviously she hadn't seen him. Well, he couldn't blame her for going in. It was becoming much colder. He could feel the icy chill on his body as his sweat dried. Suddenly he felt very alone.

The cottage was still deserted, the front door locked. He stared at it in disbelief. Perhaps it wasn't Kate he had seen after all? It must have been someone else. But who else would be out there on the beach in this weather at this time of day? It had certainly been neither Alison nor Diana. One was too short, the other too well-built. Although the figure he had seen had been too far away to recognise he had been able to see that she was tall and willowy, her figure emphasised by the way she had pulled her coat tightly around her.

Disappointed, he turned away from the door. He might as well walk up to Redall Farmhouse and see if he could cadge a cup of tea there. Maybe that was where she was anyway. Pulling his collar up more tightly around his ears, Bill set off towards the trees.

XXXVI

'Where is Allie?' Diana looked around the kitchen as though it was only the first time she had noticed her daughter's absence. It was two hours since they had finished lunch – a meal to which Kate had been invited without hesitation and one which she had accepted with equal alacrity. Alison had appeared for the first course but she had barely touched it and, making her excuses, had retired upstairs to sleep. 'Run and see how she is, Patrick, will you, dear?' She and Kate had finished the dishes together and a new kettle of water was brewing on the Aga. 'She ought to eat something.'

Patrick vanished upstairs. Diana smiled. 'I know I'm being silly to worry, but I can't help it. She's not right yet.'

'Do you think you ought to take her to the doctor?' Kate lined up six mugs on the table.

Diana's reply was interrupted by Patrick's shout. 'Ma! She's not up here.'

Diana stared across the room towards the staircase. 'What do you mean she's not up there? Of course she is.'

'She's not. And she's not in the loo. I've looked everywhere.' Patrick reappeared.

Roger had been dozing by the fire. Pushing a heap of cats off his lap he stood up. 'She must be somewhere. This is not a very big house. You had better find her.' He could not keep the anxiety out of his voice.

'She's gone.' Diana threw down the oven glove she had donned to pick up the kettle. 'She's gone back to that bloody grave.'

'No.' Kate's whisper was lost as Roger threw his newspaper down.

'She can't have. She wouldn't be so stupid. God! It will be dark in another hour.' He strode to the door.

'Look for her jacket, darling.' Diana was standing in the middle of the floor, frozen with fear.

'It's gone.' He was rummaging through the stack of coats and waterproofs on the pegs inside the front door. 'So have her boots.'

Greg had disappeared into the study with his cup of coffee after they had finished the meal. At the sound of Roger's raised voice he opened the door and peered out. 'What's up?'

'It's your sister. She seems to have gone out.'

Greg's eyes sought Kate's. His face was suddenly very grim.

'Kate and I will go and look for her,' he said. 'We'll take the Land Rover. Don't worry, Ma. She'll be all right. She's not a fool. If she's taken her coat and boots she'll be warm enough and it shows she is being sensible.'

'I'll go with you.' His father was reaching for his own coat but Greg put his hand on his arm. 'No, Dad, no need. Honestly. Kate and I will find her. You stay here with Ma. You never know. She may just have gone for a walk in the garden. We may be panicking for nothing.' He smiled into the silence. None of them believed that; they all knew where she had gone.

The Land Rover was cold. Hauling herself into the passenger seat Kate dug her hands deep into her pockets, waiting in the silent vehicle as Greg walked round to the driver's side and pulled open the door. He climbed in and reached for the ignition key, glancing at her. 'How long do you reckon she's been gone?'

'It could have been hours. Would we have noticed if she'd gone out while we were still eating?'

He shrugged. 'She had to come through the living room to reach the front door. The trouble was we were talking so hard I don't suppose we would have noticed her even if she had jumped up and shouted at us.' He rammed in the gear and eased the car away from the side of the house. 'Did you throw in the blankets?'

Kate nodded. Her stomach was cold and shivery. Her mouth had gone dry. 'Something out there is calling her.'

'Well, they can call away. She is not going.' Greg swung the Land Rover onto the track, feeling the tyres slipping sideways as they tried to grip the mud.

Under the trees they were suddenly aware of how soon it would be dusk. The shadows beneath the pine and larch were softly black; in the distance the wood was dark. The headlights cut a swathe through the undergrowth, lighting up patches of yellow where willow whips were already showing signs of spring to come in spite of the cold.

'Do you think we should check for footprints, to make sure she did come this way?' Kate asked tentatively. She grabbed at the door to try and stop herself sliding off the seat.

'We know she came this way,' Greg shot her a quick look. 'Fasten your seat belt, then you won't get thrown off if we tip over. This track will be impassable if we get any more rough weather.' He whirled the wheel round as the vehicle skidded sideways into a pothole.

'Perhaps if you went a bit slower.'

'We've got to get there before she does. Hell's teeth!' He hauled at a gear lever, forcing them back onto the track. A spatter of raindrops hit the windscreen as they brushed some trailing ivies and clematis, the bare, woody branches of traveller's joy already showing tiny new buds. Ahead, on the track something moved. He slowed the Land Rover and they both peered through the streaked windscreen. 'What was it? Is it Allie?' Kate leaned forward eagerly.

He shook his head grimly. 'Deer.' He pulled the wheel round. 'Christ, how far has she got?'

'Is there another way? Could she have taken a short cut?'

'I don't think so. This is the short cut. Everyone always goes the quickest way.'

Kate looked across at him. The worry was clearly etched into his face, the lines between nose and mouth drawn tight and deep, the frown lines between his eyes accentuated in the near-darkness. For all his constant bickering with his sister he obviously loved her deeply. She felt a wave of something like affection for him. Curbing her instinct to touch his shoulder in an attempt to give him some sort of comfort she stared ahead through the windscreen once more. 'She'll be all right. We'll find her.'

'Indeed we will.' His voice was grim.

They drove on for several minutes in silence, then Kate let out a cry. 'There she is! Look. Over there.'

Greg swung the Land Rover off the track towards the figure sheltering beneath a tree. They had drawn up beside it and Greg was already opening his door before they realised at the same moment that it was not Allie. The figure which staggered towards them was that of a man. Suddenly Kate recognised him.

'Bill!' She leaped out of her seat and ran round the vehicle, slipping in the mud. 'Bill, what are you doing here?'

'Watch out. He's hurt.' Greg caught her arm, stopping her in her tracks. In the light of the headlamps they could both see the stream of blood running down his face.

'Bill?' Her stomach turning over with fright, Kate put her hand on Bill's arm. 'Bill, are you all right? It's Kate.' The look he turned on her was completely blank.

'I'll get one of those blankets.' Greg turned and sped back to the car. Returning, he pulled the warm rug round Bill's shoulders. 'Can you walk, old chap? Come on. Only a few steps. Kate, open the back door. Help me boost him in. Christ, what's happened to him?'

Her mouth dry with fear, Kate helped Greg push Bill up onto a back seat. He was a big man and his limbs did not appear to be co-ordinating properly. She could feel him shivering under the thick blanket. She climbed in beside him, fumbling for his hand. When she found it she chafed it gently, appalled at the chill of his skin. 'I think we should get him to hospital, Greg,' she murmured.

Greg nodded. 'As soon as we've found Allie. Has he had a fall? Hold on. I'll get the other torch and the first aid box.' Rummaging in the box at her feet he glanced into the darkening woods. Kate was staring at Bill's face. That look of blank terror; the fixed, pinpoint pupils, the chilled skin. It was the same as Alison. Identical. She glanced at Greg who had slipped onto the narrow seat opposite them. 'This is how Allie looked when I found her.' She felt Bill give a small shudder.

'Christ!' Greg bit his lips. 'Look, can you cope in the back? We've got to go on and find her.'

'We'll be OK. He's not quite as cold as she was.' Even so, she could hear his teeth chattering. She bent to open the first aid box. It was difficult rummaging in it in the unsteady light but she managed to find antiseptic and some dressings. As gently as she could she swabbed the blood off his forehead, wincing at the bruises on his hairline. He sat unmoving, seemingly oblivious to what she was doing, though he flinched once or twice as the swab did its work. Taping a dressing across his forehead, she was carefully mopping some of the blood that had dripped down his cheek when he gripped her wrist with sudden, ferocious strength. 'Alison!' he gasped.

'Have you seen her?' There was a strange cold sickness building in Kate's stomach. She left her hand in his. His fingers were very strong but they were still very cold.

Bill shook his head, bewildered. He put his hand to his temple and drew it away, looking at his fingers as though he expected to see blood. He did not seem to realise there was a dressing there. 'She hit me.'

Greg had climbed into the driving seat. He turned, his elbow over the back. 'Alison hit you!'

'I tried to stop her. She was with someone. The woman I saw on the beach.' To her horror Kate saw Bill's eyes fill with tears. 'I wanted her to come with me,' he went on. He was mumbling slightly. 'I tried to stop her. I took her arm and it was then she turned on me. Her face was –' he shook his head back and forth several times '– it was ferocious. She grabbed a fallen branch. It was a big one. Out there. Pine or fir or something. She lifted it up and crashed it down on my head. I must have lost consciousness. I don't remember anything else until you came.'

'You're imagining it! Allie couldn't, wouldn't do such a thing!' Greg said, horrified.

Kate glanced up at him.

'What woman did you see with her, Bill?' she asked.

He shrugged. 'I saw her in the distance on the beach. She was tall. Thin. I thought it was you. She was wrapped up tightly against the wind. Her hair was long, falling down, all sort of dishevelled. She was angry. I could feel her anger.'

Greg's eyes flicked from Bill's face to Kate's. He wondered briefly if he looked as frightened and shocked as she did.

She met his eye. 'You'd better drive on, Greg,' she said. Her voice had gone husky.

He hesitated for a moment. Then he nodded. Turning round he reached for the ignition.

Kate put her arm round Bill's shoulders as the Land Rover lurched forward again and she felt him slump against her, shivering. As calmly as she could she edged another blanket out of the pile Greg had thrown on the floor in front of her and tucked it round him. Then she groped for his hand again and held it tightly.

It took them another ten minutes to reach the cottage. Greg swung the Land Rover to a standstill on the grass, directing the headlights past the building, down towards the beach. Kate leaned forward, staring ahead across the back of the seat. 'I can't see her.'

Greg reached for the torch and swung his door open. 'You stay here. I'll go down to the grave.'

'I should come with you.'

'You can't.' His voice was curt. Then he relented. Coming round to the back he swung the rear door open for her. For a moment he looked into Kate's eyes. He held out his hand to help her out, and she felt him squeeze her fingers. 'You've got to stay with Bill. Take him into the cottage. Get the kettle on or something. I won't be long. We know where she'll be.'

'Be careful, Greg.'

'I will.' For a moment he stood gazing at her then he leaned forward and gave her a swift kiss on the lips.

She watched the torchlight receding into the distance. After a few moments it disappeared. The Land Rover was silent save for the ticking of the engine as it cooled. Kate swallowed. For a moment she didn't move. Bill didn't stir. Taking a deep breath she groped in the pocket of her jacket for the keys. She could see a pale glow of light from the window to the right of the front door where she had left the lamp switched on.

'Where are you going?' Bill jerked awake as she turned away.

'To open the cottage. You'll be more comfortable there. It's warm. Do you think you can walk?'

'Where's Greg?' He seemed aware for the first time that Greg had gone.

'He's looking for Allie –'

'On his own?' The fear in the man's voice made her skin crawl.

'He'll be all right. Greg's a big chap. And he knows he has to be careful because you've warned us.' She was astonished at how reassuring her own words sounded. 'Shall I go and open the door first? Then I'll come back for you.'

'No.' Bill's fingers clamped around her wrist. 'I'm coming with you.'

To her relief the house was still warm. Propping Bill against the wall, she switched on all the downstairs lights and drew the curtains. Then she looked at him properly for the first time. His face was a mass of purple bruises. There were lacerations in his scalp she had not seen in the dim torchlight. His sweater and anorak were torn and soaked with dried blood. She schooled her face carefully into a reassuring smile, hoping he had not seen her horror as she saw the extent of his injuries. 'Bill you must lie down.'

'No. No, I want to stand for a minute.' He pushed himself away from the wall. 'Can we have something hot to drink? I'm so cold.'

'Of course. She took his arm and ensconced him on the stool in the kitchen while she reached for the kettle. All the time her ears were straining for sounds outside the house. She had locked the front door and drawn the bolt.

'I ought to try and clean up those cuts for you a bit better,' she said as she reached down a couple of mugs.

'Don't bother. I'll be all right.' Beneath the bruises his complexion was returning to a more normal shade. His hands though, when he reached for the coffee, were still shaking visibly.

'Can you tell me any more about it, Bill?' she asked quietly as she sat opposite him. 'About the woman. Did she say anything?'

He shook his head. 'Not a word. She just sort of hovered in the background.'

'Hovered?'

'Well, watched. You know. Her face was impassive. Uninvolved. She didn't seem to care what Allie was doing.' His voice trembled again.

'Bill.' Kate leaned forward and touched his hand reassuringly. 'Allie is not herself. She had an accident of some sort on the beach.' She hesitated. 'I don't think she knew what she was doing. As for this woman.' She bit her lip. 'God knows who she is. Bill?' She realised suddenly that his attention had been distracted. He was staring at the curtained window, his head slightly to one side.

'Did you hear that?' he said.

'What?' She held her breath, listening.

'I thought I heard something – a shout – I don't know.' He put his head in his hands.

'Shall I go and look?' There was nothing she wanted to do less than open the front door but Greg was out there, alone.

He shook his head mutely. 'You can't help him,' he said after a minute. 'No one can.'

'What do you mean?' She stared at him, whitefaced.

He shrugged. Suddenly he laughed but she saw a tear slide down his cheek. 'I came over to ask you to supper. I bought some wine and there's a M & S gourmet meal waiting back at my place.'

She leaned forward and reached for his mug to refill it. 'That's a lovely thought. I shall look forward to it.'

'But not now. Now everything is changed.'

He was like a child talking. Working it out, plaintive that his plans had been spoiled. She looked at him, frightened. Bill was strong, reliable, always there to lean on. This shaking, shocked man was not the Bill she knew.

'We'll do it tomorrow,' she said, keeping her voice bright. 'Perhaps for lunch. I'd like that.'

'Yes. For lunch.' His voice was dull. He pressed his hand to his head again. 'I feel sleepy, Kate.'

'Why don't you lie on the sofa? I'll stay with you and keep you company.' She rose and took his hand.

He followed her through into the living room and lay down obediently, his long legs hanging over the arm. She pulled a rug over him, and arranged a cushion gently under his head. He looked very uncomfortable on the small piece of furniture, but he curled up on his side and closed his eyes without a word. She sat down opposite him, watching him uneasily. Almost certainly he had concussion; perhaps a cracked skull. And there was nothing she could do to help until they managed to get him to a hospital.

She leaned back in the chair, gazing into the fire. The house was silent. She strained her ears, trying to hear through the walls, listening for sounds from outside. There was nothing save a gentle scraping of the rose tree at the window which faced the sea. Where was Greg? Why was he taking so long?

XXXVII

Standing on the shingle bank Greg shone the torch ahead of him into the sleet. All he could see were silver needles slanting across the dark; beyond, he could hear the sea above the howl of the wind. The whole world seemed insubstantial, moving. Sand. Shingle. Water. Grasses. All swayed and shifted, formless in the torchlight.

'Allie!' Greg yelled. His voice was puny against the roar of the elements. 'Allie. Where are you?' Why hadn't they questioned her more? Why hadn't they tried to find out why she had run out into the cold at dawn to come here by herself? Why hadn't they asked her more about what happened? He shuddered violently. What had made her attack Bill, a man she had met dozens of times? Was it that she hadn't recognised him, or had the attack come from someone else; the woman with her. And who was the woman? Oh Christ, let her be all right!

He moved forward, his boots slipping on the wet stones, and swept his torch around again. Nothing. There was nothing.

Shivering, he forced his way into the teeth of the wind, emerging between the dunes onto the beach and turning towards the grave. In the roaring darkness he could see the flash of breakers and hear the suck of the water as they pulled back against the wind. Beneath his feet the ground seemed to be shaking.

'Allie!' His fear, under control in front of Kate, was rising by the second. Fear for Allie and fear for himself. He had walked on this beach a thousand times in every weather, at midnight and in the day but never before had he found it so ball-breakingly terrifying.

His steps slowed as he approached the grave. He could feel his heart thundering beneath his ribs and he felt cold and sick. The torch was slippery in his hands as he thrust it ahead of him, seeing the beam slide waveringly towards the edge of the excavated hollow.

'Allie?' His voice was growing hoarse. 'Allie? Prat! Where are you?'

It was dark in the hollow below the beam. The rushing hail and wind seemed to speed across it, leaving the gaping blackness very still.

Sliding in the wet sand he climbed to the edge and looked down, directing the beam swiftly up and down the digging. For a moment his heart stood still. A black cavern seemed to open up beneath his feet, leading down and down forever. The torch hovered for a long moment over it, then he forced it to move on and saw that it was just a trick of the light, a lie perpetrated by the shadows. There was nothing there but a slightly higher ridge in the sand, which had cast that deep impenetrable shadow. Beside it lay the usual scattering of shells and weed. The grave site was empty. He felt a rush of relief and at the same time a sharp pang of disappointment. He had half expected – hoped – to find her kneeling there, just as Kate had found her. He leaped down into the hole. The torchlight showed up every bump and indentation in the sand, but he could see no footprints, just the pitting of the rain.

Crouching down out of the wind he directed the torch at the sandface, running the beam of light along the strata. It was smooth now, wet, compacted. There was no sign that he could see of any remains. No bones. No hand reaching out from the sand, the broken fingers beckoning in supplication. He felt his body shaken by another uncontrollable shudder. Standing up he swung the torch round. Where was she? Where in the name of Christ was she?

This damn grave. If she hadn't found it all would have been well. He aimed a vicious kick at the sand and with a sharp sense of pleasure saw a large section of the sandface break away and fall. He kicked again. It would only take a few minutes. The sand was so soft. They would think it was the sea. Behind him the tide was hurling itself ever closer across the beach. Gritting his teeth, he drew his foot back for another kick at the base of the sand cliff when he heard a sound behind him. He swung round, holding his torch out before him, like a weapon.

'Allie!' His voice came out as a croak. 'Allie?' He tried again. 'Where are you?'

The destruction of the dune forgotten, he scrambled, slipping and stumbling back into the wind. The torch beam was growing less sharp. He shook it angrily and slapped it against his palm. His hands were ice cold and wet, his fingers growing numb.

The darkness was empty. She could be anywhere. In the woods; on the beach; in the marsh. Anywhere. Helplessly he turned slowly round, staring into the tearing darkness, feeling the ice-cold fingers of sleet sliding down inside his collar, fighting the battering of the wind, hearing the throb of it in his ears.

She could be back at the cottage by now. His hand tightened on the torch. Supposing she had gone there? Supposing she was hiding in the woodshed or amongst the trees, waiting for Kate to come back? She liked Kate. She seemed to trust her. Surely that is what she would have done. Turning, he began to retrace his footsteps, his back to the sea.

It was then he thought he saw a figure at the very edge of his torch beam.

It was a man.

As the figure moved sharply backwards Greg's feeble torch-light caught the glint of what looked like a knife blade before he vanished into the darkness.

207

XXXVIII

'Bill?' Kate's whisper sounded strangely loud in the silence of the room. 'Bill, are you asleep?' He was lying on his side, huddled beneath the blanket she had tucked around him, his head on the pillow she had brought down from her bed. One of the cuts had reopened on his temple and she could see a slow trickle of black blood soaking through the dressing onto the flowered pillowcase, adding to the entwined cornflowers and poppies an obscene decoration which shone slick and oily in the light of the lamp. 'Bill?' She knelt down next to him. His sleep frightened her. It was too deep, too sudden and she didn't know what to do.

She squinted at her wristwatch. It was seven o'clock. Two hours since they had left Redall Farmhouse, perhaps an hour and a half since they had reached the cottage. So where was Greg? She stared up at the curtained window, straining her ears. The whole cottage was full of the sound of the wind and the sea. The walls seemed to vibrate beneath their combined assault. Trickles of draught played across the floor, shifting the curtains uneasily, flaring the flames in the stove, teasing the fringe on one of the cushions on the chair.

Taking Bill's hand in hers, she stroked it gently, appalled by the heavy coldness. Slipping her fingers around his wrist she felt for the pulse. She thought there was something there, but it was terribly faint, barely a fluttering beneath her chilled fingers. Too frightened to touch him any more she tucked his hand under the blanket and stood up. The stone still lay on the hearth where she had put it after bringing it in earlier for Alison. Humping it up onto the top of the stove she opened the doors and pushed on another log. Then she turned to her cassette player. The Requiem was still there. As the music filled the room she glanced back at Bill.

It was a long time since she had prayed. Not since she was

a small child and had knelt beside her bed, her hands folded neatly and fervently beneath her chin, and prayed for a pony. It had never materialised and her faith which for a short time had blazed inside her, had shrivelled with disappointment and died. She wasn't sure she knew how to pray now. Our Father, which art in Heaven. Save Bill. Please, save him and keep us safe. Deliver us from evil. For thine is the kingdom. She kept her eyes open, scanning the room, trying to allow the music to soothe and comfort her. Behind her on the windowsill the puddle of water inside the frame had broadened. A drip fell from the ledge onto the floor. Then another.

The 'Pie Jesu' finished. The room fell into silence which was broken only by the sharp click as the player switched itself off. Even the wind seemed momentarily to have died away. For a while Kate sat without moving, then she stood up. She picked up the towel she had fetched from the bathroom and wrapped it round the hot stone.

'Bill?' she whispered. 'Bill? Are you asleep?' The heavy warm bundle clutched in her arms, she stood looking down at him. His face was remote, white, utterly composed. The wound on his temple had stopped bleeding now. She could see where the blood had clotted into a dried crust on his skin. 'Bill, I'll put this by your feet. It will help keep you warm.' But she couldn't. His feet were hanging over the edge of the sofa. She lifted the blanket and eased the towel-wrapped stone in near his knees. His trousers were damp. Perhaps she should try and take them off. Then, wrinkling her nose, she realised what had happened. He had peed all over himself as he lay there on the sofa. Closing her eyes she tucked the blanket back over him.

She had never tried to find the pulse in anyone's neck before, but she didn't really expect to find it. The total emptiness in the room told her that he was dead. Turning away she sat on the floor in front of the fire and wrapped her arms around her knees, as the tears poured down her cheeks.

XXXIX

He had been hiding in the reeds, lying on his stomach where he had a good view of the proceedings, close enough to see the rivulet of drugged mead running down the man's chin, dropping into the hollow of his collar bone and on down his chest. As the garotte tightened, he stood up, slowly, in full view, his hands on his hips. He saw Nion's eyes open; he saw the realisation dawn, saw the man's hands flail towards his throat as he tried to tear away the ligature and he began to laugh. 'It was not the gods who ordered your death, Nion, prince of the Trinovantes!' he shouted into the sunrise. 'I arranged it all, I and the priests I bribed. You die to avenge my honour at the expense of your own.' He could see the flesh bulging on either side of the knotted cord around the young man's throat. He could see the trickle of blood as his struggles grew more frantic. 'No man lies with my wife and lives. Not prince, not druid, not Briton, not Roman! And no god will greet you and lead you across the Styx. You die dishonoured.'

'Marcus!'

The scream from the far side of the sacrificial site sounded like that of a wild bird. He swung round, numb with shock, as behind him the priest plunged the knife into Nion's back. For a second his wife's beauty stunned him, illumined as she was by the rose gold rays of the rising sun, then the hatred congealed again in his breast and he stared at her with cold loathing as she gazed wildly past him, towards Nion.

For a moment the young man straightened, his dying gaze fixed on the sun. His hands dropped away from the garotte around his throat. As the light died from his eyes his knees buckled and he fell forward into the waiting mud.

She was standing knee deep in the rushes, her blue gown wet, clinging to her body, her hair unbraided, loose on her shoulders, her face crazed as she ran towards him, her arms upraised, her nails clawed like those of an animal.

'May the gods of all eternity curse you, Marcus Severus, and bring *your putrid body and your rotten soul to judgement for what you have done here this day!'*

As her cry echoed across the marshes a flight of duck rose from the reeds, soaring above their heads and setting off towards the rising sun, a vee of glittering green and gold as they rose into the fresh light of the new morning.

Greg was running. His breath was catching in his chest, rasping in his throat as he propelled his feet forward through the soft sand, the weakening torchbeam moving wildly back and forth in front of his pounding feet.

'Allie!' His cries were almost inaudible. His throat was dry and there was no breath left for shouting. 'Allie, for the love of Christ, where are you?'

The sea was coming closer. His feet were wet. There was a trail of seaweed clinging to his shoe. He splashed on, feeling the icy water immerse him to the knees, then draw back, leaving the cold against his flesh under the wet cloth like a burn. 'Allie!' He veered away from the sea, feeling his feet on firmer sand now, pounding up the beach. 'Allie!'

The man had gone again. Twice he had glimpsed him, a shadow in the greater darkness, and each time the torch had picked out the blade of the knife.

Stumbling to a standstill he stared round, his chest heaving, feeling the ice in the hail rasp against the delicate linings of his nostrils. His face felt raw, as though it had been flayed of several layers of skin. He bent forward, switching off the torch for a moment as he rested his forearms against his thighs, his whole body heaving with the effort of drawing in those painful, shuddering breaths. Beside him another wave toppled onto the beach, racing towards him, stopping just short of his feet, showering him with spray. He straightened, his ribs a straight-jacket of pain, and stared round. Without the narrowing, confining point of light from the torch, the horizon had suddenly enlarged. The darkness was no longer so absolute. He could see the tangled luminous lace of the white water on the heaving darkness of the sea; he could see the glint of the wet sand, the heavy umber of the clouds bellying over the water. His head throbbed and spun and he staggered as his eyes focussed in horror on the man who had appeared again only a few feet from him now. He could see him clearly. The strong, patrician face, the hair plastered to his forehead by the rain, the heavy, sodden garment clinging to his body, the forearm naked beneath a swathe of darker material with the raised dagger clutched in his fist.

ANGER
HATE

Probing, thrusting, expanding, rage whirled within the confines of Greg's brain. The torch fell from his fingers as he raised his hands to his head and tore at his flesh, trying to free himself from the pain. He stepped backwards. His foot, tangled in a lump of gelatinous weed, slid and turned over. The sudden shaft of agony in his ankle forced him down abruptly onto one knee and he felt his arms flail sideways.

The figure was suddenly closer. It was smiling and the deep-set cavernous eye sockets, which for a fraction of a second had seemed empty, blazed with light.

Greg felt all the air wrenched out of him. He could feel the suspension of his lungs – rigid, straining to take in another breath which would not come. His head was whirling. His eyes were growing dim. The white had gone from the sea. All he could feel was the cold. A strange, all-encompassing cold which came from deep inside him and was working its way, layer by layer through his body towards the surface. When it reached his brain he would die. He knew it clearly. And, just as clearly, he knew that this was what had happened to Alison and to Bill. He would die here on the beach of hypothermia and no one would ever find him because the tide was coming in. He raised his eyes to the face of the man who stood over him but the figure had gone. The night was empty. High above the bulbous obscenity of cloud a waxing moon sucked at the sea and spewed the tide ever higher across the land.

XL

With shaky determination Kate reached for her scarf and wound it around her head. She grabbed her thick jacket and her gloves, and with a last desolate look at Bill, she picked up her torch and opened the front door. She had to find Greg.

She stopped for a moment at the corner of the cottage, gathering her strength, then, not giving herself any more time to think, she launched herself down the track towards the dunes into the teeth of the gale.

The excavation was deserted. She stood at the edge of it staring down, her eyes narrowed against the cold, her back to the wind, feeling the damp seeping through the shoulders of her jacket. The wall of sand opposite her had fallen away at one point, and in the torchlight she could see huge patches of discolouration in the exposed strata. She stared at it blankly. The outline of the body was quite clear in the torchlight. It was crouching in the foetal position, exposed in the sand and peat where the wall of the excavation had fallen. She stared at it. For a moment she was too shocked to react. The torch in her hand was wet between her gloved fingers. She steadied it desperately. Had Alison seen this? Was this what had tipped her over the edge into a madness that had driven her to attack and kill a man? She swung the beam round frantically, turning into the wind again, searching for Greg, but she could see nothing in the streaming darkness. Beneath her feet the ground shuddered as the waves crashed onto the beach. The tide was high, within yards of where she stood. She could feel the spray soaking her back as each new wave thundered up the sand and shingle. She had never felt so alone.

'Greg!'

Her tears were scalding her icy cheeks; she dashed them out of her eyes with the back of her arm. Where was he? She didn't have the first idea where to look. The dunes and beach and marshes stretched for miles in both directions. Had he walked along the sea's edge looking for Allie, or had he turned back inland towards the cottage, or even back into the woods?

She swung the beam back towards the dune face. It was still there, the body, crouched in silhouette in the wet peat. Beneath it the first trickles of frothy water, thick with weed were seeping into the hollow. Unless the tide turned now the dune would be lost. She turned away. She didn't care. It would be a good thing if it were never seen again as far as she was concerned. Defiantly she began to walk along the edge of the tide, turning northwards, keeping an unsteady parallel course to the sea. If she walked north for fifteen minutes, then inland a hundred yards or so and back, still parallel to the sea, she wouldn't get lost. That would be better than wandering aimlessly amongst the dunes. Shutting off her torch, she rammed it into her pocket. The sea had a strangely luminous quality about it and she found she could see quite easily as she walked. Better to save the torch until she needed it. She did not specify to herself what such a need might be.

There was a movement in the darkness ahead of her. She stopped, squinting into the wind. Alison? It wasn't Greg, of that she was sure. She could feel her breath quickening in her throat. Alison was still out here in the dark. Alison, who had killed a man. Her hand closed over the body of the torch, but she didn't switch it on. Slowly she moved closer to the spot where she had caught a glimpse of movement.

The figure had moved. She was slightly to Kate's left now, almost behind her. And she was beckoning. Beckoning back towards the grave. It wasn't Allie. This woman was taller, slimmer and she was wearing some sort of blowing, willowy garment – a skirt in spite of the weather, and it looked like a long skirt. Kate's mouth had gone dry. She found her breath was coming in small, tight gasps. Was this the woman Bill had seen with Allie – the woman who had watched the girl attack him and not lifted a finger to help?

'Claudia?'

It was a whisper. Please God, don't let this be happening. Don't let her be real. Kate took a few steps backwards. The woman seemed to follow her. Adjusting her fingers carefully along the body of the torch until her thumb found the switch, Kate drew it out of her pocket. Sliding the switch across she lifted the torch in one quick movement and shone it straight into the woman's face. She did not react. The beam went straight through her. Kate could see the streaming grasses and the blowing sand behind her as if her figure was made of glass.

'Help!' The voice was distant, almost obliterated by the wind. 'Help me, someone! Kate!'

Keeping her eye on the woman, Kate backed away. The woman seemed to follow her. Her face was clearly visible. It was a young-ish face, pale in the torchlight, the cheekbones high, the hair unravelled, whipping around it. She could see the colours clearly for all their transparency. The bright blue of the gown with the stains upon the front, the redness of her hair, the strange golden eyeshadow on the deepset eyes.

'What is it? What do you want?' Kate's voice was shaking. She was vividly conscious of the cry from behind her but she did not dare to turn her back on the figure. It didn't seem to threaten her in any way but her own terror was so great she was incapable of doing anything other than backing slowly away from it. Slowly, the figure was holding out its hands, but at the same time it was fading. The background behind it was growing stronger. It was her torchbeam, she realised suddenly. It was weakening. 'Oh no. Please don't run out.' She switched off the beam and switched it on again, keeping it directed desperately at the figure. But the woman had gone. She directed the beam up and down, seeing it waver as her hands shook. There was nothing there. Nothing but the violence of the night. She swung round and began to run towards the place from where the voice had seemed to come, the torchbeam swinging violently up and down as she moved and then she saw him. Greg. He was sitting on the edge of the sand, almost in the water.

'Greg. Oh Greg, thank God!' She flung herself down beside him, almost knocking him backwards on the sand, tears streaming down her face. 'Greg. Greg.' She couldn't do anything but repeat his name over and over again as she clutched at his jacket.

His arm went round her and he pulled her against him. 'It's OK, Kate. It's OK. Calm down.'

'I saw her. I saw the ghost. Claudia. She was standing by the grave. And there's a body there, Greg. A body.' Sobbing, she pushed her face against his sleeve. His jacket was wet and cold, and she could feel him shivering through it. 'Greg. Bill's dead.'

The words were muffled through the green waxed material, but he heard them clearly enough.

'Oh sweet Christ.' He hugged her closer against him. 'Listen, Kate. You have to help me. Strange though it may seem I'm not sitting here with my feet in the sea for fun. Something has happened to my ankle. I've got it caught in something. Have a look, there's a love. Each time I try and lean forward to free myself I go all peculiar.'

He had lain there watching the tide rising higher and higher, swimming in and out of consciousness. He was not catatonic like Alison, nor dazed like Bill, but he knew, as he lay back, resigned to the cold that was creeping through him, that he was well on his way to unconsciousness. Then he had seen the crazily flashing light of Kate's torch for a second in the dunes behind him. The sight had given him the shot of hope which had sent the adrenalin coursing through his veins again.

Kate crouched forward. She held the torch close to his ankle. 'It's fishing line. All wound round your foot. The hook has gone through your shoe.'

She felt her stomach clench at the sight of the blood soaking into the sand around his foot. The line had tangled around a whole pile of jetsam weed which had snagged against something which stuck out of the sand. She tugged at it, careful not to touch his foot, but it was immovable, tethering him there in the path of the tide.

Greg eased himself forward on his elbow. 'Can you free it? I've got a knife somewhere in one of my pockets. Inside, here.' He tried to drag the zip down from his chin but his hands were cold and slippery and he could feel another wave of nausea and dizziness building.

'I'll look for it.' She left his foot and came close to him again. The knotted ends of her scarf were fluttering wildly in the wind. He could feel them drumming against his cheek as she knelt beside him, her eyes narrowed. 'Wait, I'll have to get my gloves off.' She gave him the torch and he saw her pulling at the fingers of her glove with her teeth. He switched off the torch. He could see how weak the battery was, and he ducked suddenly as a stronger than usual wave hurtled up the beach and crashed almost over them, covering them both in icy spray. The glove was off and she had the heavy zip in her hand now, coaxing it down.

216

He could feel the cut of the wind as it slid inside and froze his skin. Her hand followed and he felt her fingers rummaging against the jacket lining. Easing his position slightly, he lifted himself onto his other elbow and put his free arm around her shoulders, trying to borrow some of her warmth. But her jacket was slick and cold with rain. She glanced up at him, her face only inches from his and he saw her smile grimly in the darkness. 'Hang on in there. I'll find it. You've got more pockets than the Artful Dodger.'

'Keep searching. I wish I were feeling better. I'd take the chance to make a massive pass at you!' He gave a wan grin.

'In this cold I might just reciprocate.' Her hands were methodically searching each of the deep pockets on the inside of his jacket. Another wave broke across them and she heard herself gasp at the cold.

His arm tightened around her. 'It's getting closer.'

'It must be nearly high tide. It was in over the edge of the grave.'

'There's an easterly wind. It's pushing it higher than usual.' He glanced up at the sky over her head. 'Thank God the moon, wherever it is, isn't quite full. We're not into springs or I would have been a goner by now.'

The pain from his foot was hitting him in pulses, travelling up his leg and receding but always constant from his ankle down. He did not dare to try and waggle his foot. The pain when he had done that had caused him to faint. When he had woken up it was because a wave had broken across his face; he had come to, choking. He did not dare to contemplate what the pain would be like when Kate freed him. If she could free him. Perhaps he would pass out again – God's own anaesthetic. He tried to concentrate on her hand roaming the pockets of his jacket. He was not so far gone that the old system had not reacted a little to the questing hands of a beautiful woman. Her hair smelt of woodsmoke and ash from the woodburner, and her body, pressed close to his, had the slightly musty smell of wet wool, but under it all he could smell the faintest traces of whatever scent she had put on that morning – whenever that was, and her own indefinable smell, the smell that registered subconsciously and made you like or hate, love or loathe, or remain purely indifferent to every human being you met. In her case, in spite of the aggravation she had caused him, he found it extremely attractive. He lay back a little, trying to ease the weight on his elbows, jumping as the movement jarred his leg.

'Sorry. Did I hurt you?' She had noticed.

'Not you. The hook.'

'Found it.' At last her fingers had closed over the knife. She pulled it out of his pocket and sat back. Catching hold of his zip she dragged it up. 'Can't let you freeze to death.' She shook her head as another deluge of cold spray poured over them. Officially, the tide had turned half an hour before, but nobody seemed to have told the sea. She glanced at his face. 'I'll try not to hurt you.'

He forced a grin. 'Listen, if I keel over, just go on and do it. Cut the line, and get the hook out while you can and stop the bleeding.' He paused to catch his breath as another spasm of pain took him. 'Don't try and move me though. I'm heavy.' Another wan grin. 'When I come to, I'll be able to wriggle away from the sea. Then you can go and get help.'

'OK boss.' She put her hand on his for a second and squeezed it. Then she picked up the torch.

Whatever happened she mustn't drop the knife. She tried to pull open the blade with cold, wet fingers but they slipped off uselessly. Swearing, she tried again, hands shaking. Behind her Greg had lain back on the sand. His eyes were closed. His face in the torchlight was almost transparent. She breathed on her fingers for a moment to warm them and then, half unzipping her jacket, pushed her hand under the opposite arm to dry her fingers on the wool of her sweater and bring some feeling back. The next time she tried to prise open the blade the knife opened easily. With a sigh of relief she edged down his body until she was opposite his feet. His free leg was hunched up beneath him where he had tried to drag himself away from the approaching water, his other leg stretched out, the foot twisted, the patch of blood beneath it washed away now by the tide. Holding the torch close to the foot, Kate studied it. Her hands were shaking and she felt suddenly very sick. The first job clearly was to cut away the tangled fishing line where it was wrapped around the ankle. She inserted the knife blade flat against his sock and pulled tentatively against the nylon line. Nothing happened. She pulled harder. Greg groaned. Kate bit her lip. 'I'll cut away this bit from the rest.

218

That way I won't hurt you so much.' She felt around beneath his foot amongst the weed. Another wave swamped her hands and she clutched desperately at the knife, waiting for the water to draw back again. How had he got it tangled so tightly? It was as if someone had tied the line around and around the foot, tethering him to something buried in the beach. She scrabbled with her hands in the sand. There were shells and an old dead crab tangled amongst the weeds, then the ice-cold, wet sand, then her fingers encountered something hard. A balk of timber completely buried. The line seemed to come from under it. She pushed the knife blade against the timber and gave a ferocious jerk. The line parted. Cautiously, she felt for the next bit. That was easier. It came away at once as did the next. But the final strands, wound round his foot seemed to be pulled tight. Of course, he had done that himself, struggling to free his foot. Shaking the water out of her eyes she worked steadily, strand by strand until at last the final piece fell away. He groaned again. She ignored it. Gently she felt around his shoe. The fish hook in his foot was the largest of several that had been knotted into the line. Curved and barbed they lay glittering in the torchlight, all except the one which disappeared into the side of his trainer. She studied it for a moment, biting her lip. Then she turned, shining the torch for a moment onto Greg's face. 'Shall we try and drag you back away from the sea before I do anything else? I've cut the line that's holding you.'

Lifting himself on his elbows he nodded. 'I'll be too heavy for you, Kate. Just help me while I edge back.' He crooked his good leg up, wedging his heel into the wet shingle and sand and pushed. Sweat broke out on his forehead. Grimly clenching his teeth he did it again, painfully inching his body back away from the sea's edge. The drag on his bad foot was agony. He could see Kate bend over him. He knew she had gone behind him and he felt her hands under his shoulders. One more good pull and he would be out of reach of the waves, where the line of wet debris showed the tide had at last begun to pull back. The pull was agonising. He bit back a cry, then everything went black.

'Greg! Greg? are you all right?' Kate laid him gently down. 'Greg?'

His eyes were closed. She stared round in the darkness, feeling suddenly terribly alone. But she knew what she must do: get the hook out, now, while he was unconscious. Biting her lip in concentration, she wedged the torch so the beam shone on his foot and groped in her pocket for the knife. The trainer laces were easy after the fishing line; and the fabric of the shoe itself was not much tougher. Cutting carefully round the hook she managed to remove the shoe and straighten the twisted foot which was blackening and swollen. She wondered if it was broken. Swallowing the wave of nausea which threatened to overwhelm her, she gently lifted the remaining flap of the shoe and stared down at the hook. It had gone completely through his foot. There was no question of trying to pull it out the way it had gone in. The cruel barb on the end of the hook was half out of the top of his foot, wedged between two tendons. 'Dear God.' For a moment she wondered what to do. There was no choice. Taking as much care as she could not to jolt his foot further, she sliced the remaining length of line where it was knotted around the hook and began to ease the hook into the cold white flesh, pushing it right through his foot.

What kind of bastards left this stuff lying around on the beach to ensnare anyone or anything who walked there after them? She thought of the gull, drowned and cold, its feet laced together with nylon mesh. And this – a line of hooks abandoned by someone who had no doubt decided to go off to the chip shop somewhere down the coast and couldn't be bothered to take his line with him. The heat of anger which washed through her as she worked took her mind off the task she was performing. She wanted to push her hair out of her eyes – long strands of it had pulled free of her scarf – but she ignored them grimly. She had to do this and somehow bandage his foot before he came round, and before, she glanced at the torch, the battery failed. The hook slipped free surprisingly easily. Behind it the wound began to ooze with fresh, dark blood. She tore off her scarf then she fumbled in her pockets, searching for the small pack of tissues she had wedged there days earlier. They were still there. She tore several out of the cellophane and folded them carefully into two pads, one for the entry wound and one for the exit, then she bound them in place with the scarf. She wound the ends round and round his ankle, trying to tie it tightly, then she knotted it again and again. As she wrenched the last knot tight the torchbeam gave up and went out. She flopped back on the beach, wrapping her arms around her legs, her head on her knees, and sat quite still for a moment. She was shaking so much she could not move but Greg's groan brought her to her feet. She crouched next to him and reached for his hand. 'All over. The hook's out and I've straightened your foot.'

'Feels like hell.' He tried to sit up and failed. Closing his eyes he concentrated hard on staying conscious. 'What do we do now?'

Kate shook her head wearily. 'I suppose I ought to try and go for help. We can't move you.' She glanced up without enthusiasm at the stormy blackness of the shore behind them.

His hand tightened on hers. 'I don't like the idea of you wandering around out there on your own. Listen, let me get my strength back a bit, then maybe I can walk.'

Kate smiled wistfully. 'No chance. You've damaged your foot horrendously.'

Greg was silent for a moment. 'If you could find me something to lean on. Some driftwood perhaps. There's masses of stuff chucked up on the beach. If we take it slowly, I'll manage to get back to the cottage.'

The word cottage triggered something in both their minds. Kate collapsed on her knees on the sand beside him and suddenly her eyes were filled with tears again. 'Bill's at the cottage.'

'I know.' He reached over and touched her face. 'But so is the Land Rover.' Somehow he kept his voice firm. 'You have to drive us back to the farm.' He did not mention Alison. 'Have you ever driven a four wheel drive?'

She shook her head wordlessly.

'Well, that doesn't matter. It's easy enough. I was just wondering how far you could get it on the sand.' He thought silently for a moment, then he gave a deep sigh. 'No. It's not worth trying. There's so much mud and soft stuff around. If you got bogged down, that would be our last chance gone. Our only hope is walking sticks.' Somehow he forced a bracing note into his words.

'I'll go and look along the tideline.' Kate wiped her nose on her sleeve – just like a small child, he thought affectionately – and she climbed wearily to her feet. 'I'm not going far. I'm not going out of sight.' She was reassuring herself as much as him.

'There's no need. It's surprisingly easy to see when one's got one's night vision. I can see lots of junk down there now.' He

221

reached out and touched her hand. 'Only for God's sake be careful where you walk, Kate. I don't want you treading on some more of those bloody hooks.'

He watched as she made her way cautiously back down to the tideline. What had happened was a blur; a nightmare which was coming back to him in sudden flashes. He could remember putting his foot down on something slippery; he could remember it sliding away from under him and he could remember going down on one knee in the icy water. That much was clear. He had been running away from something. Or someone. He frowned, cudgelling his memory.

Kate was walking slowly away from him, bending low, groping in the mess of tidewrack. She found an old tree branch and lifted it triumphantly, but it snapped as soon as she put any weight on it and she hurled it away.

She was right at the edge of his vision now. Greg frowned, sitting up straighter, trying to keep her in sight. She was a darker patch in the darkness. Every now and then as she straightened and looked around he could see her face, a pale blur beneath the flying hair. He lost her. Then he saw her again, several yards from where she had been. She was standing upright now, staring out to sea. It was strange. She seemed taller now. Taller and broader, and something had happened to her hair. He glanced back at where he had seen her before and his heart stopped still. She was still there. She had been squatting at the tide's edge, and now she jumped back as a wave hurled itself up the beach. He could see something in her left hand. He glanced back. The other figure was there. Near her. Watching her. The man with the knife.

Christ Almighty!

'Kate! Look out!' Greg's voice bellowed out into the wind. 'Kate, for God's sake look out. Behind you.' She couldn't hear him. Her back was turned and the roar of the wind and water would have deadened all but a foghorn at that distance. 'Oh Christ!' Desperately, Greg leaned forward, trying to drag himself onto his knees. 'Kate!' The bastard was nearer her now. He was moving effortlessly towards her. In a minute he would be right behind her.

'Kate!' His voice had risen to a scream. 'Kate, for God's sake, run!'

He half rose to his feet, lurching forward, and had put his

weight on his injured foot before he realised what he had done. With a cry of despair he pitched forward onto his face. He was unconscious before he hit the ground.

XLI

Diana was stirring a pot of stew listlessly over the hotplate of the Aga. Made from leftovers from lunch to which she had added fried onions and dried herbs from the jars on the dresser, potatoes and mushrooms and carrots, it smelt delicious. The two cats were sitting side by side behind her, respectfully watching her every move, their admiration of her cooking technique obvious in every alert glance.

Patrick was sitting at the table behind her. His fingers drummed on the table top rhythmically and slowly, a drum roll for the march to the scaffold.

'Stop that, Paddy!' Diana's voice was sharp.

He stared at her and then looked down at his hand as though he did not know he owned it. 'Sorry.'

'They should have been back by now.' She clattered her pans together. 'They should have found her.'

'It's pretty stormy out there, Ma. They might have got the Land Rover stuck. Or they might have decided to stay at the cottage.'

'Or they might not have found her.' Diana turned to face her husband as he walked through towards the kitchen. 'Is the phone working?'

He shook his head. His face was lined with weariness and, as she watched, she saw his hand go surreptitiously to his chest under the flap of his jacket.

'Roger, darling. Go and sit down.' The displacement activity at the Aga forgotten she flew to him and threw her arms around him. 'Come on. Rest. You're wearing yourself out.'

'I should be out there with them, looking.' He shook his head crossly, but he allowed her to steer him towards the fire.

'I'll go.' Patrick followed them. 'I'll take the bike and see where they are.'

'No.' Diana shook her head forbiddingly. 'No, Paddy. You stay here with us.'

'Let him go, Di.' Roger threw himself down in a chair and leaned back, his eyes closed. 'He can get to the cottage and check if they're there.'

'No.' It was a wail of misery. 'No. I want him to stay here. I don't want all my children lost.' Diana sat down abruptly, blinking hard, the strain only just contained.

'I won't get lost, Ma. I know the track like the back of my hand.' Patrick put his hand on her shoulder.

Her fingers sought his and tightened over them. 'But the storm . . .'

'If something has happened – I mean if the Land Rover has broken down, or the track is blocked or something, they have no way of telling us with the phones down. If I go, I can be back in half an hour and I can put your mind at rest.'

'He's right, Di.' Roger didn't open his eyes. 'Let him go.'

Her hand slid helplessly from her son's. He gave her shoulder a squeeze and stepped towards the door.

'Take no risks, Paddy.' Roger opened his eyes. 'No risks at all. If you see anything you can't cope with, come back at once, do you hear?'

'Sure, Dad.'

'No heroics.'

Patrick grinned. 'I'm not the superman type, Dad. Besides, what am I going to find? Mud. Trees. Snow. Cheer up. I won't be long.' He dived out into the hall and came back, dragging on his oilskin jacket. 'Have we got a decent torch?'

'I'll get it.' Diana went back into the kitchen. She rummaged in a drawer. Patrick followed her. 'Don't let Dad go out,' he whispered. 'He's looking awfully pale.'

'I won't.' Finding the torch she switched it on, testing the beam. 'At least it's got batteries. Paddy, I know it's silly, but there have been some strange things going on at that cottage. You will be careful, darling, won't you?'

Patrick nodded. 'Promise.' He kissed her on the cheek and rammed the torch down into his pocket. Minutes later he had let himself out into the sleet.

The cold took his breath away. The ice on the wind felt as though it were cutting his face as he pulled on his gloves and went over to the barn, dragging back the heavy door to find his bike.

The narrow beam of his headlight lit up first the trees arching across the track as the bike slid and bucked over the potholes, then the slushy track itself where the latest set of tyre marks were clearly visible, not yet obliterated by the wet. Patrick concentrated hard on riding the machine without getting thrown off into the undergrowth, his eyes narrowed against the weather, searching out the least hazardous route, peering into the distance for a glimpse of the Land Rover. He was not feeling nearly as brave now he was out here alone. His thoughts kept jumping back to Alison, with her crazy eyes, to Kate's cottage – he thought of it as Kate's cottage, not Greg's – and the mess someone had made there. Was there someone out here in the woods? A maniac on the loose? Or was there really someone or something out there at the grave?

After a particularly bad skid in the thick mud he stopped, trying to catch his breath, bracing his foot against a tree root, aware that all his muscles were trembling with effort and shock. He stared round. The woods seemed awfully dark. The wind was howling between the trees, the sound sometimes rising to a banshee wail, sometimes falling to a moan. Leaning forward, he gripped the handlebars tightly and taking a deep breath, pushed off once more, forcing the pedals round with every ounce of strength he possessed. He would not think about the darkness where the light beam did not reach.

It was with enormous relief that he saw at last the squat outline of the Land Rover parked outside the cottage, silhouetted against the rectangle of a lighted window. Leaning the bike against the wall he hammered on the door. He waited, rubbing the back of his wrist against his nose, pushing his wet hair out of his eyes, then he knocked again. He frowned. Splashing his way through the puddles, he made his way to the front window, but it was curtained and he could see nothing. He turned back to the door and knocked again, hammering this time with his fist. 'Kate! Greg! Hey, let me in!'

At last he heard a sound. Somewhere inside a door banged.

'Kate! Greg! Come on. It's bloody freezing out here!' He paused, sniffing, to listen again. The silence inside the cottage was absolute, in contrast to the roar and scream of the elements outside.

Suddenly he was frightened. 'Kate! Greg! Why don't you open the door?' he shouted once more. He began pounding on it again with both fists. 'Come on. Please.' His voice cracked and slid up into the alto range, something which normally would have embarrassed him terribly. As it was he didn't even notice. He could feel tears pricking at the back of his eyes. He ran back to the window and knocked, pressing his face against the glass, but the flowery curtains with their pale sun-stained linings obscured any view of the inside of the room. He turned back and ran past the door, making this time for the windows at the side of the cottage. The bathroom window was slightly open. He inserted his arm and jiggled the arm of the latch free, letting the window swing outwards a little. The wind caught it and slammed it back against the wall, but it didn't matter. The gap was large enough for him to climb in. He tried to get his knee up onto the narrow sill but his oilskin caught. Swearing to himself he unzipped it and tore it off, feeling the rain and wind blast against his body as he bundled the unwieldy garment up and tossed it in in front of him. Then he levered himself up onto the windowsill, and, holding his breath, squeezed himself in, dropping awkwardly onto the floor. The bathroom was dark. He scrabbled around the wall until he found the door and beside it the pull cord for the light. Tugging at it, he switched it on and stared round. The bath had a scattering of dark wet earth in the bottom. The tap was dripping slightly and he could see the trail scoured by the water in the soil. He frowned. Kate struck him as the sort of person who would meticulously wash out a bath after her, but perhaps like Greg she was also the type to get easily distracted when she was being creative; he forgot to change his clothes and wash and even eat when he was painting.

Tiptoeing across the floor again he opened the door a crack and peered out into the hall. It was dark out there, but he could see a thin line of light showing from the living room. Opening the door further he peered up the stairs. Everything there was dark and silent.

Suddenly he was shy of having broken in. It seemed a terrible intrusion to be in someone's house without their knowledge. He cleared his throat loudly, then realising how frightening that might be if Kate were on her own in there, he called out nervously. 'Kate, are you there?' He knocked on the door and jumped

227

himself at the loudness of the hollow sound he made. 'Kate, it's Patrick.'

He crept across the hall and pushed the living room door open. The room was empty save for a figure lying on the sofa, covered by a rug. He felt a rush of relief. She was asleep. That explained it. He had crept right into the room before he realised that the feet and legs hanging over the arm of the sofa were those of a man.

'Greg?' He moved closer. The air in the room was stale and faintly unpleasant. It was very hot in there. Glancing at the stove he registered that it was glowing with heat. 'Greg?' He pulled the corner of the blanket away from the man's face and gave a small cry of horror. The flesh of Bill's face was discoloured and puffy; his eyes, half open beneath flaccid lids, were glassy and dim. A small stream of saliva had run from the corner of his mouth onto the pillow where it had dried in a sticky trail amidst the black crusts of blood. He was very obviously dead. Patrick reared back, repelled, swung away from the body and vomited onto the floor. 'Oh God! Oh God – oh God – oh God!' He leaned over and vomited again. Groping in the pocket of his jeans for something to wipe his mouth on, his fingers encountered the oily rag which he had used earlier to wipe the dipstick on the Volvo as he checked the engine for his father. He brought it to his face, mopping his mouth and his brow and his eyes, leaving a smear of dark oil across his cheeks. His eyes on the body he backed away from it towards the door. Where was Kate? He reached the hall and slammed the door shut, leaning against it. He felt desperately cold and shivery despite the heat in the house, and his legs were shaking violently. For a moment he thought they were going to collapse under him. He sat down on the bottom step of the stairs and took a deep breath, followed by another. Then he half turned, screwing his neck round so he could gaze up into the darkness of the upper landing. 'Kate?' His voice was husky, barely a whisper. 'Kate, are you up there?'

Somehow he hauled himself to his feet and he began to climb. Above him a door slammed again. 'Kate?' His voice wavered unsteadily. 'Kate, it's Patrick.' He could hear the wind more clearly up here. It was howling around the windows and behind it, a deep, subliminal beat, was the roar and crash of the sea. He reached the landing, straining his eyes into the darkness as he scrabbled along the wall for a light switch. He found it and flipped it on. Both bedroom doors were wide open. The air up here was ice cold in contrast to the fug downstairs. He frowned. In some recess of his mind he was registering that heat rises. It should be hotter up here, unless a window was open somewhere.

'Kate?' He tiptoed towards her bedroom door. Then he stopped. As the shock of what he had seen downstairs wore off a little his brain had begun to function again and the significance of what he had seen dawned on him. No fall could have caused the injuries he had seen on Bill's head and face. The man had been beaten to death. Bill had been murdered and the murderer was wandering round in the dark, perhaps up here now. He thought about the sound of the slamming door. Both doors on the landing were open. He swallowed, tasting once more the sharp, bitter flood of bile in the back of his throat. Kate. What had happened to Kate?

Taking a deep breath he flung wide the door to her bedroom and stared in. The light was on. The room was empty. He looked round, his hand clutching the door handle so tightly that his finger joints cracked. Apart from the bed which had been stripped of its blankets, the room seemed undisturbed. Peaceful. It was full of the scent of some unidentifiable perfume – not Kate's. He sniffed, puzzled. It was pleasant. Nice even, but it disturbed him. He could feel the hairs on the back of his neck stirring, like the hackles of a dog. He didn't like it. He turned away from the door and went across the landing to the other room. The light showed it to be empty with only a few stacked suitcases and cardboard boxes piled near the window on the far side of the floor. There was no sign of Kate. The windows in both rooms, he noticed suddenly, were tightly shut. So which door had he heard banging, and why the cold? He shuddered.

The kitchen. He hadn't checked the kitchen. 'Kate!' Suddenly he found his voice again. 'Kate, where are you?' Taking the short flight of stairs two at a time he threw himself at the kitchen door. The room was empty. He stared round frantically. She had to be here. Please God, let her be here somewhere.

But there was nowhere for her to hide, nowhere else she could be. On the table in the middle of the room he noticed suddenly the bottle of Scotch they had given her. It lay on its side, empty. The lid, he found after a moment's hunting, was on the floor in the middle of another patch of damp wet earth; a cautious sniff told him the damp was whisky.

'Oh God! Kate! Greg!' He glanced round wildly, then turning on his heel, he ran to the front door and tore it open. All he could think about was getting home as fast as possible. Dad would know what to do. Dad would somehow make it all right.

Outside, the darkness was opaque, wet, like the bottom of the sea. He could see nothing, hear nothing but the wind. He was searching frantically for his bicycle when he heard the door bang behind him. Terrified he looked round. The bicycle wasn't there. He couldn't find it. It was gone.

For a moment in blind panic he thought of taking the Land Rover. He had driven it before, on the track. He ran towards it, scrabbling at the door handle and, dragging it open, looked inside. There were no keys in the ignition. With a sob of frustration he slammed the door and looked round again.

Where was his bike? It must be here. Desperately he ran a few steps up the track and suddenly he saw it, right in front of him. He couldn't stop in time and he had fallen over it before he knew what was happening. It bruised his shins, and he felt the warm trickle of blood down his leg, but he ignored it, dragging the machine upright, fumbling numbly for the pedal. It was only when he was once more on the track through the trees, his face streaming with rain and tears that he realised he had left his oilskin where it had fallen on the bathroom floor in the cottage.

XLII

Half-way back along the track the back tyre of Patrick's bicycle punctured. The machine ploughed deep into the mud and stopped. Panting, Patrick tried desperately to force it on, then, giving up, he dismounted and let out a string of expletives. It was impossible to ride with a flat tyre when the track was in this state. He was nearly in tears. Around him the woods seemed to be closing in. He grabbed the front lamp and slid it off its bracket, directing it around him in a long sweep. The trees hung over him, Arthur Rackham fingers clawed, ready to snatch at his flesh, their trunks twisted into leering faces, sleet dripping from their boughs like acid, trying to eat away his face.

With a sob he hurled the bicycle away from him and began to run, his boots slipping and sliding, his body pouring with sweat, the cycle lamp, clutched in his hand, illuminating the puddles, throwing blinding reflections from the black, treacly mud, sparkling from the sleet crystals which had caught in the undergrowth. After a hundred yards or so he had to stop, doubled up with an agonising stitch in his side. He put his hand to his hip, gasping. It was then he saw a figure in the shadows.

He froze, the stitch vanishing as though by magic. Slowly he straightened. He fought the urge to switch off the torch. Whoever it was would have seen where he was by now anyway. Slowly he swept the light around in an arc, playing it on the slick black of the branches, seeing the shadows shrink back and regroup just beyond the reach of the beam. He was holding his breath. If it was Kate or Greg they would have come forward at once when they saw him. The picture of Bill's battered, dead face swam up before his eyes and he thought for a moment he was going to black out. He took several steps backwards, feeling twigs and thorns tearing at his jersey, but he felt safer with the narrow trunk of a spruce at his back, solid between his shoulderblades.

231

At least no one could get him from behind. Under the tree the smell of resin was clean and sharp and strong. It cleared his head a little. Once again he swept the torch round. There was no one there. No one in sight. He crouched lower trying to steady his breathing which sounded deafening in his ears.

He wasn't sure how long he stayed there. Perhaps five minutes, perhaps much longer, but suddenly he realised that he was shivering violently. The sleet was soaking into his thick sweater and he was ice cold. There was no sign of any movement in the trees. Whoever it was had long gone. Cautiously, he forced his cramped legs to move, crawling out of his hiding place and straightening up. He swept the rapidly-dimming lamp round once more. Nothing. He looked left and right up the track, seeing it disappear into the distance and he felt a sudden moment of total terror. Which way was home? In his panic he had lost his bearings completely. He closed his eyes. Idiot. Nerd. Keep calm. He knew this track like the palm of his own hand. Look for a landmark; he had always prided himself that he could recognise any tree in the wood.

He swept the lamp around again, concentrating this time on the vegetation. But it all looked so different in the dark; so sinister. For a moment he was afraid he was going to cry. His eyes were stinging suspiciously; he had never felt so desolate or so lost in his whole life, but as he cast one last desperate glance around, he spotted the lone pine. It was a tree they all knew well – a tree which rose head and shoulders above the others in the wood, an ancient Scots pine whose distinctive shape had been out of range of his torch as he flashed it around. With a sheepish grin of relief he headed towards it, realising that he was barely ten minutes from the farmhouse.

As he rounded the barn he caught sight of someone crouched in the lee of the wall and he stopped abruptly. Whoever it was was not moving. He glanced at the house, reassured by the comforting sight of light pouring from the downstairs windows, then he looked again at the figure. His cycle lamp had barely enough strength to light the path at his feet, but he shone it warily in the direction of the barn wall.

'Allie?' His voice was hoarse. 'Allie, is that you?' He took a few steps closer. 'Allie?' He ran towards her. 'Allie, what is it? What are you doing out here? What's wrong?' Catching his sister by the arm he swung her to her feet.

She stared at him. Her eyes were hard and blank. There was a deep scratch down one side of her face from her temple to her jaw and her hands, he saw as he pulled her towards him, were raw and bleeding.

'Come in, Allie.' His voice was urgent. 'Come in. Quickly. ' He glanced over his shoulder. There was a murderer out there in the woods and by the look of things he had already attacked his sister.

Pushing open the front door he half carried, half dragged Alison in. 'Ma!' He propelled her into the living room. 'Ma!'

Diana flew towards them. 'Dear God! Alison! What happened to her?'

Patrick bit his lip. He shook his head, for a moment unable to speak, watching as Diana guided Alison towards the chair next to the fire and knelt beside her, chafing her hands.

Behind him his father had risen from the kitchen table where he had been staring blankly at *The Times* crossword for the last forty minutes. After a first horrified glance at his daughter, Roger turned to his son. He was appalled at the expression on Patrick's face. Putting his arm round the boy's shoulders he guided him back to the kitchen and sat him down at the end of the table. Without a word he reached into the cupboard and produced a bottle of brandy. Pouring a quarter of an inch into a tumbler from the draining board he pressed the glass into his son's hand. 'Drink first. Then tell me,' he instructed.

Patrick took a sip from the glass. His eyes started to stream. 'It's the brandy. Making my eyes water,' he whispered. 'It's the brandy.'

His father's hand was on his shoulder. 'It's OK old chap. It's OK. Take your time.' Roger glanced over Patrick's head towards his wife. She was tucking a blanket around Alison's knees. The girl had not spoken or moved since she had sat down.

'Give her some brandy, Di.' Roger called. He pushed the bottle across the table.

Diana looked at him. Her face was white as she left Alison's side. She stood for a moment staring down at Patrick. 'What's happened to them, Roger? What in God's name has happened to them?'

Patrick took another gulp from his glass. He was clutching it so tightly his knuckles shone white through his chapped skin. Taking a deep shuddering breath he looked up at his father. 'Bill Norcross is dead. He's at the cottage. He's been murdered.' His eyes flooded with tears again and this time he made no effort to hide them. 'His head is all bashed about, and his face . . .' He drank again, the glass trembling so much in his hands his parents could hear it banging against his teeth. 'I couldn't find Kate or Greg. I called and called. The cottage was empty so I came back, then I got a puncture and I saw someone skulking in the woods . . .'

Roger sat down abruptly. His face was grey. He closed his eyes as a wave of pain shook his body. 'Try the phone again, Di. Perhaps by now they've reconnected it.'

For a moment she didn't move, then she turned and ran towards the study.

Alison watched her with blank eyes. 'The truth has to be told,' she said slowly. She pushed the blanket away and staggered to her feet.

Her mother stopped abruptly in the doorway. 'Allie? What do you mean. Did you see what happened?'

Alison smiled. 'It was Marcus. She's told me everything. It was Marcus. He killed them all.' Stooping, she picked up Serendipity who was curled up on the sofa, and cuddled him in her arms.

'Killed them all?' Diana whispered. Her mouth fell open in horror. 'Killed who?'

Alison smiled again. She kissed the top of the cat's head. 'All of them. All in the same grave.'

'Who?' Roger was suddenly there behind them. He grabbed his daughter's arm and swung her to face him. The cat gave a yowl and fought free of her grip, leaving a long scratch along her arm but she didn't appear to notice. 'Alison! Answer me. Who has been murdered? Where is your brother?' Diana's gasp of horror was lost in his next shout. 'Alison! Can you hear me? Who has been murdered?'

'All of them.' She smiled vaguely. 'Did you expect him to let them live?'

Roger swung round to face his son. 'What does she mean? Did you see the Land Rover? Did Greg get to the cottage?'

Patrick nodded. 'It was parked outside.'

'So he must have seen the –' he paused. 'He must have seen Bill there.'

'I suppose so.' Patrick took a deep breath. 'Someone had put

234

plasters on his face. He was tucked up on the sofa. Someone had tried to look after him.'

'Greg and Kate perhaps.' Diana clutched at the thought. 'They must have found him. Tried to help him.'

'We need the police.' Roger frowned. 'Did you try the phone?'

Diana shook her head. She was staring at her daughter who had not moved. Alison was standing before the fire, her arms hanging loose in front of her. From the scratch on her left forearm the blood dripped slowly and steadily onto the carpet.

Roger strode past her towards his study. In thirty seconds he was back. 'It's still dead.' His face was grim. 'I'll have to take the car and try and get help from Joe's.'

He glanced at Patrick who was still sitting at the kitchen table, staring deep into his empty tumbler.

'Paddy!' His voice was sharp as he used the baby name for his son which Patrick hated so much.

Patrick jumped. He looked up at his father. There was bewilderment in his eyes.

'Patrick, your mother must stay here and look after Alison. I'm going to leave you here to take care of them both. I want you to lock the door behind me, and bolt it. You are not to let anyone in. Anyone at all, do you hear?'

'Dad, you can't go.' Patrick rubbed his sleeve across his face. He was shivering again in the soaking wet clothes. 'Let me take the Volvo. I know how to drive it.'

'He's right, Roger. You can't go.' Diana looked from Alison to her husband and back in an agony of indecision. 'It should be me.'

'No. Alison needs you.' Roger shook his head.

'I can do it, Dad,' Patrick said quietly.

The fact that Roger hesitated even for a second showed more clearly than any words just how weak and ill he was feeling, but he shook his head slowly. 'Not in this weather. It's too dangerous. And it's not as though I have to do anything but sit there and let the car do the work. I'll drive it up to the road and along to Joe's. Joe will do the rest and bring me back.' He hesitated, seeing the strange mixture of emotions cross his son's face and reading them all. Relief that he did not have to go out again; worry about his father; indignation and mortification that he was not considered old enough to cope.

235

Roger sighed. 'Get the car out of the barn for me, there's a good chap.' He smiled. 'I'll get my coat.' He took Patrick's arm and drew him to one side. 'You'd be more use here, old chap. If anything happens.' He glanced at his son's face and knew that the sop he had just thrown to the boy's pride was in fact the truth. 'You're stronger than me. You can protect them better. I want you to load the shotgun and keep it in here near you.'

Patrick stared. Then he nodded. 'I'll get the car.'

Unhooking the keys from the small rack behind the door he pulled it open and peered out. He didn't want to go out again. Outside was hostile and frightening. It had lost all the safety and charm he had known all his life – the secret wonder of the black sky sewn with stars, the rushing clouds, even the rain and snow. He had loved them all for that special clean fresh smell that comes at night, that quietness which enfolds the countryside and wipes out for a few hours all the brash horror of the twentieth century.

Shutting the door behind him Patrick sprinted across to the barn. Pulling open the heavy double doors he groped for the light pull and dragged it on, flooding the huge, shadowy building with a harsh blue light from the double strip of lights which hung, crazily crooked, from their chains and electric cables twenty feet above the ground. There was an uneasy rustle from above him in the rafters and he heard a querulous piping cry. Some bird, roosting there out of the wind, was bitterly resenting his intrusion.

He opened the door of the car and slid behind the steering wheel, slamming the door behind him and ramming down the locks. It was bitterly cold in there. His breath fogged the windscreen. Glancing through it with a frown he pulled out the choke and turned the key. The faithful old car started first go and he sat there for a few minutes, teasing the accelerator with his toe, feeling the cold engine warm slowly into life. Frowning with concentration he engaged reverse gear, and craning over his shoulder, he backed the car out through the impenetrable trails of its own exhaust and swung it backwards towards the house, parking it neatly outside the front door. Mission accomplished.

Climbing out he hesitated for a moment then he reached in and turned off the engine. Locking the door, he let himself back into the house. No point in leaving the car there, engine running.

He watched his father wrap himself in coat and muffler, and turned away, pretending not to see Roger slipping a bottle of pills into his pocket. He didn't need reminding that his father was in terrible pain. The strain of his face and the pallor of his skin told it all.

'Here.' Roger handed him a key. 'The gun cupboard. I'm serious, Paddy. Load it and keep it near you. And check every door and window is locked and bolted after I've gone. I'll be back as soon as I can.'

'Be careful, Roger.' Diana ran to him and threw her arms around his neck. 'I shouldn't be letting you go like this. Oh, darling, be careful.'

He smiled grimly. 'I will. Don't worry.' He turned to the door and pulled it open. In the few short minutes since Patrick had come in the sleet had turned to snow. It whirled down out of the sky and already it was settling in the sheltered corners of the garden. He frowned as he peered through it then he turned. 'Where did you leave the car?'

'Right there. Outside.' Patrick gestured past him. He frowned and took a step past his father.

The car had gone.

Patrick's mouth fell open. He stared round helplessly. 'But I left it here. Here.' He stood where he had parked it. In the light spilling out from the front door the faint rectangular outline in the snow where the car had been parked was clearly visible. He looked up at his father, distraught.

'You didn't put the brake on,' Roger said slowly. He was frowning. The patch of gravel where the car had been was totally level.

'I did.' Patrick contradicted hotly. 'Of course I bloody did! And I locked it. It's been taken. He must have been watching me all the time.' He could feel the hair standing up on the back of his neck. 'He must have broken in and hot wired it.'

'It only took me three minutes to come out after you parked it, Patrick,' his father said slowly. 'No one could break into a car that fast. Not without taking a sledge hammer to the window and we'd have heard that. The brakes can't have been on.' He was staring down at the ground.

In the thin covering of snow there was no sign of any car tracks.

XLIII

Marcus stared at the woman who was his wife and his eyes were hard.
She had never looked so beautiful. Her hair was wild, loose in the wind,
her eyes fiery as she ran towards him. He gave a cold smile, his arms
folded across his chest, aware of the priests drawing away from them,
aware of the body sinking slowly, face down, in the soft mud of the
marsh. The blood red of the sunrise spilt across the reeds, reflecting in
the still waters around them. She was running towards him, but it
seemed to take forever for her to reach him, to lift her hand, her nails
clawed, towards his face, to duck beneath his raised arm and snatch the
sword snugly sheathed at his belt. He stepped back to protect himself and
she laughed. The sound made his blood curdle. She raised the sword.
'Curse you, Marcus. Curse you. Curse you. You will not keep me from
him.'

The sword seemed to catch for a moment against the flimsy stuff of her
gown. Then it was free, sliding into her belly like a knife through cheese.
She stood for a moment, upright, strong, proud, her fists still clenched
around the hilt as she pulled it towards her, not acknowledging the pain,
a daughter of Rome, then slowly her knees began to sag as the blood
splashed out over her skirt.

Kate swung round, her eyes straining in the darkness. She had
the feeling someone was standing behind her. 'Greg?' She glanced
round wildly, but she couldn't see him; she had walked farther
than she thought. The beach was deserted. There was no sign of
him sitting on the sand. Her heart began to pound unsteadily as
if she had been running and she felt her mouth go dry. She
clutched the piece of driftwood she had picked up from the tide
edge, feeling it cold and wet and solid against her fingers and
slowly she began to retrace her steps, straining her eyes into the
darkness. Dear God, where was he? She could feel little trickles
of panic running up her back. He couldn't have gone. He wouldn't

have gone. He had to be there somewhere. She dashed the sleet out of her eyes, realising as she did so that it was more like snow now, light and feathery, caressing her skin where before it had been hard and sharp.

There it was again. The strange conviction that there was someone near her. Someone beside her, close beside her, so close she could feel the heat of his body, sense his bulk. 'Idiot!' In her fear she spoke out loud. She veered towards the sea trying to free herself of the feeling and felt a wave breaking over her boots, showering her with spray. She jumped back out of reach of the next and felt it again – the absolute conviction that there was a man standing beside her. She stopped walking and stood quite still staring round. There was no one there. It was some trick of the wind and the weather. Gritting her teeth she turned her back on the sea and began to walk up the beach. 'Greg!' Tucking the piece of wood beneath her arm she cupped her hands around her mouth. 'Greg! Where are you?' Trudging wearily on she scanned the darkness again. She frowned. She had suddenly realised that she was heading back towards the sea. Somehow in the dark she had turned completely round and, without noticing it, she had strayed back below the high water mark in a lull between waves. The roar of the sea and the wind had disorientated her and now she could see a wave racing towards her. She froze. It towered up above the rest like a tidal wave. Tsunami. The word flashed into her mind unsought. Desperately she turned to run but she couldn't. She seemed to be rooted to the spot. It was as if someone were holding her, forcing her forward towards the onrushing water. She could almost feel the grip on her arms, propelling her onwards.

'Greg!' She heard her voice rising into a scream as the towering water seemed to lift above her head. 'Greg!'

As the water crashed forward over her, knocking her backwards onto the shingle the last thing she heard before the roaring filled her ears was a man's laugh.

She awoke to find Greg bending over her. 'Thank God you're all right. Oh Christ, Kate, I don't know what's going on.' He was lying beside her, she realised, his body shielding hers, one arm across her almost as though they had been making love. He must have dragged himself towards her over the wet shingle, his poor useless foot agony as he moved. 'I saw the wave. I saw him push you. I thought you were dead.' He clutched at her hand, holding it against his chest.

Desperately she tried to clear her head so she could think. 'Who pushed me?'

'Marcus. It was Marcus, Kate. I saw his toga, his cloak, I saw his sword. He was beside you, then he pushed you towards the sea and I saw that great bloody wave rising up . . .' He leaned forward and laid his head on her chest. It was a strangely comforting feeling – completely unsexual. She reached up and stroked his hair.

'Marcus doesn't exist, Greg. He's not real. He's a statue. A joke. An imaginary ghost.'

'There was nothing imaginary about him.' He was mumbling into her jacket. 'He was real. I saw him push you. I saw you shoot forward towards that wave. He was real, he tried to take over my mind. He's done it before, and each time I've pushed him away. I didn't realise what was happening; I didn't understand. But now, for some reason he wants us both dead.'

She lay back for a moment, staring up at the sky, her eyes narrowed against the softly drifting snow. It was falling harder now, settling higher up the beach out of reach of the water, clogging the dunes, drifting before the wind. 'Why? Why does he want us dead?'

He shook his head. 'I don't know. It's something to do with that bloody grave. We've disturbed him.'

'It's not his grave. He's buried in Colchester.' She rolled towards him, dislodging his head so that he was lying face down next to her. Gently she put her hand on his back. 'Can you turn over? Let me help you to sit up. We've got to try and find some shelter.' Where was her carefully garnered piece of wood? She glanced round but there was no sign of it in the darkness. The sea must have snatched it from her before it tossed her back on the beach. She dragged herself up to her knees, groaning. Her whole body seemed to be one big bruise. She was soaked to the skin and already she could feel herself growing seriously cold. If they were not careful they were both going to die of hypothermia.

Greg, with a small sigh had lain back on the sand and closed his eyes. For a moment she felt total panic. He was dead. He had just died, next to her, between one moment and the next, like Bill. 'Greg!' Her voice rose to a scream.

He opened his eyes and smiled. 'You have a plan?'

Her relief was so overwhelming she nearly kissed him. 'We have to keep moving. However much it hurts you. It's the only way to stay alive. Sod Marcus. If he comes near us again we'll pray or something. Doesn't that chase off ghosts? We'll make the sign of the cross. The sign against the evil eye. They are always doing that in historical novels and it always works.'

Greg's smile deepened. 'Do you know what the sign against the evil eye is?' He seemed to be content to lie there. Like her, a moment before, he could feel the soft engulfing peace of the snow closing over him.

'I'm sure I can work it out. Come on, Greg. Move. You've got to move. Try and roll over. If you crawl, you can keep your weight off the foot. Come on. You mustn't give in.'

With a groan he obeyed her, swinging himself over until he was lying with his face pressed into the cold, wet sand. A shaft of pain shot through him and he felt the heat of his own sweat like a mantle flowing over his cold body. With a grunt he dug his elbows into the sand and dragged himself forward a couple of feet. Falling flat again he groaned out loud. 'It's going to take me a while, like this.'

'It may take all night, but we're going to do it.' She was grim. 'If you can't do it that way you'll have to stand up and lean on me.'

'It's tempting, but I think if I try and stand I'll pass out again.' He clenched his fists and with a superhuman effort dragged himself forward again. Then he collapsed. 'It's no use. I can't do it. You've got to go for the Land Rover. It can't be far to the cottage.' He raised his head with an effort and squinted into the whirling snow, willing it into view.

'I can't leave you, Greg.' She was kneeling in front of him.

'You must or we'll both die. I'll be OK. I'll keep moving forward, like this, parallel with the sea. Don't attempt to drive down onto the soft sand. Keep to the firmer stuff away from the dunes. Just get as near as you can. Realistically, we'll only survive if we get into the Land Rover. I've had it and you're soaked through. Even if it does get bogged down we'll have a chance in there and they'll find us more easily.' He dragged himself up onto his elbows. 'Do it, Kate. Here, take the keys. They're in my pocket.' He groped painfully inside his Barbour and withdrew them with numb

241

fingers. Dropping them into her palm he forced himself to smile.

Her hand closed over them. She looked at him in despair. He was right. He couldn't get back on his own.

She climbed to her feet and began to drag off her jacket.

'No, don't be a fool.' He shook his head angrily. 'You need it as much as I do. The slightest move leaves me pouring with sweat. I'll be all right. You keep it on and get back as fast as you can.'

She nodded grimly. For a moment longer she hesitated, then she turned and began to run unsteadily back down the beach, the wind behind her now, which made it easier, without the snow and sleet in her eyes.

Her exhaustion seemed to have reached a plateau where pain and chill had withdrawn behind some automatic programmed response. On and on she went, sometimes slowing to a walk, sometimes jogging, faintly aware that part of her was listening over her shoulder for the sound of pursuit. But pursuit by whom? Marcus?

Snatching great lungfuls of air, she pounded on, driven by her fear. She had to get back to the cottage. She had to find the Land Rover. There was no question of getting lost with the sea constantly at her left hand, crashing on the shore, drawing infinitesimally back, worrying the sand like an animal reluctant to abandon its prey, yet glancing up the beach again she found she was beginning to panic. Where was the cottage? Surely she should be able to see the lights from the windows by now. She had left them on. She remembered distinctly. She had left them on because she could not bear to leave poor Bill in the dark. Tears flooded her eyes and she brushed at them with the wet, icy sleeve of her jacket and stopped.

Bending double she drew in great rasping gulps of air, not daring to look behind her, keeping her eyes strained into the darkness. Then, suddenly she saw it. The rising silhouette of the dunes against the white of the distant trees, and the angular black shape which was a roof. There was no sign of any light from the upstairs windows.

She swallowed, willing her heartbeat to slow down as she turned her back on the sea and looked for the track between the dunes. The cottage garden was white with snow; beneath the wall it had drifted in the wind and was heaped into shallow piles already several inches thick. Not giving herself time to think she followed the wall towards the front and peered round it. The Land Rover stood where they had left it. She closed her eyes and sank against the wall, weak with relief. It was only at that moment that she realised that she had half expected it to have gone. Leaving the shelter of the wall she walked towards it, then she stopped abruptly. The front door of the cottage was wide open.

'Bill.' Her lips framed the words silently. Her stomach was churning suddenly and her legs seemed incapable of co-ordinated movement, but somehow she forced herself to walk towards the door. Light poured out of the hall, showing the snow white and clean. There were no signs of any footprints.

She crept to the door and peered in. The sitting room door was open and she could see the curtains blowing against the window. The cottage stank of vomit. 'Allie?' Her voice came out as a croak. 'Allie?' she tried again. 'Are you there?'

The effort of will required to force herself to walk forward and peer into the room was enormous, but somehow she managed it. It was as she had left it. Bill still lay on the sofa; nothing had been touched. Cautiously she stepped inside. The woodburner had cooled down. There was no welcoming glow from it now. The room was distinctly chilly. She took another step forward, pressing her forearm against her mouth and nose in an attempt to filter out the evil smell in the room and stopped, overwhelmed with horror and disgust. The blanket which she had drawn over Bill's face had been pulled back. His face, blue and puffy was turned towards her, his eyes half open, staring blindly straight at her. In front of him on the floor was a pool of vomit.

Turning she ran back towards the front door, trying desperately to control her own retching. She tore out of the house and running to the Land Rover, slumped over the bonnet, her head cradled in her arms, her stomach feeling as though it were somersaulting against the back of her throat. For several seconds she stood still, fighting her nausea, her legs trembling, then at last she managed to grope in her pocket for the keys. She found them and staggered to the driver's door, trying desperately to insert one in the lock. It was several seconds before she realised that the door was not locked. Dragging it open she pulled herself onto the seat and slammed it shut. Then she burst into tears.

Her glasses. She had lost her glasses. Sniffing frantically she groped in her jacket with shaking hands until at last she found them, pushed into an inner pocket. Rubbing her eyes with her wet sleeve, she put them on and leaning forward she inserted the key into the ignition. Fumbling with the unfamiliar gears, she slammed the gearstick back and forth until she managed to find first and at last she pulled the heavy vehicle round to face the sea and jerkily she began to drive towards the dunes.

'Come on. Come on. Please don't get stuck, you bastard, please don't get stuck,' she begged, her voice husky as she peered forward desperately through the streaked windscreen.

The Land Rover lurched across the grass and down onto the sand, its tyres slipping and sliding but somehow keeping a grip on the shifting, wet surface of the beach as she threaded her way at a snail's pace between the dunes, the headlights catching a whirling wall of sand and snow and sleet. When at last she saw the sea, it was a barrier of angry white rising in front of her, hurling itself at the land. Biting her lip she tore the wheel round, heading north now, keeping the vehicle moving at a steady walking pace, every muscle tense as she willed the wheels to keep their traction. Where was he? Oh please God, let her find him. She had never felt so lonely in her life, with her eyes straining frantically ahead, scanning the beach and the dunes to her left as she looked for Greg's hunched figure on the sand. She hadn't been too long, surely? She cursed the time she had wasted weeping like some useless, spineless feeble fool, and desperately she pulled the vehicle further away from the sea as it lurched into a weed-strewn rutted pool and ground to a halt. 'Oh, no!' She juggled the clutch and accelerator desperately, trying hard not to drive in deeper. 'Please. Please, come on.' She wrenched the gear levers back and forth frantically as the car rocked forwards and lurched to a standstill again, the wheels spinning. 'Damn you!' She hit the steering wheel in fury. 'Come on. Come on!' In the cold remorseless beam of the headlights the beach was unrelentingly empty of life. Sleet whirled in the double light beams, the sand gleamed coldly and beyond it, even above the sound of the engine, she could hear the angry roar of the sea. Biting her lips in concentration she tried a new combination of gears and suddenly, wonderfully, the old vehicle lurched into life and dragged itself out of the hollow, shaking itself free like some great hippopotamus which had been wallowing in the mud. 'Be careful.' Kate was talking to herself openly now. 'Be careful you silly cow. Look where you're going. Next time you won't get out.' Her hands gripping the wheel so tightly her knuckles cracked, she leaned forward again, peering into the shadows at the edge of the head-light beams.

Midnight: the witching hour, in this empty, godforsaken, lonely place.

Where in the name of God was he?

XLIV

'Allie?' Diana leaned over her daughter's bed. 'Allie, can you hear me, darling?' The child was cold again, her skin clammy, but she wasn't shivering. After her first outburst she had said nothing at all as her mother led her upstairs, ran a hot bath and helped her undress. Normally Allie would have protested wildly at the thought of Diana even coming into the bathroom while she bathed but now she stood meekly while Diana undressed her, lifting her arms obediently like a small child as her mother pulled off her sweater and tee shirt, and stepping quietly into the bath. Sitting down she drew up her knees and hugged them, resting her chin on them, eyes closed, as Diana sponged her back with warm water. 'Do you want to lie back for a bit to thaw out?' The child was so thin. How had she not noticed that she was losing so much weight? Diana went on sponging, watching, horrified, as the scented water trickled down Allie's staring ribs and around the prominent knobs of her backbone. 'Allie, did you hear me? Do you want to lie down and have a bit of a soak?'

The shake of the head was barely visible.

'Come out then. Let's get you into bed,' Diana spoke briskly. 'Then I want you to tell me what happened. Did you see Greg and Kate?'

Alison stood woodenly whilst her mother towelled her dry and moved her limbs with the same automaton jerkiness as before as her nightshirt was pulled over her head. Obediently she allowed Diana to lead her to her bedroom and there she climbed into bed. It was only as Diana put the teddy into her arms that she showed any emotion at all. Clutching the toy against her chest she turned on her side, pulling her knees up below her chin until she was curled in the foetal position, and she began to cry.

'Allie, sweetheart.' Sitting on the bed beside her, Diana put her hand on the girl's shoulder. She felt helpless and afraid. 'Sweetheart, please. Don't cry. You're safe now.'

But Alison went on crying, sobbing into the teddy bear's fur until at last she fell asleep.

Diana sat there for a long time, her hand on her daughter's thin shoulder then at last she stood up. Turning off the main light she left the small bedside lamp burning and, leaving the door ajar, she tiptoed out of the room.

The living room was empty. 'Roger? Paddy?' She went quickly to the study. That too was empty. 'Roger?' Her voice rose in panic. 'Patrick? Where are you?' She retraced her steps to the front door and pulled it open. The front garden and the grass which led down to the saltings were a uniform white beneath the whirling darkness. There was no sign of her husband or her son. Closing the door again she bolted it and walked slowly back to the fire. They must have both decided to go up to the main road after all. She stared round the room. The two cats were sitting together on the sofa, a pair of recumbent lions, shoulder to shoulder, staring into the embers of the fire. The sight of them reassured her, but for the first time for years she found herself wishing they had a dog. If there was someone out there in the woods a dog would at least alert them. Her gaze went thoughtfully to the shotgun which Roger had left propped in the corner, a box of cartridges on the chair beside it.

Unable to sit down and relax she walked through into the kitchen and began to tidy it. She was on automatic pilot. Her entire concentration was fixed outside the house, listening.

'We should have brought the gun, Dad.' Patrick was scared. He kept as close as he could to his father as they walked up the track. At their feet the torch beam was searching the ruts for any sign of footprints or tyre marks.

'It's not thick snow. It's hardly settled here, under the trees. If he'd come this way we would have spotted something by now.' Roger was indignant rather than scared.

He did not believe that there was a murderer skulking in the woods. Whoever had attacked Bill would be long gone by now. He stopped, glaring down at the pale circle of torchlight as it rested on a patch of muddy pine needles gleaming with watery sludge. It made no sense, all the same, to take unnecessary risks.

The car had not come this way. Of that he was convinced. And they had left Diana alone in the farmhouse. Better to go home and search again outside the door where the car had been standing. A stranger might after all, have driven off across the garden. No, he halted that train of thought. There had been no trail of destruction through the bare flowerbeds. The other possibility was that he had driven across the lawn and down onto the marsh. The garden was more exposed on that side of the house. Perhaps the snow had indeed hidden the tracks or they had missed them in their initial panic at finding the car gone.

He led the way back, swinging the torchlight left and right this time, scanning the darkness between the trees, conscious that Patrick was so close beside him that he could feel the boy's shoulder brushing his own. He found himself wishing suddenly for both their sakes that Patrick was small enough to be held by the hand.

Outside the front door they stopped. Roger drew a deep sigh of relief. The pain was coming back. He could walk no further. He followed Patrick to the door and waited, leaning against the wall while Patrick banged on it, thankful that the darkness hid his face.

The door opened within seconds and Diana fell on them both. Hugging them to her she dragged them to the fire. 'Thank God! Did you get through? Is the doctor coming? And the police?'

She looked from one to the other and her face fell. 'You didn't get there, did you,' she said in a small voice. She sat down abruptly.

Roger sank down beside her and took her hand. He shook his head. 'The car's gone, Di. It's been stolen.' He leaned back and closed his eyes.

'So he was here. Right here outside this house.' Her eyes went to the curtained window near her. She closed them weakly, slumping against Roger's shoulder. 'What are we going to do?'

'Nothing. Not tonight.' Roger was suddenly so tired he could hardly speak. 'We'll just have to pray that Greg and Kate are together and safe. Greg will look after her . . .'

His voice trailed away as he thought suddenly about Bill. Bill was a man; a big man and he had not been safe.

'It will help no one if we go searching for them in the dark. Far better to keep ourselves safe here until daylight. We'll check again that all the windows and doors are locked and wait it out. There is nothing else we can do.'

'I'll check, Dad.' Patrick had been standing looking down at his parents. He fought off the wave of fear which had been building inside him as he realised suddenly and completely that they were as helpless and afraid as he was; that for the first time that he could remember they were not going to be able to bail him or themselves out of the situation.

His father looked up at him and their eyes met. 'It'll be OK.' Roger gave a wan smile. 'We'll sort it all out in daylight.'

'Sure, Dad.' Patrick turned towards the stairs. Then he stopped. 'Greg's going to be all right, isn't he?'

'A great big chap like Greg? Of course he is.'

'But he wasn't in the cottage.'

'I expect they were looking for Allie.'

'And he doesn't know she's safe.' Patrick's voice rose unsteadily. 'They'll go on looking, Dad. Greg won't give up.'

'They'll be all right, Paddy.' Diana forced herself to stand up. 'Greg is not a fool. He'll realise there is nothing he can do in this weather. He and Kate will go back to the cottage or they'll come here. Now you go upstairs and check everything's all right, while I put the kettle on. Don't wake Allie, but double check her window too.'

She watched her younger son nod and turn away. Then she glanced down at her husband. His face was grey, his eyes shut. Miserably she pulled the rug from the back of the chair where she had folded it that morning – yesterday morning, she corrected herself as she glanced at her watch – and she tucked it round him, then she went to the Aga and slid the kettle onto the hotplate.

XLV

Kate stopped the Land Rover and closed her eyes. There was no sign of him. She had driven up and down the beach three times slowly, edging the vehicle closer and closer to the water's edge, taking it as far to the north as she dared, far beyond the area where they had walked. He must have wandered up into the dunes where, she knew, she did not dare to try and drive. All she could do was go back slowly, further from the tideline this time, hoping he had seen her lights and was even now trying to drag himself towards them.

Cautiously she let in the clutch, turning this time towards the sea for one last sweep of the boiling waves with the headlights. It was then she saw him. He was kneeling at the water's edge, waving at her.

'Greg!' Incautiously she accelerated towards him and for an awful moment she felt the wheels lose their grip and spin, then she was near him. Drawing to a halt she leapt out. 'I couldn't find you.' Shaking her hair back out of her eyes she ran to throw her arms around him.

For a moment he didn't move then she felt him return the hug, his mouth against her hair. 'Kate. Oh, Kate,' he murmured. For several seconds they clung together, then gently she freed herself.

'Come on. Try and stand. We'll put you in the back so you can rest your leg along the seat.' He was desperately cold. She could feel the chill from his body through his wet clothes. 'Come on, Greg. You've got to stand up. I can't lift you.'

He was staring at the vehicle. 'But I saw you. I saw you out there.' He gestured behind him, towards the sea. 'I heard you call me. I was crawling towards you, then this wave came and drenched me again.'

She glanced up. 'You've lost your bearings and come right back

250

down the beach. Come on. Stand on your good leg. I daren't bring the car any closer to the edge. You'll have to hop.'

'I can't.' He subsided onto the wet sand again with a groan. 'I've had it. I can't move.'

'You can. You've got to.' She gritted her teeth. 'Come on. You can't give up now.' She hauled at his arm. 'I'll find something for you to lean on. You've got to try, Greg.' She was growing frantic.

'OK, OK.' He tried to shake his head. Spray and sleet were cold on his face; tears and sweat, hot. The salt mixture ran into his eyes, blinding him. He could see someone standing behind her. Why didn't she help? It was a woman. Not Allie. Not Ma. 'Give me a hand. Please.' His words were slurring. He felt Kate's arm strong under his; then her shoulder as he hauled himself up. The other woman was helping, no, she was gone. Where was she? He felt his knees buckle. He could not put his left foot on the sand. The rush of the waves filled his head; dimly he could see the outline of the Land Rover. The back door was open. Inside it was safety, warmth, rest. With a superhuman effort he launched himself towards it with three massive hops on his good leg, throwing himself half in through the door. Then he lost consciousness again.

'Greg! Greg!' Kate bent over him. 'Come on, one more effort.' The car was a haven. She wanted them both inside and the doors locked. Behind them the beach was hostile, threatening.

She glanced over her shoulder and saw the shadow; the woman hovering near them. Her skin crawled. The blue dress was still stained; it did not blow in the wind; the sleet did not seem to wet the woman's hair, but she was watching them and Kate could smell her scent. Over the wind and the sleet and the salt smell of sea and sand and weed she could still smell that flowery perfume. She felt sick. Her terror was so great she could not move for a moment. Only a groan from Greg jerked her back from her terrified fascination. She turned. 'Get in, Greg. Get in quickly,' she said urgently. 'Just crawl. Quickly.'

Something of the panic in her voice reached him through the black haze. His hands scrabbled at the seat in front of him; somehow he dragged himself along it and lay, panting, clawing at it to give himself purchase. Behind him Kate caught him round the hips and shoved at him with all her might. Without regard to his injured foot she caught his knees and folded them in behind him and slammed the door on him.

Spinning round she stared out into the night as a new flurry of snow whirled in across the beach. Where was she? She could see nothing now. Desperately she turned and fled round the car, grappling with the driver's door handle, dragging it open and flinging herself into the seat before slamming the door behind her and banging down the lock. With a cry of relief she slumped back to try and get her breath.

The white shape which hurtled onto the bonnet was so close in front of her she let out a scream. She saw a huge, bloodshot eye. Something crashed down on the windscreen and she saw a splintering crack shiver down the glass. 'No!' she flattened herself against the back of the seat, bringing up her arm instinctively to protect her face. 'No! Please! *Greg!*'

Greg stirred. He found himself lying face down on the rough rug spread on the back seat. He clutched at it convulsively and felt an agonising pain shoot up his left leg which appeared to have been folded in half beside him on the floor. 'Kate?' His voice was indistinct, muffled in the rug. 'Kate, where are you?'

'Here!' Her whisper barely reached him. 'Greg. Help! Look!' The fear in her voice reached him through the swimming veil of pain. With an enormous effort he raised his head. Somehow he managed to move sideways, dragging himself up into a sitting position. His teeth were chattering and his body was seized by a wave of violent rigors as he tried to focus on Kate. 'I'm here. I'm here.' He clutched at the back of the seat.

Her eyes still fixed on the windscreen she did not turn round. 'Look.'

It was still there – a huge, flapping white object. Again she saw the eye, yellow, threatening, and then a vicious curved beak. Kate flinched, raising her arm to protect herself, closing her eyes in terror as with a resounding clang a sharp blow descended on the already shivered windscreen.

'Kate –?' Greg's voice was blurred and indistinct.

'It's a gull!' She was sobbing with fear and relief. 'It's a huge gull.' For a moment the whirl of flapping wings and the cruel eyes and vicious beak resolved themselves into a clear outline, the webbed feet scrabbling for a foothold on the bonnet, and then it had gone, launching itself off into the wind and out of sight.

Kate reached for the ignition. Her hands were shaking so much she could hardly start the engine. Frantically she grabbed at the gear lever and shoved it forward. The Land Rover jerked and stalled.

'Well done.' It was almost a chuckle from the back. Kate started the engine again. Forcing herself to be calm she engaged reverse gear and let in the clutch with more care. The Land Rover backed away from the sea, the headlights sweeping the beach. 'I can't see it. There's no sign.'

'I don't think we'll send out a search party. Let's get out of here. Can you see all right? See if you can get back to the track.' Greg gritted his teeth as a new wave of pain hit him. Ignoring it he pulled at the rug on the seat and dragged it around his shoulders. The dim interior of the Land Rover was beginning to swim around him once more.

'I think we're on our way.' Kate glanced back at the sea. Was the tide retreating at last? It seemed to be farther away, certainly, and the force of the wind seemed less. Cautiously she turned the vehicle south, keeping parallel to the waves, and began to drive back towards the cottage. Straining forward to see through the slivered glass, she watched the beach; it was impossible to see where the sand was firm. All she could do was pray as at last she swung the wheel and headed up towards the dunes. It all looked so different in the headlights; the snow and the spinning sand eddies shifted and disguised the landmarks. Nothing was where it should be. She felt the Land Rover lurch sideways suddenly and she clutched at the wheel. For a moment she thought they were going to stop, then the wheels regained their grip and they were on their way again. Moments later she saw the lights of the cottage in the distance behind the dunes and muttering a short prayer of thanks, she headed doggedly towards them, threading her way round the dunes, following the path she had taken so often on foot, until at last she felt the vehicle drag itself onto the snow-covered grass.

The front door was still open but she ignored it. She had no wish to go in there again, with poor Bill still lying on the sofa. Instead she headed up the track towards Redall Farmhouse, driving more quickly now as they lurched uncomfortably over the ruts and skidded in the ice-fringed puddles, once or twice crashing over fallen branches as she drove on with gritted teeth. The petrol indicator, she had just noticed, was bouncing around the empty level. She could not believe it. They could not run out of petrol now. Not here. 'Hang on, you bastard. Just hang on.' She chewed on her lip furiously, ducking automatically as they brushed beneath the low overhanging branches of a stand of larch and slithered back onto the main track.

Through the cracked and murky windscreen she didn't see the shadow which appeared right in front of them on the track until it was barely feet from her front bumper. She slammed on the brakes, fighting to control the sliding vehicle, spun the wheel and heard with a cry of misery the resounding crack as they crashed into a tree. She was wearing no seat belt and the jolt sent her flying forward against the windscreen.

It was several seconds before she sat up, feeling herself cautiously. There was a bump the size of an egg on her forehead and she felt as though she had been kicked in the ribs by a horse but she was alive.

The headlights were directed at an angle up in the air. They had landed against a tree, with the back wheels in some sort of ditch. Even from here she knew there would be no way of getting the car out. 'Damn.' She struck the steering wheel with the flat of her hand. 'Damn, damn, damn! Greg? Are you all right?' She dragged her aching body round to look at him. He had been thrown to the floor by the impact and lay there huddled below the seat not moving. 'Oh God!' Stiffly she groped for the door handle and tried to push it open. It appeared to be jammed. She peered out again. What was it she had seen in front of her like that? She shivered. Whatever it was had gone – a figment of her overwrought imagination probably – and now the woods were empty as before.

'Greg. Greg? Are you all right?' She wrestled with the handle. 'Greg. Can you hear me?'

It was no good. She couldn't open it. She glanced across at the other door. It looked as though it might be easier to open. Climbing across into the passenger seat she pulled at the handle. After a moment it swung free and she managed to climb out. One glance past the headlights showed the front wing was buckled, the radiator had gone and the front tyre was flat. 'Damn!' She kicked the tyre as hard as she could, then she turned and dragged at the rear door. It was locked. Shaking with panic she crawled back in the front, knelt on the seat and reached down towards him. In the darkness she couldn't see his face. 'Greg? Greg, can you hear me?'

Her small torch was still there, in her pocket. Switching it on she directed it down. He was lying face down on the floor, his body hunched, his arms trapped beneath him as though he had made no effort to save himself at all when he was flung forward. Somehow she managed to scramble over the seat and putting her arms around him, she propped him up on the floor between the seats. He groaned but he did not open his eyes. For a moment she sat still, gazing out at the harsh beam of the headlights which lit up the woods. Soon the battery would fade and they would go out. She glanced at her watch wearily. It was after two. There was nothing for it. She was going to have to leave him and go for help on foot.

Gritting her teeth she wedged the torch into her pocket, tucked the rug more closely round Greg, lowered her window half an inch for air and climbed out into the cold. 'I'll be back as soon as I can. Hang on,' she whispered. She glanced up and down the track, shining the puny, swiftly-fading beam into the trees. The only sound was the drip of melting snow and the occasional rattle of leaves.

It couldn't be more than a quarter of a mile – ten minutes' walk at most. She set off up the path, keeping to the middle of the tyre ruts, feeling her boots slip repeatedly in the icy puddles and frozen mud. Her shoulders were crawling with terror. Tensely she hunched them, sure that any moment she would feel a hand reach out and touch her, turning round repeatedly as she walked, to look into the dark. There was no one there. The silence grew deeper as the sleet slackened and the dripping of the leaves began to diminish, but always with her was the sound of her own laboured breathing and the steady flap and squeak of her rubber boots.

The sight of a light in the distance was so sudden, so wonderful, she stopped and rubbed her eyes. It was a square light, pale blue, a light shining through an upstairs window at Redall Farmhouse. With a sob she began to run, squelching through the slush, brushing the wiry branches of larch and spruce out of her way as they tangled and whipped across in front of her.

She was gasping as she ran across the snow-covered grass and flung herself towards the door, reaching frantically for the bell.

For several seconds there was no response to her frenzied ringing, then she heard footsteps on the other side. 'Who is it?' Patrick's voice was muffled.

'It's me, Kate. For God's sake let me in.'

She listened to the sound of locks being turned and the two bolts being drawn, then at last the door was open and she fell into the hall.

'Kate, thank God you're all right. But where's Greg?' Diana, still dressed, her face drawn with exhaustion, clutched at her arm.

'He's in the Land Rover. I skidded into a tree. He's hurt his foot, and I think he may have knocked his head. It's only a few hundred yards up the track. You've got to help me bring him home.'

'Dear God!' Diana looked helplessly at her younger son. There was only Patrick left to help. Roger had gone to bed at last with two of his painkillers and when she had glanced into their bedroom an hour ago he had been fast asleep, his face still white and drawn as he lay clutching the pillow in the light of the shaded bedside lamp. Allie too was asleep, breathing harshly, her mouth a little open, her expression strangely hard, although her colour had returned to normal. Quietly shutting the door on her, Diana had walked downstairs thoughtfully. The sight of her daughter had filled her with unease.

Patrick had been asleep in the chair by the fire. She had pulled a rug over him and left him there, near the comforting embers. She had been sitting at the kitchen table drinking her third cup of coffee when Kate's frenzied knocking and ringing had startled her to her feet, awakened Patrick and sent them both into the hall to stand behind the bolted front door.

'Sit down, child and get your breath back,' Diana commanded as Kate staggered into the living room. She was soaked and muddy and her hair hung in tangled rats' tails around a face that was transparent with exhaustion.

'I think he's safe for now. I locked the doors and he's got a rug, but after Bill –' Suddenly she was crying. 'You don't know about Bill –'

'We know, Kate.' Diana put her arm round Kate's shoulders. 'Paddy went over to the cottage before the snow got so bad. Paddy, fetch the brandy, quickly,' she commanded. 'Don't try and

256

talk, Kate, till you've got your breath back. Then we'll work out how to fetch Greg.' Her eyes went to the window. He was alone out there. Alone and injured.

'Alison –' Kate said suddenly. She tried to sit up but Diana pushed her back against the cushions. 'Don't worry about Alison, my dear. She's safe. She came home by herself. She's upstairs in bed now. All we've got to do is fetch Greg, then we can all rest.'

There was a moment's silence. They were all thinking about Bill. Poor, kind Bill. Kate wished he wasn't alone at the cottage. But there was nothing they could do for him, whilst Greg needed help urgently.

'Did Alison tell you what happened?' She opened her eyes and studied Diana's face. Exhaustion and worry were etched on the other woman's features.

'Not really. She was too cold and tired. Time enough to question her in the morning.' Diana was silent for a moment as Patrick reappeared with a tray. On it were three glasses and a bottle of cognac. He poured them each a liberal dose and handed one to Kate, then another to his mother. The fact that she said nothing when he took the third himself filled him with misgiving. He sipped it cautiously and felt his eyes stream as fire spread down his throat. 'How can we fetch Greg? Could we somehow use your car, Kate?'

Kate shook her head. 'The track is almost impassable. That's why I skidded.'

'Is there any way he could walk? You said it was only a few hundred yards.'

'He's hurt and he's got no strength left. We've got to carry him, somehow.'

'Carry him?' For a moment Greg's mother was stunned. She looked at Patrick and then at the exhausted young woman sitting on the sofa. There were three of them. Could they do it? Greg was a tall, sturdily-built man. He weighed at least fourteen stone. But if the alternative was to leave him out there all night . . .

'We'll carry him,' she said firmly. 'It's not far. Between the three of us, we'll manage. Once Kate has got her breath back and downed that brandy. I'll get my boots and gloves.'

'Aren't you going to tell Dad?' Patrick asked. He was biting his lip with anxiety.

'Your father is asleep. We'll be back before he even knows we've gone,' Diana said firmly. 'There's no need to disturb him. We can lock the house. Allie is asleep too. They'll be quite safe.'

Kate took a sip of brandy and closed her eyes. She could feel warmth flooding back through her veins, but with it came a wave of total exhaustion. She did not think she could even stand again, never mind help carry Greg back to the farmhouse. She was willing energy back into her body as she took another sip. When she opened her eyes Patrick was watching her. 'You OK?' he asked quietly. 'Ma's gone off to get her scarf and things.'

'I'll manage.' Kate grimaced. 'Paddy, could I borrow some warm socks? I've had half the North Sea in my boots and my feet are so cold they don't even recognise me any more.'

'Sure.' He grinned, thankful to be asked for something so easy to achieve. 'I'll get them.'

As soon as he was gone she leaned back against the cushions and closed her eyes again, feeling the room spin and tilt suddenly. She opened them hurriedly as Patrick came back with a pair of thick woolly football socks and a towel. 'These warm enough?'

She nodded, suddenly realising that she was sitting there in their living room with her muddy, wet boots stuck out in front of her on the rug. Patrick followed her gaze. 'Don't worry. Ma didn't.' He grinned again. 'Shall I pull them off for you?'

'Would you? I don't think I have the strength.'

She lay back as he bestrode her legs with his back to her and professionally drew off first one boot then the other. A shower of muddy wet sand fell on the rug. Kneeling down he peeled off her socks. Her feet were white and wrinkled and ice-cold.

'Poor feet.' He smiled. Reaching for the towel he rubbed them vigorously until she snatched them away in agony, then he pulled on the socks. 'I'll see if I can find some new boots. What size?'

'Five and a half. Six.' She sat forward on the edge of the sofa. 'I think I'll wash my face. That will wake me up a bit.'

'O.K. I'm sure I can find something that'll fit you. At least they'll be dry.'

In the bathroom Kate leaned over the basin towards the mirror and stared at her face. She was drawn, grey, her eyes hollow and haunted. Pushing her hair back with both hands she splashed cold water over her face for several seconds then she reached for a towel. She would make it. Whatever it was out there would not attack three of them. She would see to it that Patrick took his gun – she had not missed the fact that he had it in his hand as they opened the door to her earlier – and they would bring Greg back. The whole exercise would be over in less than an hour and then they would all be safe.

It took two. He was conscious when they finally reached the Land Rover and he was able to greet his mother with something like good humour, forgetting the terror he had felt when he came to, to find himself alone. A combination of the fireman's lift, a sling seat made out of the rug and frequent rests, brought them back to Redall Farmhouse shortly after four in the morning.

Diana unlocked the door and walked in first, glancing round nervously as Greg stood on one foot in the doorway, clutching at the door frame. 'Everything looks all right. They must still be asleep.' She put her shoulder under Greg's arm. 'Come on, big son. Come and sit down. Let's look at you and see the damage.'

Behind them Patrick quietly rebolted and locked the front door and leaned the gun in the corner. He had seen the way Kate kept looking over her shoulder, and the relief on her face as they reached the farmhouse again. And he had felt it too, the atmosphere out in the woods; the certainty that they were being followed.

A large purple bruise had developed on Greg's forehead where he had hit it on the back of Kate's seat when the car skidded, but apart from that and his exhaustion and chill he seemed remarkably unscathed. Only his foot was badly damaged. He had been tucked up on the camp bed in Roger's study, heavily dosed with aspirin against the pain, when Patrick spoke quietly to Kate at last. His mother had gone upstairs to check on Alison.

'You'd better tell me what happened.'

'I have told you.' Kate frowned at him. Her face was white and drawn. She picked up the mug of hot chocolate Diana had made her and sipped it, blowing the steam gently.

'No you haven't. Not what happened before. Where did you find Bill?'

Kate took another sip of the chocolate, feeling the sharp sweetness flood around her mouth, comforting her with its memories of childhood.

'He was near the track, on his way here. He'd been to the cottage to find me and when he found it empty he thought he'd try Redall Farmhouse.'

'Did he . . .' Patrick hesitated, overwhelmed suddenly by the image of the dead man lying on the sofa in the cottage, 'Did he manage to tell you what happened?'

Kate hesitated. 'He was very confused. Almost unconscious.' She took a deep breath as though to speak then paused again. How could she tell Patrick that Bill had accused Alison of attacking him? 'He seemed to think it was two women,' she said at last guardedly.

'Women?' Patrick repeated, shocked.

Kate nodded. 'He was in an awful state, Patrick. I don't think he could remember much. We put him in the Land Rover and took him back to the cottage, then Greg went off on his own to try and find Allie. As you can imagine we were very worried.' She paused again. Her hands had started shaking quite badly. Clutching the mug of chocolate against her chest she gave Patrick a shaky smile. 'I didn't know what to do for Bill. I kept him warm and still and tried to stop the bleeding, but he lapsed into unconsciousness.' Suddenly she was fighting her tears. 'I didn't know what to do. If I'd known something about first aid . . .' She put down the mug, mopping at the tears which were streaming down her face. Patrick stood up and quietly fetched a box of Kleenex from the kitchen. He put it beside her on the arm of the chair. 'I saw him, you know,' he said softly. 'I don't think first aid would have helped. I should think he had a fractured skull. You musn't blame yourself.' Kneeling in front of the fire he reached for the poker and prodded the logs. 'Allie said it was Marcus who killed Bill,' he said after a minute. He was staring into the smoky embers. 'She said he had killed some other people as well.' His voice was flat and tired, beyond expression.

'Marcus?' Kate replied automatically. She did not sound convinced.

'Someone must have done it.' Patrick's face crumpled suddenly. He screwed up his eyes furiously, fighting his own tears, keeping his back to her as he stabbed at the logs.

'There's nothing we can do until daylight anyway.' Levering herself to her feet, Kate came and knelt beside him. She put her arm around his shoulders, feeling the boy's trembling body go

260

rigid beneath her touch. 'We ought to try and get a couple of hours' sleep,' she said after a pause. 'We're all safe here. Whatever – whoever it is – can't get in; the doors are locked and you've got a gun. Why don't you go to bed.'

He shook his head wordlessly.

'Lie on the sofa then. With the gun beside you.'

'What about you?' He still had not looked at her. She could see the wet trail of tears on his cheek.

'If you're down here, can I borrow your bed?' Her fatigue was so great, she realised suddenly, that it was doubtful if she could make it up the stairs.

'Of course.' He looked at her at last and gave a watery grin. 'Sorry. I'm being pathetic.'

'No you're not. You're being very brave.' She dragged herself to her feet. 'Try and get some sleep. We'll need to have our wits about us in the morning.'

Somehow she pulled herself up the stairs. Every bone and muscle in her body was aching; her head throbbed and her feet hurt as she dragged herself up the final steep steps and made her way towards Patrick's room. At Alison's doorway she paused and peered in. A dull light was spilling out across the landing from the bedside lamp. Diana was sitting on the girl's bed, looking down at her sleeping form. She glanced up and put her finger to her lips. Then she stood up and tiptoed to the door.

'Patrick said I could use his bed for an hour or two,' Kate whispered.

Diana nodded. She took Kate's arm and ushered her down the passage and into Patrick's room. Switching on the light she stared round at the mess of books and papers and for once without comment shook her head before swooping on the bed and dragging a pile of books and tapes into a heap on the floor. 'I'll get you some sheets,' she offered wearily.

'No. Please. Don't bother.' To forestall her Kate threw herself down on top of the duvet, still fully dressed. She was too tired to think, to move, to stand another second. She shut her eyes. Immediately her head began to spin unpleasantly, as though she had had too much to drink. She forced them open with a groan as Diana pulled a cover over her.

Diana looked down at her for a moment, then she turned away and switched off the light. 'Rest, Kate. We'll talk in the morning,' she whispered, and she tiptoed out and pulled the door shut behind her. Somewhere outside a pheasant shrieked its alarm call into the pre-dawn darkness and fell silent again.

XLVI

The heavy ornate brooch was solid silver. A crude native design, but it had been his; the Briton's. He had known it all along. Bending over her he tore it from her gown and pinned it onto his own cloak with a sneer of triumph. Stupid bitch. Had she thought to frighten him with her curses? Did she really think she could pursue him into eternity?

He stood looking down at her for a moment, wondering how he could have loved her so much, making no attempt to draw the sword out of her body, anger and hatred boiling in his veins like vitriol, then he stooped and picking her up under the arms he dragged her towards the edge of the marsh. One thing he could do for her, sweet wife of his, companion of his bed, mate of his loins, mother of his son – send her to Hades with her seducer. With a massive heave he lifted her from the ground and hurled her a few feet into the marsh, watching with satisfaction as her body fell almost over the spot where her lover had disappeared. She lay there for a while, her blue gown spread across the mud, the sword still protruding from her body, her hair a splash of auburn in the light of the rising sun, then slowly, almost imperceptibly, she began to sink.

Hands on hips he watched, a sneer curling his lip. Vengeance; sweet, healing vengeance. And no one would ever know. Slowly the clouds were drawing back; the sky was turning blue. It was going to be a beautiful day. He put his hand to his belt and felt for the dagger he wore there, opposite the empty sheath which had held his sword. Taking the hilt between his fingers he stroked it for a moment, then he drew it out, feeling the weight and balance of a well-loved, trusted weapon.

Then he turned towards the priests.

'Are you and Alison going to work on your projects together today, Sue?' Cissy Farnborough looked at the top of her daughter's head, which was all she could see as the girl sat at the table, her face buried in a fat paperback.

Don't read at table. She wanted to say it, but how could she with Joe sitting there on the far side of the cornflakes packet, as deeply buried in the *Sunday Telegraph*. She sighed. 'Sue!' she tried again, louder this time, more irritated. 'Did you hear what I said?'

Sue looked up. Her unbrushed hair stood out round her head like a disorganised halo; her nightshirt, adorned with a particularly ugly picture of some hirsute pop star's face in close up, was crumpled and distinctly grubby. 'I don't know what she's doing. She missed school last week. I'll ring her later,' she said ungraciously.

'Please do. I should like to know if there is someone extra for lunch.'

'You always make too much anyway,' Sue commented tartly. She buried herself back in her book. Cissy pursed her lips. She turned to the kettle and switching it on, reached for the jar of coffee. Her husband and her daughter had tea at breakfast, and as usual Joe had insisted on a full, cooked, death-by-cholesterol blow out. She shuddered as she glanced at the greasy frying pan. He wouldn't even let her grill his bacon. 'I work for my living, woman,' he had growled when she suggested a slight moderation to his diet. 'These namby pamby doctors don't know anything about life on the land. They're writing for city folk; desk pilots. Men who never shift their backsides off their chairs from one end of the month to the other. They should try and do some real work. See what that does for them!' She had given up. It was a well worn theme. A combination of rural arrogance and resentment against her father, who had been an accountant in London before he retired. Spooning the coffee into her cup she stirred it thoughtfully, rehearsing her own dissatisfaction silently as she turned to look out of the window. She had married beneath her; both her parents had thought so. And unfortunately they had made no secret of their opinion. She had defended Joe, stuck up for him, passionately supported him, slept with him and finally married him, and of course they had been right. He had gone to a minor public school in Suffolk but he was not what she would call educated; he was not interested in anything but the farm; he never read anything except the Sunday newspapers and he despised education in others – especially his wife. Susie was different. Nothing was too good for her, but even there he never supported Cissy when she tried to make the child do her homework. 'Leave the girl alone,' he would say impatiently every time Cissy tried to get Sue to switch off her Walkman or the television and concentrate on work. 'She's pretty. She'll find herself a man soon enough. She doesn't need all this crap!'

'There's no marmalade, Ciss!' Joe emerged from the paper looking wounded, the lid of the jar in his hand.

'Blast!' Cissy mouthed the word silently. Why, why, why did he always manage to find fault. Why was there always something she had forgotten?

'Don't call me Ciss,' she snapped back. Cecilia Louise. That was what her parents had christened her. But Joe had never called her Cecilia in his life. At first she had thought it funny to be called Cissy, but the joke had soon palled. Now it just added to the weight of resentment.

'Go and ring Alison now.' She turned on Sue as always, her anger and helplessness directed against her daughter instead of its true target. 'And get dressed. You look like a slut.'

To her surprise Sue got up at once, and she saw Joe glance at her surreptitiously from behind the paper. Perhaps she had spoken more forcefully than she had realised.

'I will put marmalade on the list,' she said calmly. 'You will have to wait until I go to the shops again. There's plenty of jam in the pantry.' She smiled at her husband. 'Or Marmite.' She saw him shudder visibly, but to her surprise he said nothing. Meekly he larded his toast with butter and ate it plain. Well, if that was supposed to make her feel guilty it was not going to work. What were another few ounces of butter going to matter after the load of fat he had ladled into his body over the years?

She turned and looked out of the kitchen window. It was vile outside. The sky was almost dark even though it was after nine. The wind from the east was flattening the trees in the orchard beyond the kitchen garden, and there were thin, melting drifts of snow over the grass. She shivered. It was still sleeting. On the bird table outside the window a flock of small birds fought over the bowl of melted fat and seed she had put out for them. The only thing about Joe's diet which did please her was the amount of fat which dripped from his food and which she could make into bird pudding. She half smiled as she watched two robins squabbling with some sparrows. On the snowy grass beneath the bird table about fifty small birds foraged about for the seed she had scattered there.

'Mum! Their phone's out of order.' A querulous wail came from Sue as she slammed down the receiver. 'Hell and shit and fuck!'

Joe looked up. 'Go to your room, Susan,' he bellowed.

'But Dad. Allie's got my notes. I've got to speak to her.'

'I don't care what she's got.' Something had at last pierced his lethargy. 'No child of mine uses language like that in my house.'

Cissy sipped her coffee, for once uninvolved. Let them work it out. Sue's friendship with Alison was one she cultivated assiduously. The Lindseys were a pleasant family. Well spoken; well educated. Their lack of money was not their fault – poor Roger was so ill – but still Diana managed to run that house with a grace and style which Cissy envied.

She turned away from the window and surveyed the thunderous scene at the table. 'I'll drive you down to Redall Farmhouse when I've put the lunch on,' she said peaceably. 'Then you can collect your notes and Allie can come back with us if she wants. In fact, they all can. I've got a huge joint this week. As you say, there will be plenty for everyone and it would be nice to have them over. In weather like this it's not as though anyone can be doing anything outside.' She smiled at her husband and her daughter, suddenly cheerful. Her depression had lifted as swiftly as it had fallen. The Lindseys would cheer them all up.

XLVII

Kate awoke suddenly with a start and lay staring up at the ceiling wondering where she was. Her head was spinning. Nothing about the room was familiar; she could not place it at all. A dull light was filtering through the closed orange curtains. She stared round at the overflowing shelves, the untidy desk with its computer, the posters on every inch of available wall space and then she closed her eyes again, defeated. She hadn't the energy to sit up, but she knew she must. She lifted her wrist towards her face and squinted at her watch. A quarter past nine. She realised suddenly that under the duvet she was fully dressed. Cautiously she moved on the bed, easing herself nearer the edge, with a view to swinging her legs over the side, but every part of her body ached and for a moment she lay still, trying instead to force her brain into gear. What had happened last night? Why couldn't she remember?

She turned her face towards the door as a faint knock sounded. It was Patrick. He grinned. 'Sorry it's such a mess in here. I've brought you some tea.'

Of course. Suddenly it was all flooding back. The horror and the fear; the cold and exhaustion. She levered herself up onto her elbow, and pushing the hair out of her eyes reached for the cup. 'You're a saint. I didn't realise how thirsty I was. How is everybody?'

'Alive, I guess.' Patrick pulled the chair out from his desk and swivelling it round sat astride it, facing her. 'What's happening to us? What are we going to do?'

She sipped at the scalding tea and thought for a moment.

'We're going to have to get up to the main road. We need help. A doctor; the police.' She paused, frowning. 'How is Greg?'

'His foot is all inflamed. Mum says he ought to be in hospital.'

The wave of anguish which swept over her surprised her. Greg was the only strong one amongst them; the only one who could protect them if . . . If what? If they were attacked?

Almost as though he had read her thoughts Patrick shook his head. 'Whoever murdered Bill must be long gone by now. In our car. It was stolen yesterday. I'm going up to the Farnboroughs' on foot. It won't take me more than an hour.'

She drank some more tea, feeling it flowing through her veins like some kind of elixir of life. 'You can't go on your own. I'll go with you. A quick wash and something to eat –' she was surprised suddenly to realise just how hungry she was, '– and I'll be ready for anything. What's the weather like?'

Patrick stood up. He leaned across his desk and pulled back the curtains, letting in a dim brownish light. 'Not very nice. It's still windy and there's been quite a bit of snow. They are forecasting blizzards –' He broke off suddenly.

'What is it?' The lurch of panic in Kate's stomach told her she was not nearly as calm as she had thought. All her fear was still there, under the surface, waiting to flood back through her.

'The car!' Patrick's voice was strangled. Putting down the cup Kate lurched out of bed and went to stand beside him. 'Where? Damn it, my specs are in my jacket.' She screwed up her eyes as she looked out across the snow-covered grass towards the edge of the saltings.

'Out there, on the marsh.' Patrick's voice was awed.

The Volvo was standing some hundred yards from the grass and sand at the edge of the salting, balanced on high sections of grass-topped mud. Beneath its wheels, the tide was rippling merrily out of the creek leaving a curtain of weed draped on the car's bumper.

'Is there anyone in it?' Kate could only make out the outline from this distance.

'I don't think so.' Patrick sounded distracted. 'How could it have got there? No one could have driven it.'

'Not even at low tide?'

'Kate, look at the height of the ground it's standing on! Those are like little islands. At high tide those grass patches are above sea level. They must be four feet off the ground. There is no way that car could have got there, no way.'

'The tide must have carried it. There was a terrific wind last night –'

'Blowing this way. Off the sea. That's a car, Kate. A bloody great Volvo. It's not a Dinky toy. If it got in the sea it would sink.'

'Yes. Of course.' She pushed her hands deep into her pockets, aware that she was shivering. 'Can we walk out there? When the tide's gone out a bit?'

He nodded absently. 'I'll have to tell Dad.'

'I'll come downstairs.'

She stood back and watched as he headed for the door. He was in a daze. She glanced back at the window. The car was still there, the windscreen glittering in a stray, watery ray of sunshine.

On her way downstairs she glanced into Alison's room through the open door. The girl lay unmoving, her hair spread across the pillow. The teddy lay on the floor, a hot water bottle near it. Kate stood for a moment watching her. She had a feeling Alison was not asleep.

'Allie?' she whispered. 'Allie are you awake?'

There was no reply.

Roger was sitting at the kitchen table, a cup of coffee in front of him, which judging by the skin on the top was cold and unappetising. Diana was standing near him watching the toaster.

'Did you manage to sleep?' She smiled at Kate and indicated the coffee pot on the hob.

Kate made for it gratefully. 'A bit.'

'Pour Greg one too, will you Kate, and take it through to him. I think he'd be glad to see you,' Roger said. He mustered a valiant smile. 'Then you and I and Paddy will grab a bit of breakfast. By then the tide will be low enough to make our way out to the family barouche. Those bastards. I can't think how the hell they got it there, but it won't be worth a tinker's ha'penny after the tide has been in it.'

'The insurance will pay, Dad.' Patrick had emerged from the study.

'Let's hope so.' Roger's face was grim as he watched Kate make her way across the room with the two mugs of coffee.

Greg was propped up against a pile of pillows and cushions on the camp bed in the study. Someone had made a makeshift cage across his foot to keep the weight of the bed-clothes off it, and though Kate could see the pain in his face as he grinned at her, he looked immeasurably better than he had the night before.

269

'How are you?' She knelt to hand him the coffee, and then sat down on the floor beside him. 'I hear the foot is not too good.'

'I'll live.' He reached out a hand to her. 'And that fact I owe to you. It hasn't escaped me that you saved my life about five times last night. That's some debt I owe you.'

'Don't be silly.' Embarrassed she looked down into her coffee. It was thick and black and rich.

'I know. Anyone would have done it.' He was laughing.

'Probably. Yes.'

'Well, thanks anyway. If I had been you I would probably have left me there to rot and thought it served me right after the way I've buggered you about.'

She smiled. 'Poetically put.'

There was a moment's silence. Then Greg reached out to her again. 'Kate, I had the most peculiar dream while I was asleep. I think we are all still in terrible danger. I've told Paddy and now I'm telling you. You'll think I'm hallucinating; you probably think I was hallucinating last night –'

'If you were, then we both were,' she put in softly. 'We both saw that figure.'

'Was it because we were expecting to?' He shook his head and releasing her hand, reached for his coffee cup again. 'When you came here I decided to scare you away. You know that. The joke, if it was a joke, got rapidly out of hand. We all began to imagine things . . .' He paused, his attention riveted to the depths of his cup. 'In that state, maybe, what I saw was dictated by my own mind . . .' He paused again. 'Thomas De Quincey puts it rather neatly, if I remember it right. "If a man who only talks about oxen becomes an opium eater, then he will dream about oxen" – is that right?' He cast her a quick glance under his eyelashes, and did not miss the look of astonishment in her face. '"And if a man who is a philosopher has an opium dream then it will be . . . *humani nihil* –"'

'"*Humani nihil a se alienum putat.*"' Kate finished for him. 'Well, well, I would never have suspected that you had read *The Confessions.*'

He smiled, the look of mischief cutting across the greyness of pain. 'Well, I used to be quite literate, you know. I even know what it means. "He believes nothing human strange" – yes?' He waited for her comment. When she said nothing he went on, 'I even read up my Byron when I heard what Lady Muck was up to in my cottage.'

'Lady Muck?' She was even more astonished.

'If you'd known I called you that you would have left me to the sharks.'

'Indeed I would.' Thoughtfully she took a sip of coffee. 'You haven't told me yet what you dreamed of. What phantasmagoria haunted you?'

'Marcus.'

She bit her lip. 'Who else.'

'He tried to get me, you know, on the beach. He tried to take me over. I fought him . . .' He paused. 'In my dream he was trying to get inside my head again.' He shifted his weight uncomfortably in the bed. 'It was the most awful dream I have ever had in my life, and yet I can't remember more than a few bits.'

'You were awoken perhaps by a stranger from Porlock.' Kate smiled at him, trying to tease him out of his bleak mood.

'All right, all right. Believe it or not, I know that one too. All I remember is that he was trying to get inside my head, and that if I had let him he would have got into this house. And that was what he wanted. To get to us. Because we know his secret.'

She was watching him. 'And what is his secret?'

He glanced at her looking for signs of disbelief or scorn. 'That he killed Claudia. But there's more to it than that. Much more. Otherwise why would he be so angry? And so desperate?'

The silence in the room grew uncomfortable. There had been no humour in his eyes; no relieving lightness. What she had seen there, behind the narrowed grey-green irises, was fear. She swallowed, plaiting her fingers together nervously.

'Who do you think killed Bill?' she asked at last. Her voice was husky.

Greg heaved a sigh. 'I don't know what to think. Has Allie said anything, do you know?'

'Patrick told me she said it was Marcus.'

'Did you tell them what Bill said?'

'No.'

Greg eased himself higher against the pillows. His foot was throbbing painfully, stabs of hot pain shooting up as far as his knee. He had not needed to see the inflamed, discoloured flesh to know it was infected. 'Has she woken up?'

'I don't think so. She was fast asleep when I came down. Greg, I think the important thing is to get a doctor here for you – and for her. Patrick and I are going to walk up to the main road.' She glanced at the window. 'It doesn't seem quite so frightening in daylight.'

He reached out and touched her hand again. 'I'm so sorry this has all happened, Kate. Poor old Byron.'

She gave a rueful smile. 'He'll wait.'

'You know,' he hesitated. 'I think I'm quite glad you came after all.' Leaning towards her he kissed her forehead gently. He ran a finger down the line of her cheek. 'You've got good bones. When all this is over I'll paint your portrait.'

She smiled, surprised at the shiver of excitement which had whispered across her flesh in spite of her exhaustion. 'Am I supposed to take that as a compliment?'

'Oh, yes. People who know me well would kill for such a compliment.' The humour in his eyes was hidden very deep – a mere quirk of the eye muscle.

She studied his face for a moment, then half reluctantly she stood up. 'We know where the car is.'

'Oh?'

She laughed. A tight little laugh which hovered for a moment on the edge of hysteria. 'It's out on the saltings; in the middle of the water. No one could have driven it there.'

He said nothing, his gaze holding hers, then he too gave an uncomfortable laugh. 'Well, well. Perhaps he was only used to driving chariots; a Volvo must be a bit different.'

'You don't seriously think –'

'I don't know what I think.' His patience snapped. 'For Christ's sake, what can I do from here? Just be careful. Make Paddy take the gun and watch every step of the way. We don't know what we're dealing with. There is someone out there who is out to kill. It seems to me it doesn't matter much if he's a real flesh-and-blood homicidal maniac or a ghostly one, the effect seems to be the same.'

'So you don't think it was Alison.' She had turned towards the door.

'Of course it wasn't Alison. She wouldn't have the strength even if she wanted to kill someone. And she had nothing to do with the car.' He slumped back, overwhelmed by helplessness

272

and frustration and pain. She looked down at him, hesitating for a moment longer, then silently she opened the door and slipped away.

Roger pushed a fresh cup of coffee at her across the table as she walked back into the kitchen. 'Allie is awake. Diana and Paddy are with her.' He gestured her towards a chair. He looked only slightly more rested than the night before; there was still an alarmingly blue tinge about his lips as Kate sat down opposite him.

'How is she?'

He shook his head. 'I thought I'd wait till they came down. She doesn't want us all up there crowding into her room.' Besides, I can't face climbing the stairs again, not yet. The thought, though unspoken, showed clearly in his eyes.

Kate looked away, painfully aware how sick he was. 'As soon as Paddy comes down I think we should go for a doctor.'

'And the police have to be informed.' He looked down into his coffee mug, stirring thoughtfully, watching the movement of the liquid, with its miniaturised reflection of the overhead lamp. 'I know you all have some crazy idea that there is a ghost out there, Kate. Get real, as Allie would say. Ghosts do not beat large, strong men to death.' He looked up at her at last. 'Be careful. Please be careful –' He broke off, and she saw his face light with a smile which hovered around his mouth for a few seconds and then died. Following his gaze, she swivelled round on her chair. Alison was standing by the staircase door. Wearing her nightshirt, her hair tumbled on her shoulders, she was staring round the room as though she had never seen it before.

'Allie?' Roger stood up, pushing his chair back over the floor tiles with a scraping sound which tore at the nerves. 'Are you all right, sweetheart?'

She moved her head slightly, as though she were having difficulty focussing, and looked towards them vaguely, her body swaying from side to side. Behind her, Patrick appeared in the doorway. His face was white. 'Allie?' He dodged round her. 'Allie, sit down. Sit down and I'll get you something nice to drink.' He gestured at Roger and Kate frantically behind his back.

They glanced at each other. The atmosphere in the room was suddenly electric. Alison took another step forward, placing one foot in front of the other with enormous care as though the floor

273

were swaying like the deck of a ship. As she moved towards them the two cats, who had been asleep near the fire, leaped off the chair where they had been entwined and streaked across the floor. Within seconds they had both disappeared through the cat flap. Kate stared after them, puzzled. Their eyes had been wild; their hackles and tails fluffed up in terror. Frowning, she glanced back at Alison who had stopped again and it struck her suddenly that the girl looked as though she was drunk.

Roger had the same thought. 'Alison?' His voice was sharp. 'What is the matter?'

'She attacked Mum.' Patrick murmured, his voice husky. He reached the table and slid behind it, putting it between him and his sister. 'She's gone mad. Oh, Dad, what's happening?' His face was white and strained. He looked frightened.

Roger flicked a glance at him and then looked back at his daughter. Her face was completely blank. She took another step forward, her hands out in front of her as though she were groping in the darkness.

'Alison!' Roger's voice rang out loudly. 'Answer me! What's wrong?' He shot a look at his son. 'Where is Di? Is she hurt?'

Patrick shook his head. 'Shocked. She's coming –'

He was interrupted by a sudden, slow laugh. The sound, he realised with a sudden shiver, came from Alison, but it was not her voice. Kate felt the hairs on the back of her neck stir as she stared at the girl.

'No one,' Alison spoke slowly, her voice husky. 'No one is going to leave this house. No one is ever going to find out what happened.' Behind her Diana appeared in the doorway. Kate heard Roger's sharp intake of breath as he glanced at his wife. Her face was discoloured with a massive purple bruise. She slid into the room, and stayed where she was, her back to the wall, her hurt and bewilderment and fear obvious in every angle of her body.

Roger swallowed. 'Allie, darling. I think we should have a talk. Why don't you sit down. We'll all have a hot drink –'

She did not appear to have heard him. Slowly and painfully she took another step. Kate was watching her eyes. They were blank; totally blank.

'Roger.' She stepped closer to him, her voice barely a whisper. 'I think she's asleep.'

Roger glanced at her sharply then he looked back at his daughter, narrowing his eyes. 'Dear God, I think you're right! What do we do?'

'Isn't it supposed to be dangerous to wake them?' Kate threw a pleading look towards Diana.

It was Patrick who acted. 'If she's asleep she can't see us,' he said quietly. He took a cautious step towards his sister, and then, as she failed to react he took another. Slipping round behind her, he put his hands lightly on her shoulders. 'Come on, Allie, back to bed.' She ignored him. 'Allie. Come on. You must lie down –' He increased the pressure slightly, trying to turn her round. She tensed, then suddenly she swung round out of his grip, letting fly with a massive punch which grazed Patrick's shoulder as he leaped out of the way.

'All right, Alison, that is enough.' Roger moved with surprising speed. He caught her wrists, and pulled her towards a chair. 'Awake or asleep you are not behaving like that in this house.' Taken by surprise she took two steps with him then she stopped and shook him off. He reeled back. Though weak with illness he was a tall man, and still fairly heavy and his daughter had flicked him away as though he were half her size. Her face was still blank; all expression completely wiped from her features.

'She's like a robot,' Patrick whispered. He slipped across to his father's side. 'Are you OK, Dad? She hasn't hurt you?'

Roger shook his head. They all had their eyes fixed on Alison's face which remained impassive. Kate frowned. Was she asleep? Or was it something else? The girl stood immobile for several minutes; no one moved or spoke, then out of the corner of her eye Kate saw Diana slip from the room. Moments later she reappeared, a canvas belt in her hand. As they watched she tiptoed up behind Alison and gently she began to slide the belt around her, over her arms, obviously intending to pinion them at her sides. Alison did not react. Gently, Diana pulled the belt tighter, just above the girl's elbows. 'Fetch a blanket, Roger. Wrap her up tightly,' she commanded. 'Quickly. Before she wakes up.'

Alison stepped forward at the sound of her voice as if becoming aware of the restriction for the first time. She tried to move her arms and a look of frightened puzzlement flashed across her face to be followed immediately by a roar of rage. She turned round, lashing out with her hands and almost without effort, snapped

275

the belt. The expression on her face was one of pure anger. She turned towards the table and reached out. Too late Kate saw the bread knife lying beside the loaf; she jumped to move it but Alison was there first and her hand was on the knife handle before Kate's. Kate grabbed her wrist, and for a moment their eyes met across the table. Kate felt a shaft of terror stab through her; the eyes which bore into hers were not Alison's; they were no longer expressionless; no longer asleep; they were cold, calculating and very angry.

'Allie –' She gasped. 'Please.'

Alison laughed. A deep throaty laugh. Twisting her arm effortlessly beneath Kate's grasping fingers she snatched the knife up and turning, lunged at her mother. She missed and for a moment she was off balance. Seizing his chance Patrick threw himself at her and they fell to the floor, wrestling.

'Paddy –' Diana's scream rang across the room as the blade caught his forearm and a splash of blood flew across the rush matting, but he did not let go. They fought on furiously, Patrick kicking and struggling as Alison began surely and steadily to overpower him. 'Roger, do something!' Forgetting her husband's weakness Diana screamed again but it was Kate who snatched up the folded tablecloth from the dresser and flung it over Alison's head. At the same moment Patrick wriggled free of his sister's arm lock and put his foot on her wrist, pinning it to the floor while he snatched the knife from her. It was only then that they realised that Greg was in the room, hobbling on a walking stick, his face white with pain.

'Here.' He handed something to his mother. 'Quickly. It's Dad's sedative.' Her hands shaking visibly, Diana opened the box he had given her and took out a syringe. She glanced at Roger, then filling it she approached her writhing daughter and, pulling the night shirt up, planted the needle in the girl's buttock. Alison let out a scream of rage, only half muffled by the tablecloth Kate was holding round her head. It was followed by a stream of abuse which only very slowly subsided into silence. It was several minutes before her clenched fists relaxed and she slumped to the floor. Cautiously Kate removed the tablecloth and looked down. Alison's face, flushed from the struggle was relaxed at last; she was breathing quickly and lightly, her hair spread across the floor. Slowly Patrick stooped and pulled his sister's nightshirt down to cover her bottom, then he turned and picking up a drying up cloth from the draining board he staunched the blood flowing from his arm.

'Don't, Patrick. That's germy,' Diana's comment was automatic; her eyes had not left Alison's face.

'Did you hear what she was screaming?' Greg lowered himself into a chair, his head swimming from the effort of dragging himself from the study.

'It was some foreign language,' Roger said after a moment's hesitation.

'Not just any foreign language.' Greg looked at Kate. 'Go on. Tell them. What was it?'

Kate shook her head. 'I'm not sure –'

'Of course you're sure. You heard what she said. It was some sort of Latin. Go on admit it. You heard her.' He stared round at them all. 'You all heard her. It was Latin!'

Patrick bent down to pick up the knife. He stared at it for a moment as though he couldn't believe he held it in his hands. 'Allie would never have done that; she couldn't have done that. No girl could be that strong.'

Diana picked up the broken belt. It had snapped in two places. They all stared at it. 'How long will that injection last?' Roger asked softly. He glanced up at his wife. The sedative had been left by the doctor for him.

'Not long. I didn't expect it to work so quickly. She was looking down at Alison's slumped body. 'I only used a tiny dose. Oh, Roger, what are we going to do with her?' Her voice shook with tears.

Roger moved to put his arm around her shoulders. 'I don't know.' His whole body was slumped with defeat.

'There is something you should know.' Greg looked from one to the other and then at Kate. His face was full of compassion. 'Before he died Bill told us that it was Alison who had attacked him.'

'No!' Diana's protest was half a scream, half a moan.

'I'm afraid that is what he said,' Kate added. 'But it wasn't Alison, was it? We all know that. Those eyes weren't Alison's.'

'What are you saying?' Diana rounded on her.

'You know what she's saying,' Greg said. He stared down at his sister's recumbent form. 'She's possessed.'

'No.'

'What do you call it then?' He reached across towards her but she drew back. He shrugged. 'That was not Alison speaking; they are not Alison's actions. Kate's right. They are not even her eyes.'

Diana burst into tears. 'What are we going to do?'

Greg looked at Kate and then at his father, who had sunk into the chair at the head of the table, his face grey with fatigue. 'We have to find a doctor.'

'No!' Diana turned on him. 'We are not getting a doctor, or the police. I am not having Allie taken away from here –'

'What about my foot?' Greg's voice was mild. 'And Dad. I think the doc should look at him.' He paused. 'Allie needs help. Badly. You know she does.'

'No.' Diana shook her head. Tears were pouring down her cheeks. 'No, we'll sort this all out ourselves. It will be all right. Allie will be fine when she's had a sleep. Your foot will be all right, Greg. It's better already, you said so yourself and your father only needs to rest –'

'Di.' Roger looked up. He rubbed his hands wearily across his cheeks and they all heard the rasping sound of his palms on the twenty-four-hour beard. 'We can't handle this ourselves. You know that better than I do. There is a dead man out there in the cottage. A dead man, Di. He's not imaginary. He's not going to sort himself out.'

'Allie didn't move the car, Ma,' Patrick put in suddenly. 'There must be someone else out there.'

'Patrick and I will go and phone from the Farnboroughs'.' Kate stood up. 'I think we should go now.'

'Take the gun, Paddy.' Roger nodded. 'Greg and I can take care of things here.'

Patrick looked from one parent's face to the other, uncertainly, then he turned to Kate. 'OK?' he whispered.

XLVIII

The kitchen was spotless, the joint in the oven, the potatoes roasting slowly beneath it. Cissy looked round with a pleased smile. Even Joe's Sunday papers had been marshalled into a more-or-less tidy heap at the far end of the kitchen table. There would be nothing now to jog her conscience if she and Sue drove down to Redall Farmhouse and had a cup of Diana's wonderful specially ground coffee from the shop in Ipswich, by her untidy, ash-spattered inglenook.

She often wondered why she liked Diana's house so much; the living room at Redall was just that – a room for living, always knee-deep in newspapers and sewing and cats, with Greg's paints and Patrick's books lying around in heaps. The untidy and often dusty surfaces were always filled with fresh flowers, though; even in the depths of winter Diana managed to find something in the woods and the house always smelled of coffee and home-baked bread and drying herbs, and even if there was the occasional whiff of cat, it was all wonderful.

She sighed, looking round her own kitchen. However hard she tried she could not be comfortable with Diana's mess. Not in her own house. She had tried to dry flowers, but they dropped shrivelled little petals all over the floor; she tried to bake bread, but the sight of the cloth-draped pans of dough rising on the side irritated her; and the results, though smelling good, were as heavy as lead.

'Sue!' She stood at the foot of the stairs and called up. 'Do you want to come down to Redall?'

'Coming.' For once Sue was in contact, the Walkman for some reason (no batteries, her mother concluded) abandoned on her bedside table. Available for human communication, Sue appeared. 'Great. Are they coming back for lunch?'

'I hope so. Get your gloves darling.' Cissy looked critically at

279

her daughter's attire – black leggings, black tee shirt, black jumper which came to her knees in front and only just covered her bottom behind, black scarf knotted around her head and black eye liner – and she sighed. When she had got up that morning the child had looked like a pretty teenager. Now she looked like a zombie from the swamp.

With an exasperated sigh Cissy collected the keys of the Range Rover from the hall table and led the way outside. It was a cold, damp morning, the sky heavily overcast; any moment the snow would start again. They climbed into the Range Rover and Cissy started the engine, letting it run for a few moments as she switched on the windscreen wipers to clear the screen, and rubbed at the condensation with a duster.

'I hate this weather.' Sue leaned forward to turn on the radio, flicking through the stations.

Her mother winced as Radio One blasted into the quiet cold. 'Must you?'

'Oh come on, Mum. You'll be telling me you want to hear the birds next.'

'Why not?' Cissy shrugged, unequal to the argument. With a sigh she released the handbrake and swung the heavy vehicle out of the yard and onto the road. The sanders had been down in the night and the two-lane road was slushy with yellow mud; there were no other cars in sight as she drove cautiously the couple of miles to the turning which marked Redall Lane. 'I hope their track is not too bad,' she murmured as she turned in. 'I can't think why Roger doesn't get it tarmacked. Anyone would think they wanted to get cut off from the world, down here.'

'They haven't got enough money for things like that,' Sue put in. She crossed her ankle across her knee, leaning against the door, trying to be casual and comfortable as the car lurched over the potholes. 'If Dad was any kind of a neighbour he would do it for them. It wouldn't cost him anything – he's always doing the farm roads and it would make no end of difference to the Lindseys.'

Cissy caught her breath, about to retort that things didn't work like that – Joe would never do it, and Roger would never accept anyway – when she thought better of it. The young sometimes saw with shining clarity what needed to be done, and often they did it. It was adults who loused things up with their dithering and self-imposed rules. She bit her lip at the choice of words which had spilt into her mind. A fuck up. It described so much of her life; and Joe's. A fuck up from beginning to end. Well, why shouldn't they help someone else for a change? Joe could easily say he had over-ordered gravel or tarmac or whatever they used to make roads; a white lie to save Roger's pride.

'What are you smiling at?' Sue was staring at her, defying her to tell her to sit in a ladylike fashion. Sue smiled even more broadly. Well, fuck that too. The child could sit how she liked. It was her life.

The Range Rover slithered round the first of the steep corners without mishap and moved steadily towards the next. Daringly, Cissy accelerated a little, longing to be there. Overhead the trees arched beneath a fine mist of snow, their leaves crumpled and stripped to skeletons by the frost. The wet ruts gleamed darkly, reflecting no light from the sky, She flicked on the headlights with an irritated exclamation. The next moment she let out a scream as the arcing flash of the lights illuminated a figure in front of them on the track. Jamming on the brakes she wrestled frantically with the wheel as the heavy Range Rover began to slide.

'Oh God!'

Desperately she fought for control, conscious of Sue being flung sideways against the window with a resounding crack.

'Oh God!' her voice rose to a scream again as the figure seemed to fill her vision, his hands raised, then the car swung sideways over the edge of the track and spun into the ditch, slamming Cissie's head against the steering column as the engine stalled.

In the silence that followed the voice of Bruce Springsteen floated suddenly from the radio over the sound of the ticking engine and the hiss of steam from the shattered radiator.

XLIX

Patrick was clutching the gun under his arm. He was breaking all the rules; it was loaded and it was unbroken, but Kate had not commented on the fact as she followed him out of the door and they heard Diana bolt it behind them.

'Shall we go and look at the car?' Patrick turned to her questioningly. His face was pinched and white and she was astonished to feel a wave of something which she suspected was quite maternal. For all his attempts at being grown up he was still a little boy in some ways and he was looking to her to be the adult. Great. She wanted someone's hand to hold too.

She stopped and listened. The air was raw and cold; it smelt of damp pine trees and mud, catching in her throat, clammy against her face.

'We might as well,' she said slowly. 'It will only take a few minutes.' She was not anxious to set off up the dark track any more than he was.

They made their way across the rough grass to the sandy strip of ground which bordered their garden and the marsh and stood for a moment looking out across the mudflats. 'The tide is out far enough. I'll go and look.' Patrick handed her the gun. 'Will you wait here?'

She nodded. The gun was surprisingly heavy; she doubted if she could raise it to her shoulder and hold it steady even if she had to, but it felt reassuring in her gloved hands. Watching steadily, she narrowed her eyes against the wind as Patrick, protected by long boots, leaped from tussock to tussock, making his way out onto the mud, splashing every now and then through narrowing streams of water, scrambling up sandy, muddy dunes which rose out of the sea like little islands. He reached the car and she saw him peer in through the windows, circling it cautiously. He groped in his pocket and, producing the key, he unlocked the passenger door, easing himself inside. She held her breath, watching. Behind her the garden was totally silent. She imagined Diana and Greg watching from the kitchen window and the thought comforted her.

Only seconds later Patrick was climbing out of the car again. Carefully he relocked the door – something which struck her incongruously as being immensely funny, and began to make his way back towards her. He was muddy and out of breath when at last he stood beside her again.

'It was locked. There was no sign of anyone forcing the door and pulling at the wires under the dashboard. Everything was as it should be. No mud; no water; no scratches. In perfect nick.'

'Should we be pleased?' Kate asked wryly.

Patrick bit his lip 'How did it get there, Kate?'

She shrugged. 'Better not to ask at the moment. Let's concentrate on getting up to the road.' Pushing the gun at him she turned away from the sea.

He nodded. 'There's a short cut. Let's take that. I'll show you.' He led the way back across the grass.

In the house Greg turned away from the window. Behind him, his father had thrown himself down on the sofa. Within seconds he had fallen asleep. With a compassionate glance at Roger's exhausted face, Greg hobbled back to the kitchen. 'They've gone. Listen, Ma, what are we going to do about Allie? She is not going to sleep for very long.'

He gave her a careful look under his eyelashes, knowing what he would do – lock her up somewhere safe – and knowing that his mother would not hear of it. 'We have to accept that she might be dangerous. I know it's not her fault; it's not her, for Christ's sake, but we have to be careful.'

'What are you suggesting?' Diana's voice was hoarse with fatigue.

'Is there a key in her bedroom door?'

'You know there is. She's always locking herself in.'

'Then it won't be any hardship for her if we take her up and lock the door when she's safely tucked up in bed. For our own peace of mind.'

To his surprise she merely shrugged. 'All right.'

He glanced at his father and then back at her. 'You and I are going to have to do it, Ma.'

She nodded. For a moment she sat still, visibly wilting, then as he watched she straightened her shoulders and looked up. She gave a brave attempt at a smile. 'Sorry, Greg. I'm being no help. You're right, of course.' She stood up. 'I'll get her upstairs.'

'You can't do it on your own.'

'Of course I can –' Diana stopped short. For a moment neither of them had been looking at Alison but now, as they spoke, they realised that the girl had opened her eyes.

'Allie?' It was Greg who spoke first. 'Are you all right?'

Her eyes were wide, frightened, bewildered. Her own. He glanced at his mother and saw that she had seen too. She went towards the girl and kneeling put her arms round her. 'Allie, darling. You gave us such a fright.'

'Did I fall over?' Alison struggled to sit up, leaning against her mother.

'You had a dizzy spell, old thing.' Greg replied. He grinned at her reassuringly. 'Better now?

'I . . . I think so.'

'Bed, sweetheart.' Diana's voice was firm. 'Then I'll bring you up something to eat.'

Alison climbed unsteadily to her feet and stood for a moment, rocking slightly, looking around her in a daze. 'He's gone, hasn't he,' she said at last.

'Yes, he's gone.' Greg shook his head sternly at Diana as she opened her mouth to speak. 'Nothing to worry about any more little sister.'

Alison smiled. 'Nothing to worry about,' she repeated obediently. She still looked dazed.

Diana took her arm. 'Come on, darling. Upstairs. You'll catch cold down here.'

Greg watched as they crossed the room, then he sat down, aware again suddenly how badly his foot was throbbing.

It was several minutes before Diana reappeared. 'She lay down at once and she seems to have gone to sleep again.'

'Did you lock the door?'

She nodded. 'Oh, Greg, I hate to do it.'

'It's not going to hurt her. And better that than a repeat of – whatever happened before.'

She nodded. Pulling herself together she moved purposefully towards him. 'Right. Let's look at that foot.'

'Shouldn't we wait for the doctor?'

'So he can amputate? Come on. Put your leg up on the chair.' They both knew she had to keep herself busy somehow.

Gently she pulled away the bandages. They studied the swollen foot. 'I'm going to have to drain that.' She glanced up at him.

He managed to muster a smile. 'Can you face it?'

'Of course. I'll get the first aid box.'

It was in the study. Switching on the light, she peered round looking for the box she had left on the desk. It did not seem to be there. With an exclamation of annoyance she began to search the room then suddenly she stopped. It was cold in there – extra-ordinarily cold – and she could smell earth; damp earth. She frowned, fighting a sudden urge to run out of the room. 'Greg? What did I do with the first aid?' Her voice was unnaturally loud as she called over her shoulder. The door behind her was closed. Surely she hadn't closed it? She almost ran towards it, grabbing at the handle. It wouldn't open. 'Greg!' Her voice rose to a scream. 'Greg!' There was someone behind her. Someone very close to her. She could smell a strange perfume; sweet, cloying, and the cold was even more intense now, cutting into her fingers as she wrestled with the door latch. 'Greg!' Her voice broke into a sob. Whirling round she raised her arms in front of her face to ward off whoever was there.

The room was empty. She stared round, stunned. She had been so certain; she had heard her, felt her, smelt her; a woman. She knew it had been a woman. Sobbing with fear she turned back to wrestle with the latch. The door swung open with ease.

'Ma? Are you all right?' She could hear Greg's voice calling her; not worried, not afraid, just curious. Hadn't he heard her screams then? Swallowing hard in an attempt to steady herself, she looked back into the room. The first aid box was on the shelf by the door where she would have seen it straightaway if she had looked. Grabbing it she slammed the door behind her and went back into the living room.

'Couldn't find it for a minute.' She gave Greg a bright unnatural smile. 'Right. What I need is some boiling water and the TCP and I'm ready for you.' She hunted out a towel from the drawer while the kettle boiled, putting it gently under Greg's foot, fussing about laying out her equipment on the table.'

He put a hand on her arm. 'Are you OK?'

She nodded. 'I'm fine.'

'It's going to be all right.' He gave her a reassuring smile. 'There's an explanation for all this; nothing can bring Bill back, but I know it had nothing to do with Allie. Once the police get here they'll sort it all out, you'll see.'

She nodded again, concentrating on sorting out her dressings and bandages.

She boiled the razor blade for several minutes, then, washing her hands first with soap and water, then in the TCP she waited for it to cool before picking it up. 'Don't look.'

He grinned. 'If I don't look I might find you've chopped my foot off.' He gritted his teeth as she laid the blade against the stretched swollen skin. She hardly seemed to apply any pressure at all but suddenly the wound was erupting in a froth of yellow-green pus. He swallowed hard, averting his eyes in spite of himself, wincing as he felt the pressure of her fingers pressing out the last of the poison. She swabbed the wound again and again, holding the cotton wool with a pair of tweezers, then at last it was over. He felt the cool, clean dressing on the fiery skin, and then the bandage.

'Thanks.' He spoke through gritted teeth, amazed to find he felt dizzy with pain.

She had noticed. 'Rest a minute and I'll make us both a cup of tea.' She was gathering the swabs and throwing them into the bin, clearing up the mess, wiping down the table. Collecting the kettle, she was half way to the sink when the lights went out.

'Shit!' Greg stared round. 'It must be a fuse.'

'Don't you move.' Diana put a hand on his shoulder as he started to get up. 'Wait there and I'll go and look in the cupboard.'

The room was dim without the lights; the windows allowed a grey, dismal daylight to filter in from the garden where, they realised suddenly, it had started snowing again – soft white flakes this time, drifting down out of the heavy sky.

The loud crash upstairs made them look at each other in alarm.

'Allie!' Greg said. 'She's woken up.' He glanced at his father. Roger had not stirred, his head cushioned on his arm.

'I'll go.' Diana put down the kettle, horrified and ashamed to find that she was afraid – afraid of going to her own daughter.

'Be careful. Remember she's not herself,' Greg said softly.

She glared at him. 'Who are you suggesting she is?'

'I don't know. No one. I'm just saying, take care. She's been through a lot and she's had awful nightmares and I don't think she knows what she's doing half the time at the moment.'

Another crash followed the first and they both looked up. 'That came from Patrick's room,' Diana whispered.

'Take the rolling pin.' Greg murmured as she moved towards the upright studs which divided the living room from the kitchen. 'Just in case.'

'To hit my own daughter?' She stopped.

'If necessary, yes. For both your sakes.' He levered himself to his feet. 'Damn and blast this foot. I'm coming with you.'

'No, Greg –'

'Yes. Give me a walking stick from the hall. I'll be fine as long as I don't put too much weight on it.' He was staring up at the ceiling.

She brought it without further argument and then led the way to the staircase, pulling open the door which hid the dark stairwell. Looking up she listened, aware that Greg was right behind her, breathing painfully as he tried to balance with the stick.

Holding her breath she began to climb the stairs. At the top she peered cautiously down the passage. It was empty. Alison's bedroom door was closed as she had left it. The key was in the pocket of her trousers. She closed her hand around it and with a glance over her shoulder towards Greg, she moved stealthily towards the door and listened. At the far end of the passage the door to Patrick's room stood slightly ajar.

Biting her lip as she tried to move soundlessly, Diana led the way down the passage towards it. Behind her Greg felt the sweat break out on his forehead as he forced himself to walk softly after her. Without lights the upper hall was almost dark; the black beams threw wedges of shadow across the soft pink of the ceiling. The curtains, though open, blocked whatever light filtered in from the heavy sky. The garden was totally silent. Even the sound of the wind had died. Diana tightened her grip on the rolling pin, slowing as she approached the door, reluctant to go in.

Behind her Greg frowned. He could feel the skin on the back

of his neck crawling. He put his hand out and gripped his mother's arm. 'Let me,' he whispered.

She did not argue. Flattening herself against the wall, she let him pass and watched as very slowly he pushed open Patrick's door with the end of the stick. Peering over his shoulder she could not at first see anything, then slowly her eyes began to make out the dark interior of the room. 'Hell, look at his books.' Greg spoke out loud. He pushed the door back against the wall and took a step inside. The contents of every bookshelf had been tipped into the centre of the floor. There was no one there.

'Allie did this? Why? How did she get out?' Diana spoke in a whisper. The room smelled faintly of lavender.

Greg shrugged. He ran his stick under the bed, grunting with pain as his foot caught his weight, then he pulled open the cupboard door. There was nowhere in the room for anyone to hide. Pushing past him Diana pulled back the curtains, letting in a little more light. It revealed nothing but the shambles of books in the middle of the carpet. 'Some of them are torn,' she said sadly as she stood surveying the mess. 'He'll be so upset.'

'Where is she?' Greg turned and hopped back onto the landing. One by one he threw open the other doors – his own room, his parents', the bathroom. All were empty. It left only Alison's. 'She must be back in there.' He glanced at his mother. 'Shall I look?'

She nodded bleakly. He put his hand on the door knob and turned it. Nothing happened. 'It's locked,' he said in a whisper. 'Is there a bolt on the inside?'

She shook her head. 'I've got the key.' She put it into his hand. He frowned. With only a slight hesitation he inserted it into the lock and turned it as quietly as he could.

Alison's room too was dark, the curtains closed, the light which had been on beside her bed now off like the others. Greg stood in the doorway peering into the darkness, trying to see. If only they still had a torch that worked. His ears, straining in the silence adjusted to the sound of breathing. It was slow and steady and came from the bed. He groped in his pocket suddenly as he remembered his matches. Pushing his stick at his mother, who was immediately behind him, he struck one and held it high. The light was small and barely touched the room, but it was enough to see the hunched form of his sister in the bed. Wincing with pain he took a shuffled step forward and held it near her face. For a brief second, before it went out, he saw her closed eyes, the dark lashes on her cheek, her fist, clutching the blanket below her chin. Holding his breath he waited, half expecting her to leap from the bed with a scream, but nothing happened. The silence extended and filled the room again. All he could hear was her slow, heavy breathing, and behind him his mother's, quicker, lighter, exuding fear. Carefully he withdrew another match. The rasping sound as he struck it seemed to echo deafeningly as it flared and steadied, but Alison's lids did not flicker. He watched her for several seconds before raising the match high and glancing round the rest of the room. As far as he could see it was as it should be: her clothes lay in heaps on the floor, tapes and books in confusion on the chairs and table, but nothing seemed out of the ordinary. Nothing but the smell. As the frail light went out again he sniffed. The room was full of the heavy, spicy odour he had smelt before in the study. His mouth dry he began to back out. Diana moved with him. Without a sound he pulled the door closed and relocked it, then taking his mother's hand, he led her towards the staircase.

Safely downstairs he subsided into one of the deep armchairs beside his sleeping father. He realised suddenly that he was shaking again. A sheen of sweat iced his skin as the pain, which had seemed dulled upstairs, swept up his leg and took hold of him again. He lay back and closed his eyes, fighting to remain conscious.

'I'll check the fuses.' Diana's voice reached him through the roar in his ears. She groped in his pocket for the matchbox, paused for a moment to rest a gentle hand on Roger's head, then she had gone.

Greg had allowed himself to slide away into the spinning kaleidoscope of pain, settling deeper into something approaching sleep when he felt a glass being pushed into his hand. 'Brandy.' The voice was crisp and commanding. 'Come on, Greg. I'm sorry, but I need you awake.'

He opened his lips obediently and felt the fire on his tongue. For one more minute he resisted, then, choking, he felt himself propelled into full consciousness.

'There are no trips out and I've tried all the fuses. Nothing works.'

Opening his eyes he realised the room was full of candlelight. He was still disorientated. 'Did you smell the perfume?'

'What perfume?' She sounded irritated. 'Did you hear me, Greg? The electricity is off. All of it. And I can't find out what's wrong.' Her voice rose slightly and he realised that it was fear that he could hear. Desperately he took a grip on himself and swigged another mouthful of the brandy. Fire shot through his veins this time, and he felt his head clearing rapidly. 'It's the wind and the snow,' he said as steadily as he could. 'You know we are always being cut off when the weather's bad. We've got the fire, and the Aga and candles. There's nothing to worry about.'

'No.' She didn't sound convinced. 'What happened upstairs, Greg, it wasn't Allie, was it.' She sat down on the arm of the chair beside him. He could feel her trembling as she leaned against his shoulder. He reached for her hand and pressed it gently. 'No. It wasn't Allie.'

'Then who – ?'

He shook his head. 'The wind? An earth tremor? Perhaps the shelves were under too much stress. Perhaps it was the cats. Where are they? Those two are quite capable of knocking a million books when they play scatty cats round the house.'

'When they were young, perhaps.' She sniffed. 'Not now. Not for ages. Normally they are here, by the fire.' Suddenly her eyes filled with tears. 'I haven't seen them since Allie came back.'

Greg frowned. Now that he noticed, their absence was a tangible thing. He took it for granted that one or the other or both would always be there, in the chair where he was sitting now, or on the sofa with his father, or on the rocking chair beside the Aga. The room without them was unfurnished; empty. Threatening. 'I expect they've gone out before the weather worsens,' he said, trying to comfort. 'They won't have gone far, not when it's like this. They're soft little buggers, for all they like to think they're so tough.'

'Oh Greg!' A sob escaped her in spite of all her efforts to sound calm. 'What's happening? The car; the cats; Allie; Bill – I can't bear it.'

He put his arm around her. 'Just a sequence of strange coincidences,' he said as firmly as he could. 'And some bastard out there who will be behind bars before much longer if Paddy and Kate have anything to do with it.'

'They will get through?' It was a plea.

'Of course they will get through.' He wished he felt as positive as he sounded.

L

Sleet hit the side of the dune, lodging in the crevices of sand, standing a moment, half snow, half ice, then melting into the cracks and crannies. A further lump of sand fell away, and behind it the black peat, spongy, sweet, no longer encased in its jacket of airtight clay and meeting daylight for the first time in nearly two thousand years, began to wash in a black streak down the face of the excavation.

Deep down the great golden torc, symbol of Nion's royal blood, settled further into the subsoil. Torn from its silver companion by its weight and accepted by whichever gods there were in that black underworld, it would never again see the light of the sun.

Far above, the sea was meek, restless, the waves brown from the sandbanks which the storm had chewed over and rearranged in the night. Overhead a skein of geese, flying low and fast, sent their ringing bugle cries out into the wind where they were lost.

Another high tide, another storm and the dune would be gone, the peat and the clay mingling in the churning depths of the North Sea, its secret hidden forever. Another slice of soft black soil peeled off and slid away and the air, corroding, acid, insidious, touched the arm which lay there cushioned on what had once been a raft of flowering rushes. Around the humerus, loose where once it had clung tightly, lay the twisted semi-circle of a priestly arm-ring.

'Come on, through here.' Patrick turned and gave Kate his hand. They were both panting now, exhausted from the scramble through the tangled, wet undergrowth.

'You are sure you know where this short cut goes?' Kate climbed after him, hearing her jacket rip once again on a trailing bramble as she levered herself up the slippery bank to stand beside him in a clearing.

'Of course. Greg and I used to come this way all the time. It doesn't go anywhere near the lane; it cuts off the whole corner and comes out just below the Farnboroughs' place.' Patrick looked round. It was quite dark in the clearing; the trees, glistening with sleet, hung low above their heads and they could hear the hiss of rain on the leaves of a holm oak. The air smelled of wet earth and beech mast and rotting leaves.

Kate shivered. She glanced at Patrick again. He had slung the gun across his back; in his hand was a stout staff which he had pulled from a thicket as they dived into the woods. Both gave her comfort. She glanced behind her again. Not for the first time she had the feeling that they were being watched. Her fist tightened on her own stick. Not as long as Paddy's, but just as sturdy, she held it in front of her as she looked from side to side into the shadows.

Patrick saw her glance. 'There's no one around.' He did not sound very confident. 'If there were we'd hear the birds go up. Pheasants. Pigeon. They make a hell of a din if they are disturbed – you heard when we set them off. And there are magpies down here. They would all let us know if there was anyone around – or anything.'

She nodded. 'I wish we had a dog with us all the same.'

Patrick nodded. He grinned. 'A detachment of paras wouldn't go amiss either. Come on. It can't be much further. Once we're on the road we'll feel better.'

So, he was feeling it too. Kate looked behind her again. There was no sign of the way they had come. The tangle of brambles and dead brown grasses and nettles had closed without leaving any sign of where they had forced their way through. She felt a moment of panic. 'Which way?'

'Upwards. The road is quite a lot higher than Redall. It's uphill all the way, I'm afraid. We're bound to hit the road somewhere between Welsly Cross and the Farnboroughs'. We can't get lost.'

'No?' she grinned wanly. 'I hope those aren't famous last words.'

He was about to set off again when he stopped. He gave her a long look, his thin face drooping with exhaustion. 'You look absolutely whacked.'

She smiled. 'So do you.'

'It will all be over soon, won't it?'

'Of course it will.' Trying to reassure him did nothing for her own confidence. She glanced up at the sky. Where she could see it, between the interlaced branches of the thicket, it was growing increasingly black. 'We ought to get on.'

'I know. It was an excuse to get my breath back.' He hitched the gun higher onto his shoulder then he turned and led the way with more bravado than confidence up the high slippery bank which led out of the thicket and, he hoped, towards the north.

Ten minutes later he stopped. 'There ought to be some kind of path. But I suppose it could be overgrown.' He sounded doubtful.

'Have you got a compass?' It was the sort of thing all boys in the country festooned themselves with as far as she could remember.

He shook his head. 'I know this path like the back of my hand.'

She refrained from comment.

He bit his lip. 'It's getting so dark.'

'I know. There's more snow on the way. You can smell it.'

He smiled. 'And to think Greg thought you were Lady Muck from the town. You know more about the country than he does in many ways.'

'I can believe it –' She broke off as she saw a movement out of the corner of her eye. She spun round, staring into the shadows of the trees. 'What was that?' she whispered.

'Where?' He swung the gun off his shoulder.

'I thought I saw something move.'

They stared in silence for a moment, side by side.

'Probably a rabbit or a deer,' Patrick said softly.

He slipped the safety catch off the gun with a barely perceptible click.

She strained her eyes into the distance, trying to penetrate the murky depths of the scrub. There it was again, a shadow against the shadows, upright. Human. 'There.' Her whisper was scarcely audible. Inside her warm jacket she could feel her skin growing cold. 'There is someone there.'

'What shall we do?' Patrick's voice rose in panic and she was reminded suddenly that he was only a schoolboy and that he was probably far more scared than she was. If that were possible.

'I don't know. He must have seen us.'

'Do you think he's got a gun?'

She shook her head. 'I doubt it. We'd know by now.'

'Shall I shoot at him; try and scare him off?'

'I don't know.' She had started to shake again. 'Supposing it makes him angry?'

'If it does and he comes at us, at least we'll see who he is. And I can shoot him for real.' She saw Patrick's finger curling round the trigger.

She had only taken her eyes off the shadow for a second. Now as she looked back it had moved closer. It was tall; dark. To her horror she saw that it was moving quite swiftly, seeming to have no problem with the rough, tangled undergrowth. 'Yes. Go on, shoot.' She could hear her voice shaking with fear.

The report from the gun was colossal. It reverberated through the woods, echoing from the trees, temporarily deafening her. A pheasant rose shrieking into the sky, followed by a pair of pigeons, their wings smacking loudly. Patrick lowered the gun cautiously, feeling in his pocket for his cartridges. 'Where is he now? Did I hit him?' To his chagrin he didn't know whether or not he had aimed at the shadowy figure. He had been too frightened to think.

'I can't see.' She stared into the trees, forcing her eyes to focus into the darkest corners. There was nothing there.

With shaking hands Patrick reloaded the gun. 'If I've killed someone I'll go to prison.'

'Not if he murdered Bill, you won't.' She touched his shoulder reassuringly. 'I don't know if it was anyone. It could have been a shadow.'

'Should we check?'

She hesitated then she shook her head. 'Let's get onto the road and fetch the police. They can look.'

Slowly, more nervously now, they began to make their way forward again. Minutes later Paddy stopped so suddenly Kate cannoned into him. 'Look.' He pointed ahead.

She followed his finger and caught her breath. He was there again. On the rabbit track in front of them. Beside her Patrick raised his gun. She saw the barrel wavering as he felt for the safety catch and slid it back.

She stared at it. It was no more than a shadow; she could see no features – no face at all, just a silhouette. But it was a man.

He had disappeared before Patrick could move his finger to the trigger. 'Where is he?' He was frozen, the gun to his shoulder.

'Gone.' Kate could feel herself trembling. 'He vanished as I was watching. Paddy, keep the gun at the ready. Let's walk on slowly.'

She stepped forward, so close to Patrick he could feel her jacket brushing against his arm.

'One shouldn't walk with a loaded gun,' he whispered.

'This is an emergency. Just don't trip up.' They were there already; where it had been standing. She looked down. There were no footprints in the mud.

'Marcus?' She breathed the name out loud.

Patrick lowered the gun. 'I don't like this, Kate. And we should have been at the road by now.' He glanced over his shoulder. 'We're lost.'

'How big are these woods?' She was still scouring the ground for signs of footprints. She could see rabbit here and there, where it was soft, and the deep, sharply-cut slots of a deer, but none that had been made by a man.

'Hundreds of acres. The other side they're conifer plantations. They go for miles.' He shivered visibly.

'Can you find your way back to Redall?' She glanced at him. The boy was near to tears.

He shook his head. 'I don't know where we are.'

'Right.' It sounded confident. 'Let's think. Your original plan of following the rising ground sounds a sensible one. We can't stay out here all day; we've got to keep moving. Let's do that. Let's move only upwards, then, if as you say, we cross the road we'll be fine.' She was trying to picture the map in her head. The sea would be to the east; the estuary to the south. That left only two directions: north where the road ran east-west towards the coast, or due west where presumably the woods spread out until they reached the bleak, agricultural prairie lands east of Colchester and south of the soft wooded folds of the Stour valley.

'Come on. We can't get lost, Paddy. Not here. This is hardly uncharted country. We're just getting tired and cold.'

'And frightened,' he put in. She wished he hadn't.

'All right, and frightened.'

'You think it's Marcus, don't you.'

She shook her head. 'I don't know. I don't know what to think. I don't want to think any more. Let's save our strength for walking.'

He hesitated, about to say something, then he changed his

mind. Breaking the gun he lowered it to his side. 'OK. Lay on Macduff. Which way would you say is up?'

She glanced round. 'Straight on up this rabbit track. Shall I go first?' It was only wide enough for them to go in single file. She saw him hesitate, and knew he was longing to say yes, but chivalry or male pride, or the possession of the gun or a bit of all three won and he shook his head. 'I'll go. You can protect my rear.' The giggle he gave was a little hysterical.

Two minutes later he stopped with a gasp of terror. The shadow on the track was barely ten feet in front of them. A swirl of icy wind swept round it, whipping leaves and soil off the ground, howling up through the branches of the trees, gaining in strength until it rose to a scream as the hatred and anger hit them like a tangible force. Kate heard Patrick cry out and she saw him reel to one side, the gun flying into the air. For a moment she couldn't breathe. She could feel a constriction round her throat. Her feet refused to move. She wanted to run, to run faster than she had ever run in her life before but she couldn't take even the first step. There was an enormous bang somewhere inside her head and suddenly everything went black.

LI

Fat, confident, unsuspecting, the priests died like sheep, their throats cut like butter, their indignant, protesting whimpers still on their lips as they fell. So much for the power of their gods! He wiped his knife on a fold of his cloak and sheathed it with a triumphant smile. That was the end of the matter. The Britons, the whore, all dead, all gone to Hades and perdition. No one would know. The land would not tell. The men of the Trinovantes, who would give an arm each for a reason to fall on Rome, would never find reason for rebellion from him. This small drama would die as it had flourished on the edge of the mud. If men had disappeared, it would be assumed that the gods had called for more than one sacrifice; they were greedy these British gods; they lapped blood like dogs in the arena.

He folded his arms and stared out across the marsh, towards the eastern sky. It was clear now of cloud. The sun shone cold and hazy, clean like the blade of his knife, the light incising the wind. The heaviness of salt was in the air, overshadowing the flat, sallow smell of mud, cleansing it, purifying it with the incense of the northern seas. His eyes flicked down at the rushes which grew at the marsh's edge; they were green, the ends tipped with spiky, iridescent flowers. Nothing disturbed them. There was no sign that anyone had passed that way at all. He flexed the muscles of his fingers slowly, staring down at his hand. Four lives, snuffed out like flames, as though they had never been. And no one would ever know.

It was the sound of a shot which awoke her. Loud, close, exploding in her brain. Then silence. A long long silence where she floundered painfully in nothingness. A shot. It couldn't have been a shot. Who would be shooting? The sound must have been in her head. A part of the nightmare. A part of the pain. Giving up the struggle to make sense of nonsense Cissy slept again.

'*Mummy!*'

A cry this time, floating into her head like a dream. 'Mummy, I'm hurting. Help me.'

The sound spun round and round, and finally lodged in some part of her brain which was capable of a reaction. Cissy forced her eyes open with a groan. 'Susie?' She tried to move. There was a tight band around her ribs, preventing her from breathing properly. 'Susie?'

'*Mummy.*' The word was followed by a sob.

The sound cut through the last of Cissy's confusion. Christ! She'd crashed the car. She lifted her head with difficulty and stared round, trying to make sense of a world upside down. No, not upside down. On its side. The car was on its side and she was hanging from her seat belt. She looked down. Red. Blood. An awful lot of blood. Dear God, had Sue been wearing a seat belt at all? The child was below her, huddled in the well in front of the passenger seat.

'Are you all right?' Somehow she managed to make her voice work calmly in spite of the pain in her ribs which was, she realised, excruciating.

'We've crashed!' The reply was couched in the tone of a complaint.

'I can see that, darling.' Cissy bit her lip, trying to keep herself under control. 'Darling, I don't see how I can move. Are you hurt? Try and move each one of your arms and legs in turn. See if they're all right.' Her eyes were heavy. She wanted to close them, to slide away from the pain.

'They're OK.'

'And your head. Does that hurt?'

Sue moved it from side to side experimentally and her eyes filled with tears. 'Yes.'

'And your neck?'

'Yes.'

'But not so badly you can't move.'

'No.'

'Is there any way you can climb out?' The windscreen had gone, she realised hazily. That was why it was so cold. She was shaking now, her whole body shuddering in tight, agonised spasms. 'If I undo my seat belt I'm going to fall on top of you.'

'Is the car going to explode?' Sue was crying so hard she had not heard anything.

299

'No, darling, of course it's not going to explode. Range Rovers can't explode.' If they could, presumably it would have done so by now. 'Please, Susie, I want you to try and be brave. We have to get ourselves out of here. See if you can wriggle out of the windscreen. Then see if you can stand up.' She was finding it hard to breathe now. 'This is an awfully big adventure.' Who had said that? Peter Pan, was it? But he was talking about death. 'Please, darling. You must get out. If you can't help me, you have to go down to Redall and get help. If I . . .' she swallowed and choked, '. . . if I pass out, you musn't be frightened. I think I've broken some ribs. It's not serious –' please God '– but it's very painful. I think we've got to cut the strap.' Everything was spinning round her. She frowned, trying to focus. She couldn't see Susie at all now. Or hear. Why couldn't she hear? She tried to lift her head and look round, but her eyes were blurred with tears. Hands. Where were her hands? Why couldn't she use her hands?

'I'm out, Mummy.' Susie's voice was further away, but it seemed to be stronger. 'I think I'm all right.' Suddenly her face was there, close to Cissy's. 'Can you climb out?'

Cissy tried to think. Climb out. It seemed like a good idea, but how? She seemed to be suspended by her pain, swimming in space.

'I . . .' She tried again. 'I'm all right. My ribs. I think my ribs are hurt.'

'It's the seat belt. You're hanging in the seat belt.' Susie's voice was extraordinarily strong. 'I'll see if I can cut it with something.'

'No.' Shaking her head hurt. Perhaps her neck was broken too. Her thoughts were scattered, like a flock of pigeons after a bird scarer has gone off. Regroup them. Bring them in. Make sense. 'Can't cut it. You've got to undo it.'

'Mum, I can't. Look, you're pushing down on the slot.' Susie's hair was sweeping her face. 'We've got to lift you up somehow. 'Can you pull yourself this way?'

The girl's hands were cool, competent. She would make a good nurse. Cissy pondered her hands for a few seconds. 'Mummy!' The voice was cross now; impatient. 'Concentrate. You can't hang there. We've got to get you out. Put your hand up here. Where mine is. That's it. Now hold on. There. Tightly.'

She's make a good commander too; firm. Positive. Calm. Lost

in her endless pop music, it was easy to forget what the child was like as a person. She had become a shadow, walking round the house jerking to an unheard rhythm –

'Mummy!'

Silly girl. Giving orders. Silly orders.

'Mummy! Put your hand here.'

Impatient too. Stroppy little cow her father called her. Joe. Joe! Where was Joe?

She must have called out loud. Susie's face was there, in front of her again. Concerned, swimming in brightness. 'Dad will come soon, but we have to get you out.'

Susie had seen the slight dribble of blood at the corner of her mother's mouth. It terrified her. It should be Cissy comforting her, not the other way round. She glanced yet again over her shoulder into the dark trees. There had been no sign of him, the kook who had stood in the middle of the track in front of them and caused her mother to skid, but he must still be out there. He must have seen them crash.

Marcus

The name floated into her mind. Allie's Marcus. The dead Roman from the grave on the beach.

'Mummy!' Her terror gave her strength and she turned back to the smashed windscreen, leaning against the bonnet, trying to get a purchase on her mother's shoulder. 'When I say, try and take as much of your weight as you can here, on the doorframe. I'll see if I can free your belt.' She took a deep breath and reached into the car through the shattered glass. There was blood on the seat belt; the catch was slippery, hard to press, the belt strained beneath her mother's weight. She curled her fingers round the release and braced herself. 'Now. Now, go on, lift yourself as much as you can. NOW!' Frantically she pressed, wrenching the catch. Nothing happened. 'Don't let go. Pull up harder!' It must open. It must.

Pull. Cissy closed her fingers around the windowframe where Susie had positioned them. Pull. Good idea. Take her weight. Take the strain off her ribs. She pulled again and the pressure had gone.

'Done it!' The shriek in her ear was ecstatic. Then she was falling. Frantically she clung on again. Susie's arm around her took her full weight and she felt the girl stagger; the arm closed

301

around her and the pain was renewed in force but somehow she was half out of the windscreen. Flailing with her hands she felt grass and brambles; her weight was sliding her out of the car across the bonnet to the ground and suddenly she was lying on the mud, huddled, hips high, hugging her pain.

'Well done!' Susie was triumphant. 'Now sit up comfortably. Lean against the bank here.'

The girl glanced up into the trees again. There was something there. It moved slightly in the darkness of the shadows. She stood up, letting her mother slump back to the ground, her eyes straining to see what it was.

'Who's there?' Her voice was shaking. 'Greg? Paddy?' Please let it be one of them. They must be near the farmhouse. She glanced round, confused. How far had they come before they crashed? She couldn't remember.

It was there again. The movement in the trees. She could feel her mouth, dry as sandpaper; she couldn't breathe properly. Her knees were beginning to shake. 'Mummy.' It was a reflex action, this desperate whisper for help. She knew her mother couldn't hear her. 'Mummy, can you see him?'

The figure was tall; the face, dark, aquiline, cruel. Strange, she had always thought ghosts would be transparent, insubstantial, traversable should they cross one's path. Without fully realising she had done it, she sank to the ground beside her mother and reached for Cissy's hand. 'Mummy. Help me. He's coming.'

Cissy heard her. She tried to move her fingers but they didn't seem to work; her words of reassurance were lost as blood seeped into her throat.

LII

Joe frowned and glanced once again at his wristwatch. Strange that they weren't back.

He could smell the beef. The whole house was full of appetising scents which made his juices flow. Perhaps she didn't realise the time; she always got carried away, did Cissy, when she went down to Redall; something about that house that made one forget the time – he had felt it too. But if she was bringing them back, surely they should be here by now? He glanced at his watch once again; it was after three. The meat would be ruined. He glanced at the oven and shook his head. Tempted though he was to start without them perhaps he'd better get down there and see what was wrong. Grabbing an oven cloth off the rail he pulled open the door and pulled out the meat pan. The meat was dry, shrunk on the bone, the potatoes almost black. He shook his head sadly and pushed the trays of food onto the counter. Spoiled anyway.

Outside he glanced up at the sky. The light was nearly gone already, the cloud black and threatening, the wind – he sniffed knowledgeably – coming a degree or so round to the north. That would bring real snow; the kind they hadn't seen for four years on this coast. Thoughtfully he hauled himself up into the old Land Rover which stood by the barn and leaned forward to turn the key.

At first he didn't recognise what he saw; his eyes refused to make sense of the axles, the wheels, the exhaust which were all he could see of his Range Rover, on its side in the ditch. In the headlights, through the driving sleet, all he could see was a pattern of shiny mud and steel. Then he realised and his stomach turned over. He skidded to a halt, and leaving the headlights trained on the wreck, he levered himself out of the driving seat and jumped down into the slush. 'Cissy?' Dear sweet lord, where were they? 'Susie my love?' He jumped into the ditch and clambered round to the far side of the vehicle, his boots sliding and squelching, catching in the brambles.

The black silhouette of the wreck cut out the powerful beam of his headlights and it was a moment before his eyes adjusted enough to the dim light to see Cissy, sitting, leaning against the bonnet, her eyes closed. Susie was curled up close to her, her arms wrapped around her knees, rocking slowly from side to side.

'Susie?' Joe called.

The girl tightened her grip on her knees. 'She's dead.' She did not look up. 'She's dead.' Tears were streaming down her face.

Joe scrambled closer and knelt down beside her, his craggy face white. He could hardly see for tears himself. 'No. No, baby, no.' Tearing off his gloves, he reached past her and gently he took Cissy's wrist in his own. It was cold. 'Ciss? Ciss, my love? Come on.' His fingers were rough and split, no good for this sort of thing. Persistently he felt all over her wrist, pressing the soft cold skin until suddenly he felt a faint flutter.

'She's not dead, Sue.' He was trembling as much as his daughter. 'Nearly, but not quite. Help me lift her. We'll get her into the back of the Land Rover.'

He scooped her up into his arms as though she were no weight at all, and slipping and sliding, carried her back to the track. The open back was full of old tools and sacks and bits of twine. 'Hop in, Susie. Take your Mum's head in your lap. Keep her comfy.' His calmness now that there was something to do was infectious. Susie obeyed him, sitting on the floor, pulling sacks over her mother's inert body.

Joe walked back to the driving seat and pulled himself into it. One look at the steep, icy track down which he had slithered only minutes before told him they were unlikely to make it back that way. 'I reckon we'll take her down to Redall. Diana will know what to do to keep her comfy. She used to be a nurse. Then if their phone is still not working I'll get back on the back lane to phone for an ambulance. Hold her now, Susie my love. You'd almost got there, you know. We're only a few hundred yards from Redall.'

He refused to consider the possibility that she might be dead. He had felt a pulse. He was sure of it. Letting in the clutch with infinite care he dragged the Land Rover back onto the track and headed on down towards the farmhouse.

Diana had seen them coming, but not until Joe emerged from behind the wheel did she open the front door. 'Joe? Thank God! Where are the police? Are they coming?'

'The police?' Joe shook his head, preoccupied with his own sorrow. 'I haven't called them yet, nor the ambulance. I reckoned I'd leave her here with you and try and get back up through a side track. It's all too slippery up there even for this old girl.' He slapped the vehicle with a gnarled hand as he walked round the back and tenderly lifted Cissy out.

'Cissy!' Diana cried. 'What's wrong with her?' Behind her Roger rose wearily to his feet. He peered over her shoulder.

'We crashed the Range Rover.' Susie scrambled out after her mother. 'She's dead. I know she's dead!' She burst into tears again.

'Bring her in. Quickly.' Diana glanced out into the darkness of the woods. Dusk was coming early. The snow was feathering down out of a bruised, blackened sky. The woods were silent.

'Put her down on the sofa.' She stared down at Cissy's white face, and then, as Joe had done, reached for her wrist. 'Where are Paddy and Kate? Didn't you see them?'

More practised than Joe, she found a pulse almost at once. It was faint but steady.

Behind them Greg emerged from the study. Quietly he shut the front door and bolted it. The candles in the living room flickered.

Standing around the sofa Greg, Roger, Susie and Joe stared down at the still figure lying there. Diana sat beside her, cautiously running her hands over her still form, refraining from any comment about the way Joe had manhandled his wife out of the Land Rover. If her neck or back were injured it was too late to say anything now. There were bruises on her face, a cut on her lip – please God that was where the blood was coming from – livid bruises on Cissy's shoulders and ribs as Diana opened her blouse.

'Joe, I think you should go back and phone for an ambulance now,' Greg said as he watched his mother's hands. 'And we need the police. Somebody has beaten Bill Norcross to death.'

The action of Joe's jaw lifted his scalp until his whole face seemed to slip back in surprise, but still he did not take his eyes off his wife. 'You reckon they attacked Cissy?' He looked at Greg at last, a deep flush spreading up from his neck across his face.

'No, Dad. We skidded. There was a man –' Susie stopped short.

'A man?' Greg turned to scrutinise her face.

'What man, Susie?' Joe grabbed her and turned her to face him. 'You didn't say anything about a man.'

'He . . . he appeared in front of us.' Susie started crying again. 'Mummy jammed on the brakes and we began to spin round. I banged my head on the window.'

'What did he look like, Susie?' Greg kept his voice gentle.

'He was dressed in a long cloak thing. He had a sword . . .'

'A sword!' As Greg and Diana looked at each other Joe's words were an incredulous echo.

'And you saw no sign of Kate or Patrick?' Diana was feeling down each of Cissy's legs. Nothing broken there at least.

'No.' Susie shook her head violently.

'They had a gun,' Greg put in.

'I think I heard a gun going off,' Susie broke free of her father's hands and went to kneel beside her mother. 'Just after the crash. There was a big bang.'

Diana closed her eyes briefly. Somehow she managed to keep her hands steady as she took the rug which Greg handed her and pulled it up over Cissy's inert form. Standing up she turned to Joe. 'You must go and get help, Joe. We'll look after her as best we can but she needs a doctor. I think she's only bruised, but she might be concussed. She must have an X-ray.'

'But she'll be all right?' Joe looked down at her miserably. He felt lost and abandoned.

'I hope so.' Diana smiled at him; she rested a hand on his arm. 'Susie can stay here; I'll take care of them both, Joe, I promise.'

He nodded. For a moment he hesitated self-consciously, wanting to stoop and kiss his wife, then awkwardly he turned away.

Greg hopped after him. In the hallway he spoke in low, urgent tones. 'Joe, there's a maniac out there. Be careful for God's sake. Paddy and Kate set out hours ago to ring from your place. Keep your eyes open for them, and tell the police what's happened.'

Joe nodded curtly. He reached out to open the door. 'You take care of them all here.'

'I will, don't worry.' The grimness of Greg's tone was reassuring.

Joe paused on the doorstep. The world was totally silent,

wrapped in whirling snow. For a moment he hesitated, unwilling to cross the few yards of white ground to his Land Rover, then shaking his head, he strode forward, hearing Greg bolt the door behind him.

Walking round to the back he reached in over the tail gate for his gun, wedged into clips which had been screwed onto the vehicle's frame. Wrenching it free he pushed back the lid on the box which sat beneath the side seat. His cartridges were there; left after the last shoot. He could lose his licence for carelessness like that, but who was to know. Almost kissing them he stuffed them into the baggy pocket of his jacket and climbed behind the wheel. Laying the gun on the seat next to him he reached for the key which he had left in the ignition, his eyes on the windscreen which was blanked out with snow.

The key clicked uselessly.

He turned it again and again without success. Behind him the door of the house opened again. Greg had obviously been watching from the study window. 'What's wrong?' His voice was muffled by the snow.'

'Darned battery's flat. Hold on, I'll try the starting handle.' He climbed out, glad that someone else was there. The silence of the woods was becoming oppressive.

The metal was cold through his gloves as he inserted it and swung it round. The engine remained dead. 'Damned bloody thing!' He tried again, feeling the sweat start on his forehead.

Behind him Greg was watching the trees. He could feel his skin prickling with fear. Someone – or something – was watching them. He was sure of it. 'Joe,' he called quietly. 'Joe, bring the gun and get in here.'

'I'll just give it one more try.'

'No, Joe. Don't bother. Grab your gun and come in.'

There was something in the urgency of Greg's tone which stopped Joe in his tracks. He straightened. He could feel it too now, a building panic crawling across him. Leaving the handle where it was he reached in and grabbed the shotgun, then turning, he sprinted the few yards back to the farm house. Greg slammed the door behind him and threw the bolts across. Both men stood for a moment in the small hallway and listened. There was no sound from outside. 'You reckon he's out there?' Joe whispered.

Greg nodded.

'You've seen him?'

'Kate and I saw him down on the shore.'

'And Norcross is dead?' It seemed only just to have sunk in. 'Are you sure?'

'Quite sure.' Greg's tone left no room for doubt. 'What the hell do we do now, Joe? We have to have help.'

'I could take your car. I reckon that old Volvo would have a good chance of getting up the back lane.'

Greg shook his head. 'Our old Volvo is out on the marsh, Joe. Don't ask how it got there, and our Land Rover is smashed up; it hit a tree.'

Joe stared. 'You mean there are no cars working? None at all?'

'And no phones.'

The two men stared at one another. 'You reckon he did it. He caused Cissy's crash.'

'And Kate's. He tried to kill me on the beach.' Greg paused. 'Wait, Joe. I've just remembered. Kate's little car. The Peugeot. It's in the barn. I don't know if it would make it up the lane, but it might be worth a try.'

'Right.' Joe dug down into his pocket and came up with two cartridges. 'I'll put a couple of these up the spout, then we'll have a go. Is the barn unlocked?'

Greg shrugged. He rummaged in the drawer of the table. Two small padlock keys on a large ring appeared and he pressed them into Joe's hand. 'I'll come with you. Hold on while I get my boots.'

'No.' Joe shook his head. 'I reckon I'll be quicker on my own. You look after your dad and the women.'

'I don't know if she left a key in it.'

'If she didn't I reckon I'll smash the window and hotwire it. I'm sure she'll forgive me in an emergency. My Cissy needs a doctor. No car door is going to come between me and that.'

Once more Greg unbarred the door and pulled it open. It was beginning to grow dark. The shadowed woods were in stark contrast to the brilliant whiteness of the lawn. Somewhere in the distance a pheasant let out its manic alarm cry. Joe tightened his grip on the gun. He gave a quick thumbs up sign to Greg then he turned and ran towards the black barn.

The padlock hung open from the hasp. Joe stared at it. His

hackles were stirring again, like the back of a frightened dog. Cautiously he put his hand to the door and pulled it open a fraction. There was a strange smell in the barn. He sniffed. It smelt hot, petrol, with something else – like cordite. And smoke. There was smoke. He had time only to step back half a pace before a fireball of yellow and gold heat erupted out of Kate's car and blew him backwards into the garden.

'Christ Almighty!' Greg had not had time to close the door when he saw the man's figure fly backwards away from the barn doors. Fire and smoke were already erupting from the barn roof, sparks jumping into the air to be lost in the snow.

'Greg? What is it? What's happened?' Diana ran to join him followed by Susie. Behind them Roger closed his eyes. For a moment he stood without moving, then slowly he dragged himself after them to the door.

'Daddy!' Susie's hysterical cry was followed by a wild sob as she saw the figure on the grass begin crawling towards them. 'I'll go.' Diana pushed past Greg. In seconds she was kneeling beside him.

'I'm all right. I'm all right. Just shaken.' Joe was coughing violently, his eyes streaming. 'Find the gun. Quickly. Find the bloody gun. And be careful, it's loaded.' He staggered to his feet and began to move towards the house.

Greg watched in an agony of frustration, seeing his mother running towards the blazing building. 'Get me my stick,' he yelled at Susie. 'Quickly. Get me my stick!'

Grabbing it from her he had begun to hobble towards Diana when he saw her duck into the smoke and reappear a moment later, the shotgun under her arm.

Pushing past his son, Roger ran out into the snow. 'Di–'

'Get in, Joe.' Greg thrust the man behind him and ran after his father, his eyes on the barn. Smoke was pouring through the roof; a series of small explosions were rocking the building. Diana reached them, gasping. For a moment they all stood staring at the fire then Greg took his mother's arm and pulled her away. 'Get back inside quickly.'

'Oh Greg.' Her eyes filled with tears. Miserably, she went to Roger, who put his arm around her and guided her back towards the house.

In his impatience Greg had put his foot down for a couple of steps. The pain sliced through him like a knife and he swore viciously. 'Just thank God the wind is blowing away from the house; the snow will damp down any sparks. But we've lost the barn, Dad. Nothing can save it.'

They stood in the doorway for a moment watching in despair as the first flames licked out through the black boarding. Diana's eyes filled with tears. 'I loved that barn. It was lovely. And my roses! My poor roses. They'll be burned.'

'I expect their roots will be all right.' Roger tried to sound reassuring. Gently he pulled her in and closed the door. 'Go and sit down with Joe. Greg, can you manage to get us all a brandy?'

'Are you hurt, Joe?' Trying to forget the pain of her precious plants, and the small birds who always roosted in the barn at dusk Diana turned towards him, scrutinising the black smudges across his face.

He shook his head. 'Just bloody shocked.' He sounded angry more than anything else. 'What bastard would do a thing like that? That place must have been booby trapped!' He threw himself down on a chair. 'I reckon I could do with that brandy, thanks Greg.' He looked at Cissy. 'How is she?'

'Much the same.' Diana sat down beside her and put her hand on Cissy's forehead. Aware that her own heart was thundering in her ears with the shock of what had happened she slipped her fingers down to take the pulse beneath Cissy's ear. It was stronger now and steadier.

She looked up to find Greg standing behind her with a glass.

She reached up for it. 'So. What happens now?'

'I'll go on foot. That's what happens now.' Joe swallowed his brandy in one gulp and held out the glass for a refill. 'I'm not letting any murdering bastard do that to me and get away with it.'

'You can't go in the dark, Joe.' Greg glanced at the windows. 'It would be madness. Kate and Paddy will have reached your place by now. If they can't get in, I'm sure they will hitch up to the Headleys' or Heath Farm. They will get help far more quickly than you can.'

'And if they haven't made it?' Joe's question was brutally direct. 'What if he got them?'

'He hasn't got them, Joe.' Greg looked at his mother. 'Paddy had a gun. He wouldn't be afraid to use it.'

His eyes strayed thoughtfully to Sue. She said she had heard a shot. But you can't shoot ghosts. The thought kept straying back into his mind. A gun would have no effect on Marcus. No effect at all.

As if she had read his mind, Diana glanced at him. 'A ghost couldn't set fire to the barn, Greg. Or move the Volvo. That must have been a real man.'

'A ghost?' Joe stared at her. 'What does a bloody ghost have to do with all this? Are you telling me a bloody ghost ran my wife off the road?'

'I don't know what we're telling you, Joe. I just don't know.' Greg was white with frustration. He threw himself down on the chair again. 'Oh, Christ, I wish I could walk! Where are Kate and Paddy?'

LIII

Kate was lying on her face, her head cushioned on her arms, aware slowly that a small trickle of blood somewhere in the hair above her left temple had dried into a crust. How long she had been lying there she wasn't sure, but in the interval she had grown very cold. Cautiously she raised her head, expecting to feel at any second an icy hand on her back, but there was nothing, just the long, lingering catch of the bramble which had scratched her head as she fell. Her hand closed in the mud, crisp now with incipient ice, and she realised she was shaking.

'Paddy?'

There had been no sound since the gun went off. Her terror had led to paralysis of will. She could not move or speak. Some atavistic instinct told her that shamming death was her only protection. How long that state had lasted she didn't know. She moved her hand slightly, trying to bring her wrist, with the narrow, gold watch, within sight without raising her head more than a few inches.

'Paddy?' She tried again, louder this time.

'Here.' His voice was muffled, but not too far away.

'Are you all right?'

'I think so. I've lost the gun. I fell.' She could hear tears in his voice. 'Has he gone?'

'I don't know.' She raised her head higher, trying to see. 'I think so.'

'Where are you?'

'Here.' She rose cautiously to her knees, wishing she could stop herself shaking. She could actually hear her teeth chattering. 'I'm here. Keep talking and I'll see if I can find you.' The light had nearly gone.

There was a rustling somewhere to her left. She swung round. 'Is that you?'

'Yes. I'm OK. Here.' He clung to her for several seconds and she could feel the chill of his body against her own. 'He's gone,' she whispered. 'I can't feel him around any more.'

'Which way do we go?' He pulled away from her and she could feel him grasping at his dignity almost as though it were armour, and shrugging it on again.

'We should have brought a compass.' She tried to make the remark light. 'We can still follow the contour of the land, though. Keep going up.'

'That doesn't seem to work.'

'Paddy, what else can we do? We can't stay here all night.' She had only just realised that it was snowing again; proper snow this time, light and feathery and relentless; a pale glimmer at her feet showed where it was settling.

'Do you know any prayers?'

The question caught her by surprise. 'Well, the Lord's Prayer, of course, everyone knows that.'

'That's what one says to ward off evil, isn't it? To keep him away.'

Kate reached out and took his hand. 'We could say it together if it helps. You're right. It's supposed to keep evil spirits away. I'm not much of an authority on prayer.'

'Or evil spirits, I expect.' He forced a small laugh. 'Do you know it in Latin? *Pater Noster.* All that. He must speak Latin if he's a Roman. We don't do Latin at my school.' Again the strained little laugh. 'It never crossed my mind that I might need it.'

May the gods of all eternity curse you, Marcus Severus, and bring your putrid body and your rotten soul to judgement for what you have done here this day.

Kate rubbed her face with her hands. The words were trapped in her brain. They were not external. If they had been Paddy would have heard them too. And the words were in English.

'I think he understands our language,' she said carefully. They had both accepted, she noticed, that it was Marcus they had seen, not some flesh and blood intruder in the woods. 'I think if we are communicating with him or with anyone else it is in our heads.'

'But you could tell him to sod off in Latin?' He said it so hopefully she heard herself laugh out loud.

'I did the kind of Latin one learns in the hope that it will

313

facilitate one's grasp of literature,' she said apologetically. 'I don't think I ever learned to say sod off.' She paused. 'I do know the *Pater Noster* though.'

'Say it.'

'*Pater Noster, qui es in caelis, sanctificetur nomen tuum. Adveniat regnum tuum. Fiat voluntas tua, sicut in caelo, et in terra. Panem nostrum quotidianum da nobis hodie. Et dimitte nobis debita nostra, sicut et nos dimittimus debitoribus nostris. Et ne nos inducas in tentationem: sed libera nos a malo . . .*' She stopped.

There was a moment's silence. 'Go on,' he whispered.

'That's it. Or at least, that's all I can remember. But that's the important bit. *Libera nos a malo.* Deliver us from evil.' It didn't matter. There was no one out there listening now. She was sure of it. He had gone. 'Paddy, let's try and find the gun. It can't have gone far.' It was almost dark. The light was failing fast.

'I think it fell over there. Don't tell Dad it went off. He'll never let me use it again.'

'It probably saved our lives,' she retorted tersely. 'I can see it. There. In those nettles.'

The snow was thicker now, drifting down, here a pale drifting cloud, there driven by the wind into a stinging curtain.

Patrick retrieved the gun cautiously, and broke it under his arm. He looked round. 'There's no sign of a path. I can't even see which way we came.'

'This way.' Kate didn't hesitate. She pushed through some brambles and began to climb a small incline, her borrowed boots slipping in the snow.

'Wait.' Patrick was staring round. 'Look. Through the trees.'

'Where?'

'There. I can see a light.'

'Thank God!' It was a heartfelt prayer. Side by side they scrambled towards it, sliding and slipping downwards now, out of the eye of the wind into the shelter of the woods again.

'It's gone. I can't see it.'

'There. There it is.' Patrick stopped. 'It's Redall. Oh, Kate, we've come round in a circle. We're back where we started. He's not going to let us escape.' The disappointment and fear in his voice were palpable.

She bit her lip, angry with herself as much for the stupidity as for the overwhelming rush of relief which had swept over her.

314

'Can't be helped. We'll go back in and see if we can find a compass.'

'Right.' He nodded firmly.

'Then we'll have to try again. And this time we'll stay on the main track.'

'Agreed.' He gave her a broad grin. 'A hot drink first, though. Yes?'

'Yes.' She put her arm around his shoulder.

LIV

Jon opened the door of his flat and peered in. It smelt stale; unlived in. Cyrus, he had heard only yesterday before he flew out of Kennedy, had stayed there just two days before having a massive fight with the sponsors of his London visit, and flying back to the States.

Dropping his bag on the floor, Jon pushed the front door closed behind him with his foot and stooped to pick up his mail. Wearily he walked across to the table and threw it down. On the window-sill a vase of dead flowers stood in a circle of sticky yellow pollen. He went to pick it up and carried it through to the kitchen, wrinkling his nose at the stench from the stale water. On the worktop was a set of keys. Turning on the tap so it ran into the vase, flushing away the slimy green deposits which clung to the rough porcelain he picked up the keys and looked at the tag. A small black cat. Kate's keys. He smacked them down on the counter. Two days! Two lousy days Cyrus had stayed and he had as good as thrown her out for that! Well, he had paid back the first half of her money now, at least.

Going back to the living room, he flung himself down on the sofa and reached onto the table beside him to punch the answer machine. The calls went on and on. He listened wearily, his eyes closed. The procession of voices through the cold half light of the afternoon was like a review of his life. 'Hi Jon. Call me when you get back' . . . 'Jon, if you're there around the 18th we're having a get together . . .' 'Jon, don't forget, twelve thirty on the 23rd at the Groucho . . .' 'Jon . . .' 'Jon . . .' 'Jon . . .'

He stood up and went to pour himself a Scotch. The bottle – all the bottles on the tray, he noticed wryly – were empty.

'Shit!'

'Jon. This is Bill. Just to let you know all the phones down at Redall seem to be out of commission. I'm going down this morning – it's about ten on Saturday morning now – to see what's going on.'

Jon switched off the machine. Reaching for the phone he dialled Bill's number. It rang on in the silence. He redialled – Bill's cottage this time. 'Come on, answer.' Jon drummed his fingers on his knee. Abruptly he cut the connection. He tried the Redall Cottage number. The line was still dead. Swearing under his breath, he dialled the Lindseys'. That, too was silent. He slammed down the receiver and stood up. What the hell was going on up there?

Turning to his bags, he found the bottle of duty free Talisker he had picked up at the airport. Uncapping it he poured himself a slug.

Why the hell did he care so much anyway? Kate was part of history. They had not got on. The affair was over. Finished. Kaput. There was nothing left to rekindle. She wasn't interested in him any more, however friendly she had been on the phone. That was just politeness; typical Kate, not wanting to hurt anyone's feelings. He would probably never see her again.

He drained his glass and poured some more. Outside the window with its veil of sooty net the London street grew dark. A steady wet sleet had begun to fall. Setting down his glass Jon went to switch on the tall, chrome lamp in the corner. Then he reached for the road map.

LV

raging inside her head. There were no words, no form; a mael-strom of whirling pain.

'*Mummy!*'

The cry was muffled, agonised. It fell into the black silence of the room, unheard.

'*Mummy, help me!*'

They were inside her head, locked in battle. He, Marcus, always the stronger, tearing at the core of her brain, wanting her, using her, needing her voice, her arms, her strength.

And she. Claudia. She would not give in. The truth must be told. Nion. Betrayed. Insult to the gods. *Nion. Nion. Love of my life, partner of my soul.*

Tear them out. Be rid of them. Be free of them. Nails. Rip them out with her nails. Tear her head open.

'*MUMMY. HELP ME!*'

'*Let the truth be told. I will have the truth told.*' The scream is louder now. Claudia is gaining in strength. '*The grave is open. The secret is out. The people of Britain shall avenge our death. The fall of the Empire will not be revenge enough. May the gods of all eternity curse you, Marcus Severus Secundus, for what you have done . . .*'

'No, no, *NO!*'

Alison sat up violently, her hands to her temples. Her nails were red with her own blood. She stared round the room. The lights were no longer on, but she could see quite clearly. The woman was standing by the window, her blue gown moving gently as though the wind were blowing from behind her, her feet in the soft dune sand, her hair tangled in its combs. She seemed to see right through the wall, through the house, through the darkness and the snow.

Alison cowered against the wall. Blood. There was blood everywhere; down the front of the woman's dress; on the floor on her own sheets and – she looked down suddenly, seeing without trouble in the darkness, all over her own hands.

Her own scream blocked out the sound of voices. She screamed on and on, out of control, out of her head now, watching herself from the doorway, watching the group of people downstairs rise from the kitchen table, pick up their candles and head towards the stairs. Diana was there first, the flame of her candle shivering and trailing smoke.

'Alison. Alison, darling! Oh Christ, what's wrong with her?'

She could see her mother's arm around her, see her mouth moving, but she felt nothing. He was there now, inside her head again. Laughing. Why was he laughing? Laughing at the blood and the pain. Laughing at her: the woman by the curtains. She was indistinct now, a shadow from a distant past. Nothing more. Disappearing. Vanquished. Crumbling back into the sand. Part of the forgotten time . . .

'*Pater noster* . . .' It was Patrick's voice, trembling, in the shadows. '*Libera nos a malo. Ave Maria. Libera nos a malo.*' The words slid into a sob of pain.

'Her face. Christ, Di, look at her face.' Breathless, Roger had joined the group on the landing, peering over his wife's shoulder. 'Shut up, Paddy!' He turned on his son. 'I won't have that sentimental crap uttered in this house!'

'Go away, all of you.' Diana tightened her grip on Alison's shoulders. 'Go away. I'll see to her.' She glanced up, scarcely able to see through her tears. 'Kate, will you stay. The rest of you go downstairs.'

For a moment Roger opened his mouth, about to speak, then he changed his mind. He handed Kate his candle and turned away. He was shaking visibly as he ushered the others down.

Obediently Kate went to the bathroom for a facecloth and, wringing it out brought it back to the bedroom. Diana wiped the blood from Alison's hands, then gently she guided her back to bed. 'You're safe now, sweetheart. Quite safe.'

'What about her face?' Kate was holding the candle steady.

'I'll leave it for now. They're only superficial scratches.' Diana glanced at her wearily. 'I'm not letting you and Paddy or Joe leave this house again tonight.'

'Someone must get help, Diana.'

'Time enough in daylight. Everything must wait until then.'

'But what about Greg? What about Cissy?' Kate had been appalled at the sight of Cissy Farnborough lying, barely conscious, on the sofa by the fire.

'She'll be all right. I can take care of her. There is someone trying to kill us all out there, Kate!' Diana pulled the sheet up around Alison's chin and tucked it in. 'I am not letting anyone else set foot outside this house.'

Kate looked down at Alison. The girl was quiet now, lying very still on her blood-stained pillow, breathing long, even breaths as though she were asleep again. 'What do you think happened?' she asked in a whisper.

'She had a nightmare.' There was a desperate set to Diana's chin.

'I think it was more than that.' Kate walked further into the room. The small intimate space, lit by the two candles was icy cold. On the floor in front of the curtains lay a scattering of sand. Kate stared down at it for a moment, frowning, then she turned away. 'Why did your husband swear at Paddy for praying?'

'He doesn't believe in God. He stopped believing the day he discovered he had cancer.'

'And does he believe in evil? In possession? In ghosts?'

It was Diana's turn to shiver. 'He's a reductionist and a fatalist. He believes in nothing that cannot be scientifically proven.'

'How strange.' Kate's eyes were fixed on Alison's face. To her, Roger had come across as a man with poetry in his soul. And he was a man who still, in extremis, cried out the name of Christ even though it meant nothing to him.

'Do you pray?' Diana sat down on the edge of the bed and laid a gentle hand on her daughter's forehead. It was very cold.

'Not very often. But it was me who taught Paddy the words to say. Outside in the dark it seemed the right thing to do. He thought Marcus would understand the Latin.'

'And did he?' The note of irony Diana was aiming at somehow failed to materialise; the question came out straight.

'I don't know. But the words made me feel better. A shield. A talisman against evil.'

'He's got us trapped here, hasn't he.' Diana looked at her suddenly and for a moment she could no longer hide her panic. 'Every one of the cars is damaged; the phone won't work; no one knows what's happened. Bill and Cissy tried to help us and look what happened to them.' A tear slid down her face. 'And Allie. What's happened to Allie?'

Kate knelt beside her and took her hand. 'I think we should take Allie downstairs. I think we should all stay together.'

'She's right.' Greg's voice from the landing made them both jump. He hobbled in and stood looking down at his sister. 'I'll ask Joe to come and carry her down then I think you should make a huge cauldron of soup for us all.' He was looking at his mother. He glanced at Kate who was still kneeling on the floor. 'Everything will seem a bit less fraught in the morning, then we can send for reinforcements.'

Kate gave him a watery smile. 'You make it sound easy.' The flickering candlelight, made her face look ethereal. She had, he noticed not for the first time, a frail, pre-Raphaelite beauty, emphasised by her disordered, tangled hair and helped, he supposed wryly, by the submissive posture, on her knees at his feet.

'It will be easy. Everything is always better in daylight.'

'Don't tempt providence!' As if realising that her position put her at a disadvantage, she scrambled to her feet. Standing, she was as tall as he. 'Greg.' She put her hand on his arm, her voice barely a whisper. 'Look, by the window. On the floor.'

He raised an eyebrow, then picking up the candle, he limped across and surveyed the carpet.

'Sand. It could have come from Allie's shoes.'

'But it didn't. I was up here earlier and it wasn't here.'

'How can you be sure?'

'I just am.' She shrugged. 'I notice things like that. After the cottage.'

'What are you saying?' Diana turned to look at the carpet.

'She's saying that some sand has blown in the window and that it would be better if we all went downstairs and sat round the fire,' Greg said firmly.

'Don't patronise me!' Diana snapped. She stood up. 'What does the sand mean?' She looked at Kate.

'All right, I'll tell you,' Greg said slowly. 'It means that I don't think we are dealing with a human killer. I don't think there is anyone out there in the woods or on the beach. I think our enemy is a man who has been dead for nearly two thousand years; a man who is very, very angry because we have disturbed a grave in the sand. And I think we are all in terrible danger.'

LVI

'I must have been mad to come, quite mad!'

Anne Kennedy walked along the line of small cars, the keys in her hand as she peered through the driving snow to try and find the vehicle she had been allocated. In her other hand were the handles of a large canvas holdall, a road map bought from the car hire desk in the airport terminal, the strap of her shoulder bag, and there were three books balanced in the crook of her elbow.

It had not been snowing in Edinburgh. This was ridiculous. Sisterly love had overstepped the bounds. There it was. Number 87. A small, neat, bright red Ford Fiesta. With relief she slotted the key into the lock and pulled the door open. The car smelled of plastic and air freshener. It was blessedly spotless. Tossing her bag and her books onto the back seat she climbed in and closed the door then she fumbled for the light switch. She had to find out how to get from Stansted out to the east coast before the snow piled too thick in the country lanes.

Her last conversation with Kate had worried her a great deal, as had the fact that Kate's phone was still out of order. It had been with enormous relief that she had found two visiting lecturers to look after her flat and wait upon C.J's every whim, so that she could head south for a three-day break to reassure herself that all was well. Now she was not so sure that she had done the sensible thing. England, with its usual paranoia about any weather pattern one or two points either side of the norm showed every sign of closing down completely. The forecast was becoming increasingly hysterical and to make matters worse, Kate was not even expecting her, thanks to the incompetence of the telephone engineers who swore each time she rang them that the line had been checked and was working perfectly.

She took one last look at the road map, memorised the formula

– A120 east towards Colchester, A12 north towards Ipswich and then A120 again – switched on the engine and turned out the light. It would take, she reckoned, about an hour, perhaps an hour and a half at most. She glanced down at the dashboard clock. It was nearly nine already.

The roads were unpleasant but by no means impassable as she drove east, the windscreen wipers carving arcs in sleet which turned white and sparkling in the reflected headlights of on-coming cars. The road was more or less straight and she made far better time than she expected, bypassing Dunmow and Brain-tree and turning north at last on the main dual carriageway which cut through the flatlands of East Anglia towards Suffolk. The radio played quietly in the background with once a break for the weather forecast – dire: overnight snow would thicken with easterly gales tomorrow causing drifting, and piling high tides onto the beach with the full moon – and a news update, then it lapsed once more into Brahms and Schumann.

It was ten past ten when she pulled into a layby in front of a multi-armed signpost and, flicking on the light, consulted her road map again. It showed Redall as a small dot on the shore. Leading to it was a broken line which denoted a track of some sort. To reach the track she had to negotiate about four miles of intricate lanes. She scowled. The snow was harder now and though the little car had bowled gamely through the worst it could throw at her so far, there were signs of it drifting now she was on a deserted road. There were no car tracks visible; and at the foot of hedges a deceptively soft bank was building up on both sides of the road.

'Oh, well, plough on.' She muttered to herself. She had already pinpointed a pub on the mainish road which looked as though it was only half a mile or so from Redall. Perhaps she should make for that first.

The tyres slithered uncomfortably as she engaged first gear and pulled out into the middle of the carriageway, but once she got going the car held the road. Left. Left. Right. She repeated the turnings to herself out loud as she negotiated each increasingly narrow lane with more and more care. She should be nearly there now. There should be a pub on the next bend.

There wasn't. She drove on. The turning she knew should appear within a couple of hundred yards did not materialise. The

324

lane turned inland again and wound infuriatingly back on its tracks, climbing up and down steep hills which had no right to be there at all. She must have missed a turning somewhere. 'Damnation!' She pulled up and consulted the map again. It looked so straightforward on paper. Left, left, right. A straight bit, a bend, the pub and then a few more bends until the top of the track. She wound down the window and stared out. The wind was ice cold, clean, cutting. Ice crystals seared her skin. All she could hear was silence and then, almost subliminally, in her bones, the distant moan of the wind. Hastily she wound her window up again. She preferred the steamy, incestuous fug of the little car with its canned music – Schumann had now given way to a Beethoven Sonata.

She had begun to ponder the possibility of having to spend the night in the car – not a pleasant prospect without rugs or thermos – when she saw the lights of a house loom out of the snow ahead. It was no pub, but at least the occupants might be presumed to know where they were.

They did, and it was a good five miles from Redall. 'You turned the wrong way back there, my dear.' The elderly man who opened the door in his dressing gown had invited her into his hallway to consult her map with her. 'What you had better do is go on down here,' he stabbed at it with a nicotine-stained finger, 'and then turn back along the estuary road.'

'Are you on your own?' A pale wispy woman in a worn eau-de-Nil bathrobe, her straggly hair in rollers, appeared at the top of the stairs. 'You shouldn't drive around on your own on a night like this.'

'I know.' Anne managed a bright smile. 'I didn't realise the weather was going to be so bad.'

'Would you like a cup of tea before you go on?' The woman was descending the stairs now, one step at a time, painfully.

Anne was sorely tempted but she shook her head. 'It's kind of you, but I think I had better go on. It's settling quite deep and I don't want to get stuck.'

'Well, you go carefully,' the old lady nodded. 'And you watch out for the Black Dog on the marsh.' She chuckled as she watched Anne pull up her collar and run out to the car.

'Black Dog!' Anne muttered to herself as she restarted the engine. She had heard of the phantom Black Dog of East Anglia;

she gave a wry grin. She had not expected to run into the supernatural quite so soon.

As the car slithered down the lane and turned at last onto a slightly broader road which showed signs of having been recently sanded, the snow lessened and a patch of clear sky revealed a high, cold moon, only a fraction off the full, sailing amongst a trail of huge, bulbous clouds. Cautiously Anne accelerated a little, following the winding road with care. The woman had described this as the estuary road, and suddenly Anne saw why. A steep incline, where the car tyres spun wildly for a moment gave way to a flat straight stretch and she found she was looking down on a broad river estuary, glinting like silver in the moonlight. She brought the car to a standstill and stared. It was breathtaking. A landscape of white and silver and polished steel. And completely deserted. She had not, she realised, seen another car for over half an hour now. Turning her back with regret on the view, she set off again, more slowly this time, determined not to miss the turnings which would take her across the arm of land which led behind Redall Bay.

The track was in the right place. There was no doubt she had reached it at last, but it was obvious that that was as far as the little car was going. The wind had piled the snow across the turning in heaps four feet deep. She climbed out and looked round in despair. The moonlight was so bright now that the road was clearly visible in both directions for several hundred yards. She had passed a farmhouse some half a mile back. Perhaps she should drive back there and ask their advice? She glanced at her watch. It was after eleven. Not too late, surely, to knock on the door.

But the farmhouse, when she reached it, was in darkness and her repeated knocking brought no answer.

She shivered. The moon was half veiled now and the clouds were building once more. In another few minutes it would have gone. Climbing back into the car, glad of its lingering warmth, she sat back for a moment and thought. There were only two alternatives. Either she could drive on to the next village and beg a room at the pub or she could leave the car on the road and walk down the track to Redall.

Pulling back onto the road she drove slowly back to the top of the track and stopped. It was clearly visible, in spite of the

326

snowdrifts, winding into the trees. She put on the light again and stared down at her map. The track could not be more than half a mile long, less probably. She measured it with her thumbnail. It was crazy to go away now she had got here. She glanced up at the sky again, peering through the windscreen. The moon was clearly visible now, lighting the whole place like day. The banks of snow cloud she had seen over the estuary did not seem to have advanced at all. It would be easy to see her way down the track.

She made up her mind. Climbing out of the car she pulled her bag out with her. There was a bottle of Laphroaig in there, produce of Scotland. She had not forgotten her sister's fondness for malt whisky and if she fell in a snowdrift, to hell with all the received wisdom about cold and alcohol, she would drink it herself. Turning off the lights she locked the car and, shouldering the bag, with a rueful glance down at her far-from-waterproof Princes Street boots, she turned towards the trees.

For the first twenty-five yards the moonlight lit the path with brilliant clarity and it was easy to put the thought of Kate's poltergeist out of her mind. The snow was soft but not very thick and she found the going easy, though it was strange how quickly her bag grew heavy. Then abruptly the track turned at right angles into a densely growing copse and the moonlight, deflected by the trees, shone elsewhere. The path at her feet was black. In spite of herself she glanced over her shoulder into the deeper shadows. It was very quiet. The wind had died and she could hear nothing but the steady crunch of the snow beneath her boots.

She stopped to swing her holdall onto the opposite shoulder. Without the steady sound of her own footsteps the night was eerily quiet. No wind; no patter of leaves; then, in the distance she heard the manic tu-wit, tu-wit of an owl, followed by a long wavering hoot. It was a primitive sound which brought a shiver to the back of her neck. She walked on, unaware how tightly her knuckles were knotted into the straps of the bag on her shoulder.

Her eyes were used to the darkness now and she could make out more detail. The gnarled oaks, their solid profiles clearly recognisable, the tangled mass of less easily identifiable copse which crowded to the edge of the track, the dense curtain of some creeper or other – traveller's joy, perhaps – which hung in clusters over the path. The track turned again and she found the snow at her feet bathed in moonlight once more. With a sigh of relief she quickened her pace, slithering out of control as the track steepened, staggering to keep her feet.

It was then she saw the upturned car. Cautiously she approached it, her heart thumping uneasily, pushing her way through the broken branches. The skid marks were still visible beneath the snow, and the dark stains which in daylight would probably be blood. Her mouth had gone dry as she peered round the upturned bonnet. There was no one there. Relieved, she touched the cold metal and saw the drift of snow which had settled on the inside console. The crash must have happened a while ago and whoever had been in the car had gone.

The loud crack of a breaking twig stopped her in her tracks. She looked round. She could hear her heart thundering in her ears. She glanced up at the sky. The moon was almost gone. In another few seconds it would be swallowed by the thick, snow-heavy band of cloud which was drifting steadily in from the sea. It was nearly midnight and she had never felt so lonely in her life.

The skin on the nape of her neck began to prickle as she walked on. She tried to view the feeling objectively. It was a primitive reaction to fear of the unseen; or was she sensing something out there in the dark? Something watching her. Swallowing hard, she made herself go on. Surely it could not be far now to the farmhouse? A flicker in the strength of the moonlight made her glance up again. Only a few seconds more and the moon would be gone. She held on to her bag more tightly, refusing to quicken her pace. A fear of the dark was an irrational primitive throwback; this was the twentieth century. There were no wild beasts out there, queuing up to eat her, no enemy tribes, no evil spirits, no ghosts. She was a rational, liberated modern woman; a scientist.

But in at least one of the books in her bag there was a very convincing argument that ghosts and spirits were real entities.

The darkness when it came was total. Her step faltered – a logical reaction to sudden blindness which would pass as soon as her night sight came back. She knew the path was clear; she had been able to see twenty feet in front of her a moment before, so why had she stopped? Why was she convinced that there was someone standing there on the path immediately in front of her? Why did she have this terrible urge to turn and run back the way she had come?

'Come on, Anne!' Like her sister she was prone to addressing herself out loud. 'Get a move on. Your feet are getting cold!' The sound of her voice seemed shocking in the silence; an intrusion. 'You'll be singing Onward Christian Soldiers in a minute,' she went on conversationally. 'Go on, you bastard.' She was no longer addressing herself. 'If you're out there, show yourself, whoever you are.'

This was ludicrous. There was no one there. No one at all. She gritted her teeth and walked on, concentrating grimly on the wild beauty of the night. She could understand Kate's enchantment with this place. The silence, the clean pure air which came, she supposed, straight from the arctic ice, the occasional glimpses before the moon had gone, of glittering, still water through the trees. She pictured the cottage where Kate was by now probably tucked up cosily in bed. A warm stove, oak beams, pretty, chintzy curtains, an old bed with a soft feather mattress and an old-fashioned patchwork quilt. When she arrived there would be coffee and food and whisky of course, and a long night of gossip with their toes tucked up near the fire –

She snapped suddenly out of her reverie. In the distance she could hear the sound of galloping hooves. It was coming closer. The creak of leather, the hiss of breath through a horse's nostrils. She flung herself back off the path, feeling the ground shake beneath the rider as he hurtled up the track and then he was gone. Shocked, she stared back the way she had come. She had seen nothing. How could anyone ride at that speed in the dark? And why? What was so important?

With a heavy sense of foreboding she slithered back onto the track, renewing her grip on her bag, aware suddenly of a new smell in the fresh coldness of the air. A foul, acrid smell. The smell of burning.

She stood for a moment looking at the still smouldering barn, feeling the heat striking out from the black stinking ashes, then she walked slowly towards the farmhouse and banged on the door.

For a long time nothing happened. No lights came on. There was no sound. She was beginning to panic that there was no one there when at last she heard the sound of a door opening somewhere inside.

'Who is it?' A man's voice sounded strangely hollow from behind the door.

'Hi. I'm sorry to arrive so late. My car couldn't make it down the track. I'm Anne Kennedy. Kate's sister.' It felt faintly ridiculous, speaking to a bolted door. She wished they would hurry up and open it. There was something not right out here, something frightening in the air. 'Please. May I come in?' She tried to keep the panic out of her voice.

'Wait.' The voice was curt. Almost rude.

Anne stared at the door in disbelief. It had not crossed her mind that they might not let her in. She glanced behind her at the dull white sheen which was a snow-covered lawn.

'Anne? Is that you?' Suddenly Kate's voice came from behind the door. The flap of the letter box rose and a torch shone out into the darkness. 'Crouch down, so I can see your face.'

'For God's sake, Kate. Of course it's me. I sincerely wish it wasn't!' The last of her stamina was going. Anne bent over and stared into the letter box. 'What is the matter with you all?'

'It's her. Let her in.' She heard the muffled words as the letter-box sprang shut followed at once by the sound of bolts being drawn back.

'Quickly. Come in.' Kate pulled her over the threshold into a darkened hall. Anne was dimly aware of a guttering candle on a saucer as someone closed the door behind her and shot the bolts across once more, then she was ushered into a candlelit living room. It was warm, and smelled of wonderful cooking and it was full of people.

She stared round, doing a double take. 'It's like the hospital at Scutari,' she blurted out. 'Kate, love, what's been happening?'

A woman, wearing a sling and with a black eye lay on the sofa; a girl, wrapped in rugs was lying on pillows in the corner; a man, his bandaged foot propped up on a stool sat beside the fire. Behind her the two men – one man and a boy, she corrected herself as she glanced at them – who had opened the door with Kate were standing staring at her as if she had just appeared from Mars. Two other people and a girl stood nearby, all looking at her. 'What is happening here? What's wrong?'

330

'Oh, Anne!' Kate threw herself into her arms. 'I've never been so pleased to see anyone in my life!'

'The *dea ex machina*, come to rescue us, I presume.' The words came from the man with the injured foot.

Anne stared at him blankly then she turned to Kate. 'You'd better explain,' she said.

LVII

He rode fast, leaning forward on his horse's neck, the brooch, the native brooch which had pinned her gown, holding his own cloak now against the wind. The prince of the Trinovantes had paid the price and gone to his gods and the hell-cat woman with him, with her curses and her hate. Well, let her curse. Who would ever know what had happened here today? There were no witnesses, no survivors. Her sister, simple docile girl that she was, would believe him when he told her Claudia had fled with her lover to his brothers in the west. She would be shocked, but she would believe him. And she would understand the need for divorce. He smiled as he rode, and raised his hand to flog his horse on faster as it scaled the rise in the track, its hooves throwing up clouds of dust. He had already decided that he would remarry. Her sister was much like her to look at, much younger and more biddable by far. She could take over his household and raise his son; provide him with more sons if she did her duty well. And he would see to it that the prince's tribe came no more to Colonia Claudia Victricensis. They incubated sedition and plotted with the Iceni against Rome. A burning straw would ignite the mood against their overlords, but it would not be his straw; no uprising would be of his instigation. Nor hers. Claudia. The woman he had treated as a goddess. No one would ever know what had occurred here today. She would never tell; she had taken her betrayal and her fury with her to her muddy, inglorious death.

'There are ten people in this house.' Roger stood with his back to the fire, looking down at the others as they sat round him. Allie still had not spoken. She was asleep on a pile of cushions and pillows in the corner and no one suggested waking her. Sue was sitting beside her, holding her hand, her eyes closing as she nodded sleepily in the warmth of the room. 'I cannot believe that we can't vanquish whatever is threatening us here tonight. Anne. You are, I gather, the expert,' he bowed in her direction. 'And we seem to be agreed that our enemy is not human. Can I ask you to take the floor and tell us what the hell to do!' He moved to his chair and sank into it with a groan.

Anne felt a thousand times better than she had walking on her own through the woods, but now that the full horror of the situation had been explained to her even a bowl of hot soup had not managed to dispel the chill which had settled in her stomach. She shook her head. 'I'm a psychologist, not a psychic. I know very little about ghosts. As far as I know I've never seen one.' Then what or who was the mysterious horseman who had thundered past her on the track? No one in the house knew anything about him.

'You must help Allie, Anne,' Kate put in from her seat on the floor. She was leaning against the side of Greg's chair, gazing into the embers. His hand was resting lightly on her shoulder.

'I think she's possessed.' Greg said quietly. 'Her strength, her voice, her actions. None of them belong to Alison.'

'Greg. Don't!' Diana's voice was anguished. She glanced across at the two girls. Sue's head had fallen forward; her grip on Alison's hand had loosened and her fingers were slack. She was dozing. Alison moved her head restlessly from side to side and then lay still again. Her eyes were not properly closed. Beneath the half-open lids the whites showed as pale slits.

Anne bit her lip. They were all looking at her and she didn't know what the hell to say. 'Has she been seen by a doctor recently?' she asked at last. 'There are quite a few conditions which could fit some of what has happened to her. For instance, has she had a head injury in the last few months? Even quite a mild knock could do it.' She looked from Diana to Roger and back. Diana shook her head. 'And there has been no organic damage at any time as far as you know? Cysts, lesions, tumours, anything like that? Has she complained of headaches?'

'Yes, she has.' Patrick and Greg spoke simultaneously.

'But you're on the wrong track there,' Greg went on. 'Quite wrong.'

'Not necessarily.' Anne looked at him seriously. 'There could be a medical reason for her suffering these strange blackouts and we need to rule them out if we can.' Again she looked at Diana. 'Is there any family history of schizophrenia or genetic disorders as far as you know?'

Diana shook her head.

'And there is no possibility that she is taking drugs?'

'None at all.' Diana pressed her hands to her cheeks. 'I was a nurse, Anne. Do you think I haven't thought of these things? Besides, Allie is not the only one to have had strange experiences.'

Anne paused. She bit her lip. She had felt on reasonably safe ground talking in medical terms. 'OK.' she went on carefully. 'Let's explore some other possibilities and find out exactly what we are talking about. I take it that nothing has happened actually inside this house.' Her eyes rested speculatively for a moment on Greg's hand on Kate's shoulder.

'Except for Allie going peculiar; but that probably happened, as Kate said, on the beach.'

'And my books on the floor,' Paddy put in.

'And I smelt her perfume. It was in your study, Roger.' Kate hugged her knees more tightly.

Roger raised an eyebrow. 'What does she use? Chanel?'

'Something with flowers – jasmine and musk and amber. And with it there is always the smell of wet earth.'

Anne looked at her carefully. 'How often have you smelt this?'

'Often. In the cottage too.'

'And it always precedes some kind of phenomenon?'

Kate shrugged. 'Not always. Sometimes that is all there is.'

'And him. Marcus. Does he have a smell too?'

Kate looked up at Greg. He shook his head. 'I can't say I've noticed. When he's around one is too shit-scared to notice anything.'

'Is it mass hysteria?' Diana said slowly. 'Are we all infecting each other?' She was shivering in spite of the heat of the fire.

Anne shrugged. 'It's possible. How many of you have actually seen something?' She looked at Roger, who shook his head almost regretfully. 'Diana?'

'No. It's all hearsay – except for what happened to Allie, of course.'

'Kate and I have seen both Marcus and Claudia,' Greg said slowly. He caressed Kate's neck gently. 'Cissy and Sue saw him clearly. Allie obviously has seen them both. Paddy –?'

'I felt him,' Patrick said slowly. 'And we saw him out there. I shot at him. And he wrote a message on my computer.'

'He wrote it, or you wrote it without knowing you'd done it?' Anne asked.

'I don't know. I don't remember doing it. But how would a Roman know how to use a computer?'

Anne smiled. 'He wouldn't.'

'I wrote something strange on my computer too,' Kate added. 'A curse. ''May the gods of all eternity curse you Marcus Severus Secundus for what you have done here this day . . .'' '

She spoke the words quietly, but they hung in the room for what seemed an uncomfortably long time. Kate sat still, her eyes on the fire. 'I wonder what he did to her.'

'It must have been something pretty awful,' Greg said softly.

'Murder. I think he murdered her. Her dress is covered with blood.'

'And it's her grave Alison has uncovered in the dunes.'

Anne shivered. Pulling one of the cushions from the end of the sofa she threw it down in front of the fire and sat down on it, hugging her knees just as her sister was doing. 'Just supposing you are right,' she said thoughtfully. 'What are we assuming here? That Alison's excavation has uncovered a long-dead crime? That a murdered woman is still crying out for vengeance after two thousand or so years and that for some reason she and the man who murdered her are attacking everyone in sight. That they are capable of clubbing a man to death, burning down a barn, throwing a car into the sea, cutting off the phone, manifesting soil and maggots and perfumes and physically threatening anyone foolish enough to go outside?'

'It sounds a pretty grim scenario, put like that,' Roger commented wryly. 'But for want of a better theory, and because it is more or less midnight, which is traditionally the witching hour, and because whatever has happened has scared the daylights out of a fairly large, responsible group of people, most of whom are otherwise sane adults, I would say it sounds fairly convincing for now.'

'Perhaps Kate is right and we should pray,' his wife put in tentatively. 'I appreciate your intellectual opposition to prayer, darling, but it would seem to be the only option left, and traditionally, to use your word, it is the only sensible response.'

'It's the only possible response,' Patrick muttered.

'Rubbish,' Roger retorted. 'The sensible response is for us all to

335

get some sleep. In the morning we will have some breakfast and some of us will walk up the track with Joe and call the police. There has, after all, been a murder committed. If there is anyone out there, and I doubt if by now he is still there, my judgement is that he is human. Some kind of maniac on the loose from somewhere. Poor Bill happened to be in the wrong place at the wrong time. The police will get him. But for the rest of us to end up basket cases because of what has happened is insane in itself. I am sure we will find a concrete explanation. You do what you like. I am going to bed.' He stood up.

No one else moved. 'There aren't enough beds for everyone, Roger,' Diana put in absent-mindedly.

'Then whoever wants to can stay down here by the fire. There are lots of rugs. No one need be too uncomfortable.' Roger stooped and threw a couple of logs onto the fire. It roared up the chimney in a shower of sparks. 'Joe. I suggest you take my son's bed as he shouldn't climb the stairs. Kate, you and Anne –'

'We'll stay down here, Roger, thank you. I'm very comfortable by the fire.' Kate smiled at him.

'Me too.' Patrick put in.

Kate glanced up at Greg. 'You go and lie down in the study, Greg. Rest your foot. We'll keep watch. If anything happens we can call you.'

He reached down and put his hand on her shoulder again. The touch was only light, a brush, no more. 'Thanks, but I think I'll stay here. I'm too comfortable to move.'

When the elder members of the group had gone upstairs, Anne seated herself on the chair Roger had vacated. 'Have any of you heard the weather forecast?' she said quietly. 'It's unbelievably bad. I don't know whether being near the sea makes it better, but they are predicting blizzards for tomorrow. It's not going to be easy to go for help.'

'You think we should try now, before it gets too bad?' Greg leaned forward.

She shrugged. 'I don't know what to think. I just wanted to warn you.'

'I don't think we should go out again,' Kate put in. 'We've been lucky so far.' Her eyes strayed down to Greg's foot. 'But I don't think we should risk anything else.'

'I think we should open a bottle of wine.' Greg levered him-

336

self to his feet. 'If we're going to stay awake we may as well enjoy ourselves, and if it helps us sleep that would be no bad thing.'

He hobbled across to the kitchen. Then he stopped suddenly. 'Where are the cats?'

Paddy shrugged. 'I haven't seen them.'

Greg frowned. 'Are they upstairs?'

'If they're like C.J. they will be in the middle of the best bed,' Anne commented. 'No cat is going to be anywhere else in this kind of weather.'

'They don't usually go upstairs.' Greg bent down and hauled a bottle out of the wine rack in the corner. 'It's too cold most of the time. The cosy places are all in here round the fire or the Aga.' He took the corkscrew out of the drawer and tearing the foil seal off the bottle, he began to wind into the cork. 'We're all used to fifteen blankets and duvets each and night storage heaters and things but that is hardly up to feline standards. Here, Paddy, carry this for me, there's a good chap and we need some glasses.' He hopped back to the fire and sat down again with a groan. He put his hand on Kate's shoulder again, more firmly this time, and he let it rest there. 'Cheer up, we're all safe now.'

She shook her head. 'I keep thinking of poor Bill in the cottage, all alone.'

She accepted a glass from Paddy and took a sip. 'I can't believe any of this has happened. It's ridiculous. It's not possible. Things like this don't happen to people in real life.' Greg's hand was still on her shoulder. Without thinking, she reached up and grasped his fingers. They were warm and reassuringly strong as they returned her grip.

'I'm afraid they do happen to ordinary people,' Anne put in. She smiled at Patrick as he gave her a glass. 'But I'm glad to say there is usually a mundane explanation for even the strangest phenomenon. I'm inclined to think that most of your weird goings on here have been a combination of ordinary things. Cars skid in bad weather; they crash on steep icy lanes. People imagine they see things when the weather is bad. Oh, yes they do, Kate. And people infect one another with something like hysteria very easily when they're scared and you've had something real to be scared about. A man has been murdered.'

'But before he was murdered. When I phoned you. All the

337

things we discussed.' Kate shifted slightly to lean against Greg's good knee.

'Poltergeists.' Anne nodded. 'Centred on Alison. I think that is very possible. She seems to be emotionally very disturbed at the moment.' She glanced at the two girls who appeared to be sleeping soundly on their makeshift bed in the corner.

'So you consider poltergeists to be real?' Greg asked.

'Yes. I do, in that they are an outward manifestation of inward conflict; the energy created by the brain is quite astounding, you know.'

'Astounding enough to throw a large car out into the saltings? Astounding enough to set fire to a barn?'

'The latter could easily have been a prowler, Greg.' Kate had accepted the loss of her car with astonishing calm; after everything else that had happened it seemed almost unimportant on the scale of things.

Paddy was half way through his own glass of wine when he looked up suddenly. 'The cats couldn't have been in the barn, could they?'

'Of course not. They never went there except bird-nesting in the summer. They can't get in when the door's locked anyway.'

'Of course they can. There are – or were – loads of holes they could get in through.'

'They won't have been there, Paddy, don't worry,' Anne put in, hearing the panic so near the surface in Patrick's voice. The boy was very near the end of his strength. 'The first hint of trouble and they would have been away. Cats are psychic about these things.'

There was a moment's silence then Greg let out a short bark of laughter. 'Not entirely a happy choice of words under the circumstances.'

She grimaced as she hauled herself to her feet. 'Sorry. Listen, is there a loo downstairs? I don't want to disturb anyone who's asleep.'

'Just across the passage, behind the study.' Kate gestured towards the door. 'Here, take this candle.'

The passage was very cold after the heat near the fire. Sheltering the flame with her hand, Anne pushed past the coats and boots, past the closed study door. She could feel the draught from the front door on her neck. They should have a curtain for it. The passage was cluttered with things: carefully she held the candle up, trying not to trip over baskets and shoes, walking sticks, a box of cat food, an old electric fire – heating this house was obviously a problem – a box of what looked like stones, some rolls of Christmas paper and a box of decorations, obviously ready to go up, and – she stopped. Something had moved ahead of her, just out of candle range. It must be one of the cats. She raised her hand a little trying to throw the dim circle of light a little further from her. There it was again. Something in the shadows. But not on the floor; this was full height. Human height. 'Who's there?' To her disgust her voice was shaking.

There was no reply. No sound save the slight moan of the wind under the front door. She could no longer hear the voices from the living room.

'Who is it?' she repeated, louder this time. She was rooted to the spot. Without going closer the weak candlelight would not reach the door; without light she was too afraid to take even one step closer. 'Oh, shit, come on. Don't mess about. Who is it?'

She could smell it now. The perfume. Rich, exotic, crude, with a strong overlay of wet earth. She swallowed, conscious that her hands were shaking; the candlelight had begun to tremble.

'OK, Lady Claudia. Let's see you.'

Somehow she forced herself to take a small step forward. Her stomach was churning, her knees wobbly. The candlelight licked across the doorway, showing another row of hooks, another huddle of raincoats and jackets. Nothing more. No ghost. No Roman lady. She took a deep breath, feeling her hands ice cold and clammy as she reached for the doorhandle and pulled it open. The small cloakroom was neat, with pale green curtains, a thick rag rug, a green towel, and soap. She wedged the candle onto the high windowsill and turning, began to unzip her trousers. It was then she looked down into the small handbasin. There was a scattering of black soil in the bottom and amongst it, throwing fat, unwieldy shadows in the candlelight, wriggled several maggots.

LVIII

Snow had settled in the dunes. The streaming moonlight cast long, colour-less shadows over the sand. As the clouds drifted inexorably in from the north-east, the sky, backlit to opal and then to dull pewter, lowered closer to the land. No night birds called; only the wind in the trees behind the cottage disturbed the silence of the grave as it lay now lapped in its mantle of snow.

The young man looking down at it cast no shadow; he left no footprints. Like the woman he loved he sought revenge. No kind god had received his soul as sacrifice, for with his dying breath he had vowed to return and that vow had kept him from his love. There was no need to comb the furthest galaxies; Marcus Severus Secundus was anchored to this spot by blood. The blood of his victims. His hate had kept them apart through the centuries. The young man smiled. They had all three been released by the meddling of the girl and through her this secret charnel house would be made known to the world and his vengeance would be made sweet.

In front of him the moon was shrouded suddenly in a cloak of cloud. The darkness had returned to the land and with it came the snow. Thick, white, whirling, dissolving the shadow which was all that remained of the druid, Nion, save his need for revenge and his love.

There was a hair in her mouth. She pawed at it, screwing up her face, and opened her eyes to find a head next to hers on the pillow. Frowning, she stared at it. Sue. It was Sue, her tangled hair strewn across the pillow, fast asleep, cuddled up beside her on the floor. Alison moved her head slightly. A violent pain slammed away behind her temples, but she could see dimly in the candlelight. Candlelight? Had they been to a party? A disco somewhere? Why was she on the floor? 'Sue!' She shoved at the girl next to her with her elbow. 'Sue!' The whisper was louder this time. Somehow she managed to sit up, her head spinning.

She could just see Sue's mother asleep on the sofa. Why? Why were they all asleep by the fire in her own house? There was no one else there. The fire was burning merrily – she could feel its warmth. 'Sue!' Not a whisper this time, but a peremptory call.

Sue opened her eyes. 'What?'

'How long have you been here?'

'I don't know. Hours. Are you all right?' Sue sat up and looked at her hard.

'Of course I'm all right. Why?'

'They said you'd gone funny.'

'What do you mean, funny?'

'I don't know. All kinds of funny things are happening. Mum crashed the Range Rover, look at my bruises! And we saw your ghost. The Roman. He was horrible.'

'You saw him?' Alison's eyes rounded. She sat up and hugged her knees with a shiver. 'Is that why you're here?'

'I think so. Dad found us. He wasn't even angry. I think he's scared.'

There was a moment's silence as they considered this. Sue bit her lip. 'Mum's asleep.'

They both looked at the sofa.

'Where's everyone else?'

'I don't know.' There was a rising note of hysteria in Sue's voice.

'They can't have gone.'

'Of course they can't have gone.' Sue did not sound too sure. 'Shall I look?'

'No! Don't leave me!'

Hugging one another, the two girls stared round, frightened, as on the sofa Cissy muttered in her sleep. Inside the room the silence was overwhelming. Even the fire seemed quiet, the sweet smoky smell of burning apple logs slowly giving way to the overpowering aroma of wet earth.

LIX

Greg and Patrick were peering down into the washbasin in disgust. Behind them in the dark corridor, Kate stood clutching Anne's hand. 'You saw her, didn't you. Claudia.'

Anne shrugged. 'I didn't exactly see her . . .'

'But you smelt her scent. You sensed her. You saw the earth, the maggots that drop off her everywhere she goes!'

Anne swallowed hard. 'Let's go back to the fire. Surely you've seen enough.' The candlelight was flickering crazily on the ceiling of the small cloakroom as the two heads bent over the washbasin.

'Yuk!' Patrick's one word said it all.

Greg turned with a grimace of pain, balancing on his stick. 'You're right. Let's go back.'

They made their way into the candlelit living room to find Alison and Sue sitting upright in their rugs. Both girls looked dishevelled and scared.

'Greg? What is it? What's happening?' Alison's voice had taken on a strangely high timbre.

He gave her a long searching look, then he lowered himself back into his chair, wincing as he lifted his foot onto its cushion with a grimace of pain. 'We seem to be orphans of the storm!' he replied. Somehow he managed to keep his voice cheerful. 'So, how are you both feeling?'

'Lousy. I've got a really grotty head.' Susie's face was whiter than her companion's.

'And you, Allie?'

Alison shrugged. 'I feel a bit spaced out. Tired. Who's that?' She had noticed Anne.

'Sorry. I forgot you hadn't been introduced,' Kate put in quickly. 'This is my sister, Anne. She picked a really vile weekend to come and stay with me.' She walked over to the two girls and

342

knelt beside them. 'Do you want anything to eat? Diana made some soup. It's on the stove.'

Alison shook her head vehemently. 'I couldn't eat anything. I feel sick.'

'So do I.' Sue's whiteness had by now progressed to a shade of green. 'In fact, can we go and sleep in your room, Allie?'

'No!' Patrick's shout startled them all.

'Why not?' Alison stuck out her chin.

'Well . . .' Patrick floundered with a desperate look towards Kate. 'Won't you be warmer down here, near the fire?'

'I don't think they'll come to any harm upstairs, Paddy,' Greg put in quietly. 'Not if they're together. Why don't you go up, girls. It's a good idea. Take those rugs with you to keep you warm. Sue's had a nasty shock with the car crash, and Allie's probably still suffering from exposure. A warm bed is the best place for both of you.'

The others watched in silence as the two girls climbed to their feet, and collecting armfuls of rugs and cushions, made their way to the door. Their unaccustomed silence was unnerving as they disappeared upstairs.

'You shouldn't have let them do that, Greg,' Paddy said as soon as the staircase door shut behind them. 'You know it's not safe.'

'What's not safe?' Cissy's voice from the sofa was weak but perfectly lucid.

Greg grimaced at his brother. 'Paddy was thinking about the noise those two make when they get together. It is the middle of the night.'

Cissy lay for a moment staring at the ceiling. 'I was on my way to ask you to lunch,' she said suddenly. 'Someone jumped out in front of the Range Rover. I remember trying to miss him, and skidding . . .' She looked up at Kate who sat down on the edge of the sofa beside her. 'Did I hit him?'

Kate smiled reassuringly. 'No. No one was hurt except poor old you.'

'Joe . . . ?'

'Joe is upstairs asleep. Where you should be.'

'Have I broken my ribs?'

'Diana thought they were only badly bruised. You need to rest. I'm afraid we couldn't get hold of a doctor – the phones are still not working – and it's started to snow so hard Joe thought it better to stay here till morning.' It sounded convincing and it was, after all, the truth.

'The joint,' Cissy cried suddenly, distracted. 'My lovely joint will be burnt. What a shame.' She put her hand to her head suddenly. 'Oh, God, I'm so tired –'

'You could sleep in Paddy's room, Mrs Farnborough,' Greg said. 'If you feel you can manage the stairs.'

She did. With Kate and Anne to help, Cissy washed her face, painfully removed her torn, bloody blouse, wrapped herself in Diana's bathrobe and subsided into Paddy's bed. In spite of her pain she was asleep almost as soon as her head touched the pillow. On the landing outside, Kate and Anne looked at each other, their faces shadowed by the candle in Kate's hand, then Kate opened the door of Alison's bedroom and peered in. The two girls were huddled in the narrow bed, their heads very close on the pillow. Both were fast asleep. 'They seem all right,' Kate said softly as she closed the door on them.

Patrick had thrown on a couple more logs and the fire had sprung back into life. Kneeling before it, the poker in his hand, he was prodding it viciously as the two women returned to the room.

'Everything all right up there?' Greg asked.

Kate nodded. 'Everyone seems to be asleep.'

'No strange smells or earth where there shouldn't be any?'

She shook her head.

'Thank God. Perhaps we can settle down for some sleep too.'

'I think we need to talk.' Anne said thoughtfully. 'And besides, I don't think we should all sleep. The unconscious mind is very vulnerable when it is asleep. We need to stay on our guard.'

'So you admit all this is supernatural.' Greg watched her through narrow eyes as she settled on a cushion near the fire.

She shrugged. 'I was trying to keep an open mind, but I certainly saw something out there . . .' She paused. 'I think you were right, this is some kind of phenomenon which is centred on Alison. I read some books about ghosts and poltergeists after I spoke to you, Kate. Your story intrigued me. There seem to be two theories: one, that all the strange events occurring are somehow centred on or created by the unconscious mind of, in this case, a teenage girl. That doesn't make them less real, but they are subjec-

344 ·

tive rather than objective phenomena. The second theory is that real spirits or ghosts – however you define them – are involved. In other words, external forces.' She hesitated. 'There are respected authorities who believe that poltergeists are actually disembodied spirits who feed off the emotional energy of people. Pubescent and teenage kids often have a lot of that to spare. If one believes one of those theories, one must also believe that the forces at work are powerful – powerful enough to light fires, move heavy objects and manifest physical symptoms like the soil and maggots which keep turning up here.' She glanced from one to the other. 'Poltergeists don't usually hurt people. They are mindless and mischievous rather than malicious, perhaps taking their character from the person upon whom they are centred.' Again she looked round. The others were watching her in silence. 'Spirits, ghosts, whatever you call them can be a different matter. But even there, in the books I was reading anyway, where deaths have occurred, it is usually through a heart attack or a fall as someone ran away or reacted in terror – something indirect. Nowhere did I read of an actual physical attack, where someone was beaten to death.'

'Unless the spirit had possessed a human and was using his or her strength to do it,' Greg said slowly.

'If we are assuming Marcus possessed Alison,' Kate interposed. 'But surely it's the other way round. He was feeding her with his own strength. That is the point. She could never have done what she did on her own.'

'Does it matter how she did it?' Patrick put in suddenly. 'What matters is how to stop it happening again, and to make Marcus go away.'

'You're right, Paddy.' Anne drew up her knees and wrapped her arms around them, gazing into the fire.

There was a long silence.

'So?' Greg said at last. 'How do we do it?'

Anne shrugged. 'I wish I knew. If we had a priest we could try bell, book and candle. Holy water. That kind of thing.'

'We haven't got a priest.' There was irritation in Greg's voice. 'Even if we believed in all that mumbo jumbo. We have got a psychologist – someone who understands the human mind. So, why don't we assume that Alison is behind all this – that somehow she has attracted this ghost – and approach the problem through her.'

Kate glanced at her sister, and then at him. 'He had a go at you, Greg, didn't he? You said you felt him trying to take you over.'

Anne shot him a quick look. 'Why didn't you say before?'

'Because I'm still not sure it wasn't my imagination, that's why.'

'Tell me how it felt.'

Greg frowned. 'It felt like someone going ten rounds with boxing gloves on inside my head. It felt unspeakably frightening. I was overwhelmed with rage and hatred which weren't mine.' He stared thoughtfully at the burning logs. 'The first time it happened someone came up to me and he left; the second time I fought him off. I wondered if I was going out of my mind.'

'And Allie couldn't fight him. She didn't know how to start,' Kate put in quietly.

'He used her until he had drained her energy,' Greg went on thoughtfully. 'So, how do we fight him?' He looked at Anne.

Anne closed her eyes. 'The trouble is I'm not a clinical psychologist. I'm not a psychotherapist. I'm particularly not a parapsychologist. I'm not sure that I know where to start.'

'Start by talking to Allie.'

She shook her head. 'That's easy to say, but heavy-footed probing can be terribly dangerous.'

Paddy got up. He wandered restlessly over into the kitchen and picking up the kettle, he carried it across to the sink and began to fill it. 'You said we shouldn't go to sleep. You think Marcus might possess one of us?' He was trying not to let his fear creep into his voice.

'I think it unlikely, but I think we should be on our guard.'

'What about the others upstairs? They are all totally unprotected.'

Kate bit her lip. 'Shouldn't we go and wake them?'

Anne shrugged. 'Your father and mother didn't seem worried about the risk. Nor Joe. They are older, of course. Maybe they don't have any energy to spare. Susie and Cissy –' She frowned. 'It may be that their experiences have already depleted their energies so much that they would be no use to him anyway.'

'I'll go and look at them all again.' Kate climbed to her feet.

The staircase was cold and dark as she stood looking up, the candle in her hand. She shaded the flame as it flickered and put her foot on the bottom step. Behind her, through the open door, she could see Paddy filling the teapot. By the fire, Anne and Greg stared morosely into the flames.

She took another step and then another, staring up ahead of her. The landing smelt as it usually did, clean and slightly mothbally – from the linen cupboard she guessed. She stood, waiting for the candlelight to steady, watching the shadows running along the pink walls. From behind the closed door to Greg's room, she could hear a steady, throaty snore. Joe. Taking a deep breath, she put her hand on the latch and gently pushed the door open a fraction. The room was pitch dark, but the sound of the snore, suddenly loud in her ears, was reassuringly steady. She pulled the door closed and turned to the end of the passage. The master bedroom. All was silent. She hesitated. It seemed a terrible intrusion to look into Diana and Roger's room, but she knew she must. None of them could rest until they were sure all was well. Steadying her shaking hands as best she could, she pulled down the latch and pushed the door open. A small nightlight burned on the bedside table. By the light of its flame she was just able to see the two heads on the pillow. All seemed quiet. That left Alison and Susie. For the second time in an hour she opened their door and looked in, walking right into the room and holding her candle near the bed to see the two sleeping faces. Both were peaceful, their cheeks slightly flushed, their faces poignantly young and vulnerable as they slept. Tiptoeing out of the room, she glanced behind her at the dark square which was Patrick's door. Cissy.

The room was still a mess. Paddy had taken one look at his tumbled books and had turned and walked out of the room. He had not, as far as she knew, been back. She could see the hunched form of the woman in his bed. She was moving restlessly, and as Kate watched, she began to murmur. Kate froze. Her hand was shaking violently as she held the candle and she saw the shadows leap and dance across the walls. The temperature had dropped several degrees.

Who are you?

The words hovered on her lips, but she said nothing out loud. Secretly glad no one could see her, she made the sign of the cross over Cissy's head and closed her eyes for a moment in prayer. When she opened them again the room seemed to be warmer. Backing out, she closed the door silently and left Cissy to it.

Putting the tray of mugs down on the hearth in front of the

fire, Paddy threw himself down in a chair. His face was grey with fatigue as he glanced at his brother. 'It's going to be all right, isn't it, Greg?' His voice wavered for a moment.

Greg studied the boy and his expression softened. ''Course it is.'

'Try and get some sleep, Paddy.' Kate slipped into the room, closing the staircase door behind her. Reaching for one of the mugs, she cradled it against her chest, hoping they would not notice her shaking hands.

The boy nodded. Leaning back in his chair he closed his eyes.

Silence fell over the room. Greg too could feel his lids drooping. He glanced from Anne to Kate and back. There was a strong family resemblance between them. Their colouring and build were similar as was, at this moment, their look of total exhaustion. He sighed. Sleep. That was what they all needed. Sleep and tomorrow to awake and to find it had all been a ghastly nightmare.

LX

Jon woke with a start. He stared round, trying to locate the sound that had startled him; the phone, the quick, imperious tone of an English telephone, so different from the depressing monotone of the American. With a groan he dragged himself to his feet and pulled on his robe. Christ, what time was it? He stumbled across the bedroom and reached for the light switch as he made his way into the living room.

'Jon? My dear, I'm so sorry to wake you at this hour.'

So it really was the middle of the night. For a moment he couldn't place the voice, then it dawned. Kate's mother. 'Hello Anthea. How are you?' He tried to keep the weariness and jet lag out of his voice.

'I'm well, dear. Forgive me for ringing you so early but I'm so worried.'

'About Kate?' Hadn't she told her parents that they had split up?

'About both of them. Anne was supposed to be flying down to stay with Kate in this cottage she's rented. I can't get in touch with either of them and apparently the weather is appalling over there on the east coast.'

Jon leaned across and lifted the curtain with a cautious finger. The street light outside showed thick snow drifting down; it was settling. He frowned. If it was as bad as that in London, what on earth would it be like in deep country? 'I'm sorry, Anthea. I only got back from the States yesterday. I haven't been able to contact them either. The phone down there is out of order.' He tucked the receiver under his ear and reaching out for the whisky bottle unscrewed it deftly. 'I'm sure they're all right.'

'You really think so?' There was a slight quiver in the woman's voice. 'I've had this bad feeling. I can't explain it, but I'm sure something's wrong.'

He poured a double into the unwashed glass left on the tray from the night before. Then he put it down untouched. 'Anthea. Did Kate say anything to you about what's been happening out there? Anything to worry you particularly?' Would she have mentioned the burglary? Knowing Kate, probably not, if it would worry her mother, but then he hadn't spoken to her for several days. Supposing something else had happened?

'She rang me a couple of times. She said she was very happy, but I could tell she was keeping something back.'

Jon smiled grimly. So much for hiding things from one's parents. He could still remember the unerring way his mother unearthed his misdeeds when he was a boy, homing in on them like a bloodhound.

'Jon, dear. I know you and Kate weren't getting on very well. She told me she was probably not going to move back to your flat. Is that still true?'

'I don't know, Anthea.' He raised the glass to his lips at last. 'I was hoping I could talk her into changing her mind.'

'You know there's a man down there.'

'A man?' The tone of her voice had implied volumes. He found his body was reverberating suddenly with shock.

'An artist. Anne thinks she's fallen for him. Jon, I spoke to Anne yesterday before she flew south. She was very worried about Kate. She said all kinds of awful things had been happening. She said Kate sounded upset and frightened. She said someone had broken into her cottage and smashed it up. Apparently she was talking about ghosts and evil spirits and things –'

'Hey, slow down.' Jon frowned. Anne obviously did not share her sister's compunction about frightening her mother. 'I'm sure she was exaggerating. Kate told me about the break-in. It wasn't that bad. Kids, the police thought.'

'Evil spirits. Anne said evil spirits. Jon, please. You have to go there and see everything's all right. Please.'

Jon glanced at the window. 'The weather is appalling, Anthea. I doubt if I'd make it. They were telling people to stay off the roads –'

'Please, Jon. I know you're worried too.'

He thought for a moment. 'As you said, Kate and I aren't together any more.'

'I see.' Her voice was very small. Disheartened. 'So you don't care –'

'Oh, come on, Anthea. Of course I care.' It was true. He finally acknowledged the truth of the statement. He did care, very much indeed. 'Look, I'll tell you what. I'll ring the station and see if the trains are still getting through. If they are, I'll see how near I can get, and see if I can find someone locally who can get me out there. But I can't promise.'

'Snow doesn't last very long at this time of year, Jon. It's too early. The ground isn't cold enough. It'll all be gone by tomorrow.'

Jon gave a wry smile. 'Not quite tomorrow, Anthea. Look, I will do my best.'

The trains were running. Just. But it was afternoon before he eventually reached Colchester and there the train stopped, disgorging dozens of disgruntled passengers into the snow. By the time Jon reached the front of the queue there were no taxis to be seen. He shivered, humping his canvas carryall higher onto his shoulder, and looked round. If he found a taxi at all he was going to need one with the courage of a madman to take him out to the coast. He glanced at the payphone. Should he ring Anthea and tell her he had got this far? One look at the queue of disconsolate people waiting for the phone made his mind up. He would call her tomorrow.

The taxi driver who eventually picked him up was more help than he had dared hope. After studying Jon's map with him, he looked up and smiled. 'They've got the main roads cleared, mate. I can get you pretty close.' He glanced down over the back of the seat at Jon's shoes. 'Do you want to stop off and get some rubber boots before we start?'

Jon grinned. 'Sounds like good advice.'

He bought boots, a torch, a half-bottle of whisky and a long woollen scarf whilst his driver waited unrepentantly on the yellow lines ('Can't see 'em, mate, with all this snow.'), then he climbed in beside him, loaded with shopping bags.

'Scott of the Antarctic.' The man grinned again.

Jon laughed. 'I just got back from the States. It was pretty bad there too.'

'But they can manage, right?' The driver pulled away from the kerb. 'Here the whole bloomin' country grinds to a halt after an hour's snow. And me. I reckon I'll pack it in after I get you there.'

'If you get me there.'

351

'I'll get you as far as The Black Swan on the main road. It's as good a place as any to give up if you're going to. You might hitch a lift with a farmer. Their tractors can get through anything.'

It was a comforting thought as the car slithered its way east, the windscreen wipers pushing laboriously at the wedges of caked snow which clogged the glass. Jon shivered. He was tempted to broach his whisky, but it seemed unfair to drink alone and he wasn't about to offer it to his driver, not while he was still driving at any rate.

Every now and then a pair of headlights, dim against the white-out ahead, approached them, passed and disappeared into the murk. The driver was sitting forward, leaning over his wheel, staring ahead.

'It's getting bad, isn't it?' Jon voiced his worry at last.

'You're not wrong.' The taxi did a little shimmy sideways and the driver spun the wheel. 'Stupid thing is, we're nearly there. Can't be much further.'

'Do you think we should stop?'

'Not here. No. Pete Cutler doesn't give up if there's a decent pub within sniffing distance!' The broad shoulders quivered as he chuckled. 'We'd freeze to death if we stopped here, mate. I reckon it's about another two miles. Yes!' He let out a whoop of triumph suddenly as some landmark loomed in the distance and vanished. 'Hang on. We'll make it.'

From the way Pete locked the taxi and followed him inside the long, low, pink-washed pub, Jon had the feeling his driver was not about to turn round and drive back to Colchester. He was right. 'I'll ring them back at base and tell them I'm camping down here at the old Sooty Swan for the night. Mine's a pint of strong.' He winked and disappeared into the passage beyond the saloon bar. Jon pushed open the door. A fire was burning brightly in the huge hearth, but the room was empty. It was several minutes before a figure appeared behind the bar. 'Didn't think I'd see anyone in tonight,' the landlord greeted him cheerfully. 'How did you get here? Hitched a ride with Father Christmas, did you?'

Jon smiled. 'Something like that. A whisky for me, please, landlord, and a pint of strong for my mad driver and something for yourself.' He hitched himself up onto a bar stool. 'I don't suppose there is any way I can finish my journey from here, is there? I'm trying to get to Redall Bay.'

The landlord was concentrating on drawing the pint. He frowned and sucked in a lungful of air through the gap in his teeth. 'Tricky one, that. You'd need a four-wheel drive, I reckon. You going to see the Lindseys, are you? Or are you a friend of Bill Norcross? I saw he was down this weekend.'

'I'm a friend of Bill's, yes. And of Kate Kennedy. I don't know if you've met her? She's staying at the cottage.'

'Writer lady?' He set the glass on the counter and began to draw a second pint, presumably for himself. 'He did bring her in here, yes. A week or so back.'

'They've been cut off without phones for a couple of days, so I couldn't ring.'

'Unaccountable things, phones.' The landlord put the second glass on the counter. 'Always ring when you don't want them, and won't when you do. Do you want something to eat, sir, while I have a think about what you can do?' He selected another glass and held it up to the row of optics.

'I'd love something.' Jon was cheering up by the second. He turned as the door opened. 'Your drink, Pete.' He took a moment to survey his companion who until now had been no more than a pair of broad shoulders and a round, red face, with a huge, lopsided grin. Pete was a large man altogether – not the ideal shape, Jon thought idly, for a life cramped behind the wheel of a cab. His brilliant blue eyes, surrounded by the gold wire rims of his spectacles, were topped by thick sandy eyebrows and he was wearing two clashing bright red sweaters beneath his anorak.

The two men moved to the fire and sat down. 'Food.' Jon handed him the menu. 'The least I can do is buy you a meal after you got me this far.'

'That's uncommon nice of you.' Pete grinned. 'Any luck with a tractor?'

'The landlord is thinking.'

'Straining himself, is he?' Pete leaned back on the settle with a hefty sigh. 'I've known Ron Brown here for six years. He's a good bloke. He'll fix you up. You know, I reckon I'm starting to enjoy this.'

A chicken pie with baked potatoes, several drinks and much mutual backslapping later, Pete had wheedled Ron into lending them his old Land Rover. 'I'm a professional driver, mate!' he said, not for the first time. 'You know it'll be safe with me.'

'In this weather and with you pissed as a newt? I'd lose my licence letting you have it.'

'Then what say we borrow it without telling you.' Pete heaved a contented sigh and patted his stomach. 'I've had a nice time here. And I've heard a good story. I reckon I would like to go and do a spot of ghost hunting to round the evening off. In fact, why don't you close up and come too? You're not getting any more customers tonight.'

Both men had listened avidly to Jon's story about Kate's ghost, a story he had shamelessly embellished in the interests of camaraderie.

'No fear, I'll head for my bed, thanks.' Ron shook his head. 'I don't fancy going anywhere in this and you wouldn't either if you had any sense at all.' He stooped and groped under the counter, standing upright again to toss a bunch of keys to Pete. 'Just get it back to me in one piece tomorrow, boys, OK?'

Jon stood up. 'Thanks. We will.'

On the doorstep they nearly changed their minds. The wind had risen and the snow was driving straight at them; there was a sting in it which cut into Jon's face.

He hesitated. They could always wait until morning, when the sanders had been through, and go then. He glanced at Pete who was obviously thinking the same thing. Their eyes met.

'A bit of an adventure?' Pete said with a grin.

Jon nodded with a sudden surge of high sprits. He was right. This was an adventure.

They found the old Land Rover (the registration made it more than twenty years old, Jon calculated) in a lean to garage round the back of the pub. Facing away from the wind, it was surprisingly sheltered round there, and little snow had driven in under the roof. The two men climbed in and Pete, who had patted the bonnet as though greeting an old friend, inserted the key into the ignition.

'Are you sure you're OK to drive?' Jon looked at him dubiously. He wasn't worried about there being any other cars on the road, but he was imagining what it would be like if they skidded into a ditch.

'Right as rain.' Pete started the engine first go. 'Don't worry. I blotted up that beer with chicken pie and coffee. I'm all right. Not that any one will be driving their best tonight. You just keep your eyes skinned for this track down to the bay.'

The Land Rover backed out easily, its huge tyres holding their own in the slippery yard and gripping the road easily. They backed out past Pete's taxi – now covered in snow – and turned onto the road again. The pub behind them, with its thatched roof and string of coloured lights looked reassuringly cosy as it faded abruptly behind them and disappeared.

'A mile, he said.' Jon leaned across to peer at the milometer. He snorted. 'I wonder how many times this baby has been wound back.'

'Probably only once. I reckon Ron has had her most of her life.' Pete was leaning forward again, a frown between his bushy eyebrows. He did indeed seem remarkably sober suddenly.

'A mile will be a guess, I suppose,' Jon went on thoughtfully. 'People are notoriously bad at judging distances.'

'No, I think he's right. Look.' Pete slowed the Land Rover down in the middle of the road and stopped. They peered out into the darkness. A track led down steeply into the trees on their right, the features of the route flattened and hidden by the snow. Nearby was a notice, the message obliterated. They could see a car, almost hidden under the snow, parked close in beneath the trees.

'Private road to Redall Bay?' Pete glanced at Jon. 'Want to take a shufty?'

Jon let himself out onto the slippery tarmac with its coating of impacted ice and snow and slid across to the notice. Brushing off the snow with his sleeve he peered at it. 'Private R—d to Red– -ay. The words, blistered and worn were just visible. He walked over to the other car. Pushing the snow from the windscreen he peered in. 'Europ-car.' He could just read the sticker on the windscreen.

'That's it.' He climbed back in. 'And that must be Anne's car. She must have hired it at the airport. She got this far safely, anyway. What are we going to do? Try and drive?'

Pete screwed up his face. 'Ron said it was a bastard of a track even when the weather's all right. I can't think why folks put themselves through such sweat. Why not get someone to come in and flatten it for them and tip a load of tar? It wouldn't cost the earth and they'd save a few axles.' He pulled the Land Rover into the side of the road. 'I vote we walk.'

'All right by me.'

Jon grinned at him. His relief when Pete had enthusiastically volunteered to join in the expedition, had been so overwhelming it had surprised him. He had not realised how much he had been dreading the thought of braving a long walk from the pub through the darkness alone. He did not believe in Kate's story about a ghost for one minute, but the incredible loneliness of the night, the snow, the silence, the wind, were all a bit unnerving.

Tucking the Land Rover in under the fir trees next to the red Fiesta, they reached into the back for the canvas holdall – Jon's – and a plastic carrier containing four cans of lager, donated by Ron as a farewell gesture. They locked up and stood looking down the path.

'Ready?' Pete grinned at his companion.

'Ready.'

Jon forced himself to smile back, but suddenly he had begun to shiver.

LXI

They were there again. Nightmare voices. Hatred and anger, forcing her from her bed, until she stood, listening, in the centre of the room. Listening to something far away. The sea. The sea was the danger now. She could hear the roar of the waves, see the walls of spume crashing across the dunes.

Tell them. Tell them my story.

Claudia was the stronger now. Her voice rising above his in the howl of the wind.

Tell them. Tell them. Let the people judge.

Then he was there. Marcus. His voice the louder. Hatred. Anger.

'*No!*'

Spinning round slowly, Alison raised her hands to her head and clutched at her hair. They were fighting; fighting inside her; fighting for the last of her strength.

The grave. She must go to the grave.

She must save it from the water.

She must die.

Die with the bitch whore in the clay.

Live.

Die.

The door opened quietly and she walked out onto the landing, her bare feet warm on the thin carpet. Turning towards the stairs, she began to walk down, seeing nothing but the vision in her head. In the dark at the bottom of the stairs her fingers went unerringly to the latch on the inside of the door, though it was pitch dark there, without lights. The door opened and she stepped into the living room. Silently she moved between the sleeping figures towards the hall.

By the fire Paddy stirred uncomfortably in his chair, but, worn out, he did not open his eyes, even when the cold draught from the open front door stirred the logs into flame in the hearth.

Still barefoot she stood on the doorstep staring sightlessly out into the snow. Something made her pause – in her sleep some inner guardian directed her to step into boots and jacket – then she was gone, closing the door softly behind her.

In the living room the others slept on.

LXII

Their boots sliding in the snow, Jon and Pete tramped slowly down the track. Pete's cheerful patter had finally died away and apart from the occasional heartfelt curse as he slipped in the hardening ruts, he had fallen silent. Jon stopped every now and then to stare gloomily ahead. The snow had lessened now, and he could see clearly all round them. The moon, high above the clouds cast a flat, white radiance across the woods. He was sure they were lost.

The track they had been following seemed suddenly to have petered out and they had been forced for the past twenty minutes or so to follow what could have been a rabbit path through the undergrowth. Whatever it was it was narrow and full of brambles, and the thick snow had on several occasions piled in over the top of his boots.

Behind him Pete cursed again. Jon grinned. Stopping, he turned. 'Can't be far now.'

'No? I reckon this place of yours is like some kind of Brigadoon. It only appears every hundred years or so.'

'Please God, you're wrong.' Jon's reply was heartfelt. He shuddered as a gust of wind tore at his clothes.

A hundred yards further on the woods began to change. The thick oak and hawthorn copse became more sparse. The air grew if anything colder and, turning a bend in the track Jon and Pete found themselves at the edge of the dunes.

Narrowing his eyes against the wind, Jon stared round. 'Now where?'

'I can hear the sea.' Pete cupped his hand around his ear. 'Just over that sand. Bloody hell, it's close.'

They scrambled up to the top of the dune and found themselves overlooking the beach. Huge lines of angry breakers creamed up the shore, crashing onto the sand, and over the water they could see racing towards them the brown, bellying clouds which carried the snow.

'Another five minutes and we'll have a white-out.' Jon turned to Pete, worried. 'Which way do you think?'

'Left.' Pete spoke unhesitatingly. 'You said the farmhouse looked over the estuary. We've come too far to the east. We've got to the sea for real here.' Turning he began to tramp along in the lee of the dune. 'Come on. We'll get some shelter down here. God help us when that lot hits land.'

It seemed like hours before they saw the cottage looming before them in the darkness. Eyes screwed up against the snow Pete grabbed at Jon's arm and pointed. 'Found the bugger!'

Jon grinned with relief. At last. Thank God. Kate.

Hurrying now with new energy the two men fought their way up the dunes and across the snow covered garden, ever aware of the crash of mighty waters behind them. The tide, as the forecast had warned, was going to rise and rise.

Ducking round towards the front door they found themselves sheltered at last from the wind. 'I hope to God she's there.' Jon didn't like the look of the dark windows. The cottage felt empty. Even from here he was pretty sure that they would find no fire; no one at home. And who could blame her? If he was living here, within spitting distance of the North Sea and he had heard a forecast like the one they were broadcasting today he would have packed and moved out on the spot.

The snow in front of the front door was smooth and clean. No sign of footprints. Raising his hand to the knocker, Jon surreptitiously crossed his frozen fingers.

The door swung open. His heart sank. 'I suppose this is the right place?' There should have been locks and bolts. There were locks and bolts. His hand located them on the inside of the door as cautiously, he pushed it open. 'Hello!' He called. 'Kate?'

Silence.

He took a step in. 'Kate, are you there?' His searching fingers found a light switch and he clicked it up and down several times. 'No light.'

Pete had followed him into the hall out of the wind. 'Bit ripe in here, mate.' Pete sniffed hard. 'Somebody's puked.' He reached into his pocket for the torch and shone it around the hall. 'There's obviously no one here. I reckon your girlfriend moved out – for the night at least.' Stepping forward, he pushed open a door and shone the light inside. 'Kitchen. Bloody electric cooker. No electrics.' He was trying that light switch as well. He turned and made for the door on the opposite side of the hall. 'Living room. With a wood stove. We could light that at least. Oh my God!' The roving beam of light was directed at the sofa.

'What is it?' Jon pushed through the door behind him and peered over his shoulder. 'Oh Christ!' Both men stood where they were for a moment, their eyes fixed on the shape beneath the blanket on the sofa. It was Jon who stepped reluctantly forward. Behind him Pete shone the torch onto the battered face.

Jon closed his eyes. For a moment he thought he was going to throw up, but somehow he controlled himself as he turned and staggered out of the room. There was no need to check if the man was dead.

Pete followed him. 'Know who he is?'

Jon nodded. 'Bill Norcross. The friend I was telling you about.'

'Shit.'

'As you say.' They moved back into the kitchen and Jon sat down at the counter, his gloved hands to his face. 'What the hell happened in there?'

'I'd say he'd been beaten. Bloody hell, Jon, mate. Where's your girl? Where's her sister?'

Jon shook his head. Suddenly he was shaking like a leaf.

Pete reached onto the dresser. The fading torch beam had revealed a whisky bottle lying in a mess of earth. It turned out to be empty. 'You sit here, mate. I'll take a look round the rest of the place.'

Jon shook his head. 'I'll come with you.'

'There's no need.' Both men were thinking the same thing. Were Kate and Anne up there somewhere?

'No. But I'll come all the same.'

They took the stairs two at a time. It was Pete who pushed open first one door then the other. Both rooms were empty. They stood in Kate's bedroom and stared round. Sand and earth had drifted across the floor. The bed was unmade – blankets piled in a heap in the middle of it, and there was earth there as well. The room was full of the sweet, damp smell of it. And something else. Scent. The overpowering stench of it had completely blocked out the unpleasant smell that was seeping up the stairs from below.

'No one here.' Pete stated the obvious. 'I reckon they got out all right.'

Jon sat down on the bed. His fingers trailed across the disarrayed sheets and he found Kate's nightshirt, tangled amongst the pillows, beneath which presumably she had folded it at some point. He recognised it. It was blue with cheerful scarlet stripes. Smart. Almost masculine. He remembered the way her long, slim legs emerged from the indecently high hemline. Oh, God, Kate. Where was she? 'What do we do?' Holding the nightshirt against his chest, he found he was suddenly feeling very weak.

'Go and look for this farmhouse. It shouldn't be too far away. That's where they'll be.' Pete's voice was strong. Confident. Not for the first time, Jon thanked whichever fate had dictated that this particular Colchester taxi driver should be with him tonight.

Closing the front door behind them again, they stood outside the cottage and stared round. There was no clue to which direction to go. Any path there might have been had long since been covered by the snow. Pete shone the torch around once and was about to switch it off when he saw the tracks. A set of footprints. Recent footprints which had passed close to the door and went on across the snow back towards the sea.

'Someone's been past here within the last ten minutes or so, while we were inside,' he commented.

Kate? Anne?

The two men bent their heads towards the wind and set off the way they had come, heading back towards the snow covered dunes.

LXIII

'Where is she?' Roger burst into the room and stared round at the sleepy figures sprawled around the fireplace. 'Where in God's name is she?'

'Who, Dad?' Greg stretched with a groan. They had all fallen asleep in the end, Anne and Kate and Paddy too. In the hearth the fire had died to cold embers. He shivered violently.

'Alison. Where is Alison?'

'She's not upstairs?' Greg asked the obvious.

It was Paddy who stood up first, stretching. 'I'll go and look.'

He disappeared through the door into the hall. Roger threw himself down in Paddy's vacated chair and bent forward, rubbing his face wearily in his hands. He seemed to have aged ten years in the last few hours.

Kate stared at the greyness of his skin, the transparency of his face and she bit her lip. 'Shall I make us all some tea?' she said, standing up. 'And let's get the fire going.' She walked across to the window and pulled back the curtain. It was still dark. Thick snow had fallen and judging by the sky, there was more to come. She could hear the wind buffeting against the glass. In the distance the trees were thrashing their branches, and she watched as a cascade of dislodged snow fell to the ground.

She was filling the kettle when Paddy came back into the room. 'She's nowhere through there. Her boots and jacket have gone. I can't believe she came past us in the night, but she must have, while we were all asleep. Sorry, Dad.' He slumped on the sofa, crestfallen.

'Sorry!' Roger roared. 'Sorry! Is that all you can say?' Behind him Susie had appeared in the doorway. Her hair was tangled and her face was still crumpled with sleep. The large bruise on her forehead from the car crash had turned a deep blue.

'Sorry! You know where she's gone, don't you! God only knows how long she's been out there. Go outside, Paddy. See if you can see footprints.'

'Outside?' Patrick looked at him doubtfully. He nodded. Dragging himself to his feet again he disappeared and moments later they all felt the rush of cold air as he pulled open the front door.

'There's no sign.' He called from the hall. 'No tracks at all. Just birds and rabbits and a fox.'

They heard the door slam.

'Not that it matters. We all know where she's gone.' Roger's face was livid suddenly, the dry skin flushed with colour. 'To that damn beach. I'm going to have that dune bulldozed. I'll have it destroyed utterly!'

Was it Kate's imagination or was there a sudden frisson in the air, a charge of fear – and triumph. With a shiver, she hunted for the tea caddy. 'That's what he wants,' she said over her shoulder. 'That's what Marcus wants.'

'And once he's got what he wants, perhaps he'll leave us alone!' Roger rocked back in the chair, and threw his head back, closing his eyes.

'He might, but Claudia won't.' Paddy came and sat down next to his father. 'The only way to put an end to this, Dad, is to get the dune excavated properly. Then we'll know the truth.'

'And you think that will put a stop to all this horror?' Diana had appeared in the staircase doorway. She was still wearing her crumpled smock; there were smears of blood on it, but whose, Kate could not remember. She turned to the kettle which was steaming gently, willing it to boil. 'I can't believe you are all sitting there, doing nothing, when Alison is outside in all this snow. For pity's sake is no one going to do anything? I'm going to find her!'

'No, Ma.' Paddy staggered to his feet again. The boy was white with exhaustion himself. 'You've got to stay to look after the others. I'll go.' He looked mutely at Kate.

'I'll come too.' She found she had spoken automatically. 'Of course I will.' She glanced regretfully at the kettle.

'No, Kate. Drink something first.' Roger's voice was suddenly very weak. 'Both of you. And have something to eat. For all we know she has been out there for hours. Five minutes isn't going to make any difference.'

364

'I'll go with you, too.' Anne stepped forward. 'Safety in numbers, and all that.' She gave a weak grin.

It was nearly ten minutes later by the time they had all drunk mugs of steaming tea, eaten a wedge of bread and marmalade each and dragged on boots and coats and scarves. As they headed for the door, Paddy glanced at the gun.

'Take it.' Greg had hopped after them. His foot was stiff and throbbed agonizingly this morning. 'We'll be all right here.'

Paddy looked at his brother. Greg gave a watery grin, then he punched him gently on the shoulder. 'Take care of yourself, Paddy; and take care of the girls.' He turned to Kate and touched her hand. She smiled at him, but it was a thin, tired smile. She had no strength left for more. The air was bitingly cold. She wondered how she would summon the strength to go even ten feet, never mind the best part of a mile.

Greg watched them go. All three were exhausted, he knew that. His brother could hardly lift the heavy gun he had so bravely hefted onto his shoulder. He glanced beyond them towards the woods. Was there anyone there, watching them, or were they as deserted as they seemed? He shuddered. The wind was increasing, coming from behind the house, tearing in across the marsh from the sea.

He watched until they were out of sight, then turning, he closed the door. Shooting the bolts across seemed a terrible act of treachery with them outside, but there was nothing for it. He hobbled back into the living room and stared at his father, shocked. Roger was lying back against the cushions, struggling to catch his breath. His face was blue and he was sweating profusely. Diana was bending over him.

'Ma –'

'It's all right, Greg.' Her face was as white as a sheet. 'Your father has had a bit of a turn, but he's OK now.' She stroked his face gently. 'Rest. love. She'll be all right. They'll find her.'

'They will, Dad.' Greg knelt by his father's knees. The syringe, empty now of painkiller, was lying on the arm of the chair. 'They'll all be fine. It's broad daylight now, and the weather is a bit better.' It was a lie but he doubted if his father would know it.

Roger managed a slight grin. He patted Diana's arm as she pulled a rug over him. 'Better now, love,' she whispered. She kissed the top of his head. He had relaxed visibly, lying back against the cushions and his colour was better. Taking Greg's arm she pulled him towards the kitchen end of the room.

'I'm fairly sure he's had a slight heart attack,' she whispered.

Greg started back towards his father but she caught his sleeve. 'No. I'm sure he knows, but don't say anything. Can you go upstairs and wake Joe? He's got to try and go for a doctor.'

Greg nodded. With a glance at his father's white face he dragged himself across to the door and pulled it open. The staircase was dark. Putting his hand on the rail he set his teeth grimly and somehow he hauled himself to the top, sweat pouring off his face as he dragged his injured foot up, step by step, after him. Joe was snoring loudly when Greg limped into the darkened bedroom and shook him awake but it took him only a few minutes to shake off the deep sleep and climb to his feet. 'Right. Don't worry. I'll get there.'

He too was fortified with a marmalade sandwich and a mug of scalding tea before letting himself out into the cold.

'I hate to see you going out on your own, Joe,' Greg murmured as he stood with him on the doorstep. He was leaning heavily on his stick.

Joe smiled grimly. 'Don't you worry about me.' He carried his gun, broken, beneath his left arm. 'You take care of the others. Your Dad and Cissy and Sue. I don't like leaving you on your own here –'

'We're safe here, Joe.' Greg did his best to sound confident. 'Don't worry about us. Just get us some help for Dad.'

Joe nodded. Pulling the collar of his coat up around his ears he stepped out into the dark.

LXIV

The footprints were filling up as they watched, disappearing beneath a new layer of snow. Pete was slightly ahead, walking fast, his head down against the wind. Around them the landscape was uniformly white: shore, sea, sky, a formless, cold frame without definition.

'She went this way,' Pete had slowed almost to a standstill. He was casting around him, like a dog searching for a new scent. 'Then the footsteps seem to stop.' They stared around desperately, both men doubled over, studying the snow. 'I can't see . . .'

'Here.' Jon had walked closer to the sea and suddenly he spotted the tracks again. Lighter this time, and scuffed, as though she had been running.

Kate.

He shaded his eyes against the imagined glare and stared past the dunes towards the sea. The beach stretched in both directions, the shape of the dunes flattened by the snow, and in the cold emptiness nothing moved.

'Kate!' His shout was swallowed by the wind, muffled by the snow. It had no resonance, as though he had shouted through several layers of cotton wool. The sound would not have carried more than a few yards. 'Kate!'

Pete made no comment. He had moved on, head down against the wind, his face immobile now with cold, trying to see new footprints through the whirling snow.

'She was heading towards the sea,' Jon shouted at him at last. 'Why?'

'Lost her sense of direction? Panic?' Pete had stopped, his hands rammed down inside his pockets. 'Poor woman must be in terror of her life.' He shook his head. 'Shall we go on?'

'Of course we go on.' Jon was shaking. 'We go on until we find her.'

He plunged on, across the snow, sinking now and then through the white blanket into softer sand. 'Kate!' His voice rose and dissipated into nothing, whirled to shreds on the wind. 'Kate!'

The voices were still warring inside her head. Standing staring down into the snow-filled grave, Alison saw nothing of the snow, nor of the two figures floundering against the wind.

'Kate!'

The word whirled past her and was lost. It meant nothing.

Whore

Murderer

They were inside her head, both of them, sucking her energy. Soon she would be drained and they would go.

'It's not Kate!'

She did not hear the words; did not see the two men who stood now, one each side of her.

'Who then?'

Jon shrugged. 'I don't know.' Tentatively he reached over to touch her arm. 'Are you all right?'

Alison ignored him. She did not see or hear him. Her gaze never left the drifting snow at her feet.

'Hey, kid, are you OK?' Pete's touch was stronger. He took her by the shoulders and shook her gently.

Alison did not react. Claudia's face was white against the snow, her gown, still stained with blood, as blue as the sky. She could feel the woman's need, the longing, the fear and hate: *May the gods of all eternity curse you, Marcus Severus Secundus, for what you have done here today.*

She was winning now: Claudia.

'What's wrong with her?' Pete glanced at his companion. 'God knows, but the kid's freezing.' Jon wriggled out of his jacket and wrapped it around Alison's shoulders. 'Let's get her back to that cottage.'

'I don't know that that's such a good idea.'

'Maybe not, but where else can we take her?'

The two men looked at one another for a moment across Alison's bowed head.

She could not hear them. He was there now, his fury blistering inside her skull. *The grave. Destroy the grave!*

With a sob she wrenched herself free of Jon's arm. Staggering a few steps from him, she aimed a kick at the snow-covered sand.

'Destroy it!' The voice which came from her lips was guttural; low pitched. A man's voice, for all the words were clearly English.

Jon stepped back in surprise. Then, regathering his wits, he moved forward again to pick up the jacket which had slipped from her shoulders and wrap it once more around her. 'Come on. You must keep warm.' His own voice was shaking with cold.

'No!' She shook him off with ease. 'Keep away from me.' She threw the jacket down on the snow and leaped down into the shallow hollow below the dune with a sudden, last surge of energy. 'The sea will take it soon.' She threw back her head and laughed. 'The sea will take it at last! Two thousand years it has taken for the tide to come and tonight it will wipe the slate clean!' She stood staring at the sea, her hair streaming back from her forehead, her eyes fixed on the horizon. Jon and Pete, surprised into silence, stared with her. The wind was strengthening from the east, whipping the snow in across the water, building the waves, pushing the sea higher and higher up the beach.

'Alison!'

The cry barely reached them. For a moment none of them reacted, then Jon turned. Three figures were hurrying towards them, heads down into the wind, almost lost in the white whirl of snowflakes.

'Kate?' As he recognised her Jon felt his heart leap inside his chest. Relief, joy, worry – all three seemed to swirl around his head as he stepped towards her. She was accompanied by a young man – a boy he saw as he looked closer – and Anne.

'Jon?' Her astonishment stopped her in her tracks.

'Hi.' He found he was smiling. He shrugged. 'It's a long story.'

She stared at him for a moment, overwhelmed with relief, wanting to throw herself into his arms, then her glance moved on past him, resting briefly on Pete before she turned to Alison.

'Allie? Allie, are you all right?' Her questions to Jon could come later. The fact that he was there, on the beach in the snow, spoke volumes. She slid down the side of the dune after Patrick who had thrown his arms around his sister.

Alison shrugged him off viciously, and he staggered back, bewildered. 'She's gone, Kate.' There were tears running down his face. 'She's gone. She's not here. It's not her.'

'Allie!' Kate took Alison's hand and chafed it in her own. 'Allie, come on. Fight it. Please. You have to fight it. Come back to us!'

'What's wrong with her?' Pete slid down beside them.

'She's ill. She doesn't know what she's doing.' Pushing her hair out of her eyes, Kate began to button the jacket across Alison's chest. 'We have to get her back out of the wind. She's no strength left.'

'She seemed to have plenty of strength to me, love.' Pete grimaced. 'She nearly pushed me across the beach.'

'But don't you see, that's not her!' Kate cried. 'That's not her strength. He's possessing her. He's draining her. We have to get her away from here.'

'I'll take her.' Jon did not waste time asking her what she was talking about. He lifted Alison off her feet and turning, began to tramp inland, with his back to the wind.

He knew the exact moment when the strength went out of her. He could feel it draining away as he walked. Physically, she seemed lighter suddenly – a bag of bones in his arms where moments before he had held a rigid, angry body. He clutched her more closely, glancing down at her face as he cradled her against his chest. Her eyes were closed, her face white, a child's face, when a moment before it had seemed to belong to someone else entirely. He shuddered and suddenly there was a hand on his arm. He glanced sideways and met Kate's eyes. She smiled as she stumbled along at his side. 'Thank God you're here.' Did he hear the words against the wind or did he imagine them? He wanted to reach out and touch her, but all he could do was smile and stagger on, feeling the weight of the girl dragging at his arms. Suddenly, her head lolled back and her eyes rolled open. He stopped, horrified, staring down at her face. She was limp now, cold inside the roughly-buttoned jacket.

'Jon, what is it?' Kate was beside him, looking down at Alison's face.

He met her eyes. 'We've got to get her inside quickly, Kate.'

Wordlessly she nodded. Tucking the jacket more closely around Alison's inert body, she followed as Jon walked on across the snow through the dunes, his shoulders hunched against the wind.

In the cottage he carried her straight upstairs and laid her gently on Kate's bed, then he stood back as Kate pulled the blankets over the girl and chafed her hands.

Pete appeared in the doorway behind them. He had pulled the

370

front door closed, and then, firmly, shut the door to the living room before climbing the stairs.

'What happened to Bill?' Jon asked softly. His eyes were fixed on Alison's face.

Kate did not look up. 'He was attacked. In the woods near here.'

'Attacked?'

She went on rubbing Alison's hand. 'He said it was a woman. Two women. We brought him here. But the phones were out. We couldn't get help.' Her voice was shaking; he saw a tear fall onto the blanket. Stepping forward he put his hand on her shoulder and gave it a gentle squeeze. 'Judging by the bruises on his face no one could have helped, Kate. I should think his skull was fractured in a dozen places.'

'He said Allie did it.' The words were out before she could stop them. She heard both men gasp and at last she looked up. 'She couldn't have done, could she? She couldn't ... He was a big man. She's only a child ...'

The room was very silent. The girl on the bed, her face white, her hair strewn damply across the pillow, did not move. Her hand in Kate's was limp and cold. Kate leaned back against Jon, her eyes closed. She was suddenly so weary she couldn't move. Alison's hand dropped from her fingers. For a moment it lay on the blanket where it had fallen, then suddenly it convulsed into a fist. The girl's eyes flew open. Her voice when she spoke was strong and triumphant.

'Listen,' she said. 'Listen. The tide is rising at last.'

LXV

*When Boudicca swept across the country and burned the city she still
called Camelodunum, he was one of the few who managed to escape.
Taking his new wife and his child, he rode out of the town in good time
and waited in safety as the smoke of rebellion rolled across the country.
A spark had ignited the revolt as he had known it would. But it had not
been his doing. Claudia's curse had not touched him. The sacrifice of an
unknown, unsung prince to the gods of a British bog had sunk unnoticed
into the mists of time. He was triumphant. Later, when the revolt was
quelled and Nion's tribe had gone, lost in the slaughter of a proud and
rebellious people, he would obtain the land.*

*He asked for the marsh where the whore he had called his wife had
died, as a reward for his services to Rome and it was given to him with
much more. He grew rich and fat; he bought more land; he owned two
villas. He watched his son grow; the boy who had rich auburn hair and
eyes of glass grey like his mother, and once a year he rode east, to the
edge of the land and he stood looking down into the marsh, staring at
the irises and bog cotton which blew in the knife-blade wind. Others,
unseen strangers, still offered sacrifices to the gods of the marsh – pots of
coins, small pieces of jewellery, even weapons. He offered nothing. He did
not throw down a rose to commemorate the love which had gone; he did
not hurl a dagger to the gods of hate. He merely stood and stared at the
shifting, watery scene glittering in the sunlight, and, before he turned to
go, he spat upon her curse.*

'The storm is getting worse.' Diana turned from the study
window, letting the curtain fall. She looked down at the bed
where her husband lay. His face was grey with pain. His hands
were clawing restlessly at the blanket she had pulled over him.

'Don't worry. Joe will make it.' His voice was growing notice-
ably weaker. 'He's a stubborn old bugger. I can't see him letting a
mere blizzard get the better of him. And the kids will be all right.'

Diana forced herself to smile. 'I know.' She turned back to the window so that he couldn't see her face. Drawing back the curtain a little she peered once again into the whirling snow. He was out there somewhere. Marcus. She could feel him. Evil. Waiting. Waiting for what? To use them? To draw on their energy? And no door could keep him out. She turned back to Roger. His eyes were closed and she watched him for a moment. The energy was draining out of him almost visibly. Their evil visitor would find no food in him. She shuddered. He was dying. She could not pretend to herself any longer. He was dying before her eyes. She wanted to throw herself at him and hold him, to will her own strength into him, but she couldn't. She could do nothing but wait and watch. Shaking her head miserably she tiptoed towards the door and let herself out of the study into the cold hall. She could feel the draught blowing under the front door. It was icy; a drift of snow had somehow slipped under the draught-proofing and lay in a white veil across the stone tiles. Closing the door behind her silently she went through into the sitting room.

Cissy and Sue were seated on the sofa near the fire, side by side. Automatically her eyes went to the chair nearest the inglenook where normally in weather like this the two cats would be lying, in a heap of black and white fur. There was no sign of them. Greg was standing in the kitchen, leaning on the back of one of the bent oak chairs. He seemed to be gazing into space, 'How is he?' he asked as she wandered listlessly over to him.

She shrugged. 'Not good.'

He looked at her hard. 'Joe will get through, Ma.'

She tried to smile. 'I'm sure he will. But I don't think it will be in time for your father, Greg. We have to prepare ourselves.'

He put his arm round her, pulling her close against him. 'It was bound to happen one day. We knew he hadn't got long,' he said gently.

She nodded dumbly.

'He always said he wanted to go here and not in hospital.'

'I know.' It was a whisper.

'Shall I go and sit with him for a bit?' He dropped a kiss onto the top of her head. 'You get some sleep; you look completely flaked out. I'll call you if he needs you.'

She nodded. With a glance at the two dozing on the sofa, she went to the door at the foot of the staircase 'The moment he needs me, Greg,' she repeated softly.

'I promise.'

The staircase was cold and the upper floor of the house dark as she climbed wearily up to the bedroom she had shared with Roger for so many years. For a moment she stood in the doorway looking round, vividly aware in some inner part of herself that he would never walk through this door again. On the floor, in the corner, a pathetic reminder that Christmas was barely two weeks away, a pile of presents lay, partially hidden by a rug.

She walked across to the low window and stared out. It was growing light, but the snow was thick now, whirling through the air, blotting out the horizon. In this east-facing bedroom you could usually see across the dunes towards the sea, but today she was conscious of nothing but grey and white – a moving, whirling mass of nothing. Disorientated, she turned – and stopped short.

The woman by the bed was so clear she could see every detail of her clothes, her hair, her skin, her eyes. For a moment they stood there, their eyes locked together and for the first time Diana knew that Claudia could see her as clearly as she could see Claudia.

'Sweet Blessed Jesus!' The words were out of her mouth before she knew she had spoken. 'What do you want?

For a fraction of a moment longer they stared at each other, then Claudia was gone.

'Ma.' Greg's voice from the foot of the stairs was urgent. 'Ma, come quickly.'

Diana whirled back to the door conscious with some part of her brain that the room smelled of a sweet, sickly perfume. 'What is it? What's wrong?'

'He wants you.' Greg hobbled ahead of her towards the study. Roger was lying propped up against the pillows and cushions. He was breathing with difficulty and his cheeks, which for so long had been colourless, had a livid, painful colour to them.

'He's here, Di,' he said slowly. 'That bastard is here, in this room. He's real.'

Diana glanced at Greg.

'Marcus,' Greg mouthed. 'He's seen Marcus.'

Diana knelt at the side of the makeshift bed and took Roger's hand. 'He can't hurt you, love.'

374

'Too damn right. I've nothing for him. It's the kids he wants. He wants their energy. But he's not going to get it.' He gripped Diana's hand so hard she winced. 'I'm going to fight him on his own ground.' The breath was rasping in his throat.

'Roger –'

'He didn't bargain for that, did he. I'm going after him. To hell, if necessary.' He looked from his wife to his son and back. 'Don't worry. I'm sane. Dying, but sane. I've never believed. Not in heaven or hell or God or Satan until now. But this bastard has made me realise there is somewhere out there. If his soul can survive there, black as it is, then so can mine!' He laughed weakly and Diana buried her head in the blanket near him, trying to smother her sobs. 'I'm going to find out what it's all about. And if he can come back then so can I. I shall return to tell you.'

'Dad –' Greg tried to interrupt, but Roger talked on, his words slurring together now as the drugs took a stronger hold on his pain.

'No, my mind is made up. I am going to find out why she cursed him. She's here, you know, in the house now. She was his first wife. She's come to help me. She wants me to find him. I shall get him. I shall win –'

'Dad!' Greg knelt down stiffly on the other side of the bed, wincing as his foot dragged on the ground. 'Dad, don't talk like this.'

'Why?' Roger turned and looked at him. His eyes, though unnaturally bright, were perfectly lucid. 'After what that bastard has done to my daughter, you think I am going to let him get away with it?'

'No, of course not, but –'

'But nothing. My mind is made up. I am going after him. A quest. A glorious quest through the realms of the afterlife. How do you like that idea?' He sounded delirious as he laughed again, clutching at Diana's hand. Then he began to cough.

'Roger –' Desperately she tried to soothe him. 'Get some water, Greg, quickly. Roger, darling, please, calm yourself. You're going to be all right.'

'Balls!' The word was gasped through another spasm of coughing. 'Do me the kindness of treating me like an adult, Di. I know. You know. Greg knows.' He paused, breathless, and sipped gratefully as Greg held a glass of water to his lips. 'Thanks son. Look.

Better this way than lingering for months in some goddam awful hospice. I love Redall. All of it. I was born here. My father was born here. Not many families can say that nowadays. I'd like to think that you or Paddy will make your home here too. This place is in our bones,' he smiled grimly. 'Who knows, perhaps we are descended from Marcus himself. I'm bound hand and foot to this place – its history is in my blood.' He looked at Diana. 'What I'm trying to say, love, and making a frightful hash of it, is that I'm happy to die here. And I'm not going anywhere. I'll still love you, whatever happens. And I'll stick around. Not to frighten you. Just to watch over you and keep Marcus in line.' He closed his eyes, exhausted.

Diana looked up at Greg. Her eyes were blinded by tears. 'Greg –' She mouthed his name but no sound came.

Greg was biting his lip. Neither of them said a word as, holding a hand each, they watched Roger's face lose the colour which had animated it, as he dozed again. Around them the room seemed to grow darker in the candlelight.

'A quest,' Greg said at last, trying to keep his voice steady. 'I like that idea.' He frowned. If it were possible – to travel through time and space – to treat death as a mere doorway – that would only be comforting if one expected to find angels on the other side.

But Marcus was a demon.

LXVI

The waves threw off the snow, thundering up the beach in clouds of spray. The sea had reached the soft sand now, the sand which was never covered by the tide, sucking greedily at the ground and spitting out the residue with each successive incursion. Peat and soil swirled and dissolved; sand turned to brown liquid, dispersed and vanished, to be deposited again on a distant shore. In the dune the grave welcomed the first deep wave which seeped into its heart, whisking away a trowel and a brush, tearing at the remaining bones, grinding them, stirring them, flushing out every trace of what had been. Another followed and then another and then the sea overwhelmed, passing onwards towards the calm, ice-bound estuary where, long before, the geese had gone, flying inland away from the storm.

Joe stood panting at the top of the track and wiped his forehead with his sleeve. He could barely see now for the weight of snow on his eyelashes; his face was frozen stiff and his tears seemed to turn to ice as the wind whipped them from his eyes. He looked round, exhausted. Two cars were parked at the edge of the road. Drawn up under the trees. Anne's he supposed; but whose was the other? He walked over to it, and swept the snow off the snow-covered bonnet. Ron's Land Rover from the pub. He frowned and glanced back the way he had come. Whatever Ron had come for, he had left no trace. His tracks had long ago been covered over.

Wearily he turned up the road and began to trudge towards home. Twice he stopped and looked behind him. A dozen times in the wood he had had the feeling that he was being followed. Each time he had stopped and raised the gun, sweeping it menacingly around at the undergrowth. But there had been no one there. No one at all. Only the silence and the wind and the occasional crash of snow falling from the trees.

It took him another hour to trudge the few hundred yards home, grope in his pocket with deadened hands for the key to the back door, and let himself into the blessed warmth and stillness. The house was very quiet. Stamping the snow off his boots he shrugged himself out of his coat, leaving it where it fell on the kitchen floor and he went over to the wall telephone. Picking it up, he listened. The familiar dialling tone rang out almost deafeningly in his ear.

Nine nine nine.

He had never dialled it before. Shaking his head wearily, he waited for a moment before asking for police and ambulance. The woman on the other end of the line was dubious. 'They'll be with you as soon as possible Mr Farnborough, but the weather is so bad! They're still forecasting hurricane force winds and blizzard conditions. The helicopter can't take off. It will be down to the police to try and get through with a medical team.'

'Do your best, love.' Joe found he had sunk down onto the wooden chair left neatly against the wall. Near him Cissy's apron hung on the back of the door. He shook his head. 'Things are bad down there. Very bad. There's a man murdered. Another man dying. Please. Help us.'

He sat still for a long time after he had hung up. There was nothing more that he could do. He could not go back. He had agreed to wait so he could guide the police vehicle down to the farmhouse. Leaning his head against the wall he closed his eyes wearily.

In two minutes he was fast asleep.

LXVII

Kate glanced up at Jon as they stood side by side looking out of the bedroom window of the cottage. She still wasn't entirely sure how or why he had appeared – explanations would come later – but she was comforted and happy that he was there. Behind them Alison was sleeping deeply. Downstairs in the kitchen Pete and Patrick were rummaging in the drawers of the dresser for candles and matches.

Patrick didn't like being down here. He was acutely conscious at every moment of the dead man lying on the sofa in the next room. Bill who in life had been a genial, popular visitor at Redall Farmhouse was in death a terrifying threat.

They were half-way up the stairs when Alison screamed.

'Shit, what was that?' Pete was close behind Patrick who stopped dead, his face white. 'That was Allie.'

'OK, son, I'll go. You wait here.' Pete pushed past him, taking the rest of the stairs two at a time.

In the bedroom Jon and Kate were standing over the bed. Kate had clutched at Jon's arm – her fingers were white as they sank into his sleeve. Alison was lying on the bed thrashing back and forth as though in pain, her hands clasped to her head. 'Mummy!' she screamed again. 'Mummy, help me!'

Anne sat down on the bed. She caught Alison's wrists, trying to pull them away from the girl's face. 'Allie. Allie, please, listen to me. You're dreaming. Don't be afraid. Wake up. Allie, wake up.' Alison was raking at her temples with her nails. A streak of blood appeared across her forehead, then another. 'Allie, don't, you're hurting yourself. Please.'

Alison did not hear her. They were there again, inside her head. Only this time he was laughing. *Gone! Gone under the sea at last! Now you're forgotten. Forgotten forever, you and your priest lover!*

Claudia's screams inside her head were so loud she thought her brain would burst; pain and anguish swirled about her; a tide of blood washed back and forth behind her eyes, and now, suddenly, there was another voice – a man's voice – the voice of Claudia's lover. At last he had come. He was there with them. And he was strong; stronger than Marcus, his fury uncontrollable.

With a groan Alison pulled at her hair, sitting up, rocking back and forth with such violence that Anne slipped off the bed to the floor. 'Alison!' She scrambled to her feet. 'Can you hear me? Listen!' She grabbed at the girl's hands again. 'You must be strong. Come back to us, Allie. Open your eyes and come back. Whatever it is you're fighting, you must be strong.' She gasped as Alison tore her wrists free and went back to attacking her own face with her nails. 'Alison, please!' She looked wildly at Jon. 'We've got to tie her hands. She's going to scratch herself to pieces. Please, help me, quickly.'

Jon looked round wildly. It was Kate who pulled the belt from her bathrobe which still hung on the back of the door. It took three of them to hold her still, but somehow they managed it, tying her wrists together and tucking her firmly down with the sheets. When they had finished both Anne and Kate had been badly scratched themselves. 'She's as strong as three men!' Anne stared down at the girl who was still throwing herself back and forth beneath the sheets. She rested a hand on Alison's damp forehead.

Alison did not feel it; she did not know what was happening to her. There was no room for thought inside her head now. No room for her at all. She had ceased to fight them. They had her strength. That was all they wanted.

Jon was shivering. The temperature in the room, he realised suddenly, had dropped violently. Surreptitiously he retrieved his jacket which had fallen to the floor when they put Alison into the bed. 'What is it? What has happened to her?'

Kate looked at Patrick who had slid into the room behind Pete. 'Marcus has got her.' She gave a nervous laugh. 'My Roman. Remember? He killed Claudia, who we think must have been his wife, and now he's haunting us.' She looked down at the bed. 'He's possessed her, Jon.'

'No!' Anne shouted. 'No! He can't have her. Fight, Allie, fight!' She put her lips close to Alison's face. 'Concentrate, Alison. Think! Think about anything. Use your brain. Fight.' She took Alison by the shoulders and shook her gently. 'Don't give in. Don't let him win. Oh God!' She threw her hair back off her face with a furious jerk of her head, clenching her fists in her frustration. 'I don't know what to do. I don't know how to help her! Alison. Listen to me. Fight!'

Pete, like the others, was staring at Anne. His gaze left her face at last and slid down to Alison's restless form. His mouth had gone dry. He probably looked as bad as the others. They were all white-faced, cold. He cleared his throat. 'This kid should be in hospital, Anne,' he said at last. 'Where will we find the nearest phone?'

Kate shook her head. 'The phones aren't working.' Was it her imagination or was Alison calmer now? She stared down, terrified, at the girl's tortured face.

Shadows.

Whirling shadows filled with hate.

Inside her head Allie stared into the darkness helplessly and saw the three prowling, amorphous figures. She could feel someone's hands ice cold on hers, hear a voice shouting her name, but she could not react. They were like lions circling their prey: the woman, the two men, hungry in their hatred for living energy to sustain them.

Why me?

Did she cry out loud? She didn't know, but as her mind rebelled the figures drew back.

FIGHT

A voice reached her out of the stormy roar of hatred, a woman's voice. *FIGHT ALISON, USE YOUR BRAIN.*

Too tired. She was too tired to fight. She was empty. They had sucked her dry.

In the dark the shadowy figures had begun to fade. Their concentration had left her. They were turning elsewhere; questing, hungry. Others must be found, and soon, to feed their lust for hate.

'We'll need to get back to the car.' Jon went back to the window. Anything to get away even for a moment from the torment of the girl on the bed. He took a deep breath and stared out. He found he was shaking. 'The snow is settling very thickly.' He glanced back at Pete. 'Take a look. Do you reckon the roads will still be passable?'

Pete joined him, staring down into the murky light. After a moment he rubbed his eyes. 'Tell me my eyes are going, mate,' he muttered under his breath. 'But is that the sea down there?'

In a low-lying corner of the garden, below the dunes, a line of dark water had appeared. As Jon watched it broadened slightly, strewn with ripples, lapping at the snowy grass. He craned his neck sideways, narrowing his eyes as a fresh flurry of snow hit the window. Beyond the belt of trees he could see the broad, icy spread of the estuary, the mud and dunes smothered in a uniform blanket of snow. The water was lapping higher, free of the ice, creeping round the back of the cottage as the wind drove the sea inland.

He turned to the bed. 'Patrick. Come and look at this.'

The boy came. He stared out into the garden. 'Oh shit!'

'Are we going to be cut off?'

Patrick nodded. 'Once it's here there's nothing to stop it. It must have gone over the sea wall at Redall Point.'

'Right.' Pete looked at Jon. 'That settles it. We all have to leave. Fast. We'll make a stretcher to carry the kid.'

'What about Bill?' Kate looked from Jon to Pete and back.

'We'll have to leave him, Kate.' Jon put his arms around her and held her close. 'He won't know, love. Or if he does, he'll understand. We can't take him with us.' He lowered his voice. 'Our lives are in danger. That water is coming in very fast. We have to get Alison away.'

They built a stretcher using a rake and a broom handle from the log shed, winding sheets around them to make a hammock and padding it with blankets. Pete carried Alison down the stairs and laid her down on it outside the front door. They wrapped two more blankets around her, then Jon and Pete picked her up. 'It works,' Jon grinned at Kate.

She was about to close the door when a thought struck her. She hesitated for a moment outside the door of the living room. Bill was there. But so were her notes for the book. She couldn't leave them to the floods. Bill would understand. Screwing up her courage she pushed open the door and peered round it. Nothing had changed in the room. The smell of vomit was all pervasive. As quickly as she could, she ran to the desk. Picking up her notebook, backup disks and her volume of poetry she rammed them into the inner pockets of her waterproof. One last look round and she turned back towards the door. By the sofa she stopped. ''Bye Bill. God bless.' Her voice sounded strange in the silent room.

Whirling round she ran out, closing the door behind her. Slamming the front door she ran after the others who were already disappearing into the wood. Inside the cottage the silence was suddenly intense.

Slowly the scent of jasmine drifted down the stairs and through the empty rooms.

LXVIII

'Ma, go and take a break. I'll sit with him.' Greg put his hand on his mother's shoulder. Roger was asleep, his breath coming in harsh rasping gasps.

Diana shook her head. 'I'll stay, Greg.' She looked up at him through her tears. 'It could happen at any time now.'

Greg bit his lip. Silently he knelt beside her, ignoring the pain which shot from his foot through every nerve in his body. 'It's what he wanted. To be at home,' he repeated softly.

'I know.' She laid her head for a moment on her husband's chest.

Roger opened his eyes. 'Not gone yet,' he whispered. 'I'm trying to think –' he paused, barely able to speak. 'Famous last words –'

'How about Sod you, Marcus, I'm coming to get you,' Greg said bitterly.

'Greg!' Diana was horrified.

'No. He's right,' Roger whispered. 'It gives me – a goal.' His eyes closed and for several seconds he struggled for breath.

'Hush now, love.' Diana put her hand on his forehead. 'Save your strength.'

'What for?' The grim humour kept on coming. 'I won't need strength – where I'm going.' He managed a faint smile.

'That's right. Sock it to him, Dad.' Greg had a tight hold of his father's hand.

Around them the room was growing colder. Diana shivered. The candle burning low on the table beside the bed flickered violently.

'Greg.' Roger opened his eyes again. 'Get the archaeological boys in. Get them to turn over that grave. Every inch. Find out what it is that bastard is trying to hide and tell the world.'

Another gust of wind seemed to blow through the room. The candle flared again and then went out, trailing smoke.

Diana let out a small cry of distress.

'He doesn't like it!' Roger gave a croaky laugh. 'He wants to keep that grave a secret. It's up to you, Greg. Everything is up to you now –' His voice trailed away. In the faint light flickering through the window the room was all shadows.

For a moment the silence was so profound Greg stared round, afraid. It was as though he were seeing the room through a sheet of glass. Uncomprehending, he kept on clutching his father's hand, then suddenly he realised where the silence came from. Roger's harsh breathing had stopped. Blinking back his tears he bent and kissed the cold hand in his. 'Ma –'

'I know.' She was sobbing quietly. 'He's gone. Oh, Greg –'

Neither moved for a long time, then slowly and painfully, Greg climbed to his feet. He put his arm round Diana's shoulders. 'Come through to the warm. I'll make you some tea.'

She shook her head. 'I don't want to leave him –'

'He'll be all right. You must come. It's so cold in here –'

Somehow he managed to help her up. For a moment they both stood looking down at his father's face, relaxed now, looking younger and happier than it had for a long time, then suddenly Diana tore herself away from Greg's arm.

'All right, you bastard!' She screamed into the room. 'Are you satisfied now? You've killed another man. But he's better than you. A good man, and he'll hunt you down. He'll follow you to hell and back if he has to!' She burst into tears again. 'Now get out of my house! Get out and don't come near any of us again!'

'Ma.' Greg caught her hand. 'Ma, come away. This isn't doing any good.'

'Isn't it?' Through her tears she turned on him like a spitting cat. 'Well it's doing me some good! I want that bastard Roman out of here for ever. He's not taking my house. He's not taking my children! We'll tell the world about him. We'll tell the world he's a murderer and a liar and a cheat. He killed that poor woman. He killed Bill. And now he's killed my Roger –' She broke down in sobs.

Somehow Greg managed to pull her away. In the sitting room Cissy had managed to get to her feet, her face white. 'Diana –?'

'Dad's dead.' Greg steered his mother towards the sofa and

pushed her down. 'Please, Cissy, put on the kettle. She needs some tea. And some brandy.'

'Oh, my dear, I'm so sorry.' Cissy touched Diana on the shoulder, then she limped across the room to the Aga. She was shaking violently. Her arm, roughly bandaged and in a sling, hurt like hell, but she ignored it as she manoeuvred the kettle onto the hotplate. As she did so, there was a deafening bang from upstairs. She spun round. 'What was that?'

Greg was standing over his mother. At the sound he had turned. In two painful strides he was at the door.

Behind him Susie curled up on her chair and buried her face in a cushion. Cissy ran to her and put a protective arm around her.

Diana's face was white, her eyes glassy. 'It's begun,' she whispered.

'What has?' Greg opened the door and peered up the stairs.

'Your father and Marcus.'

Greg swung round. 'You don't believe that –'

'Your father is trying to protect us.'

Greg stared at her for a moment. Then he turned, and hauling himself with difficulty up the banisters, he disappeared upstairs. There was a long silence. Three pairs of eyes were fixed on the door. Then they heard him coming back. He appeared and closed the door behind him. He was shaking with the effort of negotiating the stairs on his injured foot. 'Nothing,' he said. The words were no sooner out of his mouth when there was another bang, louder than the first.

Diana let out a sob. 'Roger. Be careful.'

'Ma –' Greg went and sat down beside her. Putting his arm around her he pulled her against him tightly. 'It's probably the house timbers expanding or contracting in the cold. It's not Dad –' He glanced at Cissy. 'The brandy.'

Cissy, her face white, nodded. She collected bottle and glasses from the dresser and brought them back to the fire. Her hand shook so much as she poured it that the liquid spilled on the hearth. She handed Diana half a tumblerful. Not noticing, Diana took a sip. She coughed violently and handed the glass to Greg who drank in turn. They were all waiting, ears straining for another bang.

The silence lengthened. It was several minutes before they realised that the familiar smell of woodsmoke and polish in the room had been replaced by the scent of jasmine.

LXIX

He saw her often in his dreams, the wife who had betrayed him. He saw her laughing. He saw her in her lover's arms. He saw her again and again in her blue gown, the splash of scarlet dripping down her skirts, her eyes open in wild agony and hate. And again and again he heard her curse him. A woman's curse. A dying curse, made before the gods themselves. He would awaken shivering, sweat sheening his body and if Augusta woke, he would claim it was a touch of the marsh fever. He was scared of dying. While he was alive she could not touch him, but in death they would be equals. And the priest. Her lover. What of him? Was he there too, waiting? Waiting to avenge the greatest betrayal of all, a false message from the gods. He stared into the darkness and he was afraid.

The second time they stopped to rest Kate felt for Alison's pulse. The girl was getting weaker all the time, her life force draining visibly as they watched. She glanced at Anne. 'What can we do?'

Anne shrugged miserably. She felt helpless. All her knowledge of the human mind had deserted her. She had no basis to work from. This was not covered by any category she had read about. This was no chemical imbalance of the brain; it was not multiple personality disorder; it was not schizophrenia; it was not any kind of manic state. Marcus was an external force, a parasite implanted inside the girl's head and she had no parameters within which to work. 'I wish I was religious. I feel a priest would be more help than anything else,' she said slowly. 'Or a medium of some sort as a go-between. Our culture doesn't give us weapons to fight this any more. I don't know what to do.' She looked at Jon and then at Pete, kneeling in the snow. The sleet, driving into their faces had turned without their realising it to rain. The wind, stronger than ever, had a warmer feel now. Behind them, like an ever-present enemy, the water lapped higher, flowing in amongst the trees, stealing imperceptibly through the undergrowth.

'Is he still there?' Kate murmured to her sister. 'Is he still inside her?'

Anne shrugged. 'I don't think so. She's calm; her strength has gone.'

'Then where is he?' Kate looked up into Jon's eyes as he bent over her to look at Alison.

Jon gave a wan smile. 'I don't know,' he said.

Anne stood up, stiffly. The woods were very silent; the trees seemed to be listening, shrugging off the hissing rain and wind.

'Perhaps with the grave flooded, he's left completely.' Patrick stood up too. Jon and Pete bent to pick up the stretcher and slowly the small procession began to move on. Kate paused a moment, staring back the way they had come. He wasn't here now. The woods were empty. But that didn't mean he had gone for good. Something deep inside her told her that he was still around, somewhere. Waiting.

LXX

'Dear God, what's happening!' Diana shrank against Greg. The room had grown dark. The rush and roar of the wind filled the chimneys, scattering ash into the room.

'Susie!' Cissy shouted suddenly, her voice shrill with panic. The girl had fallen from the chair. She was struggling on the ground, her hands to her throat as if she were trying to prise fingers loose from her neck – fingers they could not see. The candle which had stood on the table beside the sofa flared suddenly and went out. An acrid trail of smoke drifted across the room.

'Susie!' Diana flung herself towards them. 'Oh God, it's happening again.'

Susie was thrashing backwards and forwards on the rug, beating her heels on the ground, fighting for breath.

> Mine
>> I have her
> Mine
>> HATRED
>>> ANGER

She could see nothing, feel nothing but the pain inside her head as three formless shapes tried, parasitic, greedy, to fasten their empty, gaping souls to hers.

'*Mummy –!*' Her shriek of pain and fear died in her throat as she writhed once more in a spasm of agony.

'Susie!' Cissy was on her knees, pulling at the girl's wrists, trying to drag her hands away from her face.

'It's what happened to Allie.' Greg knelt down beside them. He looked at the girl for a moment then he stared round the room. 'He's here. He's here, in the room with us.' He turned back to his mother.

'Stop her hurting herself, Cissy,' Diana commanded, her voice surprisingly strong. 'You bastard, Marcus!' She turned and shouted at the ceiling. 'Can't you see, there's no point. It's over. We know. We know what you did –'

'That is the point,' Greg put in quietly. He was holding Susie's small hands in his own. 'We don't know what he did. We think we do. We think he murdered Claudia and now his conscience is making him pay the ultimate price, but we don't know.'

'No! No! NO –!'

Susie screamed so loudly that both Greg and Cissy shrank back, releasing her hands, staring down at her in fear and horror as she sat up, her body rigid, clawing at her eyes.

Greg recovered first, pulling her hands away from her face. 'He's using her in some way. The only way we can stop it is to find out what it is he is trying to say. And the evidence must be in that grave. We have to go and see as soon as the weather has improved enough to have a go ourselves. Never mind the archaeologists. This is between us and Marcus and Claudia. We need to know the truth. For all our sakes.'

'He'll try and stop you,' Diana put in softly. 'He wants whatever is in that grave to stay hidden.'

'Tough. It's not going to. Besides, he's tried to stop me before and he failed,' he grinned bitterly. 'I defeated him, remember? And I mean to get at the truth.' He climbed awkwardly to his feet, swearing softly as a shaft of pain shot up his leg from his throbbing foot. 'Do you hear that, Marcus Severus Secundus?' Like his mother, he was shouting at the ceiling. 'I'm not afraid of you, and I mean to have the truth!'

In answer the wind screamed ever more loudly down the chimney, scattering sparks.

'Where are you, Roger? Oh, please help us!' Suddenly Diana was crying. 'Fight him for us. Make him go away.'

'Ma –' Greg put his arms round her.

'No. He promised. He's there. I'm sure he's there. Help us Roger. Please.' She was trembling violently.

There was a long silence. Greg bit his lip. Wherever his father had gone, he had not lingered here. The silence thickened around them. He could feel the skin on the nape of his neck prickling.

There was a presence in the room. But it was not his father. It was a female presence. Greg shivered, staring round. Claudia. He could sense her near him, the woman in blue, the woman whose image he had so often conjured up with pencil and brush. 'Claudia's here. Speak to her.' He seized his mother's arm. 'Go on. Tell her we mean to find the truth. Tell her we will avenge her.'

'Greg –'

'Go on!' He turned round slowly himself, as if expecting to see the woman somewhere concealed in a corner. 'Do you hear me, Lady Claudia? We are going to learn the truth about your death. That's what you want, isn't it? That's what this is all about.' He paused, panting, half expecting to hear a voice answering his, but the only response came from the wind. 'Claudia!' He shouted the name again.

Surely he could smell it: the jasmine scent she wore.

And something else.

Tobacco.

He bit his lip with a glance at his mother. Had she smelt it too? It was two years since his father had given up smoking – the day his cancer had been diagnosed – but suddenly he could smell his tobacco in the room. Was he here, after all, fighting for them as he had promised or was it wishful thinking, this strange blend of scents? Ashamed at the sudden tears in his eyes he moved a few paces towards the window and looked out, trying to control his emotions.

In the space of an hour the scene out there had changed. The snow had turned to rain. The garden, so recently locked in a brittle, short-lived frame of ice had become a living, dripping sea of water. From trees and bushes the soft snow slid in lumps or melted as he watched, desperately trying to swallow his tears. The rain, sliding down the window was carrying the premature winter away with it as swiftly as it had come. The flowers of winter jasmine had freed themselves from a frosting of ice and drooped, yellow and orange from slender green stems.

Somehow he managed to get a grip on himself.

He was turning back towards Diana when out of the corner of his eye he saw a movement in the trees. He stiffened, a shot of adrenalin flooding through his stomach. Marcus? Claudia? His father? He waited, holding his breath.

His relief when he saw the small group of figures emerge from the trees, carrying between them what looked like a stretcher,

392

was enormous. 'It's Kate and Paddy,' he called, trying to keep his voice steady. He limped to the door and, fighting the bolts, he pulled it open. The blast of cold air carried the sweet, clean smell of melt water before it, as the soaked, exhausted figures staggered across the lawn. He did not question who the two unknown men were as they trooped in; enough that they were all safe.

He stared down at his sister's face and he grew cold, his relief stillborn.

'What happened, Kate?' He looked up and met her eyes.

'We found her at the grave again,' she said wearily. 'Marcus had her.' She flung herself down on the sofa beside Anne who had collapsed there as soon as she walked in. It was only then that she saw Susie lying in front of the fire. 'Oh no?' Her plea turned to a sob.

'They'll be all right.' Diana was cradling Alison's head against her breast, kneeling beside the stretcher where Pete and Jon had lowered it to the floor. Behind them Paddy bolted the front door again and then subsided where he was onto the mat, sliding down to sit with his back against the wall, staring into space. He had reached the limits of his endurance.

Blowing on his freezing fingers Jon went quietly over to stand behind Kate and put his hands on her shoulders. It was a reassuring gesture and she leaned back, grateful for his strength. Raising her eyes wearily she found Greg staring at her. His white face was stiff with shock.

'This is Jon Bevan, Greg,' she said slowly, beginning to grapple with the zip on her wet jacket. 'He and Pete came to look for us. They went straight to the cottage. They found Allie.'

'Jon Bevan?' Claudia, Marcus, even his father were forgotten as Greg, oblivious suddenly of everyone else in the room, focussed his attention on Jon's face. 'The poet?'

'That's right.' Jon stepped round the sofa and held out his hand.

Greg stared at it. He did not make any attempt to take it. 'So, you've come to play ghostbusters with us, have you?' he said coldly. 'And what are your qualifications for sending Marcus Severus Secundus back to the hell he surely came from?'

Jon lowered his hand. Slowly he began to peel off his sodden jacket. 'Perhaps a poet can communicate with the dead; I'm sure he can do it at least as well as a painter,' he replied stiffly. 'We are supposed to speak a universal language which transcends the ages.'

'I thought you and Kate were finished,' Greg pressed. He was shaken by the sudden arrival of this man whom he had thought long gone from Kate's life.

'Greg!' His mother interrupted, her voice sharp with anxiety. 'Help me with Allie! Quickly!' Alison's head had fallen back on Diana's arm and her eyes had rolled open.

Unnoticed by any of them the smell of tobacco in the room strengthened.

'Christ!' Greg helped his mother lower her to the floor. Bending low he put his ear to her mouth. 'She's still breathing.' He swivelled to face Jon, his face growing hard again. 'Well? What do we do, poet?'

Jon ignored him. He like the others, was staring down at the two girls lying near one another on the floor. Only the occasional terrified sob from Cissy punctuated the silence of the room. Diana's eyes had filled with tears. She was drained, too tired even to speak. With Alison's hand in hers she sat helplessly on the floor gazing at her daughter's face.

There was a long silence. Kate looked at Jon. She had not noticed the hostility between the two men, nor the electric atmosphere as the tension between them flared, but she could feel the cold in the room which was suddenly palpable. It was swirling clammily round them. He was there. He hadn't gone. She could feel the strength of the alien mind reaching out, the tendrils of anger and hatred threading through the air, feeding on the energy of hate.

'NO!'

She didn't realise she had cried out loud until she saw the others staring at her, their faces full of fear. 'He's looking for someone else –'

'Fight him. Don't let your mind go empty. Fight him hard. Recite something. Concentrate.' Anne caught her arm. 'Fight him. He's drained those two like . . . batteries . . .' She spluttered with anger. 'And he needs energy from somewhere else. Fight him.' She looked round. 'Where's Paddy?' Her voice sharpened with fear.

'Oh God! Don't let him have gone into the study! Don't let him have found his father –' There had been no chance to tell them

394

Roger was dead, no way of breaking the news gently. Diana scrambled to her feet and pushing past Pete, she ran to the door. She stopped abruptly. Patrick was slumped against the wall in the passage outside.

'Paddy! Her voice rose to a shriek. The boy opened his eyes. 'Paddy. Are you all right?' Flinging herself down beside him she hugged him tightly.

He nodded vaguely. 'Tired.' He could barely speak.

'Tired and very brave.' Jon had followed her out. He extended a hand to the boy. 'He's OK.' You could tell from the eyes. Alison's blank stare did not compare with this blurred, sleepy moment of disorientation. 'Come on, old chap. Stand up and come to the fire.' He smiled at Diana. 'He's OK. I'm sure he's OK. Just exhausted.'

Diana nodded. Behind the door in the study Roger lay, cold, on the camp bed. She had to tell Patrick that his father had died. She had to tell the others. Tears filled her eyes but she said nothing as Jon helped Paddy through to the fire and lowered him into a chair. Now was not the moment. She couldn't face even talking about it. Not yet.

They all stood huddled together, looking round. A spatter of rain hit the window. From the icicle above the porch a steady chain of drips began to fall onto the step. Inside, the temperature was still dropping. They stared at one another.

Anne frowned. 'He's still here. Looking for energy,' she whispered. 'I can feel him.' She shuddered. 'My God, I've never felt anything like this before.' She stared round at the frightened faces. 'Concentrate. Fill your minds with something. Think hard. Recite poetry. Anything. Don't let him in. Recite! All of you together. Now. Something you all know. Quickly.'

For a moment the room was totally silent. Then Diana, her daughter's hand clutched in her own, began slowly to intone the words of a nursery rhyme. 'The owl and the pussy cat went to sea, in a beautiful pea green boat . . .'

With a shaky smile Cissy joined her and after a minute Pete joined in. 'They took some honey and plenty of money wrapped up in a five pound note . . .'

Was it their imagination or was the room growing less cold?

'Go on. It's working,' Anne whispered.

'Again. Again. Another.' Diana had screwed up her eyes as if she were praying. 'Humpty Dumpty sat on the wall, Humpty Dumpty had a great fall. All the king's horses and –'

They all felt the sudden easing of tension in the room.

'He's gone.' Greg's whisper cut them short.

There was a moment's silence.

As swiftly as it had come the cold prowling menace had left, and with it the strange, sudden, enigmatic smell of Roger's tobacco.

For the time being the encircling shadows were empty.

LXXI

The police Land Rover slid and bucked down the track with Joe
in the front between the two uniformed constables. Behind them
Doctor Jamieson clung on for grim death to the back of the seats
as they skidded through the increasingly wet slush. 'Not far now.'
Joe peered through the windscreen. 'Down through those trees
and we're there.'

A gust of wind rocked the car sideways and the driver swore
as he fought to keep it on the track. In front of them the radio
crackled and spat with interference. The younger constable, Bob
Garth, grinned at him, his face grey with fatigue. He had already
been on duty for forty-eight hours. 'You reckon your ghost will
be waiting for us then, do you?'

Joe had told them the whole story as far as he knew it. It was
greeted with solemn interest by the two policemen. The doctor,
an old friend of the Farnboroughs', was more forthcoming. 'If I
didn't know you better, Joe, I'd tell them to breathalyse you. I've
never heard such a load of bollocks. You've all been letting the
solitude get to you.'

'I've heard stories about Redall Bay before,' Bob Garth put in.
'A lot of the locals reckon it's haunted. If not by the Black Dog
then by a whole range of sinister things. You won't catch them
going down on the marsh or the beach in the dark. When I was
up here the other night I reckoned it felt strange. There was
something very funny about all that business at the cottage.'

'The ghosts the locals are afraid of were invented by the
smugglers to keep the revenue men away,' the man at the wheel
put in. Mat Larkin had lived nearby all his life. 'You don't want
to believe a word you hear about them.'

'I suppose not.' Joe did not sound too sure. He too was local
born and bred.

'Nearly there now.' Mat swung the Land Rover expertly round

a slippery bend. The wheels skidded in the wet slush, throwing muddy white spray across the bushes.

'Looks peaceful enough now.' All four men peered through the windscreen at the farmhouse as they drew up outside. Climbing out, both Joe and the doctor instinctively hung back allowing the two policemen to go first. A face at the window showed them that they had been seen. Seconds later the front door opened.

'Come in. Quickly. For God's sake, look! He's tried to take Susie too!' Cissy, near hysteria, grabbed the doctor's arm.

Joe stood looking down, paralysed with fear as Hal Jamieson knelt and felt the girl's pulse. He pulled up her eyelid and peered at her eye and then laid his hand on her forehead. 'She's asleep,' he commented tersely. 'Heavily asleep.' He turned to Alison and frowned. His examination this time took longer. He glanced at Diana. 'Her temperature is low and her pulse is weak. She's suffering from exhaustion. They should both be in hospital – Good God! What was that?'

The crash upstairs was louder than any before. They all looked at each other. Greg gestured towards the staircase. 'Up there,' he said weakly.

Glancing nervously at one another the policemen disappeared and the others heard their footsteps pounding up the stairs and along the landing.

A few minutes later they returned. 'Nothing.' Bob Garth sat down at the kitchen table and felt in his pocket for his notebook. The sooner they had taken statements the sooner they could be on their way. He glanced up with a shiver. There was something nasty here. He could feel it.

Kate talked to him first. As calmly as she could, she related everything that had happened since she had arrived at the cottage, watching as she did so, the doctor examine Greg's foot, rebandage it and nod to himself in apparent satisfaction. He moved on to Cissy.

'And you actually saw this figure?' Bob turned the page on his notebook. His mouth had gone dry. 'You are a writer, Miss Kennedy. Are you sure you haven't imagined some of this?'

'No, she bloody hasn't!' Greg had been listening. 'You heard that bang yourself! Did you imagine that?'

'I think,' Hal Jamieson put in, 'that all this is academic at the moment.' He straightened with an exhausted sigh. 'What we need to do is to get these people out of here to hospital. Cissy needs an X-ray, Alison should have a CAT scan, in my opinion as soon as possible, and both girls need a complete checkup before I'll be happy with them.'

'We can't take everyone, sir,' Mat Larkin put in.

There was a moment's silence. Kate felt her heart sink. For a moment she had thought it was all over; that they were safe.

'I don't suppose we could get your old banger going, Joe?' Bob Garth put in. 'Supposing we give it a jump start.'

Joe nodded. 'It's worth a try.' He felt in his pocket for the keys.

Kate gnawed at her fingernail as they waited, looking from one tense face to the other as, through the closed door, they heard the sound of Joe gunning the dead engine. Nothing happened. Again he tried. Again nothing, then they heard the sound of the two bonnets slamming shut. 'No go, I'm afraid. The old girl seems to have had it,' Joe said grimly when they were back inside. 'I'm sorry.'

'OK. You take the injured to hospital, Mat,' Bob Garth said firmly, overcoming his own reluctance. 'I'll stay here to check on the cottage and see about poor Mr Norcross.'

'Yes. You must get us out of here!' Cissy clutched at Larkin's sleeve. 'You've got to get us out of here. He's after my daughter –' Her voice slid up the scale hysterically. 'You've got to save us!'

'It's all right, Cissy. We said we'll take you,' Jamieson put in comfortably. 'And Diana and the girls. And Greg. That foot is not all that good.'

'And Joe,' Cissy put in, sobbing wildly. Her voice rose dangerously again. 'You have to take Joe –'

'I'm not going,' Greg interrupted her. 'You said my foot was OK, Hal. It can wait. I'm not leaving Redall. But take Joe. That's fine by me.'

'I'm afraid that's all we can manage,' Mat put in, worried. 'The doctor has to come back with us. He's needed elsewhere, and that makes eight of us already –'

'Don't worry.' Kate caught Anne's eye and saw her sister grimace. 'We'll be all right. I think it is the two girls who are most at risk. We'll hold him off.'

There was an uncomfortable silence then Bob Garth grinned. 'I'll look after you all, Miss Kennedy, don't fret.' He would not allow himself to feel afraid.

They watched as the large police vehicle turned and churned its way up the path into the trees. 'You must have been sorry there wasn't room for you.' Greg looked curiously at Pete who had watched them from the window.

Pete shook his head. 'I reckon I'll hang around until this is all over. If you and the constable are going out to the cottage I think it would be a good thing if someone stayed here to keep an eye on the boy and the ladies.'

Greg gave a half-hearted humourless laugh. 'I think they would consider that remark patronising at the least and sexist more than likely.' He led the way back into the farm house.

'I doubt it, sir.' Bob Garth put in. 'Don't forget. We have a murderer on the loose somewhere –'

'Haven't you taken anything in!' Greg swung round on him. 'We are not looking for a man –'

'Greg.' Kate put her hand on his arm.

He shook it off angrily. 'No! We are not looking for some escaped lunatic or a robber or a psychopath. We are trying to stop a man who died nearly two thousand years ago –'

'Quite, sir.' Bob managed to keep his face impassive. 'But whoever we are looking for, dead or alive, he is still a real threat. I think this gentleman is right. Someone should remain here.'

'Well, I'm going with you.' Kate stepped forward. 'I was a close friend of Bill's, and I am the tenant of the cottage. It's right I should be there.'

'And I'm coming too.' Jon put his arm around her once more. 'I'm not letting you out of my sight again, Kate.'

She looked up at him startled. Then she smiled. Quietly she reached for his hand. She did not see the anger on Greg's face.

LXXII

Anne and Pete watched them from the window as the four figures disappeared into the trees. The house was suddenly very still. Anne bit her lip. 'Hot drink for us?'

Pete nodded. On the sofa, Paddy, tucked up in rugs, was fast asleep. He had cried when Diana told him about his father, as had Kate, but his weariness had been too much for him. As the doctor sat, stethoscope in hand, talking to him, the boy fell soundly asleep. 'Let him be.' Jamieson had stood up, folding the tubing into his pocket. 'Sleep is the best healer of all. He's exhausted and he's sad, but he's a strong chap. He'll be all right.'

Pete and Anne sat facing each other across the kitchen table. 'Rum do.' Pete grinned. His face, weatherchapped and ruddy, broke into a mass of creases when he smiled.

She smiled. 'I keep asking myself what I am doing here.'

He nodded cheerfully. 'Me too. That'll teach us to get involved. All I wanted was to make a few honest bob; one last fare before I knocked off for the night.' He buried his face in his mug and blew off the steam.

'What do you think is going to happen?' she asked after a long silence.

'The police said they'd send a van for Mr Lindsey and the poor chap at the cottage.'

'I meant Marcus.'

He ran his fingers through his hair. 'Marcus has to be dealt with.'

'You can't arrest ghosts.'

Pete gave a slow chuckle. 'I couldn't somehow see that young chap arresting anyone. He looked as though he was still collecting plastic toys from a cornflakes packet.'

'Nice, though.'

'Oh, yes, if you like that sort of thing. Uniforms turn you on,

401

do they?' It was a half-hearted attempt but he was rewarded with a token cuff on the shoulder. As Anne lowered her hand she froze. 'What was that?'

They both listened. 'Shit! I didn't expect him to come back. Not so soon.' Pete stood up. The colour had drained from his face.

They could both hear it clearly now. Footsteps upstairs. Slow, ponderous footsteps.

Quietly, Pete picked up the breadknife from the table. On tiptoe he crossed to the door with a quick glance at Patrick who was still fast asleep.

Anne followed him as, slowly, he crept up the stairs, and peered along the corridor. There was nothing there. Carefully he moved onto the polished boards and pushed open the first bedroom door. Room by room they searched the whole top floor. There was no one there at all. In Patrick's room they stopped and looked at each other. 'Can you smell it?' she said at last. 'Cigarettes.' She bit her lip.

'Not Roman.' Pete gave a short barking laugh. 'Perhaps the lad smokes on the quiet. Or perhaps it's Mr Lindsey,' he went on tentatively. 'Patrolling.'

Anne shivered. 'I'm not sure that that idea comforts me.'

'It should. Come on. Let's go down. This house is bloody cold.' Pete led the way back downstairs. At Patrick's side they stopped, and were both secretly relieved to see that he appeared to be sleeping as soundly as before, his breathing deep and regular, his colour normal.

'"Man never perceives anything fully or comprehends anything completely,"' Anne quoted softly. 'Jung said that. It's something I try to remember when I find my brain getting stressed because I can't make sense of something. It is comforting.' She flung herself down on a chair and closed her eyes. Then she opened them wide.

'I can smell her scent again.' It had been several minutes before it had been strong enough to register.

'Yes.' He had smelt the jasmine too. The tobacco had gone.

'What shall we do?'

He turned, dusting ash and dried lichen from his hands. 'What can we do? We wait.'

LXXIII

*All the time it felt less strange. He floated up the beach above the water;
he could no longer see the grave where he had lain so long. It didn't
matter. Nothing mattered now that his strength was growing. It was the
man on the shore, the tall, dark-haired man, the poet, who had given
him the energy. Silently, secretly he had drawn it from him as he stooped
over the girl, and the man had not even noticed, preoccupied as he was
with his own love and his own loss. His beautiful Claudia was here too.
Near at hand. Always with him. Her hatred and her curse had given
her strength and between them they were going to find justice at last.*

Kate was clinging to Jon's arm. Strong, independent, clever Kate,
his sparring partner, Lady Muck, was clinging to the effete poet
like a stupid bimbo. Greg, limping in front beside Constable Garth,
glanced over his shoulder again, amazed by the sudden churning
in his stomach. Why had she said it was all over between her and
this man if she hadn't meant it? He felt a sudden surge of white
hot anger. She was beautiful. Beautiful like Claudia whom he
had drawn over and over again without realising it when he was
alone at the cottage.

He hunched forward again over his walking stick, trying to
control his fury. The wind had dropped completely now, the
storm gone as swiftly as it had come. He could feel a new softness
in the air. It soothed him a little.

They were unprepared for the sight which greeted them at the
cottage. Stopping at the edge of the wood, they peered at what
had once been a pretty if overgrown garden and an idyllically
sited house. The building stood in a pool of black water which
reached halfway up the front door, almost, but not quite, as it
had been in the painting which had so upset Kate. Beyond,
towards the saltings the sea had encroached on every side, carving
new channels through the sand, extending its domain. Already a

flock of duck were paddling busily across the muddy water feeding greedily on the debris which floated in slowly spinning mats of vegetation.

'The grave must be under all that.' Greg said soberly. None of them had made a move.

'So. Marcus has won,' Kate was standing beside him now. 'We'll never know what happened.'

Bob Garth was worriedly rubbing the palms of his hands up and down the front of his jacket. 'Where was the deceased when you left?' he said thoughtfully. 'Was he on the ground floor?'

'Oh, no!' Kate buried her face in her hands.

'I'll come with you.' Greg stepped forward. 'Kate, you stay here. There's no need for you to come in.'

The water was swirling around the top of their boots as the two men, followed somewhat reluctantly by Jon, made their way towards the front door. It was several minutes before they reappeared. All three looked grim.

'The water has been in, I'm afraid, Miss Kennedy.' Garth had recovered himself sufficiently by the time he reached her. 'It's made rather a mess in there. I think you should leave it for now. We'll wait for the scene-of-crime officer and forensic to have a look round and then they can remove Mr Norcross's body.'

She nodded. She had no intention of going in.

'Shall we walk out to the grave? The water is not very deep out there and it's receding fast.' Greg had followed Garth to her side. His foot, numbed by the cold, ached dully.

She nodded reluctantly. Her own exhaustion had reached such a peak that she wondered if she would be able to walk another step. Gingerly, she stepped into the thick muddy water, feeling the soles of her boots sliding a little on what had once been a lawn. She glanced at the bush of daphne in the corner. The small pink flowers were still there, free now of ice and snow. On the topmost branch she could see a robin.

The tide was still high. They had no way of seeing where the grave was under the choppy, angry waves. Standing calf-deep in water, Kate turned slowly this way and that. The dunes had shifted. She was disorientated. There were no landmarks now to guide her, only a wide expanse of triumphant water.

Bob Garth shook his head. 'If there were bodies in the grave there will need to be a coroners' inquest,' he said doubtfully.

'Just what Marcus didn't want.' Greg was staring at the water.

Garth regarded him dubiously. He could feel it again out here; the strange certainty that all was not right. The feeling that if he were not careful he would hear or see something which he would rather not know about. 'Do you really believe all that stuff about ghosts?' he asked nervously.

Greg threw him a quizzical glance. 'You would rather believe there was a homicidal maniac loose in the woods?'

'We are looking for a murderer, Mr Lindsey.' Garth kept his voice even. 'I'll reserve judgement on who he is, for now.'

Greg did not reply. He had felt it now. The lightest brush, tentative, questing, inside his head. Marcus was still searching for a new source of energy. Angrily, he shrugged it off.

They stood looking down at the water in silence. Greg glanced at Kate. She was frowning. Had she felt it too? She looked up abruptly and caught his eye. He could see the uncertainty there; uncertainty and fear.

'Why don't we go back to the farmhouse,' he said quietly. 'There's nothing more we can do here, is there officer? We've got to wait for the water to go down.'

Garth nodded. 'May as well.' He appeared to notice Kate's white face for the first time. 'You've all had a bad couple of days out here. You wouldn't think people could get cut off like this, not in the nineties, would you?' He began to wade back towards the cottage, relieved to be moving. 'I'm supposed to seal the door before we leave. If you three would like to walk on ahead, I'll only be a minute.'

Kate hauled herself in beside Jon and leaned back, closing her eyes. He touched her hand. 'It'll soon be over.'

She nodded.

'What happened to the book? It's not still in there?'

She gave a weary smile. 'I've got the disk safely. I expect my notes are all right. I left them on the table. Oh, Jon.' With something like a sob she leaned towards him, her head on his shoulder. He put his arm round her, aware again of Greg's baleful glance as he turned to look at them. She gave Greg a weak smile. 'What's going to happen?'

'Nothing. The police enquiries will no doubt draw a blank and that will be that. No one will ever mention Alison's part in this, whatever it was. No one will ever know what happened for sure.'

'Except us.' It was a whisper.

'Except us.'

'And Marcus will rest in peace now the grave has gone.'

Greg gave a short barking laugh. 'You think so?'

'Don't you?' Kate gripped Jon's hand tightly.

'No. I don't. He's still here. I felt him out there.' Greg stopped and closed his eyes with a sigh. Oh yes, he was still there. And so was she. Somewhere. And they were both hunting; hunting for allies, for power, for the life force of a living being to sustain their hatred. The fact that the grave had disappeared meant nothing. He opened his eyes, staring back mutely at the cottage where Bob Garth was screwing a staple and hasp to the front door. There would be no stopping it now. Battle was joined. The question was, whether he was going to fight them, to stand back and watch, or whether he was going to join in. Behind him, Jon had put his arm around Kate. Did they think he couldn't see them? He pulled up his collar and folded his arms. It didn't matter. When it came to rage and jealousy he had a perfect master in Marcus.

LXXIV

Under the water the sand swirled restlessly, turning the encroaching sea the colour of the soil it invaded. The fine suspension danced to the rhythm of the waves, erasing, rearranging, sculpting a new landscape beneath the water. The coast was used to this. The sea was its enemy, ever present, ever waiting, encroaching sometimes millimetres at a time, creeping in snail-like in the soft dawn which succeeded each storm, sometimes leaping angrily on its prey and dragging it out, dismembered, to deposit its spoils on another shore.

As the water seeped deep into the clay, probing, sucking, stirring, the final shreds of leathered skin began to dissolve. Nearby, the golden torc settled more deeply into the silt and came to rest at last upon the tooth of a mammoth, a much earlier victim of the mud of the marsh.

Nion was searching now. Lost. Claudia had gone, following the people and the energy they provided. The beach was deserted. He was lonely again. He felt his anger mount. Was he tied to this place after all? Tied for all eternity? Around him the sea had grown gentle; the water had ceased to attack the land; now it caressed, a lover who had made a long-planned conquest. He had seen them: the woman and the men. The two of them loved her. He had seen the crackle of their hostility, felt its power. So, history repeats itself.

Amused, he waited. They had guessed what had happened here. They knew the Roman's secret. They hated him, but they feared him too. He was powerful, Marcus Severus Secundus. Powerful and clever, for all his craven terror when he had faced at last the moment of his death.

Anne had made soup when they returned. Cold and shaken they sat around the table gratefully: the taxi driver, the policeman, the poet, the painter, the psychologist and the author. On the sofa

Paddy slept on. He had woken once and sat up, putting his head in his hands and rubbing his face. 'Is it true, about Dad? I didn't dream it?' He had looked up pleadingly at Anne.

'I am afraid it is true, Patrick.' She sat down beside him and put her hand on the boy's shoulder, comforting him until he fell asleep again.

'So. What happens next?' Jon looked at Bob Garth.

Ten minutes before, a message had come on the constable's mobile phone that a police car was on its way to pick him up. The young man helped himself to a piece of bread from the basket and spread it thickly with butter. 'As soon as the car comes, I'll go back and report what we found. I can take you with me, Mr Cutler, if you like – and anyone else who wants to leave.' He looked from one to the other.

'You go, Anne.' Kate said quietly. 'You can't afford to be away any longer.'

'I am not leaving you here.' Anne met her eye with determination.

'Don't worry about Kate. I'm going to look after her. She's coming back with me,' Jon said firmly.

Kate shook her head. 'I'm not coming back to London, Jon. Not yet.' She was too muddled, too shocked by everything that had happened to make decisions. 'Or at least, I'll come to Bill's funeral, then I thought I would go to our parents' for a while. I was going there for Christmas anyway.'

'Kate –' Jon looked at her in sudden panic. 'Please –'

'Stay here, Kate.' Greg put in softly. 'At least until the cottage is dried out. It won't take long.'

'She's not going back there!' Jon interrupted. 'After all that's happened. You must be mad –'

'She agreed to take it for six months.' Greg's voice was very calm.

'Things have changed since that agreement,' Kate shook her head. 'I'm sorry, but I can't stay there, Greg. Not now. Not after Bill –'

A sudden imperious crackle from Bob Garth's mobile phone cut through Greg's growing anger. Unclipping it, Garth raised it to his ear. Glancing from face to face he listened to the message intently, then he grinned. 'Well,' he said. 'That's good news. The Farnboroughs are going home. Mrs Farnborough has two cracked ribs and young Susie is suffering from exhaustion, but that's all. Mrs

Lindsey is going to stay in hospital with young Alison overnight. They think she is all right, but they are going to do a brain scan just to be sure.' He stood up. 'Well, who is coming with me? Have you made up your minds?' He couldn't wait to be off.

'Go, Anne.' Kate said after a moment's pause. 'I will wait to collect my stuff as soon as they will let me in the cottage, then I'm going to Herefordshire. Allie's gone. The grave's gone. There's no more danger. I'll be all right.' She shook her head ruefully. 'I know you're worried about work – and besides, there's C.J. You go. Only don't get lost this time.' She gave a wan smile.

Anne grimaced. 'If we can be dropped off at the end of the track, Pete has suggested that he drive in front of me, at least on these lanes, to check I don't get lost!' She glanced at the taxi driver mockingly.

'That's right.' He bowed. 'And I'm going to buy her a slap up meal in Colch to send her on her way thinking a bit better about this part of the world! So don't you worry about us, folks. Just you look after yourselves.'

'I hate to leave you here.' Anne pushed back her chair. She put her hands on Kate's shoulders and hugged her. 'What are you going to do about Greg and Jon?' she asked softly. She could hardly have missed the conflict between them.

Jon did not give Kate the chance to reply. 'She'll be all right, Anne,' he said. 'I'll make sure of it.'

Anne looked him in the eye. For a minute she was silent, then she smiled. 'Make sure you do.'

When the car finally arrived, Patrick went too. He had not argued when Greg suggested that he go to Diana at the hospital and keep her company.

Kate glanced at Jon and Greg as the police vehicle disappeared up the track. Greg had turned away to throw more logs on the fire. Outside, the garden lay very still beneath the thawing snow. She bit her lip. The silence in the house had become suddenly threatening.

Greg straightened. His face was pale and strained. 'You'll have to stay for Dad's funeral, Kate. He would have wanted you to.'

They all glanced towards the door. Someone was coming later to pick up Roger's body and take it to the mortuary.

'I don't know, Greg.' Kate bit her lip. 'Please, give me time to think. Perhaps I can come back just for the day.'

'Just for the day.' Greg's voice was heavy with irony. 'How jolly.' He stiffened suddenly and stared round. The temperature in the room was falling swiftly. 'He's come back,' he said. 'Can you feel him?'

'Marcus?' Jon moved across to put his arm around Kate.

'Marcus,' Greg confirmed. He sounded almost pleased.

Kate shuddered. She looked round. 'Where is he?'

'Here.' Greg could feel the anger; the hatred. But this time the mood was different. It had changed. This time it was accompanied by fear. That was strange. Why should Marcus be afraid? Greg felt himself shiver.

For a moment no one moved, then almost defiantly Greg picked up a candle and limped to the door.

The study was very quiet and cold. His father's body lay on the bed, covered by a clean white sheet. He stood, looking down at it. Was it Roger Marcus feared? Or something – someone – else?

He turned away and picked up his last painting of the woman in blue. Claudia. It had haunted him for so many months, this beautiful enigmatic face. He stared down at the huge oval eyes. They radiated hatred. He could feel it, directed straight at him. He frowned, touching the paint with his little finger then he walked back into the living room, taking the picture with him.

'Well, what do you think?' He propped it on the chair so Jon could see it.

Jon squatted down on his haunches so that he was level with the face. 'Powerful stuff.' He frowned. It was the first time he had smelt it: jasmine. Very strongly, coming from the canvas. He sniffed cautiously. It was heady, overpowering, sexy.

Greg was watching his face. 'At last. He understands.' His voice was very soft.

Kate crouched beside Jon. 'It's a very fine painting, Jon?' She stared at him. 'Are you all right?'

'What?' He looked at her vaguely and then he focussed his gaze once more on the picture.

'The earth is cover'd thick with other clay,
Which her own clay shall cover, heap'd and pent,
Rider and horse, – friend, foe – in one red burial blent'

he quoted softly.

'Jon –'

'Leave him.' Greg's voice was a sneer. 'Poor Kate. You have a rival. You see what she can do? The whore. Her power is infinite.'

'Shut up, Greg!' She rounded on him furiously. 'Jon! Jon, what's the matter?'

Jon looked at her. His eyes looked straight past her; through her. He did not see her.

LXXV

He knew he was dying. Lying on his low bed, his wife sitting at his side, he watched the servants scurrying silently to and fro with coals for the brazier. He was cold, so very cold even though it was still summer. His eyes strayed to the shadows. They were there, waiting. Nion and Claudia. Her dying curse had after all done its work. The web was spun. Already the sticky threads entangling him reached out to the farthest corners of time. But he would evade her; somehow he would evade her – as long as there was no evidence of his crime no man on earth would censure him and, before the gods, he would take his chance like a Roman warrior, wandering the corridors between worlds where she would never find him.

He felt his lungs falter, the breath labouring suddenly in his chest, and a stab of panic went through him. Not yet. He wasn't ready yet. The tablets. He had the wax tablets under his pillow. On them the priest had written the words which would protect him and guide him to places where they would never find him. He had given orders that he be buried without cremation; that would anchor his spirit more closely to the earth. The servants had gone now. The room was empty. Hazily, he could see that his wife was dozing, her head resting on her arm. It must be midnight. The loneliest time. The loneliest place. Through the door, open to allow a draught to stir the heat from the brazier he could hear the water from the fountain in the atrium. It had a pleasant, soothing music to it; a music echoed by the stars he could not see, blazing up there in the midnight sky where, before the dawn began to dim their glory, he too would be wandering, lost in the immensity of time. He tried to move his head a little as on the table beside him the lamp flame flickered and dimmed. Suddenly the room was full of the scent of jasmine.

When Kate awoke it was pitch dark outside, but the room was lit by a small lamp on the dressing table. She lay staring round, wondering what had awoken her. Then she realised. It was the engine of a car. She lay listening, trying to summon the strength to stand up and go downstairs to see who it was, but already her eyes were closing again.

When she next opened them it was daylight.

Downstairs the living room was empty. She stared round. It had been tidied. She sniffed. She could smell coffee. Walking over to the pantry door she peered in. Jon was there, rooting around amongst Diana's jars and boxes.

'Hi.'

He jumped, then he smiled. Putting his arms around her he kissed her on the forehead. 'Hi. Did you manage to sleep?'

She nodded. 'I can't believe it but I did.' Yesterday, after he had sat and looked at the picture for what seemed like hours he had retired to the chair by the fire and scarcely spoken again that evening. He had frightened her. Greg, in contrast, had been remarkably cheerful and unthreatening and it was he who had persuaded her at last to go up and get some rest. 'Did I hear a car last night? Who was it?' she asked.

He frowned. 'They came to collect Roger. Greg saw him on his way.'

'Poor Roger. He was such a nice man. I liked him so much.' Kate bit her lip. 'This has all been so terrible, Jon.' She went back to his arms and stood there, her head resting on his shoulder, drawing strength from him. He was himself again now; completely himself. She could feel it, see it. She glanced over his shoulder into the living room. The picture had gone. 'Where's Greg?' She looked up at Jon's face.

'He went out.'

'Did you sleep down here last night?'

He nodded. 'In the chair.'

'And you smelt it: the jasmine.'

He nodded again. 'Her face. It's beautiful.'

'It's beautiful the way Greg painted it; but it's frightening too, don't you think?' She shuddered.

He nodded thoughtfully. 'He moved it. Put it away, I think.' He glanced at her. 'He's a very disturbed man, Kate.'

'Intense; artistic; sad. Not disturbed.'

'Oh yes, disturbed. He's jealous of me to the point of madness. I'm not being paranoid, Kate. I'm serious. He's a threat. A threat to you.'

'Jon –'

He shook his head. 'I know it seems absurd. Perhaps I'm being stupid, but I really believe it. There is something in his eyes – You must come away with me. Today. You know I've paid half the money I owe you into your account, Kate.' He glanced at her. 'The rest will be there by the end of January. You won't let this come between us, will you.'

'Jon, please. Don't push me too fast.' She looked up at his face. 'I'll come back to London. I'll have to anyway to get the train over to my parents.' She grimaced. 'I will have to see about the car insurance and getting a new one. But about us . . .' She wanted to go to him. She loved him, but something held her back. So much had broken in their relationship. It would take time to mend. 'I don't know, Jon. Not yet. Let's take it slowly.'

She sighed. There was an added complication. Greg. She wasn't sure how she felt about Greg. Not yet. 'As soon as they let us into the cottage I'll pack my things and we'll have to think of a way of collecting them. Then we'll go, Jon.'

Perhaps Marcus wouldn't notice that they were leaving. She walked across to the window and stared out with another shiver. 'Jon! Look! The cats.' They were sitting side by side on the wall on the far side of the lawn. 'It must be all right. They've come back. Surely, that must mean it's safe.'

Jon smiled. 'It means they think it's safe out there. You and Anne and your cat lore! I'll have to get used to it again, I can see.' He stood beside her, looking out. A stray patch of sunshine had touched the wall to a warm red, and the cats, true to their kind, had made themselves comfortable exactly in the middle of it.

A movement caught his eye. Greg had been standing on the sea wall looking out across the marsh towards the now half-submerged car. He had turned and was walking slowly and painfully back towards the house, dragging his injured foot. They saw him stop when he saw the cats. He smiled and walked towards them. They stood up, their tails raised in welcome, then suddenly Jon saw first one, then the other stiffen, fur staring. With one bound, both cats had leapt from the wall and fled. Jon glanced at Kate. She bit her lip.

They could both see the anger on Greg's face as he approached the house. It cleared as he saw them. 'Poor old car. It's had it.'

414

He walked in and eased off his boots, wincing at the pain. 'Is there any coffee?'

Kate nodded.

'I saw the police. They've gone on down to the cottage. They've advised us to keep clear for the morning. They're going to take poor Bill away, and when they've finished down there the cleaners are going in. The sea's gone down, apparently.'

'What was wrong with the cats, Greg?' Kate glanced at him as she unhooked three coffee mugs from the dresser.

'They spooked.' Greg shook his head. 'God knows who they thought I was. They'll be back as soon as Ma gets here.' He had felt it at the same moment they had. The sudden anger; the frustrated rage. And now the fear. Marcus. He sipped the black coffee gratefully. 'Are you still determined to leave Redall?'

Kate nodded. 'Today, Greg. I'm going down to my mother's until after Christmas.'

'And then?'

She shook her head. 'Then I'll see.' She sat down opposite him at the kitchen table. 'Who knows, I might come back to write about Boudicca.'

'After Christmas she's coming back to me,' Jon said slowly. 'If I can convince her what an idiot I was to let her go.'

Greg stared at him. It was there again. The rage. He took a deep breath, trying to control himself. That bastard, Marcus. He was so close. It was jealousy. That was it. He was using the jealousy as a lever. He clenched his fists. Pushing back his chair and standing up he half staggered away from the table.

'Greg – ?' Kate was looking at him, frightened.

'It's all right.' He swung away to hide his face. It was like pain. It came in spasms; agonising spasms. This was what had happened to Alison; this was how she had killed Bill. 'You go. Both of you. Go down to the cottage and pack. I'll be all right.'

He pushed through the door into the study and slammed it behind him. The sight of the empty bed with the three blankets neatly folded, brought him up short. He stood still, letting the wave of misery flow over him. Where are you, Dad? He stared up at the ceiling. Help me. Please. He moved across to his father's desk and threw himself down in the chair. For a long time he sat looking at the portrait which lay there, where he had left it the night before, on the blotter. Oh, she was so beautiful, the Lady

415

Claudia. So beautiful. So deceitful. So evil. His eyes blurred with tears.

For a long time he sat there, staring at her face. Then he stood up. He picked up the picture and slowly he brought it up to his lips. He could smell the jasmine now. The whole room was full of it; beautiful; exotic. Haunting.

He heard Jon and Kate in the hall. They were putting on their boots and coats. His knuckles whitened on the stretcher of the canvas as he listened to their quiet, almost conspiratorial voices. Then the door banged behind them and the house was silent. He looked into her eyes again. Claudia . . .

It took no strength at all to smash the canvas across his knee.

LXXVI

Kate and Jon walked cautiously into the small living room and looked round. Bill's body had gone, so had the police and after them the cleaners who had lifted the rugs, swept out the worst of the mud and opened the windows of the cottage to air. Relieved, Kate sighed. Somehow she had expected something to have remained of the aura – and the smell – of death, but the living room was more or less itself again, tidy and smelling only of damp.

She smiled at Jon. 'I'll go up and pack.' He nodded. He glanced round the room. He had grown very quiet as they neared the cottage; almost brooding, staring at her now and then with a strange thoughtfulness.

It did not take long to pack her clothes and stack her books and papers in boxes. Later they were going to borrow another neighbour's four-wheel drive to take it all back to the farmhouse. She took one last look around the cottage, listening to the silence, sniffing unconsciously for any hint of flowers or peat or Claudia's jasmine scent. There was nothing. The cottage was empty. Reassured she pulled the door closed behind them and heard the lock click home.

The water had sunk slowly back out of the garden leaving a sea of mud. On the north side of the trees and bushes, large lumps of unmelted snow lurked, cushions of white in the damp undergrowth. The south wind after the days of ice-laden easterlies was a balm to the soul – sweet, gentle and almost warm. Jon glanced at Kate. 'Do you want to see the grave before we go?'

She nodded. 'I'd like to see what happened. The sea seems to have gone right back.' Behind them the estuary sparkled in the sunlight covered by flocks of swimming birds.

They walked slowly towards the shore. Where there had been

high, sweeping dunes of sand there was now a changed landscape: small, reshaped hillocks; mud; a high, drifted beach and everywhere a covering of tangled black weed, dredged from the bottom of the sea by the ferocious waves. A cloud of gulls rose from the stinking mass as cautiously they picked their way across it towards the spot where the excavations had been. They stood surveying the beach in silence.

'It was about here, wasn't it?' Jon said at last.

Kate looked around. There were no landmarks now; the hump of the dune had gone; the declivity where she and Alison had crouched was no more. The sand all round them was scooped and moulded as though by a giant spoon into a series of smooth, scalloped humps.

She smiled, overwhelmed with relief. 'It's gone. There's no sign of it.'

She had half expected to feel something of Marcus there – resentment, anger, fear – the insidious emotions of another age – but there was nothing. The air was fresh and cool and full of the cries of sea birds and the uneasy shushing of the waves against the sand.

'It's gone,' she said again as he reached across and drew her hand into his.

To her surprise, he laughed. 'No,' he said. 'No, it hasn't gone. Not quite. Look.'

It was a piece of twisted metal, torn from the depths of the sand once again and tossed and tangled with weed. Jon stooped and picked it up. 'A torc. Your torc?' He held it out to her.

She took it reluctantly. 'I thought it had disappeared.'

A shadow on the sand, Nion waited, invisible. His torc, the torc Claudia had given to him, which he had flung as a gift to the gods lay, a twisted, corroded half moon of useless metal, in the hand of the living woman. He could feel himself drifting irresistibly towards them, the woman who held his torc and the man who loved her, the man who would give him strength.

Behind them Greg paused on the edge of the beach. Idiots. Couldn't they leave well alone? He clenched his fists. Didn't they understand? This was where it had happened. The Roman woman, Claudia, and her lover. Her British lover. Dead. Together.

He narrowed his eyes in the glare off the sea. Two men in love with one woman. A story as old as time itself.

He limped towards them slowly, and almost guiltily, Jon dropped Kate's hand.

'You realise that it was another man who came between them,' Greg said, chattily, as he reached them. 'Why else would Marcus want to kill his beautiful wife?' He took the torc out of Kate's hands and turned it round, staring down at it, picking off the sticky, clinging weed. 'Why do you suppose we haven't heard from him: the lover? Marcus did kill him as well, didn't he?' His eyes strayed from Kate's face to Jon's.

Behind them, shadows in the wind, Nion and Claudia drew closer. Soon they would be together.

'Let's go back, Greg.' Kate stepped away from him towards the sea, feeling the wind pull her hair away from her face. 'The grave itself has gone. There's nothing to see.'

Greg was staring down at the torc in his hand, his grey-green eyes veiled. 'They are here,' he whispered. 'Marcus is here and Claudia, and so is the other, the lover. I can feel them. They are trapped here on this beach together. An eternal triangle.'

'Greg –' Kate interrupted him uneasily. 'Let's go back.'

'Why?' There was open hostility in his gaze.

'Because it's late. Jon and I have to go. We have a long journey back to London.'

'No.' He turned away from them and stared out to sea. 'No, I don't think so. You don't like London, remember?'

Jon frowned, eyeing the other man with caution. Surreptitiously he put his hand on Kate's arm and pulled her away. 'Let's go,' he whispered, his words almost lost in the rush of the sea. Nodding, she turned to follow him, but Greg had noticed. He swung round and his eyes were alight with anger. 'No. You're not going anywhere.'

He could feel Marcus so clearly now. Close. Pushing. Eager.

'Don't be stupid, Greg,' Kate's voice was sharp. 'We are leaving. If you want to stay, that's up to you.' She began to walk inland, turning her back on the place where the excavation had been.

Behind them Greg was staring once more down at the torc. Suddenly his eyes were full of tears. He couldn't fight it much longer. Marcus and Kate. He couldn't cope with both. He stumbled after her. 'You can't go,' he called. 'I won't let you. This was sent here to hold you –'

Jon swung round. He released Kate's arm abruptly, his anger bubbling to the surface at last. 'That is enough, Greg! Kate has told you. She is going. You mean nothing to her.' Angrily he snatched the torc from the other man's hands. 'This has caused enough trouble. Now it is going back where it belongs.' Lifting his arm he flung the torc into the air. As it landed in the heaving greyness of the water, he felt anger sweeping over him uncontrolled.

Terrified, he tried to master it.

It was red, vicious. Blind.

Ecstatic.

He wrestled with it frantically, staggering back from the sea's edge, clutching at his head, hearing nothing but the raging of the waves. He did not see Kate's terror as the swirl of jasmine-scented dust settled over her.

'Jon!' He heard her voice distantly; it was frightened; screaming. 'Greg! Do something! Marcus has got him! Help him! Greg, help him! Help me!'

'No, not Marcus.' Suddenly Greg was laughing. 'Marcus is here. With me! Nion's possessed him.' The name had come to him so easily – the name his wife had screamed into a Beltane dawn. Nion the Druid.

The voices were growing fainter, the sound of the sea louder. Suddenly Greg was afraid. Marcus was there; Marcus was inside him. Turning, he ran towards the water. He could feel the waves icy against his ankles, taking away all the pain. The shock of the cold stunned him.

Fight. He had to fight. The water was deeper now, sucking round his knees. Cold. Clean. Powerful.

Fight. Fight the Roman.

Fight or die.

Where was Roger? He had promised. Dad, help me! Help me fight him. Dad, please. His voice rose in pain and fear and anger.

A wave slammed against his waist and the shock of it stopped him.

He turned and surveyed the beach.

* * *

Fight. Jon too was fighting, the battle in his head deafening.

Recite. Fill your head with something else. That's what Anne had said. Don't let him take hold. Recite . . .

Nion must have his revenge.

Marcus is vanquished.

Nion turned his hungry, angry eyes to look for the Roman who had caused his death . . .

Fight. Fight the anger in his head.

Recite.

Byron. She didn't know it, but he had learned Byron for her sake. 'Where'er we tread 'tis haunted, holy ground . . .' Grope for the memory. Fill the mind. 'All tragedies are finish'd by a death.' Was that Byron too . . . ? It didn't matter.

Jon stumbled away from the sea, his hands clawing at his temples. Where was she? Where was Claudia? His love. He shook his head. Kate. Where was Kate –? There was no one there. They had gone. Nion was gaining strength. Marcus? Where was Marcus? Nion had to be rid of Marcus for ever.

Recite. It's the only way. Blank the druid out. Don't let him in. He's not going to win.

Sobbing, he fell on his knees in the wet sand.

> 'She walks in beauty, like the night
> Of cloudless climes and starry skies;
> And all that's best of dark and bright
> Meet in her aspect and her eyes.
> She walks in beauty, like the night . . .'

He repeated the words again and again until he had no strength left and his voice faded in his throat.

Marcus could see them clearly now, through the eyes of the man, Greg. They were there, near him, reaching out to one another.

Nion and Claudia.

Jon and Kate.

Greg groaned as the icy water slapped around his thighs. His eyes weren't working properly. Everything was blurred.

Jon and Kate.

Nion and Claudia.

Slowly he was beginning to understand. Marcus fed on hate

and jealousy. Their strength, their love, those were the weapons he needed. Clenching his fists he took a step towards the sand. Then another.

Fight.

Fight the alien inside his head.

Fight him with love. Love that transcends time and space.

Nion and Claudia.

Jon and Kate.

Jon and Kate.

The rage was receding. Greg could feel the anger and hate inside him dwindling. He took another step towards the beach. Marcus was losing. Love would always win over hate.

In the end.

Painfully he shook his head. It was as though he were waking from some hideous nightmare. Far out at sea a stray beam of sunlight had broken through the clouds to touch the sea to silver. He stared at it mesmerised, then slowly and weakly, he began to wade back towards the shore. He had won. Marcus was going. He could feel him shrinking and weakening. He rubbed his eyes. The dream had left him now; it had gone, into the shadows of eternity with its pain.

Kate looked up at Greg as she cradled Jon's head on her knee, her eyes full of tears. The sweet scent of jasmine was all around her.

The hands on his head were gentle. He could feel them clearly, soothing away the pain.

Her voice. It was her voice. She was there. She was with him.

Weeping, Nion the Druid rested his head in the soft blue folds of her gown, and felt himself at peace.

422

AUTHOR'S NOTE

The name Nion is taken from the Celtic Tree Calendar
Beth – Luis – Nion (Birch, Rowan, Ash) depicted by
Robert Graves.

This book has many roots: the awe and fear in a little boy's voice many years ago, as we stared together through the window into a midnight garden after a bad dream; a lonely visit to Sutton Hoo on a cold afternoon in winter when the wind screamed through the firs and down across the River Deben; a long, thoughtful visit to the twisted body of Lindow Man in the British Museum and the view from my study window out across fields where Trinovantes and Romans once walked on the edge of the saltings with, in the distance, the icy North Sea, are some of the strongest.

A lost child in the Welsh borders;
a violent attack in London;
an epic battle between the Celts and the Romans.

What can possibly link them?

Read on for an extract from
BARBARA ERSKINE'S

thrilling new novel,

The Warrior's Princess

Steph put the phone down and turned back into the kitchen where Kim was frying onions and tomatoes. She was frowning. 'I've been trying all evening but there is still no reply from either phone.'

'Perhaps she's gone out.' Kim threw some sliced zucchini into the heavy pan and added more oil. With her dark hair and eyes and her plump figure – a testament to her fondness for her own cooking – Kim looked every inch the Italian mamma in the making for all she had been born in Romford and attended the same college as Jess and Steph. 'And she's forgotten to take her mobile.'

'That's probably it. I've reported the line at Ty Bran. They checked. It is broken.'

'Well, presumably someone will go and mend it.' Kim reached for her wine glass and took a sip before turning her attention back to the sauce. 'So, you can stop worrying, Steph. Jess is a big girl. She doesn't need you checking up on her all the time. In fact you never have before, so why now?'

Steph shook her head wearily. 'I don't know. I've got a strange feeling, that's all.'

'What sort of strange feeling?' Wooden spoon in hand, Kim paused in her stirring to gaze at her friend's face. 'You two aren't twins, are you?'

'You know we're not!'

'Then stop worrying. Go and see to our guests. Make sure everyone has got a drink. If you really want to know what is happening with Jess ask Carmella. She reads the cards. You'll find a deck in Stefano's old bureau.'

Steph wandered through the apartment towards the front door. From the grand reception room she could hear the sound of voices. Kim's penchant for cooking frequently led to these

427

impromptu parties where her guests marvelled at the talent of their English hostess who could cook Italian food better than any of them.

Steph resisted the urge to mention the cards, but as they sat in the *salotto* later savouring their *dolci* and coffee Kim brought the subject up again.

'Steph needs some info about her sister, Carmella. Would you read the cards for her? Tell us what is happening over there in Wales?' She levered herself out of the deep sofa and went to the bureau, rummaging around in the drawers.

There was a general murmur of interest from the other guests at the suggestion as she drew out the small box she had been looking for.

Carmella, a tall, elegant woman in her forties, held out her hand languidly and took the box. 'I haven't seen these since Stefano died. Do you remember how often we would read them?' She smiled at Kim, raising one of her startlingly black, fly away eyebrows.

Kim nodded, suddenly wistful. 'He loved to watch you do it, but he would never let you do a reading for him. Perhaps if you had –'

'No!' Carmella started shuffling the deck. 'No, don't think of that. What was to be, was to be.' She flicked her dark hair out of her eyes and leaned forward to take a puff from the cigarette lying in the onyx ashtray near her coffee cup. 'Now, let me see what the cards have to say. This is about your sister, Steph?'

Steph nodded.

'Tell me her name.'

'Jess.'

'And do you have anything of hers with you? Perhaps a letter? A piece of jewellery to make the connection.'

Steph thought for a moment. 'I have a scarf of hers. I liked it so much she gave it to me.'

'That is good. Get it.'

Steph watched amused as Carmella cut the pack and then laid out the cards on the coffee table. It was years since she had seen anyone read the tarot. Probably not since she had been a student and done it herself. Carmella did it with superb style, she had to give her that. She lay back in her chair and sipped her coffee, watching as Carmella turned up the first card, Jess's scarf lying on her knee, a splash of emerald against the black of the woman's skirt.

'Ah, *il fante di denari*. The page of coins; pentacles you call them, *si*? This is Jess. A page can represent a woman, you know that?' She glanced round. Turning back to the table she ran her finger thoughtfully over the card. The eyes of every person in the room were fixed on her hands as she turned up the next and sat staring down at the layout in front of her. She was frowning. '*Non capisco*,' she murmured to herself. 'This is very strange. There are two different people here. We have two women. You see? *Il fante di bastoni*, the page of wands. But this one represents *una ragazza*. A much younger woman. Very important in the reading. They are linked in some way.' She turned a third card. 'And here with them we have *il re di coppe al negativo*.' She paused, shaking her head. 'Here is violence, scandal, treachery. A bad man in the lives of these two women.' She glanced up, concerned. 'And here. *Il matto*, the fool. He heralds a journey for all these people. I think not literally – maybe a step into the unknown. No, also a journey in reality.' She turned up three more cards in quick succession. 'There is so much here.' She spread her hands over the cards. 'They are on a quest. Your sister, Steph, has set out on a journey she cannot escape. She travels with another woman, maybe a child, and behind them follows this man. The cards never tell a lie, but this and this –' Her hand strayed over the cards, stroking them, reading them almost like Braille. 'This is too strange. There is love here; new love. Strong love, but also danger. And fear. And threats.'

'Oh God!' Steph whispered under her breath. She and Kim exchanged glances.

'Perhaps,' Kim said suddenly, clearing her throat, 'this is not a good idea. Why don't we have another drink and forget it.'

'No.' Carmella raised a commanding hand. '*Aspetta*! No, this is important. It is telling me something very important about your sister. She needs to be warned that she is in danger.'

'Oh God!' Steph repeated. She stood up as a murmur of concern ran round the room. Everyone was looking at her. No one seemed to doubt Carmella. No one was looking superior and cynical and scoffing as they would at a dinner party in London. They were all hanging on every word.

'Carmella, stop it!' Kim said. 'That's enough. You are frightening her!'

'So, you don't want to know? You don't want to save her?'

'Yes, of course I want to know.' Steph sat down again. She ran her fingers through her hair. 'Go on.'

Carmella looked up at her for a moment, then she glanced back at the cards. 'There is another man here.' Her finger paused over the king of swords. She frowned. 'Your sister's father? He is wounded.'

'Our father is dead,' Steph put in sharply.

Carmella shook her head. 'I don't understand. This is definitely someone's father. The other girl, perhaps. Do you know who she is?' She looked up. 'And there are soldiers here.' She leaned closer to the cards for a minute. 'And here, I see danger again.' Her voice sharpened. 'Here it is clear. There are two lives here and this,' she tapped a card, 'is your sister and someone wants to kill her!' She sat back and stared at Steph, her eyes wide. '*Dio mio*, we are told never to forecast a death. Never! This is awful!'

'And it's tosh, Carmella!' Kim looked really angry. 'This was supposed to comfort her, not make things worse.' She stood up. 'Enough! Let's have some Limoncello, then you should all go home!'

'I'm going to ring the police!' Steph hadn't moved. She was sitting staring at the cards.

'Don't be an idiot! You can't ring the police because of a tarot reading!' Kim bent forward and swept all the cards into a heap. 'That's it. Finished. I am going to put them away.'

'I'll ring the Prices. Meg and Ken won't mind going over to Ty Bran and seeing if she is all right.' Steph stood up. 'Don't be angry with Carmella. I knew there was something wrong.' She headed for the telephone, in the hallway, leaving the others all staring at each other.

The phone at Cwm-nant rang and rang. There was no reply. Steph slammed down the phone. Picking it up again she tried Ty Bran's number. The line was still dead. Then she tried Jess's mobile. It was still switched off.

'Leave it, Steph.' Kim appeared behind her. She had brought a bottle from the fridge in the kitchen and a tray of liqueur glasses. Pouring one out she put it down on the hall stand beside the telephone. 'Get that down you. I'm so sorry. It was a stupid, stupid idea doing the tarot. I should have remembered how melodramatic Carmella can be.'

Steph picked up the glass and sipped it. The strong cold shot of lemon revived her a bit. 'I don't know who to ring, Kim. Jess is all alone up there. There is no one there I know well enough to ask them to drive up into the hills in the middle of the night to see if my sister is OK.'

'I bet you she's fine.' Kim guided her back towards the kitchen and onto a stool by the table. 'I tell you what. Tomorrow, if you can't contact her by then, we'll ring the police and you can explain how worried you are, OK? Honestly. I don't think you can ring them tonight. Not on the strength of a card reading. They would think you were nuts. And they wouldn't go. You know that as well as I do. There is no point in even trying.'

'And what if someone is trying to kill her?' Steph took another swig from the Limoncello.

'Why on earth should someone try and kill Jess?' Kim grabbed Steph by the shoulders. 'Think about it, you idiot! What could Jess have possibly done that would warrant that!'

'Will was trying to find her. He rang –'

'Oh yes! And Will is trying to kill her? I thought you said he was still desperately in love with her.'

Steph shook her head. 'I'm being stupid, aren't I? I know I am. Sorry.'

'At last! Sense. There was love in those cards as well, remember? Right, I'm going to send the others home. Go to bed, Steph. Sleep well. It will all be all right in the morning, you'll see. The phone will be mended and you will find that Jess has been there all the time.'

Let time stand still.
Discover even more
of the magic.

BARBARA
ERSKINE
Sunday Times bestselling author of *Lady of Hay*

On *the* Edge
of Darkness

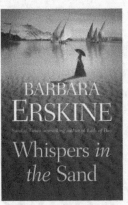

BARBARA
ERSKINE
Sunday Times bestselling author of *Lady of Hay*

Whispers *in*
the Sand

BARBARA
ERSKINE
Sunday Times bestselling author of *Lady of Hay*

Hiding *from*
the Light

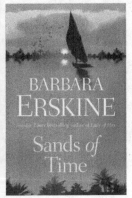

BARBARA
ERSKINE
Sunday Times bestselling author of *Lady of Hay*

Sands *of*
Time

BARBARA
ERSKINE
Sunday Times bestselling author of *Lady of Hay*

Daughters
of Fire

BARBARA
ERSKINE
Sunday Times bestselling author of *Lady of Hay*

The Warrior
Princess

Her untold life would echo through time

BARBARA
ERSKINE
Sunday Times bestselling author of *Lady of Hay*

Time's Legacy

From reality, to legend, to secret

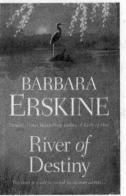

BARBARA
ERSKINE
Sunday Times bestselling author of *Lady of Hay*

River *of*
Destiny

This river is ready to reveal its ancient secrets...

BARBARA
ERSKINE
Sunday Times bestselling author of *Lady of Hay*

The Darkest
Hour

On the 30th anniversary of *Lady of Hay*,
Barbara Erskine returns to Hay, the place
that enchanted a generation of readers

Sleeper's Castle

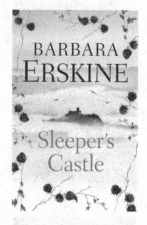

One woman sees the future in her dreams.
The other sees the past. Sleeper's Castle holds the key.
A place where history has come alive . . .

Out on 30th June 2016